Here's what's been said and written about R. Michael McEvilley's "An Irishman by Now"

Eamonn Sweeney, *literary critic, best-selling author, journalist, Cork, Ireland*
"I thoroughly enjoyed the novel and was gripped from start to finish…excellent, a rattling good story…I could see it making a fine film…a serious pleasure to read. [McEvilley is] a born storyteller."

Janet Rice, *author of "Appalachian Magic," Milton, West Virginia*
"This book is absolutely marvelous. I went through every emotion there is in reading it. It had me crying, and I *never* cry!…unbelievable! I was *there*. I was with these people!…just great. I can't see how [this book] cannot be a best-seller! A plus plus plus!"

Paula Clem-Stehlin, *Instructor, Lucent Technologies, Orlando, Florida*
"…it was great. I was glued from the very beginning…I just couldn't put it down. I could actually see the landscape and the people…a huge accomplishment."

Keran Smith, *retired banker, Somewhere in the Florida Panhandle*
"…wonderful…great…could not put it down…I laughed, cried, and dried my tears to laugh and cry some more."

William C. Schaefer, *retired executive, Ford Motor Company, Bloomfield Hills, Michigan*
"I just breezed through my first novel since college…most entertaining, captivating, and easy to read. Congratulations."

David K. Wiggins, *product consultant, Dayton, Kentucky*
"…dialogue and images so vivid, you might think you've already seen the movie!"

M. Kathleen Chappell, *businessperson, Maysville, Colorado*
"WOW!…It is really quite wonderful…I truly mean it, I was riveted. It made me laugh and cry and everything in between. It is GREAT!"

Dan Dwyer, *Insurance executive, Cincinnati, Ohio*
"...eminently readable and re-readable...awesome!"

Nicholas Cardilino, *Director of Campus Ministry, University of Dayton*
"I couldn't put it down!...gets even better as it goes on! It's a great...story!"

Lisa Bage, *retail sales, Talbots, Strongsville, Ohio*
"I was unable to put it down...IT IS FANTASTIC!...[will be a] best seller."

Karen Fessler, *Educator, Ft. Mitchell, Kentucky*
"...just finished the book. **Could not put it down**. I truly loved the book...better than most anything else...the kind of story worth losing sleep over."

August H. Eilerman IV, *businessman, Cincinnati, Ohio*
"...flat out a great book!"

Robert Gulley, *Christian Minister/Professor, Bellevue, Kentucky*
"I usually have no interest in reading this genre of work, but this book is great...couldn't put it down!"

Terrence D. Bazeley, *Attorney at Law, Cincnnati, Ohio*
"...stayed up until 4 a.m. to finish it...it was great...excellent."

Jim Melko, *Director of Learning Assistance, University of Dayton*
"...thoroughly enjoyed it...a delightful and engaging story...[that] leads to one of the most emotional, joyous, and poignant scenes I have ever read in any novel...once you've gotten to know [the characters]...you will not forget them. *They're real!*"

Jane Murphy, *author's ex-wife, Newport, Kentucky*
"I guess he is not as stupid as he acts..."

An Irishman by Now

An Irishman by Now

An American Boy's Tale of Passion and
Discovery in Rural Ireland

R. Michael McEvilley

iUniverse, Inc.
New York Lincoln Shanghai

An Irishman by Now

An American Boy's Tale of Passion and Discovery in Rural Ireland

All Rights Reserved © 2004 by R. Michael McEvilley

iUniverse, Inc.

For information address:
iUniverse, Inc.
2021 Pine Lake Road, Suite 100
Lincoln, NE 68512
www.iuniverse.com

ISBN: 0-595-30966-6 (pbk)
ISBN: 0-595-66228-5 (cloth)

Printed in the United States of America

CONTENTS

▼

Foreword.. ix

Book One County Mayo, Ireland.. 1

Book Two Cincinnati, Ohio USA... 157

Epilogue.. 221

Foreword

When I was ten years old, Grandpa McEvilley called to say that I should no longer use the name Mickey. *"Mickey,"* he explained with some distaste, "is a name for an Irish barroom bum or a prizefighter."

Wish he were alive today so that I could tell him—hey, I'm not a prizefighter.

Anyway, not many American Michaels go by "Mick" or "Mickey"—they either use "Mike" or stick with "Michael"; so it's been great fun spending time in Ireland and finding that "Mick" is a common name and perfectly acceptable. A fine name for an Irish lad. The point being, I didn't name the boy in this book "Mickey" out of any sort of egotism or conceit. I think I did it to piss off Grandpa.

—RMM

BOOK ONE
COUNTY MAYO, IRELAND

TUESDAY 6 SEPTEMBER 1977

"Did y' remember your pencils, Mickey?" she asked quietly.

"In here," he said impatiently, holding up his book bag as he stood by the kitchen table. "I have to go."

"Here's for your dinner," she said, handing him a few items from the refrigerator. "Put them in there as well."

A large, stout man stepped from the bathroom still in his underwear, passed gas and said, "You'll be home directly after school, if y' know what's good for you. There's work."

"I know, Pa," he said, as he unbolted the cottage door and let himself out.

Michael Peter Monaghan was to begin fourth class today, the first day of the new school year at St. Patrick's in Newport, County Mayo. As in the prior three years, he walked from the Monaghan sheep farm along the mile-and-a-half, single-lane, always-in-disrepair Treanbeg Road down to the main road, and then another half-mile to St. Pat's.

He was a few inches taller than average, and his farm work had made him a strong and trim 9-year-old. He was a handsome boy with brown hair and blue eyes. He carried a canvas book bag over his shoulder, empty now except for a few pencils, a box of raisins, and a cheese sandwich.

St. Patrick's school and church sat atop the highest point in the village, overlooking an expanse of farm lands and small lakes to the north, with the Nephin Beg mountain range rising as a border along the visible eastern periphery, and a

- 1 -

view to the south and west of the Brown Oak River going through and along the village center, about a half-mile from its entrance into Clew Bay and the Atlantic Ocean.

Like many of Ireland's small towns and villages, Newport was picturesque, with an array of pastel colors on its storefronts and the ancient rock architecture of its two bridges over the Brown Oak.

A light rain fell as Mickey walked the final ascent into the village, a short but steep and narrow curvature with older rock buildings—now used for storage—on either side, having the same feudal appearance as the bridges at the other end of village. At the top, the main road turned right, then immediately left in a gradual descent through the village and down to the river. Turning left, Mickey continued his climb up the lane to school.

This was a good day for Mickey. He was glad to get away from the hard work of the farm and especially from Pa, who was more a demanding overseer than a father to his adoptive and only child. On his bad days, Fergus Monaghan was a scowling drunk and frequently abusive to his wife Marian and to his son. On his better days, he was quiet and mildly unpleasant.

Whatever his mood, he seemed determined to keep his boy occupied with work projects and jobs around the farm, forbidding him to participate in team athletics and other activities that would use his time and energy, and otherwise being generally unimpressed with any accomplishments Mickey might make at school or elsewhere outside the home.

In contrast to his serf status at home, Mickey was highly regarded and well liked by the other children and by his teachers. He was no angel, but bright, and thought to be "all boy"; so this, the first day of school, was cause for a good mood.

*   *   *   *

As some parents passed to deliver their children by car, Mickey and others walked the hill to school, and he saw a commotion up ahead on the other side of the lane. In the fray, he recognized two fifth-class boys whom he disliked.

He didn't immediately pay much attention, until he noticed a little red-haired girl who was clearly upset, jumping around screaming, "Leave me alone!" as the two yanked at the braids in her hair, laughing and taunting her.

Danny O'Brien grabbed the little girl's new schoolbag from her shoulder and threw it spinning into a rain puddle. Jimmy Mitchell stood behind her and grabbed her pigtails, as Danny swept his right foot under her, tripping her to her knees.

Mickey yelled, "Get off o' her, morons!" as he ran across the lane, but he was ignored until he was right on them.

Danny O'Brien continued to poke and pull at the girl's hair as she fought to stand up, but Jimmy Mitchell turned with his fists clenched—too late—to confront Mickey. Mickey was in full stride, and he shoved both hands into Jimmy's chest, sending him backpedaling then falling into the bushes. Jimmy would need to do a little collecting before picking himself up.

Danny now turned his attention to Mickey, but he was also too late. He had barely uttered the words "Hey, stupid eejit!" when Mickey gritted his teeth and socked him in the jaw with a hard right fist, knocking him down on the spot.

"Eejit yourself, y' can o' piss!" Mickey said as he watched Danny staring up at him from the ground.

Although Danny was a troublemaker who had been in more than his share of fights, he knew that he had never been punched like that. It was rare for a boy of that age—although some fight frequently—to throw a hard punch to another's jaw. They wrestle and shove, get their opponents in headlocks, or hold them down on the ground until surrender, but they don't throw knockout punches or try to break bones. And as he dealt with the embarrassment of Mickey's being a year younger, Danny lay stunned, unable to do anything but hold the side of his face and stare.

The trouble now over, Mickey turned to the little girl, who was now staring at him as well. He picked up her schoolbag from the puddle and shook the water from it. He patted her shoulder and said, "Come on, little one. Time for school."

They walked silently up the hill as Jimmy made his way out of the bushes and helped his fellow assailant-turned-victim up from the sidewalk. Other children who had stopped to watch the action were now moving on.

*   *   *   *

As they neared the school doors, Mickey turned and said, "I'll go tell Father McDermott that you beat up those two lads, so I don't get int' any trouble, okay?"

As she turned to protest, she saw the smile on his face, and she smiled back, relieved.

"You won't get in trouble! They started it!"

With that, an older boy, in sixth class, ran by the two and into the school.

Mickey said, "Whatever did you do to them to make 'em pick on you like that?"

"I saw Danny O'Brien stealin' a pack o' fags from Chambers' market, and I told on him. He got in a lot of trouble because Mr. Chambers rang his mam to come and get him. And guess what?"

"What?"

"I know your name is Mickey. Mickey Monaghan."

"Oh, yeah, it is…how'd you know that?" he said smiling.

"I just do 'cause Keran—my sister—told me. We live down the road from you, and my name is Caitlin."

In truth, Caitlin's older sister Keran, now starting third class, was one of Mickey's admirers and had talked about him with her girlfriends while Caitlin listened attentively to the "big" girls' gossip.

"Oh, well, Caitlin, now I know—your mam is Mrs. O'Connor, who plays the organ at Mass, right? So your name is Caitlin O'Connor?"

"Yes! Caitlin Molly O'Connor! I'm six and—" Again the school door flew open, and Mr. Fogarty, who taught sixth class, ran out and headed down the hill.

"Uh-oh. Somethin's wrong. Caitlin, your hair is a bit of a mess. Maybe you should go and fix it before goin' to your classroom." Mickey opened the school door and said, "Come on, I'll show you where the girls' bathroom is."

"I already know," she said proudly. Mickey looked at her. *She's a pretty brave little kid.* "Well, then, be careful, Caitlin, see y' later."

He walked off to his new classroom as Caitlin watched him, smiling.

"Bye, Mickey!"

He figured he'd go find his new desk, and he hoped that he wasn't in trouble. Caitlin, on the other hand, went running to her sister's third-class room.

Mickey ran up the stairs and through the double doors on the left and into the hall where fourth class was located. He had some vague thoughts about little Caitlin, some nice thoughts that he didn't bother to examine. The room door was open. He looked in briefly to make sure he had the right room, and then walked in.

About two-thirds of the kids were already seated and chattering away. He exchanged quick greetings with various classmates as he went to the back of the room to sit next to his best friend, Eamonn Powers.

Eamonn leaned over to him. "Are you crazy or somethin'? Angela said you were out there fightin' with O'Brien and Mitchell! On the first day of school!"

"They were beatin' up a wee girl! From first class!"

"Sure, but they're fifth classers, and them and their buddies are goin' t' kick your arse straightaway!"

With that, the room became quiet.

Mickey looked to see Father Sean McDermott, the parish priest, in the doorway. He was a big man, about six feet two inches, two hundred pounds or so, with his black and gray hair parted and combed perfectly, as always.

As far as Mickey knew, Father McDermott never came to the classroom except to pass out report cards, a truly morose occasion. Without a hint of kindness or mercy, the parish priest announced each name, and that child stepped forward to receive his or her report. Those who had done well might get a nod or perhaps a smile, with any sort of congratulations reserved for those achieving near-perfect marks. Those who had not done well could count on the wrath of Father McDermott in lecture form; and for those unfortunate souls, report card day was no doubt among the worst of their young lives.

Father McDermott looked over the twenty or so fourth-class children until his eyes met Mickey's.

"Michael Monaghan."

He stood. "Yes, Father?"

An expressionless Father McDermott jerked his right thumb in the direction of the hallway. Mickey walked silently up to the door and continued into the hallway. He stood still until Father McDermott walked by him, and then he followed along. Through the double doors and down the stairway. Out of the school and across the lot to the presbytery. He had never seen the inside of the presbytery. This was no longer a good day for Mickey.

The priest opened one of the double doors and entered the vestibule, wiped his feet on the mat, opened an inner door, and entered a hallway. A petrified Mickey wiped his feet and stepped inside behind his silent captor.

To the left was a dark room. Mickey could only see that there was a piano in it. In front of him was a staircase. To the right, pillars about twelve feet apart marked the entrance to a large dining room.

The old cherry table was appropriately large as well, with fourteen high-backed chairs placed around it. Jimmy Mitchell sat in one of the chairs. Father McDermott motioned for Mickey to sit directly across from Mitchell, as he himself sat at the head of the table. He looked at Mickey.

"We had to send Daniel O'Brien to hospital in Castlebar. He passed out when he tried to stand up after you hit him in the jaw. Look at James' shirt, with the left sleeve about torn off at the shoulder. His parents have to pay their hard-earned money to buy clothes for their children."

Mickey sat silently. He knew he had done nothing wrong, but he didn't want to interrupt Father McDermott.

Father McDermott stood up, saying, "Your parents will be here soon, and we'll discuss this."

"No!" Mickey almost yelled as he jumped to his feet. "My pa will kill me if he finds out! He will kill me! Father, please don't ring him!"

"Now you sit back down, young man! Your folks have already been rung. And don't you think that you are going to go around attacking other students without your parents knowing about it!" He left the room.

*   *   *   *

Mickey looked at Jimmy Mitchell. He wished he had defended himself, but he *had* thought that Father McDermott would have known he was protecting a little girl in first class. And he was upset knowing that Fergus would hear about this. Jimmy wouldn't look back at him.

"Feckin' tool," Mickey said. Jimmy didn't respond.

They sat and waited. For an eternity, it seemed, but it was actually about 15 minutes before the doorbell rang. Father McDermott entered the room and went to the door.

He returned with Jimmy's mother, a frightened-looking pale woman dressed in a gray raincoat snapped to the top. She wore no makeup, used no coloring on her prematurely gray hair, and on this grim morning probably looked fifteen years beyond her actual age.

"Please tell me what's going on, Father. Jimmy, why is your shirt ripped? Was he fighting, Father?"

"Just a moment now, Mrs. Mitchell, please have a seat with Jimmy there. Now, Mrs. Mitchell, this is Michael Monaghan who is also a student here. We've tried to ring his parents, but haven't had any luck getting hold of them." She sat next to her son.

"James, why don't you tell your mother exactly what happened this morning."

Jimmy turned uneasily to his mother. "Uhm, me and Danny...we was just walkin' up the hill to school, and we was just havin' a little fun teasin' this girl that...uhm, Danny knows." He stopped.

"Go on, son," Father McDermott urged him.

"Well, uhm…so we was teasin' this girl, and this boy here comes chargin' us like he's crazy, and for no reason, shoves me into the bushes. And, uh, I didn't see him. So my shirt got torn."

"That's a lie," said Mickey.

The phone rang, and Father McDermott reached to a small wooden stand immediately behind him. "Excuse me, please, just a moment—Sean McDermott," he answered, and then listened for a moment before saying, "Oh, good, good, that's a relief. Thank you much."

He cradled the phone and turned back to his guests. Mickey quietly hoped that the good news was *not* that his parents had been reached and were on their way.

"I should explain, Mrs. Mitchell, that Daniel O'Brien was also involved in this, and apparently got quite a knock in the jaw. We sent him to hospital to make sure he's all right, and that was just the doctor telling us that he's fine. So that's a great relief."

"Well, wha—what's going on here? Did this one do that as well?" she asked, waving a hand toward Mickey.

"To be sure, that's as it appears, Mrs. Mitchell…"

She interrupted, "Why, he should be expelled, the little—"

"Well, now perhaps so, but Michael, you were saying that James wasn't telling us the truth?"

"No, sir, Father, he was not. The two of 'em was messin' with a wee six-year-old and knocked her down to the ground. *Not* teasin' her. He was yankin' at her pigtails while Danny tripped her and made her fall. I yelled at 'em to stop, but they wouldn't. And you did see me, Jimmy. You're just not fast enough."

Mrs. Mitchell scoffed, "Oh, that is not true! My son does not beat up little girls!" Jimmy wasn't talking.

The front door opened, and Ms. Costello, the first-class teacher, walked in with Caitlin O'Connor, holding her hand. Luckily, thought Mickey, Caitlin had not taken his advice. Her hair was still quite disheveled.

"Hello, Father, this is Caitlin O'Connor, whom you've asked to see."

"Caitlin Molly O'Connor," the little girl gently corrected her teacher as she curtsied.

"Hello, Caitlin," Father McDermott said kindly. "Are you all right?"

"Yes, Father."

"Did something happen to you this morning, Caitlin?"

"Danny O'Brien and this boy," Caitlin said, pointing, "*Jimmy*, I think. They were pulling on my hair, and they took my school bag, and kicked me and made me fall down—"

Mrs. Mitchell started to interrupt Caitlin, but Father McDermott abruptly silenced her with a raised hand. "Then what happened, Caitlin?"

"And then I yelled and yelled for them to leave me alone, but they wouldn't, so Mickey came and got them away from me!"

Mrs. Mitchell called out, "What do y' mean they made you fall down? Who made you fall down? How did they make you fall down?"

Caitlin didn't hesitate. "Jimmy held my pigtails while Danny kicked me and made me land on my knees!"

No one spoke for a moment. Father McDermott turned to Mrs. Mitchell, his expression offering her to question further. A little unsure, she proceeded, "So lemme see those knees o' yours that you fell on."

Caitlin lifted her skirt a little. Both knees were scraped and raw. Mrs. Mitchell turned angrily to Jimmy, shouting and smacking his head with both hands, "You...you...I am so embarrassed!"

The priest stood up, walked to Mrs. Mitchell's chair.

"All right, then, Mrs. Mitchell, you and James come with me." They walked to the front door, then outside.

"You'll keep him home for a week, Mrs. Mitchell. I'll tell his teacher."

"Yes, Father."

"James, I don't mind telling you, you should be ashamed of yourself for what you've done, and it's not going to happen again. It's a coward and a bully you are today—tormenting a little girl—and you've made your poor mother cry."

"Yes, Father."

Father McDermott returned to the dining room. "Ms. Costello, you'll take Caitlin back with you, and Caitlin, thank you for your help. Are you sure you're all right now?"

"Yes, Father."

"Good! And see if you can help her with that hair, Ms. Costello. Now, Michael, you stay here, we'll talk. Good-bye now, Caitlin."

"Bye, Father. Bye, bye, Mickey!"

*   *   *   *

Father McDermott heaved a deep breath and looked at Mickey. He sat down in the chair across from him, the chair that Jimmy had just left.

"So you hit O'Brien once, Mick—uh, Michael?"

"Yes, sir. Only one time."

The priest nodded. "Well, he's a bit bigger than you, and a year older. Must've been a pretty lucky hit. I mean, to knock him cold like that."

Mickey looked over and saw Father McDermott with a slight smile on his face. "It wasn't lucky, Father, I just wanted him to leave her alone."

"Well, fair play to y', then, son, and maybe you ought t' take up boxing." He was still smiling.

Mickey laughed just a little. "Boxing?"

"Did a little bit myself, when I was a young man," the priest offered.

"Well...I don't think I'd be allowed, what with my jobs at home and all, you know."

"Now, tell me, Mickey, you said somethin' about your pa gettin' mad at you? Are things all right down there?"

Father McDermott was well aware that Fergus Monaghan was at best an unfriendly parishioner who had moved with his wife and child to County Mayo six years ago, that he and his wife Marian—though she was many times more cordial than Fergus—had made no efforts and resisted requests to join in any parish groups or activities other than Sunday Mass. And he had heard the rumors of Fergus's drinking and abuse, so Mickey's fearful reaction at the mention of his father's being called was at once a concern to Father McDermott.

"Um, yes, sir, it's just that he don't want me in any trouble...you know, drawin' attention to myself."

"Drawin' attention to yourself?"

"Yes, sir, he says that sometimes."

"Do you know why?" Father McDermott asked with a curious squint.

"No, sir," replied the nine-year-old, unaware that both he and Father McDermott would learn the answer almost thirteen years later.

Father McDermott shrugged and said, "Well, fine then," as he stood up, and continued, "You'll come talk to me if you have any problems then, won't you?"

"Yes, Father," said Mickey as he rose to leave. He walked to the door.

"I'll go back to class now, Father."

"Yes, of course…and Mickey, that was good, what you did out there, helpin' that little lassie the way you did. But you try to stay out of fights now, you hear me?"

✴   ✴   ✴   ✴

About a half-mile down Treanbeg Road, Mickey saw Caitlin O'Connor sitting on her front porch steps. She stood and called out, "Hi, Mickey!"

He waved and said, "Hello, Caitlin."

"Father McDermott wasn't mad at you, was he?"

Mickey walked up the O'Connors' short front walk. "No, he was pretty nice to me after everybody left. He wasn't mad at all. Are your knees okay?"

"They're okay."

Mickey didn't speak for a moment; tilting his head, he appeared to be thinking about something, but he was listening. "Who is that, Caitlin?" he asked.

"Oh, that's just my mam. She's giving a voice lesson. She teaches voice and piano, and she can play my daddy's guitar—"

"Shhh," interrupted Mickey. "Let me listen just a minute." He sat on the front steps with Caitlin.

Mrs. O'Connor was singing lines from the traditional Irish song "The Hills of Kerry," and her student was repeating them after her:

The palm trees wave on high
Along the fertile shore
Adieu the hills of Kerry
I ne'er will see no more

"I like that!" said Mickey. "I'd like to sing."

"Well, my mam can teach you. She teaches other kids."

He chatted with Caitlin a few more minutes while he listened.

Keran came out the front door as Mickey stood to leave, and said, "Hey, Mickey, I heard about what you did to Danny and Jimmy. That was good. Did Caitlin thank you?"

"She doesn't need to thank me," Mickey said, a little shy.

Caitlin stood one step above Mickey, reached for his neck with both arms, saying, "Here's a thank you!" She kissed him on the cheek then pulled back with a look that said she had just shocked herself, and she giggled.

"Caitlin!" Keran scolded, "I'm tellin' Mam!"

Mickey was embarrassed now, but laughing at this funny little girl. He said, "I have to go and do my jobs!"—and he hurried away.

*   *   *   *

About forty-five minutes later, Mrs. O'Connor pulled her Renault into Monaghans' driveway, with Caitlin and Keran in tow. As the three got out and shut the doors, Mrs. O'Connor, holding a paper plate covered with aluminum foil, shushed the two girls and said, "Listen!"

As they listened, they looked up to the hill behind the Monaghan house and saw Mickey carrying a few planks over his shoulder, as he repeatedly sang,

> *The palm trees wave on high*
> *Along the fertile shore*
> *Adieu the hills of Kerry*
> *I ne'er will see no more*

"What a pretty voice he has!" Mrs. O'Connor remarked.

"He heard you singin' that today, and he says he wants to be a singer!" offered Caitlin, remembering what Mickey had said.

"Well, I'll be," muttered Mrs. O'Connor as she walked to the front door with the girls close behind.

Marian opened the door and greeted the O'Connors. "What can I do for you, Ellen?"

Fergus had heard the automobile and had walked around to the front of the house from the storage shed cater-cornered to the house in the rear. He stood about ten feet away as Ellen O'Connor spoke.

"Well, I don't know if you heard, but your brave son saved my little Caitlin from a couple o' ruffians today, and I've made him a plate of biscuits as a thanks from us," she said smiling.

As Marian accepted the plate expressing her appreciation, Fergus immediately moved to take it from Marian. He handed it back to Ellen, saying, "Y' might as well just take these with you. I'll not have the lad gettin' rewarded for his fightin' at school! I spoke to Father McDermott about it."

Ellen turned to look at Fergus's face and quickly surmised an unpleasantness that she did not care to deal with any further. She had started to speak, intending to explain that Mickey had done a good thing, but realized she wouldn't get far.

"All right then, I didn't mean to interfere," she said curtly as she turned to leave.

"I'm sure y' didn't," Fergus said, as politely as he might ever speak, "but I have rules for the boy."

Ellen was a bit befuddled, and said, "Well, I'll certainly not butt into how anyone raises their children. Come along, girls."

She had intended to comment on Mickey's pretty singing voice, and to remind them that she teaches voice, but now she couldn't get away quite fast enough. Caitlin looked up to the hill. Mickey had dropped his planks and was watching them now. He waved, and Caitlin waved back.

"Mickey's daddy's not a very nice man," Caitlin said as Ellen turned from the driveway.

"He's mean!" said Keran.

Mrs. O'Connor would have normally stopped her daughters from criticizing an adult, especially a parent, but she didn't speak.

Meanwhile, Mickey had walked down the hill to ask, "How come the O'Connors were stopping by, Pa?"

"Mrs. O'Connor had some notion that she should thank you for helpin' her little one up at the school today. You need to finish carryin' them boards across the hill for me, y' hear?"

"Well, is that all they said, Pa?"

"That's all they said, and I told 'em you'll not be gettin' int' any more fights on their account or anybody else's in the future, if y' know what's good for you. Do y' need me t' tell you again about those boards?"

"No, sir," said Mickey, and he walked back up the hill.

∗   ∗   ∗   ∗

After dinner, Mrs. O'Connor uncovered the plate of twenty-four biscuits for dessert. Caitlin didn't eat any, but snuck a half-dozen into her paper napkin, then into her new schoolbag. While her mother wasn't looking, she took her schoolbag to her room and slid it under her bed.

Ellen tucked Caitlin into bed at eight o'clock sharp, while Keran was still working arithmetic problems. She sat on the side of Caitlin's bed and recited the *Hail Mary* and *Our Father* with her.

Caitlin followed with her normal "God bless Keran, God bless Mam, God bless Daddy, and bring him home safe, and…" She squirmed a little with her lips pursed in a smile.

"Go ahead, sweetheart," Ellen urged, smiling back.

"God bless Mickey!" she squealed, pulling the covers over her head as she blushed.

Ellen O'Connor sat on the bed waiting for her daughter to come out of hiding. Caitlin slowly lowered her blankets and looked at her mother.

"Caitlin?"

"Yes, Mam?"

"You make sure that Mickey eats those biscuits when you give them to him, all right? You don't want him takin' 'em home and gettin' in trouble with his father."

Caitlin yanked the covers back over her head. Ellen pulled them down to kiss her on the cheek. "Y' hear me?"

"Yes, Mam."

THE NEXT DAY AND AFTER

Caitlin saw Mickey with Eamonn Powers in the schoolyard after the final bell, and she called to him. She gave him the biscuits, which he shared with her and Eamonn, and then he left Eamonn to walk home with his new friend.

"Do y' know the rest of the words to that song, Caitlin? 'The palm trees wave on high'? I keep singin' it, but all I know are a few lines."

"My mam will tell you. She knows lots of songs."

When they arrived at Caitlin's residence, Mrs. O'Connor was busy with a piano lesson; but, when Caitlin interrupted her with Mickey's request, she excused herself and stepped outside to meet Mickey and to thank him for helping Caitlin.

"I'll write down those words for you, Mickey, and maybe Caitlin can sing them for you. Or you can stop someday when I don't have a lesson."

Caitlin ran to find him after school the following day, gave him a paper with the handwritten words to "The Hills of Kerry," and sang them with him on the way home.

This would come to be a course of action for Caitlin: she'd have her mother teach her a new song, usually a traditional Irish folk song or ballad, then run to find Mickey after school to share it with him. They became fast friends in this way, an odd sort of twosome walking home singing and talking together—the popular, sometimes tough-guy, fourth-class boy with his garrulous little six-year-old pal.

Mrs. O'Connor was pleased to help Mickey learn melodies when she was available. A few years later, she would teach the two children to harmonize with one another; and she even let Mickey try his hand at her husband's guitar, which interested neither of her daughters, but which Mickey coveted. He knew that he had no chance of getting a guitar from his parents, and so he practiced on Mr. O'Connor's whenever allowed. In return, he would do routine yard work or handyman jobs, helping Mrs. O'Connor however he could. Keran and Caitlin, meanwhile, both studied voice and piano, and Keran, the violin as well.

He hid all of this activity from his parents, as Fergus Monaghan could barely tolerate Mickey's doing *anything* other than work at home. He had once angrily instructed his son—after beating him upon finding him helping with yard work at O'Connors'—that "charity begins in the home."

So, of course, Fergus was unaware—although Mickey constantly sang his songs of Ireland as he tended the sheep and did his work—that Ellen O'Connor was providing Mickey with free music lessons. Indeed, he would have been furious to know that his son was wasting his time on such nonsense.

Mickey had never met Caitlin's father—Fintan O'Connor rarely came home from his employment in England, where he'd been since Caitlin was only a year old. And shortly after Mickey started secondary school, he learned that he never would meet him: Mr. O'Connor had drowned, going overboard during a drunken brawl on a ferry crossing the Irish Sea from Holyhead, Wales bound for Dun Laoghaire, Ireland. And so, Mickey concluded, the rumors that Mr. O'Connor was a "wild one" were likely correct; but he chose to *not* ask Caitlin, Keran, or their mother about it, all of whom seemed to carry on as usual after the initial shock had passed. *And why not, after all,* Mickey reasoned, *he was never around anyway.*

*   *   *   *

Father McDermott kept an eye on Mickey as he grew, checking with him to see that things were satisfactory at home. He was aware that Mickey worked hard and did well in school, and also that he continued to fight with other boys from time to time. *Always* winning. The fighting was not so much a concern to the priest—boys fight, after all—as was his fear that Mickey might hurt one of the other boys; and so he occasionally warned Mickey that he should always fight fair and that he shouldn't hit the other boys in the head, as he had done to Danny O'Brien. And he also spoke to Mickey of the increasing gossip about his "improper conduct with the opposite sex."

In the late spring of 1984, Father McDermott saw Mickey, now 16, walking up Main Street in Newport and called out to him. Father McDermott had talked to Father Brennan from Westport, who had told him about a young man in his parish, Hugh Conroy, also 16, who could "outbox anyone in the county, so quick and fierce he is!" Fair Day was only weeks away, and Father Brennan was seeking an opponent for Conroy in the boxing competition.

"Now, mind, I've never seen this Conroy, Mickey, so I thought you and I could go over to the gym in Westport, and take a look while he practices. What do you think?"

"Take a look…what? Why do you want *me* to take a look at him?"

"Because I've bet Father Brennan a case of Tullamore Dew that you could whip 'im!"

"Aw, Jesus, Father!" Mickey laughed. "My pa don't want me doin' things like that—fightin' and drawin' attention to myself!"

"Listen, Mickey," the parish priest said smiling as he grabbed his shoulder, "will y' be at Fair Day anyway?"

"Sure I will," he answered, still laughing.

"Well, then, what is there to steppin' into the ring and standin' up for your parish?"

Mickey gave in, as a favor to Father McDermott, and a week later the two stood with a proud Father Brennan, watching Conroy and his sparring partner.

Father McDermott came away with misgivings, and as they walked to his car, he said to Mickey, "I don't know, Mick, the kid's awfully fast, dancin' around, movin' back and forth, up and down…maybe we ought t' forget it."

Mickey didn't answer. They walked another few minutes to the car without speaking. Father McDermott put the key in the ignition, looked over at Mickey and said, "I'll call it off."

Mickey smirked and looked back at the priest. "I'll beat him, and I'll beat him good."

*   *   *   *

When Fair Day arrived, Father McDermott stood in Mickey's corner as his manager. In the opposite corner, Hugh Conroy made lightning strikes at the air around him, bobbing and weaving to the delight of the crowd, as Father McDermott tied the gloves to Mickey's hands and adjusted his headgear. He warned Mickey to spend the first of the three rounds keeping out of Conroy's way, watching and learning his moves, and—for God's sake—protecting himself.

Eamonn Powers and a few somber others sat quietly by, near Mickey's corner. In the last row of seats, unnoticed, sat a discomfited Caitlin Molly O'Connor with a tear running down her thirteen-year-old cheek.

The bell rang, and Conroy was the showboat, to be sure, but most of his jabs either glanced off Mickey or missed him entirely. Those that connected seemed to have little effect, if any. Mickey kept himself safe, as Father McDermott had instructed; and, as the priest realized that Mickey was in no apparent danger, he began yelling out, "Go on and get him!" But Mickey just kept moving away and defending.

The round ended, and Father McDermott scolded Mickey. "What the hell's wrong with you, Monaghan? Can't you throw a punch, for God's sake?"

Mickey took a drink of water and wiped his face.

"The hell?! You told me not to!" he yelled back. "I could've thrown a lot of punches, but you said to keep away from 'im!"

"Damnit to hell! Didn't y' hear me screamin' at you to go get him!?" Father McDermott barked at him, clearly caught up in the excitement, and now convinced that Mickey could win.

"I can't hear a feckin' th—oh!—sorry, Father, but I can't hear *anything* out there with this crowd!"

"Never mind that!" shouted Father McDermott as the bell clanged for round two. "Just get out there and fight like a man!"

Mickey stood up in his corner and watched as Conroy danced to the center of the ring. He took three steps forward, avoided a jab, and caught Conroy's head with a hard right, then a left. It wasn't artful, but Mickey's strength was overpowering, and Conroy staggered backwards. Mickey walked after him, pounding him as he went, step by step, with a merciless barrage of brutal punches.

Within seconds, it was evident that the fight was over, with Conroy backed into his corner, scrunching down helplessly; but Mickey wouldn't let up at all, and the force of his blows literally kept Conroy's body up on his feet, thumping against the ropes. When the referee was finally able to pull Mickey away, Conroy dropped to the canvas like a dead man.

*   *   *   *

"So y' think y' want a boxin' match, do y'?" Fergus Monaghan roared out as he entered the cottage at about half nine. He was *woeful* drunk.

Mickey sat with Marian at the kitchen table. She was upset and angry. He had told her about his boxing as soon as he had returned from Fair Day a few hours earlier. He had semi-apologized, but told her frankly that he had decided to do it knowing that they wouldn't have allowed it, and whatever that brought him, he'd just have to take it. He was still trying to explain that they were wrong to forbid him from participating in sports, when Fergus arrived.

Marian had warned him that his pa would have plenty to say to him when he found out, and, apparently, he had.

Mickey stood as Fergus approached him. Fergus punched his arm. "Is that what y' want, boy?" he yelled. He pushed Mickey back against the sink. "Well, then, I'll show y' boxing! Disrespectful little cocksucker! Is that your thanks to us?" He jabbed at Mickey's chest.

Mickey watched Fergus carefully. He figured he'd let him release his frustration, hoping that would take care of it. *After all, I did disobey my parents. They may be the two biggest arseholes on this blessed green island, but I did disobey them.*

Fergus smacked Mickey's head, and said, "You sneak around with your priest friend disregarding my rules…little bastard! Let the fuckin' Church pay for your raisin', then!"

Mickey did not want Fergus to hit him in the head again, and he braced himself to block any further blows.

Fergus bellowed, "Let fuckin' Father McDermott buy your clothes and put food on the table for y'! Let that cocksucker take care of y'…couple o' cocksuckers, the both o' y'—is that what y' do for each other?" He tried to smack Mickey's head again.

But he had gone too far, and, as Mickey deflected the smack with a hard chop to Fergus's forearm, for the first time in his life, he yelled—actually screamed—at Fergus, "You don't speak those words about a priest of God, and you damn feckin' well don't speak them about Father McDermott!"

Mickey's teeth were clenched, his fists were clenched, and his breathing was quick and shallow. It occurred to him that he might well be on the verge…of seriously injuring Fergus Monaghan.

Fortunately for Fergus, the same thought occurred to him, and he backed up. He stared back at Mickey uneasily. He spoke cautiously, "This is my house…and I make the rules." He looked at Marian as he rubbed his sore arm, turned, and went to bed.

Fergus, and Marian at his direction, would never again attend Mass at St. Patrick's, nor anywhere else for that matter.

*   *   *   *

The Monaghans lived under a fragile truce following Mickey's act of defiance. Whether Fergus was testing Mickey, punishing him, or was simply unsettled to realize that his own days of physical superiority had ended, he seemed more determined than ever to see that his adoptive son's days were filled with hard work.

Mickey, for his part, kept to himself and did what he was told, continually daydreaming about his future and the day that he would walk away from Treanbeg Road and the Monaghan sheep farm. Knowing that his education would give him the best opportunity for success, he dedicated himself to his schoolwork more than ever.

In September, when Fergus and a neighbor, Johnny Daly, went to the sheep auctions in Maam Cross, County Galway—an annual long weekend away that Mickey had always enjoyed—Fergus left him at home for the first time, still bitter and at odds with him.

Coincidentally, however, Mrs. O'Connor had scheduled that weekend for her and the girls to repaint their house, because the paint had chipped off and faded to the point that "if it weren't for the car out front, people would think the place was inhabited by ghosts." Mickey stopped by Friday evening to see that they had already begun.

Ellen and the girls were inside eating supper as he arrived, and he walked to the side where he saw a ladder and a paint bucket. There were three distinct areas where paint had been applied, and, as Mickey examined them, he became horri- fied. Not only did the three ladies have no apparent notion of scraping, sanding or priming, but also, he reckoned, they had approximately the same amount of paint on the yard as on the house.

He knocked and let himself in.

"Ah, be-Jaysus, missus," he said with a laugh, "I hope you three musicians don't plan to continue in this line o' work!"

As he explained the futility of carrying on without proper preparation, he offered to go to Castlebar for primer, then go home to borrow paint scrapers, sandpaper, and tarps. Mrs. O'Connor listened attentively, and—now con- cerned—she found a twenty-punt note for Mickey to purchase a can of primer.

When he returned with the primer, her change, and the other equipment, he suggested they let him "get a start" with the scraping and priming, and that he'd let them know when to get back to their respective paintbrushes. He worked until their bedtime, then assured them that it wouldn't be safe to paint until he examined the wood in the morning. When he returned, he put them off further while he "tested" the paint; then further; and by Sunday afternoon, he had fin- ished the job completely.

After cleaning up, he went to the front door full of confidence and proud of his meticulous work. He was all set to be at his smart-alecky best, and to tell the three ladies, "There's one can still half-full, if you care to finish touching up the lawn and the shrubbery."

But they were ready for him. Ellen stood inside the door with Keran on one side of her and Caitlin on the other. She handed him Mr. O'Connor's guitar, in its case with a ribbon around it, and a big card that said "For the Man of Our House"; and the best he could do was to *not* cry before offering his quiet thanks.

FRIDAY 24 JANUARY 1986

Mickey was almost asleep when he heard Fergus's truck pull in about half eleven. He could tell from the abrupt braking and the slamming of the truck door that Fergus was mad drunk. *Jesus Christ, what now?*

Of course, he slammed the door as he entered the cottage, and Mickey knew that, if Marian had been asleep, she had now been awakened. *Jesus Christ!*

Kitchen cupboard doors slammed. Fergus muttered. The refrigerator door slammed, and Mickey could hear that Marian was now in the kitchen talking to Fergus. Fergus bellowed, "Name o' Christ! Why in the hell can't you keep some damn food in the damn house?! What in the hell do we have to eat, damnit?"

"Fergus, please! We had a big dinner!"

Fergus was raging. "Dinner's not the fuckin' end of the world, for chrissake! Now, *why is there nothing to eat, damnit?!*"

Mickey heard a crashing of the kitchen table and chairs, a thud, and Marian's scream. He leapt from his bed and into the kitchen. A chair was on its side, and Marian lay on the floor behind it, slowly getting up as she cried.

Mickey helped her up as Fergus continued yelling, "Get the hell back to your room! You're not needed out here!"

Mickey silently picked up the chair and slid it into place. He knew that, drunk or sober, Fergus could no longer physically hurt him, and he figured that Fergus knew it as well. Nonetheless, with Fergus's foul temper and abusive nature, especially when he was drunk, he understood that the day might come when Fergus would need the proof. This night would be that day.

Mickey was a month away from turning eighteen, and thanks to Fergus, rock solid. He stood between Fergus and Marian.

"I told you to get the hell out o' here!" Fergus yelled.

Mickey stood calmly before him and said, "You left off the part where you say, 'if you know what's good for you.' Could be y' understand that don't apply anymore."

"I'll tell you what applies in my house, you smart-aleck little bastard!" Fergus screamed as he charged Mickey. Mickey had just enough room to sidestep him and give him a shove as he passed. Fergus went sprawling on the floor.

"You're drunk, Pa. Maybe it's bedtime."

Marian tried to help Fergus up, but he roared, "Get yer fuckin' hands off o' me!" He fell again as he pushed her away, and caused her to fall again.

Mickey's anger grew, not just at this act of cruelty but also at Marian's stupidity in trying to help such a miserable bollocks. He decided to force the confrontation.

"Mr. Monaghan, if you keep bouncin' that fat fuckin' arse o' yours on the floor, you're goin' t' break the fuckin' boards, and then have me fixin' 'em for the rest of the fuckin' week. I got better things to do." *That should do it.*

Fergus stood and stumbled to kitchen counter. He grabbed a butcher knife and turned to Mickey. He looked liked a madman. He *was* a madman. "You dirty little cocksucker!" he scowled. *Yes, that did it.*

"Not so little, Pa. You better watch yourself," Mickey said evenly as he moved around the table with his back to the living room. Fergus walked after him, holding the knife, prepared to strike. Mickey allowed him to get within reach, and Fergus took a futile swipe at him as Marian screamed in horror.

Fergus, now frustrated, hurled the knife toward Mickey, then attacked him. Mickey ducked, and the knife sailed into the living room. He put his right fist squarely into Fergus's jaw, and, as Fergus veered left, Mickey's left fist hit him above the ear. Fergus was down and out.

Marian was hysterical. Mickey rang for an ambulance.

*   *   *   *

Two paramedics knelt by Fergus, gently reviving him to a groggy state. Mickey heard the one whisper to the other, "He needs feckin' mouthwash more than he needs medical help!"

As they placed him on a gurney to wheel him out, two Gardai walked in through the open front door.

"Evenin' ma'am. I'm Garda Burke, and this is Garda Kelly. What do we have here?" he said to Marian.

Marian looked at him with her left eye swollen shut and said, "Nothin' to be concerned about. Just a small argument between the boy and his father." She was extremely nervous.

"Y' all right there, sir?" Kelly asked Fergus in a loud voice. Fergus mumbled something unintelligible. "Who did this to you, sir?" No response. Passed out. Knocked out.

"We don't really need you here, officers. Just a little…just a little—"

"Aw, Christ, Ma, what the hell are you talkin' about? Tell 'em what happened!"

In truth, Marian could only think about whatever retribution might be inflicted upon her if Fergus were to be arrested and charged. God knows he didn't need more reasons for wife abuse.

"Well, *he* did it! He hit his father!" Marian said, motioning to Mickey. She cried, covering her mouth with her hands, as she stood looking at her unconscious husband.

"What?!!" Mickey said, incredulous.

"Is it true, son?" asked Garda Kelly.

"True that I hit him after he came at me with a fuckin' butcher knife slashin' away, then throwin' it at me! True that I hit him after he tossed *her* around the room like a sack o' flour. Look at her eye, for chrissake!"

"We can see that, son. Your husband did that to you, ma'am?"

"I don't know. We don't need you here!"

"What about the knife, ma'am, did you see a butcher knife?"

"I didn't see any knife. We don't need you here."

Suddenly, Fergus stirred and called out, "My fault! My fault! Leave him alone!"

The Gardai ignored him.

"Ma'am, there's been a fairly significant incident here. If your son attacked your husband for no reason, we'll have to take him with us."

"Marian!" Fergus called out from the gurney, and she hurried to him. He weakly motioned for her to lean to him so he could whisper, but Mickey was able to overhear him calling her a "stupid fool," and then warning her not to allow the police to take Mickey.

Garda Burke asked Mickey, "Where's this butcher knife you say he threw?"

Mickey turned, nodding to the living room, and he immediately saw it stuck into the far wall, still hanging. He looked back to the officers. They glimpsed at each other and shook their heads.

"I take it that's not your taste in wall decorations there, is it, ma'am?" asked Kelly.

She bowed her head and said nothing. Kelly nodded an okay, allowing the paramedics to take Fergus away, and then he went to get the knife.

Burke said, "What's your name, son?"

"Michael," he said sadly, as he stared at Marian. "Michael Peter...*Monaghan*," he added with disgust.

"Well, Michael, maybe we could let your mother go on to bed," said Burke. "She don't seem to want to help us much. Then you, Garda Kelly and I can sit at the table here and finish up our report."

They watched Marian slump off to her bedroom and close the door. She was moaning.

"You'll excuse me one moment?" Mickey asked.

"Yes, Michael, go ahead," said Burke.

Mickey opened the bedroom door to see Marian sitting on the side of her bed.

"I'll have my things out of here tomorrow morning. I feel sorry for you," he said quietly, but with contempt.

"Where y' goin', Mickey?" she sobbed.

"Away from you." He shut the door and went to the kitchen table.

The Gardai stayed with Mickey another forty-five minutes as he detailed for them the events of that particular evening, and he then gave a history of Fergus's abuse to both him and Marian. He could not tell the officers why she had refused to cooperate, but they assured him that it was not unusual for a woman to be unwilling to speak against her husband in these situations.

In truth, although he didn't mention it, Mickey was even more confused by Fergus's defending him, even though it did not seem to be quite that.

It was 1:30 a.m. when the officers finally left.

SATURDAY 25 JANUARY 1986

At 7:45 a.m. Mickey knocked on the front door of the presbytery. Father McDermott, clad in a Marquette University sweatshirt and his black slacks, opened the door to see him standing there with a suitcase. He was about to make a joke about Mickey leaving town, but he discerned the pathetic expression on his face.

"What's wrong, Mick?" he said, swinging the door all the way open.

"I need a place to live. I thought you might recommend something."

"Oh, boy! Oh, my! C'mon in, Mickey, there's coffee brewin'. What's the trouble, son?"

They walked to the kitchen. Father McDermott pulled out a chair for Mickey and motioned for him to sit. He grabbed another cup from the cupboard and placed it by the still-brewing pot.

Mickey started to say that Fergus had tried to kill him the previous night, but his voice started breaking, and he couldn't speak. As if to say "Give me a minute," he held an index finger in the air as he collected his emotions.

Father McDermott stood by him and said, "There's nothin' wrong with cryin', Mickey…well…whenever you're ready. Take your time."

"Sorry, Father." He told the story of the previous evening, explaining with frustration that Marian had preferred to lie for her "miserable shite of a husband" rather than telling the simple truth to support her son.

"Well, Mick, I can't say that I understand this, but I know the bond between a husband and wife can be strong beyond reason. That's a good thing, for the most part, o' course, but not here. Not here."

Father McDermott dismissed his first thought—to suggest that he stay with the O'Connors for a time, knowing Mickey was close to them. Mickey's ever-growing reputation for "chasing the girls" was a concern to Father McDermott, and he didn't want to be responsible for placing him in the midst of two decent young ladies like Keran and Caitlin. But then he thought, *Well, he's down there quite a bit anyway, and I know Ellen is very fond of him.*

"Mick, what would y' think if I asked Mrs. O'Connor if you could stay a short time at her place?"

"No! Never! They'll not see me as some pitiful charity case. I have some money, Father, I can pay for a room somewhere, I just don't know where. I'm quittin' school t' work."

"Aw, Mick!" Father McDermott groaned. "That's not the answer, lad! Don't go throwin' away your young life because of a fight with your ma and pa!"

Mickey said nothing, so Father McDermott stood up. "Get your bag, Mick, and follow me upstairs. There's a room up here you can use, but you're goin' t' work for it, and I'll tell you right now—no arguments—I'll be goin' down to talk to your mother and to your father, wherever he may be. And I'll be damned if I'll let 'em put me off!"

$*$ $*$ $*$ $*$

Fergus had indeed been charged with assaulting both Marian and Mickey, but Father McDermott, through his friendship with Senator Frank O'Malley, worked with the police and the Court to have the charges dropped in exchange for Fergus's promises to quit drinking—which he did for a few months—and to see a counselor, which he never did.

Knowing this, Father McDermott began making random visits to the Monaghans, although not particularly welcome, telling Fergus that—if it came up—he would represent that he had been his counselor, as long as he behaved himself; and he assured him that the charges could be refiled if he didn't.

Mickey had returned home after spending five days at the presbytery. Fergus began paying him wages for his work, and Mickey bought an old pickup truck from Johnny Daly. This allowed him to get a gig singing and playing guitar at the Brown Oak Inn in Newport, then working as part-time bartender when needed.

He applied and was admitted to the college in Castlebar, to study business, starting the fall of 1986.

When Caitlin finished secondary school in '89, unable to afford college, she started as a clerk with the Newport branch of the West Irish Bank. She planned to work a few years, then perhaps begin college classes one or two at a time, as she was able.

FRIDAY 11 MAY 1990

Caitlin and Mickey had run into each other at Chambers' Market in Newport the prior evening. Caitlin had told Mickey that she'd be organizing old records at the Bank's main office in Castlebar on the following day, and Mickey suggested that he'd buy her a noon lunch at McCarthy's if she could get away.

He walked into McCarthy's right at 12:00, and he saw that Caitlin was already sitting at a table for two with a man, about 30 years old, in the seat opposite her.

Although Mickey was only fifteen feet or so from her when he stepped through the door, she stood up and waved, "Hi, Mickey! Oh, sorry, Mr. Sullivan, here's my lunch date!"

As Mickey walked to the table, Mr. Sullivan turned in his chair to look at him, but he didn't get up.

"Mickey, this is Mr. Sullivan who works at the bank here in Castlebar. Mr. Sullivan, this is my lunch date, Mickey Monaghan."

Still seated, he extended his hand. "Bill Sullivan, Mickey. Wish we had another chair for you, but maybe some other day—ha!—just kiddin'," he said as he stood and drank from the water glass that would have been Mickey's, and then put it down in the center of the place mat.

"Good taste in lunch dates, Mickey."

He walked to a table against the wall, sat and read the paper, paying no attention, it seemed, to anything else.

Sullivan was about 5'10", maybe 185 pounds, not much of it muscle. He had about three months' growth of curly black hair that he might have run a comb through earlier in the day, and his "five o'clock shadow" was five hours early. A dowdy sort, in his rumpled maroon wool suit.

Mickey remained standing as he watched Sullivan move to the other table. He picked up the water glass that Sullivan had drunk from and walked it to the back of the restaurant. He held it far in front of him, as though it were poison or explosive, handing it through the kitchen door to a dishwasher. He hoped Sullivan had seen him. *Bastard.*

Back at the table, he said, "Who was that?"

Caitlin shuddered and made a noise indicating revulsion. "He's always lookin' at me and talkin' to me, like we're friends, or like he's interested. I know he's married. He's an auditor, and he comes down to Newport about every two weeks, you know, checkin' the books or somethin'. He just followed me down here like a stalker, walkin' twenty feet behind, and he comes in and sits down with me."

Mickey stared over at him. "Cait, I hate to say it, but I bet that's not the last trouble you'll have with him. Is there someone you can talk to about him?"

"Yes, Papa, I'll tell his mam on him," she said, and they laughed.

Mickey was aware that Caitlin, who was about to turn nineteen, was considered quite an incredible catch. Her silky mane of dark red wavy hair fell below her shoulder blades now, her 5'6" figure was perfectly developed, and her china complexion flawless. When she walked down the street, heads turned. Always. Even today, when she was in a sweatshirt and jeans to move storage boxes, she was beautiful.

Nonetheless, when *Mickey* looked at her, he saw his adoring little friend who had become in many ways his closest friend, oftentimes his music partner, a person with intelligence and common sense, a person he trusted. Sure, she was a pretty girl, but she was the same girl, with the same pretty face, that he had looked at for almost thirteen years on a regular—sometimes daily—basis.

And for most of those thirteen years, anything beyond friendship between them would have certainly been taboo. After all, when Mickey's adolescent hormones kicked in at age thirteen, Caitlin was *ten.* Even much later, when Mickey started college at age eighteen, a relationship with a fifteen-year-old Caitlin would have been unthinkable.

And he truly *liked* Caitlin. She was his kid sister in a sense. Over the years, they had sat together on Mrs. O'Connor's piano bench learning voice, piano and guitar, harmonizing and playing duets. In addition to singing on the way home from school, they had performed together at various school and church functions; and more recently, as Mickey was able to get work singing and playing guitar in the pubs, Caitlin sometimes joined him singing a few songs, and even playing piano if one was available.

At age twenty-two, Mickey stood 6'1", with 190 trim pounds of muscle from his years of hard farm work. Smart, talented, and carefree, it seemed, and a "runaround" with the girls. He kept to himself about his numerous flings and conquests, but they had become, in the gossip circles, a matter of constant update. He could never have subjected Caitlin to such chatter.

Perhaps also somewhere in his thoughts, like one of a thousand stars slipping in and out of passing clouds, may have been the notion that Caitlin—as a mate—was somewhat contentious, maybe too proud, too *something,* to be a day-to-day partner for his life. Or maybe, that in the long run, he was not the one who could provide all that she wanted and deserved out of life. But there was no need to think about that, and so he didn't.

Regardless, there was often speculation of romance between him and Caitlin, or of its future inevitability, given their known fondness for one another and their years of companionship. Caitlin especially made little effort to conceal her affection for Mickey, teasing him about taking her out, being her boyfriend, etc. But he had never considered dating her, and, to him, it was all routine small talk.

Their closeness was known and respected by their friends and acquaintances, but God help any stray young buck who, unaware and in Mickey's presence, spoke about her in vulgar terms. For instance, the visiting rugby player a month or so previous, who came into a Newport pub with his teammates on a Saturday evening following the game. When Caitlin and her girlfriends walked by the group, he commented, "Whoa, look at the shirt on you!—I'll be ridin' that milk truck home tonight!"

As the teammates roared with their laughter of approval, Mickey threw him to the floor, dragged him by a foot out of the pub, across the sidewalk and into the street. He stood over the frightened athlete and said, "Well, look at you in the gutter. Already home. Now you don't need that ride."

*   *   *   *

The waitress brought their grilled cheese sandwiches and tomato soups. Caitlin put half of her sandwich on Mickey's plate, then held the other half while she dumped her crisps on top of his.

"Aren't you playing tonight, Mickey?"

"That I am, Miss, at Seamus Kilkelly's. It's the one out in Liscarney. Nice place. Big and open, remember?"

"Sure. He's a sweetheart, Seamus is!"

"Just a real gentleman."

"If I come out there, Mickey, will you let me sing a few with you?"

"I won't let you leave until you do! We got enough, let's do a whole set! Oh, and here's somethin' I want to try on 'Fields of Athenry': rather than waitin' til the third verse to modulate, we'll go 'G' to 'A' on the second, then I got a nice riff that'll go to 'C' for the third—which *you* sing, and I'll harmonize on the chorus!"

"You're goin' 'A' all the way to 'C?'"

"Oh, you'll love it."

"Okay, I'll sing it, and then you can take me home, can't you?" she smiled, knowing that he would not likely do that.

It was the rare weekend night, according to current blather—and true—that Mickey did not find his way into the bed of a college girlfriend, waitress, shop clerk, whatever. It bothered Caitlin, because she loved him, and at nearly 19 felt their ages were now "perfect" for each other. But it was nothing new, and she was resigned to it. Their relationship, she reasoned, although not romantic at this time, was so honest that on that wonderful day when he would finally realize that they were meant for each other, all the others would immediately be forgotten.

"Stop, Caitlin," he responded to her request for a lift home.

"Yeah, Mickey, I'll help you pack up, and we'll go back to Newport together!" she continued.

"Caitlin, I'm not takin' you home. Go home however you get there!" he said, smiling back, ready for her to keep it up a bit longer.

"Well, I figure I'll go out with you!" she said.

"I'll *give* you a lift out," he said, then stopping himself, "Now, Caitlin...okay, if you want a lift out, fine, but I'm not takin' you home, and that's that!" he said laughing a bit, knowing she was probably not finished.

She leaned over her plate and whispered, "So who y' fuckin', Mickey?"

As well as he knew her, he was stunned by her question. He now leaned toward her and, without humor, said, "Caitlin, I don't want to hear that out of your mouth. That is *really* unattractive!"

She looked at him a little sheepishly, trying to smile, and said, "Well, you are! Everybody talks about it."

"Well, whether I, what the—look, Caitlin!" He was a little tongue-tied and still not smiling a bit. "Whatever I do is one thing. But you—a girl like you—you do *not* use that language, that *word!*"

"Well, what's a girl like me...what am I like?" she said, feigning sincerity.

Even knowing she was putting him on a bit, he did not want her to think he'd fail to pursue his point, but the best he could come up with was, "Well, uh, nice. You're a nice girl."

Caitlin burst out laughing. She looked back at him—holding back his own laughter at his feeble explanation—and said out loud, "We-e-ll...I'm makin' progress, aren't I?" She continued laughing briefly, repeating, "Nice, aren't I *nice?*"

"Are you comin' tonight, then, Cait?"

"Yes, Mickey, I am. Peggy O'Grady from the Castlebar branch is driving and taking me home, if she has to."

"She does, indeed. C'mon, I'll walk you back."

Bill Sullivan got up at the same time and walked out behind them.

*   *   *   *

Mickey was scheduled to play a 4-hour 8 p.m. to 12 midnight gig at Seamus Kilkelly's Pub in Liscarney, about 24 miles from his home outside of Newport.

All that Mickey could see in the immediate vicinity were a few houses on one side of the road and the pub on the other, with fallow farmland surrounding it. He had once asked Seamus if his pub was in Liscarney, or if Liscarney was somewhere in his pub.

Mickey was breaking in a new pair of steel-toed leather work boots on this night, and he hoped they'd be reasonably comfortable while he stood and sang for four hours. He arrived about 7:30 p.m. and went in to greet the owner.

"Good evenin', Mr. Kilkelly!"

"Hello, Mickey, do you need any help this evenin'?" Seamus said as he towel dried pint glasses.

He was a good-looking man, whose completely silver hair probably made him appear older than he was.

"No, sir, but thank you for askin'. Just a few things to unload. I will need to get two microphones from your closet, if that's okay?"

"Help yourself."

Mickey carried in the amplifier, speaker, guitar, and canvas equipment bag from his pickup, and he finished setting up within twenty minutes. Seamus walked over and handed him a pint of Guinness.

"Who's joinin' you this evenin'?" he said, nodding to the two microphones.

"Caitlin O'Connor, a friend of mine who was out here last time. Long red hair, she sat and talked with you at the bar for a while, if you remember."

"If I remember?"

"Yes, sir," said Mickey, knowing that his question was tongue-in-cheek.

Seamus smiled at Mickey and said, "I tell you what. The day I *don't* remember talking to Caitlin O'Connor, will you go get a gun and put me out o' my damn misery?"

"Oh, you must converse well, you and Caitlin!" Mickey said as they laughed.

"You're a lucky man, Monaghan!"

"No, no, sir! She's just my very good friend."

Seamus waved him away, as though he didn't believe him, saying, "That girl is good craic, she is, good craic altogether!"

He walked to a table-for-two near the door and placed a "Reserved" sign on it, then returned to his patrons at the bar.

Mickey started singing right at 8:00 p.m., and as usual, some rearranged their chairs or stools so they could see the source of this fine tenor voice, singing along when they knew the words.

Caitlin and Peggy walked in about 8:40 p.m., ten minutes before Mickey would take a break. Caitlin had obviously changed her clothes, as she was wearing a light green scooped-neck blouse under a dark green jacket, and a better pair of blue jeans.

Seamus called out to Caitlin, motioning her to take the reserved table.

Peggy was very pretty, about 5'3", trim with short, dark brown gently curled hair, and a sweet face that was *sweet in a sexy way,* Mickey thought as he watched them sit. He guessed she was early or mid twenties, then noticed her wedding rings. *Damn.*

Bill Sullivan walked in two, maybe three, minutes behind the girls and sat nearer to Mickey in a section of wood and leather built-in benches on either side of the fire hearth, the only seats open. *He* had not changed his clothes. The girls, it appeared to Mickey, had not noticed him.

Mickey sang "Marjorie's Ballina B&B," a humorous song that many of the crowd sang along with on the chorus, then finished his first set with an American song, "Fire and Rain."

As Mickey walked to the girls' table, he grabbed an available chair and carried it with him. From behind the bar, Seamus held one finger in the air and raised his eyebrows, clearly asking, "Ready for another?" Mickey nodded, and he sat down with the girls.

"This is Peggy O'Grady from the bank who I was tellin' you about, Mickey."

"Really nice work, Mickey. Caitlin's told me an awful lot about you," she said.

"Thanks much, Peggy." He leaned into the table as though he wanted to share something private. "So did the three of you come down together from the bank?"

"We came from my house," Caitlin said. "What're you talking about, *three?*"

"Well," said Mickey, with a sort of a smile, "let's not all invite him to join us at once, but your close personal friend Bill Sullivan walked in a few steps behind you two. He's over at the hearth."

"Wha...!" Caitlin gasped, jerking her head up to see Sullivan looking back at her. Sullivan raised his hand to wave, and smiled. She gave a slight wave in return, and then leaned back over the table. "Mickey, I don't like this!"

"Are you going to tell his mam?" he teased her, for saying so earlier at lunch.

Mickey stood to take his pint from the bar, and he asked Seamus if he knew the "dowdy fella" over by the hearth. Seamus glanced over and said, "Never seen 'im."

Mickey walked over to Sullivan. He extended his hand and said, "Mr. Sullivan, how nice to see you a second time today!"

Sullivan lightly shook his hand, while Mickey stared back at him with a look that asked Sullivan to explain himself. Sullivan said nothing, but only offered an uncomfortable smile and looked away, inviting Mickey to leave him alone.

Mickey continued, "So do you live out this way, Mr. Sullivan?"

"No, down Murrisk," he said, trying to relax.

"Down Murrisk? That's a good trek away," said Mickey.

"Little bit."

"Ten, twelve miles, I'd guess," Mickey countered.

"Might be," Sullivan said, looking a little irritated.

Mickey was getting impatient himself, and in a mockingly friendly louder tone he asked, "So what brings you down here tonight, Bill?"

"What's it to you?" Sullivan asked, letting his personality get the best of him.

Anger flashed in Mickey, and he was through with the social pleasantries. He sat down on the edge of the bench next to Sullivan, shoving his strong frame against Sullivan's maroon uniform, moving him down a few inches.

"Listen, fucker," he said calmly, "I don't know why you're here, but I know it's no coincidence that you came in on the heels of two girls who had no idea you were followin' 'em. I suspect you got some notions under that shrubbery that might not be appropriate, especially for a married man. I don't like you, Sullivan, and you're goin' t' find out how much, if you keep followin' Caitlin O'Connor around."

Mickey got up and walked back to the girls, trying to adjust his mood as he went.

"That's an odd guy. Better watch him," Mickey told them, not wanting to spoil the evening, but wanting only to stress that he didn't consider Sullivan just some run-of-the-mill pest.

"So, Peggy, where's your old man tonight?"

"Brian? He's over in Belgium at a conference."

"Oh, well, there's nothin' quite so depressin' as seein' all this jewelry on such a pretty girl's finger," he joked, picking up her left hand, "but if he's out o' town, that's a wee ray of light!"

They all laughed, and Peggy, loudly counting on her fingers, said, "Well, let's see, *one*, I'm dropping Caitlin off at 10:45, *two*, I'll be back home at quarter past eleven, *three*, you're off at midnight, yeah, I think I could have the place cleaned up and ready for you!"

They all laughed, and Caitlin smacked his shoulder, "Couple o' whores, the two of you!"

Mickey said, "Well, I can't be sure about Peggy, but God knows *I* try my best, so thanks for sayin' so!"

Caitlin continued, "We do have to leave at 10:00 after this set, though, because Peggy promised she'd ring Brian between 11 and 11:30."

Peggy excused herself for a moment to use the bathroom, giving Mickey a provocative look—he thought—that he wondered if he was misinterpreting. He had no experience with married women, and it seemed irregular that such a young and pretty married woman would seriously flirt while her husband worked out of town.

Caitlin said, "She's flyin' out of Shannon to go and meet him in Belgium at the end of next week. Wouldn't you love to fly in a plane some day, Mickey?"

"I have," he said, reacting to her question.

Whoops. Whether it was the look that Peggy had just given him, the incident with Sullivan, the Guinness, whatever, Mickey had just said something that he never intended to say. The airplane trip he had taken was immediately after Fergus and Marian had adopted him in the U.S.A. It was the flight from Chicago, he believed, to wherever in Ireland they landed. It was a part of the larger story that was off limits.

Caitlin studied Mickey's face, which appeared honest, but after a quick mental runthrough of all she knew about him, smiled and proclaimed, "You have *not!*"

This would have been Mickey's chance to simply say, "Yes, I know, I was just kidding," and his remark might have been forgotten. The fact that he could not do that would eventually change the course of his life forever.

He looked at Caitlin momentarily, then he drummed one finger on the table for a few seconds and said, "Yeah, never mind," without expression.

Caitlin looked puzzled. "You're nervous," she said, and she quickly recalculated her earlier pronouncement.

Caitlin generally knew when Mickey was teasing and when he wasn't. She knew his facial expressions and his moods. She knew, at least, that something to do with her airplane remark was really under his skin. She decided to press on.

"When did you fly in an airplane?" she asked, trying to be casual.

Again, rather than *trying* to deflect the subject with some sort of retraction, for which it was probably too late anyway, his tact could not have been worse: "Caitlin, that is something that I simply cannot talk about," he said, meaning every word of it.

She took in a breath and looked at him. She was both curious and offended—offended to the extent that she didn't know what to say. Finally, she tried: "*You*…can't talk to *me*? About an *airplane ride?*"

He looked back at her, searching her eyes for some understanding, shook his head helplessly and said, "No! I can't."

Mickey was starting to feel some irritation with himself for getting himself into this conversation, and also a little panic. He knew Peggy would be back any second, and he damn sure did not want to be arguing with Caitlin, especially about *this*, in front of a stranger. And of course he was concerned about hurting Caitlin's feelings, with the further immediate concern that she might walk out on him, leaving him upset and worried about her, while he tried to sing songs for another three hours.

Mickey and Caitlin were normally good to one another, and they usually conducted their arguments with a sense of fun. They seldom had real differences, but resolved them quickly if they did. One of them found a way. But now time was running out, and Mickey began to feel desperate.

"Caity Lin…"

"Don't *Caity Lin* me, Mickey," she snapped back. Oh, yes, he had done it, all right.

"Caity Lin" was a pet name that Mickey had given Caitlin shortly after they met. Although she had initially protested this incorrect utterance of her name, she changed her mind when her mother assured her that "he calls you that because he likes you."

He tried again, this time with what he judged to be a necessary concession: "Will you trust me, Caitlin, if I give you my word of honor that I *will* talk to you about this on another day, so that we can put it aside just for this evening?"

She stared back at him. "Another day? Another day *soon?*"

"Sure."

"Yes, Mickey, I will."

She smiled at him, knowing he would certainly not go back on his word, and fully trusting that he intended to tell her all about his airplane ride and whatever it was about it that upset him.

His intent, however, in making this promise, was to tell Caitlin in some detail *why* he could not discuss certain matters, such as this airplane ride.

Mickey looked at his watch. They were overdue. "We better get up there, Cait, where's Peg—" He stopped abruptly and looked for Sullivan. The bench by the hearth was empty. He realized Peggy had been gone much too long for a bathroom break.

"Jesus almighty Christ!" he said as he stood to run out.

They were just a few feet from the hallway where the bathrooms were located. A woman was stepping out of the ladies' room, and Mickey grabbed the door and held it open.

"Peggy!" No answer.

He ran out the front door into the parking lot. He called out, "Peggy! Peggy!"

Caitlin was immediately behind him, and by the time he said, "Where's her car?", Caitlin was running towards it.

At the end of the parking lot, from behind a hedgerow, they saw a form running away, across the field. They ran and found Peggy lying on her back on the other side of the hedge, her shirt torn open, her slacks and panties pulled down below her knees. She looked blankly at them, terrified, but did not move.

Mickey tore out after the fleeing assailant, who was not making great progress negotiating the plowed field. No doubt about it, that was Sullivan's bushy head. As he turned to see Mickey bounding after him, he realized that youth and strength were about to work a horrific revenge upon him. He decided to get on his knees and beg for mercy, but Mickey was on him and pounded a fist into Sullivan's mouth as he bent to kneel.

Sullivan choked on two dislodged teeth as he twisted to his left and fell. He instinctively rolled on the ground to avoid whatever was coming next, but a powerful steel toe crashed into the back of his neck and left him motionless.

As Mickey walked back toward the pub, he stopped at the edge of the field. He looked in every direction to make sure no one could see him. He picked up a clump of the plowed earth and rubbed it on his shirtsleeve, then on a leg of his pants and walked on.

Before Caitlin left with Peggy in the ambulance, she told Mickey that Sullivan had not been able to rape Peggy, as he tried, and that Peggy was grateful they had stopped him.

"She's very upset, but I pray she'll be okay."

Mickey and Caitlin both felt guilt, however, for whatever part they might have had in bringing her into the situation and failing to look out for her. Mickey asked Caitlin if she would attend 10:00 Mass with him Sunday morning, and he then sat with Detective Billy O'Hare in the corner of the pub, answering questions and completing reports until midnight.

Kitty O'Neill, a waitress from the Newport House Hotel, had finished her shift and arrived at Kilkelly's at 11:15 p.m. for her late date with Mickey. He stepped away from O'Hare and explained to her that he would be occupied for a while, that he wouldn't be much good as company that evening, and that she should just go on; but she assured him that he needed a friend at this time, and that she'd be happy to sip a beer while she waited.

Seamus Kilkelly was outwardly understanding as Mickey apologized on his way out with Kitty, but he wasn't happy. Who could blame him?

SATURDAY 12 MAY 1990

Eamonn Powers, now a patrol officer with the local Gardai, had looked into the incident at Kilkelly's at Mickey's request. He stopped by the farm around 6:30 p.m., after working his shift Saturday.

He had found out that Sullivan had been tentatively identified as the perpetrator of an unsolved rape 8 months earlier in Roscahill, in neighboring County Galway.

"What about him? His injuries?" Mickey asked.

"They say he's not movin', and it don't look good that he will. He's froze up for good from the neck down," he said sipping his coffee at Monaghans' dinner table.

Fergus had finished his dinner and was in the back gathering sheep. Marian sat with Mickey and Eamonn.

"Paralyzed?" she asked.

"That he is, Mrs. Monaghan, quadri-...quadriplegia" Eamonn confirmed soberly. "You might get a gold medal pinned on you for this one, Mick."

"I'll do without it. I hope Peggy O'Grady is okay. I feel terrible that that pig slipped out after her while Cait and I sat there goin' on about nothin'."

"You can't blame yourself for that, Mickey," Marian said.

"I don't know, Ma, I knew that Sull—" he started when Eamonn interrupted.

"Oh, by the way, the young lady, I found out, uh, Peggy, had stepped out to ring up her husband on the call box in the parking lot—"

"What?" Mickey said, startled.

"Yeah, she said she wanted to check in with him before listenin' to you two sing. He was away somewhere on business, but he came back today. He's worse off than she is—turns out he had to listen to some of her strugglin' and cryin' through the damn phone!"

"Christ! She was goin' t' get to fly out to see him next weekend...in Belgium, I'm quite sure. Guess that's out."

"I don't know," said Eamonn.

"You can't blame yourself for that, Mickey," Marian repeated.

"Sounds like a pint or two would do you right, Mick. C'mon down to Dunning's about 10. A few of us are meetin'."

"Nah, the old man and me will be shearin' til 10, and I'm not up for it. I got some stuff I need to think on, anyways," he said, looking at Marian, then turning away immediately.

He knew that Caitlin would likely continue to probe once he explained why there were certain topics that he could not discuss. He needed to think about how to make her understand—somehow—that the subject was closed, and to do it without hurting her feelings if possible.

"Well, 10's when we're *gettin'* there, if you change your mind," said Eamonn, as he stood to leave. "We'll be a while."

"I don't think so," said Mickey, and he walked Eamonn out, asking him if he would stop by the O'Connor residence and give them the news. He had already called Caitlin first thing Saturday morning to make sure she was okay, and he thought she'd appreciate hearing this information from Eamonn.

Back in the kitchen, he took his and Eamonn's dishes to the sink.

"What's that y' need to be thinkin' on, Mickey?" said Marian, seeming quietly concerned.

"Nothin' at all, Ma," he said, "just, uh…Sullivan and Peggy and all that."

"Well, what's to think about?" she said, unconvinced.

Mickey could tell she sensed something, so he decided to tell the best lie he could come up with, as he *really* did not want her pursuing this with him.

"Ma, you paralyze a man, I don't care how bad a guy he is, that's somethin' to think about! And Peggy's husband havin' to listen and all—that's bad! I feel bad."

She tried once more: "Well, you just now heard about all that, and it sounds to me—the way you said it—that you were needin' to think about things before that."

He was getting irritated that her intuition was correct, but he knew she'd have to be satisfied with his answers unless he chose to tell her otherwise.

"What is it you're gettin' at, Ma? I was part of a pretty bad mess last night, and I just need a little peace in my mind about it! Is that so hard to believe?" *There, that'll take care of it!*

She said quietly, "I didn't like the way you looked at me when you said it."

"Ma, for chrissake, you're one o' two people in the room! I look at him, I look at you. Now if you got somethin' else to say, say it. If not, I'm goin' out."

She said nothing, and he went out to shear.

*   *   *   *

It was almost 11:00 p.m. when he and Fergus finished cleaning up. Mickey showered and considered going directly to bed, but he was a bit on edge, so he decided to walk down the road. He walked by Caitlin's residence, and he could tell from the light that the television was on, but he opted not to socialize.

He might have stopped on another evening, but tonight he knew Caitlin would be asking about his airplane ride, and he wanted to think all of that through a bit further before seeing her. He had, at this point, at least convinced himself that she would accept his explanation.

After all, he'd tell her, this was a promise he'd made to his parents, to *not* discuss these matters. This thing about an airplane ride is just a part of all that. He'd tell her that he's sorry he'd let it slip. He was certain Caitlin could present no viable argument for a young man to betray a promise he'd made to his mother and father.

He reached an ancient pub, The Fiddler's Widow, in a small two-story stone building at the edge of Newport, and he decided to go in and sit for a while. The pub occupied the first floor, with the owner's residence on the second.

"Evenin' there, young Monaghan," said the bartender/owner Sarah Callaghan. She was an attractive strawberry blonde woman, about 42, who *was* actually a widow, but her husband had been a property tax collector for the government, not a fiddler. A middle-aged couple sat at the bar talking to her, and the place was otherwise empty.

"Evenin', Ms. Callaghan, may I have a pint o' the dark stuff, please?"

"No, Mickey, you may not. I don't serve handsome young men unless they call me Sarah."

"Well, I'll promise to call you then, Sarah" he said smiling, flirting with a woman almost twice his age.

"One Guinness comin' up," she said laughing.

The place was small, and it was dark except for the bar. Mickey sat at a candle-lit table by the window and watched for the second draw on his pint. Sarah walked it over to him, and whispered, "Stick around a bit if you can. I want t' ask you somethin' if I can get rid o' these two," she said, nodding towards the bar.

"Can't be too late," he said. He really just wanted to sit.

Nah, he thought, *Caitlin can't argue with a boy keeping his word to his parents, can she?* Not that he really understood why *they* felt so strongly about it, but he had always figured that it was merely a matter of the differences in folks, feeling one way or another on a given matter. Nothing particularly strange about that.

"You never, never tell people you're adopted, because they won't treat you well. People look down on adopted children. No one has to know that you're adopted. It's no one's business but ours! You are our son, and we are your parents."

What's the harm in that? To be sure, it won't hurt anyone else to not *know that I'm adopted; and if that's the way Fergus and Marian think, if that's the way they want it, so what?*

But Becky and John Flaherty are both adopted, and everyone seems to like them. They don't hide it. As a matter of fact, thinking about it, Mickey realized that he'd never really heard anyone but Fergus and Marian say that adopted children are looked down upon. *Why is it such an issue with Fergus and Marian?*

He argued with himself that *talking*, or "opening up," about his concerns might bring some understanding. Indeed, suppressing them might only cause him eventual anxiety. *Oh, hell,* he reasoned, *a lot of people do ignore and suppress their problems, issues, whatever…it's a common thing, and we all do it to one degree or another. Again, just differences in people. We all get by somehow.*

But was that what he wanted for himself?

No, not really. Somewhere inside, he knew that he'd prefer to share all of this with his closest friend Caitlin. He knew he could trust her, and it would feel good to let her know the truth—let her know who he *is*, for chrissake!

But, he thought, *it isn't really a matter of trust or feeling good, is it? What it all ultimately comes down to is my personal policy of keeping secrets secret. Just common sense, isn't it? If you tell your friend a secret, who swears not to tell anyone else but does anyway, whose fault is it? No need for fault, just don't tell your friend.*

Hmm. It occurred to him that, for some reason, Caitlin might not accept his rationale, but he couldn't quite imagine what justification she might use. A promise to his *parents*, he would say. Of course, they aren't really his parents, but *she* doesn't know that.

Then, he thought again, Fergus and Marian's insistence on secrecy on these matters just doesn't make much sense to him anymore; but *Caitlin* can't argue that point with him, not knowing what the secrets are. *Chicago*, and all the strange bits of conversations between Fergus and Marian he'd heard over the years. Maybe Caitlin *could* help him figure it all out…*nah, best just to forget it all.*

"Finally they're gone!" said Sarah. "Mind if I sit down?" she asked, waking Mickey from his reverie.

He smiled, "You own the joint, as I understand, Sarah!"

"Here's another pint, love, on the house!"

"*Not* on the house. I'll be happy to pay for it," he said, noting that he was her only customer.

"Well, I might have you do that," she winked, and continued, "So what do I hear, Mickey…you stopped a raper out in Liscarney last night?"

"You heard about that, did you already, Sarah? Caitlin drove out with a friend from the bank, to come out and sing with me, and this creep—who was also from the bank—was obviously tailin' behind, without 'em knowin' it. Cait's friend, poor girl, stepped outside to use the phone, and the bastard grabbed her!"

"And I hear he didn't succeed, thanks to you," she said admiringly.

"I don't know, Sarah, if I had been a bit more wary, we could've avoided the whole thing."

"But, Mickey, the way I get it, he'd done it before! So you avoid this, but he just goes out and does it again!"

"Maybe, but that poor girl…" He looked at her and smiled slightly.

Sarah now stroked the back of Mickey's hand with her finger. She smiled and said quietly, "Mmm…always hearin' stories about Mickey. Now folks are sayin' Mickey Monaghan fixed that fella so he's pretty much out o' business."

"Speakin' o' business," Mickey said as he lifted her finger to his mouth and kissed it, "wouldn't it be about time to lock up?"

SUNDAY 13 MAY 1990

"Would you like breakfast, Caitlin?"

"Not a bit, Mother," she called from her room. "I'm hopin' I can talk Mickey into visitin' over at Peggy's, and we can get somethin' before we go."

It was 9:30 Sunday morning. Caitlin came into the kitchen, ready for Mass, and said, "Maybe some tea if the water's hot?" as she found a cup.

Ellen O'Connor grabbed the teapot and motioned for Caitlin to sit. As she poured the water, she made some faint noise like "whew" with her breath, then quietly repeated "that *Mickey*" several times. She seemed concerned.

Eamonn Powers had stopped to give them the news the previous evening as Mickey had requested, and Ellen was apparently reflecting on it.

"What y' thinkin' about, Mother?" Caitlin said.

"Well, Caitlin, I'm thinkin' about your pal...I don't want you to take this the wrong way, I know you love 'im...and you know I love 'im, too, sometimes like he's my own. But did y' ever think there's somethin' about him that don't quite add up?"

"You're speakin' of Mickey, no doubt," she said, a little unnerved that her mother might be reading her mind.

"I mean, what is this, Caitlin, the fourth time for him sendin' somebody to hospital? First there was little O'Brien on your first day of school, then the boxin' match, then his pa, and now this auditor fella he paralyzed! Mind, I'm not sayin' they didn't deserve it or ask for it, each and every one of 'em...but this *kind* lad, who loves music, loves to sing, works hard, studies hard...then to fight with such fury! Is there somethin' inside o' him, Caitlin?"

The remarks seemed almost eerie to Caitlin. *And she doesn't even know this odd business about an airplane ride that, for some unreadable reason, he can't even talk about!*

"And that's not all, honey," Ellen continued, "it's all these women y' hear about! I know he's good-lookin' and the girls like him, but if you think about it, there's plenty o' good-lookin' men—"

"Not like him," Caitlin interrupted.

"Maybe not, but they don't need all that bedhoppin'! So why does he? What's he lookin' for?" She paused. "I'm not sayin' I know any of the answers, and I guess that's my point. It just doesn't all add up, when you think about it."

"Good mornin' in there!" Mickey's voice called from the front door.

"Come in," both Ellen and Caitlin called together.

Caitlin said, "Well, we've just been talkin' about you, and I'm not sure I can stand to be with you after all the horrible things that have been said!"

"Sounds to me like you need to get that red head of yours directly to Mass and do some penance!" Mickey retorted, laughing. "How are you, Mrs. O'Connor? You would better spend your time sayin' a rosary for me than sayin' ugly things!" he said as he leaned to kiss her cheek.

Ellen laughed, "I'd say ten a day, Mickey, if I thought it would help in the least!" Her tone changed, "Now, Mickey. You're all right after all that business Friday?"

"Well, yes, I am, and thank you for askin'. I'm most concerned about poor Peggy, and now about her husband, too."

"Let's go, Mickey," Caitlin said impatiently, grabbing Mickey's arm. "Bye-bye, Mother!"

As Mickey turned the key in his truck, Caitlin said, "Eamonn came by after stoppin' at your place last night."

"Mm-hmm," nodded Mickey. He did not want to have this conversation.

"Said Peggy was makin' her call to Brian when it happened."

"Yeah," said Mickey, as he pulled onto the road, "poor chap apparently heard some o' the carryin' on."

"Poor chap is right," said Caitlin, "in more ways than one. You get where I'm goin' with this, Mickey?"

"Well, I'm feelin' pretty bad about jokin' around with her, if that gives you an idea."

"Yeah," said Caitlin, as he parked in the church lot, "and what you *don't* know is that she was a little too damned—and don't correct my language if you don't mind—a little too damned impressed with your singin' *and* with how you strolled over and talked to Sullivan."

As they walked to the church entrance, Mickey fought a smile as he scratched his head and said, "Didn't she mention anything about what a fine-lookin' fella I am?"

She gave him an elbow and laughed in spite of herself. "Oh, my, do we have a lot to talk about!"

*   *   *   *

After Mass, Father McDermott greeted the parishioners at the door as they exited.

Mickey said, "Good Sunday mornin', Father," but the priest ignored him and spoke to Caitlin, "Miss O'Connor, God'll surely rush you into heaven some day for seein' that these black sheep get to Mass on Sunday!"

They all laughed, and Father McDermott said, "Now, Michael Peter, I want to have a word before too much longer, y' hear me? When can you come by?"

"Whenever you like, Father. I hope there's not a problem."

"When I see that Caitlin is still willin' to associate with you, I tend to believe there's not, but Mickey, I just want to catch up with you, and see how you're gettin' on. How 'bout lunch next Saturday noon?"

"Long as you don't fix the lunch, Father, it's a deal," he said, and Father McDermott gave a hearty laugh. Mickey remembered the meals that Father McDermott had prepared during his brief stay with him, particularly a dinner for which he had fixed roast beef sandwiches that were so gristle-filled they were inedible.

As they walked to the truck, Caitlin thought she'd take the opportunity to needle him further, and, staring up with a completely false sincerity, said, "I hope you don't think that this luncheon obligation with Father McDermott is going to reduce my agenda in any regard!"

Mickey stopped in his tracks. He turned to Caitlin with a look so serious that she was caught off guard. "C'mere," he said, pulling her against him, hugging her tightly. "I hope it doesn't, Caitlin Molly...I hope it doesn't reduce your agenda." He had never done such a thing before.

As quickly as he'd grabbed her, he spun away, smiled, and said, "Let's eat!"

One thing's certain, thought Mickey as he turned left at the foot of the village, over the huge painted white letters, *C'BAR*, at the turn to Castlebar: *Father McDermott will be speaking to me about all the gossip of my womanizing. Judging from his comments, he might even tell me that now, as I'm about to graduate, I'd do well to settle down with a nice girl like Caitlin. Yeah, that's it, I'll bet, he'll tell me how lucky I am, that such a girl seems to be genuinely fond of me, or some such thing. Well, hell, I guess I am, but settle down...?*

And, he thought, *if I surprised Caitlin there in the parking lot when I hugged her, it couldn't have been much more than I surprised myself. Things are piling up, maybe? To be sure, a married woman was almost raped while her husband listened on the phone, because I...because I what? Sullivan's the guilty one...he did it, not me. I'll graduate from college soon, and Fergus expects me to stay on at the farm, but I don't want to. I can't make a living singing and playing guitar in pubs. Caitlin's hot on the trail of these family secrets that seem crazier by the day. And I'll bet that para-*

noid adoptive mother of mine is going to be checking my facial expressions and cross-examining me on every other one!

In just a few minutes, they'd be sitting in McCarthy's with their coffee, waiting on their breakfasts, and she'd say…

*   *   *   *

"Mickey, I think I'm just going to tell you something that you know anyway, but I want it in front of you for perspective: I love you. However you want to take that…as a friend, as a brother," she giggled a little, "or as a *sister*, if you prefer!"

"And *I* love this coffee with cream and sugar…the more the better, don't you agree?" he rejoined. He was happy to keep the conversation light for the moment, but he was also eager to put this subject to rest.

She looked at him for a moment, still smiling but not joking any longer. "Mickey, I think there are things that you need to talk about, maybe not with me, but I *hope* with me."

"Caitlin Molly, do you know how many people there are in the world?"

"Mickey!" she said, a little vexed.

"I'm dead serious, Cait. Do you know?"

"I think…five billion."

"That's what I think, too. And do you know that out of those billions, there's only one that I *could* talk about such 'things' with, and she's right here with me now."

Caitlin was taken aback by his sincerity and didn't speak for the moment.

"Caity," he continued quietly, "here's what I want to tell you. There are some, well, 'family secrets' that I am under obligation not to talk about. Fergus and Marian insisted that I promise not to, and I like to keep my word. I'm sure you understand. So it's not a matter of whether I trust you or not—I absolutely trust you. And I also have a personal policy of not telling secrets, because I don't feel that I have the right to expect another to keep a secret that I can't keep myself."

Caitlin studied his face. She knew that he meant exactly what he said, and she felt anger because, in her mind, he was not keeping his word. She wanted to believe that he was about to say "however" or "nonetheless," and so she waited for him to continue, feeling increasingly dismayed.

Mickey looked at her unimpressed countenance, then carried on undaunted. "I suppose my mind was elsewhere when I confirmed that I had been in an airplane, and I apologize for that. If you'll recall, I had just come back from talking to Sullivan…"

Caitlin had tossed the napkin from her lap onto the table. She looked down angrily. He noted her unfavorable response and tried one last line: "And so Caitlin, my wonderful friend, do you understand the responsibility that I'm saving you by simply keeping all of it to myself?"

She shook her head back and forth. Finally, she looked at him. "I've never been so disappointed in someone!"

"Cait?"

"Why in God's name did you say you were going to tell me about your airplane ride, if you didn't intend to follow through? I expect better than that out of Mickey Monaghan! Now I'm embarrassed to have believed you!"

Mickey now felt a little anger himself. "Wait a minute, Caitlin! I never told you that I'd tell you about the airplane…I did say I'd talk to you about it, and that's exactly what I'm doing! If you want me to break confidences and betray the trust of my parents so that you can get a bit of gossip, well…I think your anger is misplaced!"

"There's more to it than gossip, Mickey!" she said disgusted.

"There's *not* more to it than that, Caitlin! I made a mistake! I said something I should not have said! I will apologize to you *again* for that, if you like, but who the hell are you to tell me what I meant, or whether I should keep a family secret?"

She was angry, now he was angry, and she was terribly hurt by it all. A tear came down her face, but she maintained herself without crying. She turned sideways, and said quietly, "Why don't you eat?"

Their eggs, rashers, pudding and toast had arrived a few minutes earlier, but neither had yet taken a bite. Mickey realized that this conversation had no chance of quick retrieval, so he tried to eat.

"I think you should eat as well, Cait," he offered calmly.

She tersely replied, "I'm not hungry."

He tried to be kind and said, "Caity, I'm not so hungry myself. Why don't you try a few bites, then we'll go."

"Mm. Goin' t' give me your *word* on that?" she said sarcastically.

He was upset again at that comment, but spoke quietly. "I damn well don't like your suggesting that I have not been honest with you. When I told you that I would talk to you about things, I meant it. As far as I'm concerned, I have done just that, although I might have given you a fuller explanation had you not been so damned indignant!"

He felt bad and was surprised to lose his temper with Caitlin, but perhaps no more surprised than he was at her aggressive tact.

"I'm goin' t' wait outside, Mick," she said, and walked out. She went to the truck and cried.

True, she was angry and crushed by the anger he returned; but more than that she felt humiliation at what she perceived as a lack of trust in her and his apparent shallow view of their friendship. At the outset of the day, she had felt closer to him than ever, believing that he might open his heart to her on matters festering somewhere within him. She had looked forward to new bonds between them, and, yes, even to making this big handsome lout realize that his heart and his future should belong to her. She had challenged his devotion to her, and lost.

Where she had imagined some door about to open, she instead found a wall. A brick wall with Mickey on one side, and Caitlin on the other. With the rest of the world. Where she had imagined a new intimacy, she instead found a reason to believe that such a relationship with Mickey Monaghan might not even be possible.

He got up to pay immediately, but it took the waitress a few minutes to get to the till. He trotted out to the truck to find Caitlin standing by the passenger door, crying.

"Caity, my heart is breaking to see you cry like this! This talk of ours...I don't know how it went so wrong. What I said and the way I said it...it's not what I'd have chosen, but I was just reacting to your, uhm, your disappointment, which I didn't expect. I would never hurt my little girl," he said, hugging her. She was hugging him back, but she kept crying.

"I can't believe that you and I can't reach some understanding on this, Caity. I'm not sure why you're so upset."

"I had just told you I loved you, Mickey, and you shut me out," she cried. "I don't understand any of it myself."

Mickey's first thought was, *That's not fair at all! You say you love me like a brother or sister, and now you want to use it as leverage!*

On another level, he knew that she was reaching for something deeper from him, but he refused to acknowledge it—for now, at least—knowing that it was he who would have to reach within to find whatever she was looking for. Reach within to places that were "off limits."

He wanted to again assure her that these private matters did not relate in any way to the trust between them, but what's the use? He had just told her that and made her cry.

He opened her door, and said, "Can we sit in the truck for a moment? Maybe I can explain all this a little better." She quietly stepped up and sat down.

Mickey went to the other side and got in, put the key in the ignition, but didn't turn it. He moved to his left and again pulled Caitlin close to him, hugging her.

"If I knew the right thing to say, I'd say it. Ten times. Cait...these...secrets, as I've called them—there really isn't a lot to them. It's *nothing* that *I myself* would *ever* choose to keep from you. Or even from anyone. But it's not me doin' the choosing. The information that you'd get from all this...it just really doesn't amount to much."

He knew *that* wasn't exactly true, but even he couldn't comprehend all that it would soon lead to.

Caitlin felt better at hearing this, and she was further comforted by the fact that Mickey was hugging her for the third time in one day. She closed her eyes with her head rested against his chest and said without energy, "And the airplane ride?"

Mickey answered, "...was just an airplane ride."

"Nobody killed or died?"

"No, Cait."

"Didn't crash land in the Irish Sea?" she said, being a little silly.

What a relief, he thought. "No, sweetie, just a ride in an airplane that's part of...some other equally boring...whatever."

"Guess I have to live with that," she said, still holding on.

He gently pulled back from her and smiled at her as he held her shoulders with his hands, "Well, I have to live with it, so I guess you do, too."

She took a breath and said calmly, "You don't have to 'live with it.' You choose to 'live with it.' And now you ask your best friend to please let you live your life in darkness. Well...okay."

No response.

"Mickey, I was hopin' we could go check on Peggy for a few minutes before goin' home. Would that be possible?"

"Sure, why not," he said, starting the engine.

He drove silently for about a mile, and then heard Caitlin sniffle. He glanced at her to see another tear on her cheek.

Mickey pulled over and turned the truck off.

"Caitlin? Somethin's goin' on here. I might not understand it, but I know you well enough to understand that you are not telling me what's beneath all this!

You've never cried like this when we've disagreed. You've never cried like this at anything!"

"I'll be all right," she said as she gathered herself. "But I guess you're right. And it's about *you*, Mick. Just...I need to say some things. Maybe we could talk again after we visit Peggy?"

"On the way home?"

"I'd like more time than that."

Mickey looked at her, knowing he had to decline, and said, "Caity, Fergus has me working on walls and fences this afternoon, then I have a lot of studyin' to do, but how 'bout a walk at half eight or so?"

"I can't," she said quietly. "Promised Gerry Findlay I'd play piano down at the pub with him til midnight."

Mickey was familiar with Findlay's Pub, which was owned by Gerry's parents. In fact, it was in Lecanvey, about a mile past Murrisk, where Sullivan had said he lived. And he knew that Gerry, who was 21, had recently started singing and playing the fiddle at the pub. He also knew that Gerry had been trying to win Caitlin's affections for most of the last year.

"Well, he's just doin' two hours, isn't he—10 until mid—?"

"He's takin' me to dinner down on the Quay first."

That irritated Mickey because he was trying to accommodate her, or so he told himself, but he opted to say nothing. He knew that any response he could think of quickly would most likely be inappropriate.

Finally, he started the truck again, saying, "Well, we'll get to it." As he pulled onto the road, he added, "Poor Gerry'll probably have to pay big for that dinner, what with you skippin' your breakfast." Neither laughed.

*   *   *   *

Mickey and Caitlin visited with the O'Gradys for little more than 30 minutes. Peggy and Brian lived in a stylishly decorated three-bedroom home in a new neighborhood on the outskirts of Westport, about 10 miles from Newport. Obviously, Brian, who looked to be over 30, was doing quite well in his employment.

Peggy was extremely gracious and warm, but still a bit fragile, her eyes tearing up a few times. Brian, on the other hand, seemed tense and somewhat ill-at-ease with these two folks who had escorted his wife into this catastrophe, and he loudly assured everyone several times that his wife would *not* be patronizing such places in the future.

While Peggy profusely thanked both Mickey and Caitlin for rescuing her, Brian commented that he only wished "the three of you could've watched each other a bit closer."

Mickey had heard enough of him at that point, and he said, "Well, Brian, every time I follow a woman into the toilet, it seems I get a scolding."

The three of them laughed while Brian smiled in spite of himself, mumbling something about Mickey missing his point, and then leaving the room. They heard a door close, almost slam.

Peggy was clearly embarrassed, and said, "He's just so upset."

They made small talk for a few minutes longer. Peggy told them that she had met Brian while working as a waitress in a hotel in Gwbert-by-the-Sea, near her home in Cardigan, Wales, just three years earlier when she was just out of secondary school. Brian's employer held business conferences at the hotel.

So she's just 21, thought Mickey, *and even prettier in the daylight without makeup! Damn!*

Brian, although he had been engaged to be married back in England where he was based at the time, pursued her for the entire week of his stay, then with relentless phone calls and several weekend visits afterwards.

Lured by his promises of financial success and world travel—"Although he's never been much on romance," she whispered—she accepted his proposal.

Shortly thereafter, about two years previous, Brian was assigned to a management team for construction of an upscale hotel on the Quay outside Westport. Peggy's job at West Irish Bank was "a natural," since the bank was participating in the financing of the project.

Brian re-entered the room announcing that he hated "to be a wet blanket," but that "Peggy really needs some quiet time."

It was time to go.

Caitlin and Mickey walked to the truck without talking, but glanced at each other several times, smiling.

As they drove off, Mickey joked, "Suppose if I lived with a controlling prick like that, I'd be out lookin' for some action, too!"

"Maybe *that* explains your life," Caitlin said calmly, looking straight ahead.

*   *   *   *

On the way home, they discussed when they might get together to talk. Usually, their time together these days was spontaneous, or at least not so much a matter of actually scheduling. Mickey told Caitlin that his study requirements for the coming week were so difficult that he didn't think it would be a good idea to do anything until Friday. Caitlin explained that she had a date Friday with Ray Mitchell—an older brother to Jimmy Mitchell, one of Caitlin's two bullies from her first day of school.

"Ray Mitchell? He's thirty damned years old, isn't he?"

"Twenty-six. And what do you care how many *damned* years old he is?" she said, pleased to have found a spark of, maybe, jealousy.

"You shouldn't talk like that," he said, smiling at his ridiculous admonishment, then laughing as Caitlin, also laughing, replied, "Damned right, but you shouldn't talk like that, either, damnit! How about Saturday?"

Mickey had been scheduled to play Saturday night at Kilkelly's, but he thought that that was now questionable in light of Friday night's incident, and that he would need to confirm with Seamus before heading out there.

"Are you talkin' about Saturday night?"

"I was thinkin' lunch," she said cautiously, knowing she was busy Saturday night, too.

"Can't. I'm seeing Father McDermott for a gristle sandwich and a morality lecture."

"Oh, right! Well, we could always have breakfast at McCarthy's next Sunday," she replied, being somewhat facetious after having left two full breakfasts on their table at McCarthy's an hour or so earlier.

"Yeah, that's an excellent setting for resolving differences," he deadpanned. "What's wrong with Saturday night?"

"Findlay's again."

Mickey was actually getting frustrated, but knew he had no standing to express it. He certainly couldn't ask her to cancel her dates just to chat about himself, but wasn't she the one who asked for this talk?

"Well, let me ring up your ladyship's assistant, and I'll have her pencil me into one of your open slots..."

"I'm available all week, Mickey, but I know you have to study," she said with sincerity.

From Caitlin's point of view, all Mickey had to do was to tell her, in any words he might want to use, that *he* would like to take her on a date—a real date—and she'd have cancelled anything to accommodate him. Better yet, he could tell her that he'd like to see her exclusively, and she'd never accept another date. But until that happened, she wasn't inclined to ignore suitors, for her own sake *and* as a matter of her personal strategy in dealing with her feelings for Mickey.

"Aren't you playing at Kilkelly's on Saturday anyway?"

"I'm scheduled to, but poor Seamus might not want me back after Friday's disaster. I need to ask him."

Caitlin saw a chance to tease him again. "Well, then, I'll be home by one o'clock from Findlay's. You'll finish at midnight, too, so just come by the house on your way home, and we'll have our talk!" she said, knowing he'd turn her down to be in some girl or another's bed. But he surprised her.

"One o'clock a.m. Sunday mornin'. I'll be there!"

"What!? Aren't you goin' t' be...you know?!"

"I'm goin' t' be with you. I'll bring the stout, so don't let Gerry get you too drunk."

"Mickey, are you serious? You'll come by at one?"

"Were you serious when you invited me?"

SATURDAY 19 MAY 1990

Mickey rang the presbytery bell right at noon on Saturday. He counted on some small talk over a sandwich, then the little heart-to-heart about his philandering, maybe a short lecture about how he ought to find a nice girl like Caitlin to settle down with. He also counted on having a few laughs, too, as he always did with Father McDermott.

"Michael, me boy, come right in! Glad y' didn't forget me!"

"Forget you, indeed. I'm not doin' a year in purgatory for ignorin' a lunch on the Church, no matter how bad it is!" Mickey said, and they both laughed as they walked to the kitchen.

"Well, Mickey, you're a man who lives fearlessly, I must say. If you think it's a year for missing lunch with your parish priest, just imagine the time you'll be doin' for the *rest* of your lifestyle!" he said, chuckling.

"I thought you'd let me chew my way through my sandwich before y' started in on my sins, Father."

"No, no, there's no gristle today. One of the ladies brought by a wonderful meat loaf last evening. You'll love this, Mick."

Father McDermott directed Mickey to his seat, and they both sat. Mickey looked at his plate: a huge meat loaf sandwich, pickles, crisps, and two large carrots. He looked at Father McDermott's plate: same thing without the carrots. And a pint of Guinness in front of each plate.

"Well, I think I must have your carrot here, Father," Mickey said, a little confused.

"No, those are both yours. Let me know what you think of the sandwich," the priest said, as he took a sip of his stout.

Mickey had not yet stopped smiling as he stared at the carrots—two big carrots with green stalks—which looked somehow oddly out of place, but then decided to ignore them for the moment. He took a bite of his sandwich.

"Oh, my goodness, that *is* delicious!" he said with enthusiasm. He took another bite.

"What'd I tell you? About the best I've ever tasted!"

Mickey took a sip of his Guinness. "And a pint even! I didn't die and go to Heaven, did I, Father?"

"You damn well better not have! Because if I thought Heaven was eatin' meat loaf with you, I'd get another job!" he laughed. "To be serious, Michael," he said, smiling but matter-of-factly, "that stout is to loosen your tongue, so we can talk freely about your future."

Father McDermott folded his arms in front of him as he looked at Mickey. "You're comin' up on a crossroads, you know."

"I do indeed, Father," he said taking another bite from his sandwich, "graduation just a few weeks off. Pa wants me to stay with the farm. I been lazy about makin' plans to leave—really, just concentrating on doing well in school, so that I can find a good job. A business career, that's what I want, maybe get involved with politics in the by and by."

"And wouldn't you be a good one for that, good-lookin' honest young man like you, soon as you quit your whorin'. Or is that what you're lookin' for, a life like they say JFK had over there in the U.S.?"

"No, Father, no, I'm not lookin' for that."

"Because you know it's wrong, don't you, Mick? Don't be afraid to answer that!"

"Well, all right then, of course I know it's wrong," he said, not knowing quite what to expect next.

"Mick, when I was teasin' Caitlin about still associatin' with you, let me tell you what I was really thinkin'."

Here we go.

"I was thinkin' what a wonderful thing it is that you two have kept that friendship through the years. And I was thinkin' back to the day you two met. Do you remember that I was a part of that day?"

"Yes, Father, you were the scary part," Mickey said with a smile, remembering the walk to the presbytery.

"Ah, right!" he laughed, understanding Mickey's point. "Do you remember when you were sittin' just out there in the dining room," he said, wagging a finger, "what Caitlin said when I sent her back to the classroom?"

"I don't think so."

"Well, I do! She said, 'Bye, Father,'" and now with exaggerated singing, he continued, "'Bye-bye, Mickey!' Now, Mick, I might be a Catholic priest, but even I could see the stars in that little girl's eyes when she looked at you, and I have it on very good authority that those stars are still there today! Understand what I'm sayin'?"

"Yes, and I kind of expected we'd be talkin' about that," Mickey said, taking a drink.

"Well, you be sure to eat those carrots, both of 'em! They're good for your eyes, you know, and I'm pretty sure yours aren't workin' lately!"

"Aaaaah! The carrots!" Mickey laughed. "I knew there was a reason!"

Father McDermott leaned over the table, examining Mickey's face as though it were something inscrutable, and said, "For th' love o' Saint Pat! Have y' looked at that girl in the past year, Mick?"

"Father," Mickey said calmly, trying to retard the conversation with humor, "in my search for a life partner, I try to look beyond the physical."

"The *hell* you say!" McDermott shot back. "That's what I don't understand…somebody who likes the physical as much as I hear *you* do, and you look right past the prettiest girl who's probably ever graced this village o' Newport! Newport, hell! The whole damn county!"

"To be honest with you, Father, I don't look past her, but I guess I really don't see her the same as others do. My friendship with Caitlin is precious to me, and—"

"Let me tell you something, Mick," Father McDermott said, pretty much ignoring his attempt to explain his feelings, "I'm not tryin' to play the matchmaker here. There's more to it than that!" he said, with words that seemed to evoke something Caitlin herself had said to him recently.

"In a few short days, your time as a schoolboy is over! Crossroads, remember? Like it or not, you'll be a man, tryin' to make your way through this world like the rest of us. The days and the years fly by, Mick, and you need to chart your course. I don't feel good about your spiritual life," the priest warned, "if you keep goin' down the same road you're on!"

Mickey knew the time for jokes was over. "Well, must my spiritual life involve, you know…marriage, or settling down with a family, for the time being?"

"Well, of course not! Mine doesn't, does it? But…for most—that's the life God intended. Why don't we take a stroll outside if you're done eatin'?"

Mickey nodded and took a big chomp from one of the carrots, smiling at Father McDermott as he did.

As often as both men had seen the view from St. Pat's of the farms, lakes and mountains, on this serene sunny day in May, it seemed to deliver its own message of hope and renewal.

It was not lost on Mickey that Caitlin and now Father McDermott, unquestionably the two people he respected and cared about most, were asking him to take a deeper look at himself, with obvious concerns for his future.

"Did y' know that some people are afraid of you, Mick?"

"Afraid?"

"I have a lot of sources, you know. This thing with that Sullivan fella seems to have revived talk about what a dangerous creature you can be, and I partially blame myself for that, you know, because of that boxing match. That glorious boxing match," he remembered with a grin, "but never mind that. I spoke with our friend Father Brennan over in Westport, who tells me the pubs and shops are alive with chatter about this frightful Monaghan character. I say, 'Father, he's the sweetest kid y' ever met in your life,' but o' course he doesn't know you like I do, does he, Mickey?"

"Maybe it's you who don't know me, Father," he kidded, as they walked along.

Father McDermott stopped walking, grabbed Mickey's arm with one hand, and wagged a finger from the other in his face. "Now we're gettin' somewhere!" he said. "You're jokin', but there's definitely somethin' I don't know and don't understand about such an otherwise fine young man *using* all these young women to do what *you know is wrong!* But, Mick, listen to me: what *I* understand about all that is not important—it's what *you* understand! Now, c'mon and let's walk some more," he said, releasing Mickey's arm.

"You never smoke cigarettes, do you, Mick?"

"No, sir."

"Well, you know, I smoked 'em for seventeen years. Started when I was 14. First one I ever had I stole from my mother and hid behind a bush to smoke it. Talk about doin' somethin' I knew was wrong!"

"I think I see your point, Father," Mickey said earnestly.

"Smokin' those damn things gave me a lot o' pleasure, Mick. In the mornin' with my tea, especially…but from the very first one, I knew I was doin' harm to myself. I knew it was wrong!"

"I definitely see your point here, Father."

"But Mickey—it wasn't until I went to a program to help me quit, when I finally understood just exactly what the harm was. And knowin' that, understanding that, I was finally able to convince myself to stop doin' that to myself! I want you to do a favor for me, if you will."

"Of course I will, Father."

"I want you to think, and think hard, about the way you're livin'." He stopped to look at Mickey. "Think about the harm it might be doin' to you *and* to the young ladies that you involve. Will you do that, Mick?"

"I will."

"Good! That's all I need to hear from you now!" Father McDermott said, slapping him on the back and turning back toward the presbytery. He glanced sideways at Mickey and said, "And the *not-so-young* ladies as well, y' hear?"

Mickey smiled slightly saying, "As you say, Father, you have your sources."

*   *   *   *

As they reached Mickey's truck, Father McDermott told him that Caitlin had rung him right before Mickey had arrived, asking him to tell Mickey to stop and see her on his way home.

Mickey said, "Father, I want you to know there are a few things I been thinkin' over lately. I'm not real sure they're related to what we've talked about, but it may be somethin' I could use your help on soon."

"You come back whenever you like, Mick. I'm not sure who y' confide in, and God forgive me for sayin' it, but I don't imagine you're able to share a whole lot with your parents, them bein' such…well, we'll say they're just not very *warm* by their natures. And you, you're so different from them, and, God forgive me again, that's a good thing."

What the hell, Mickey thought. "Well, I'm different from them because I'm not really their son, Father."

Father McDermott stared at Mickey, confused, and muttered, "…their son, Father—what?!"

"I'm adopted."

Father McDermott was stunned. He stared at Mickey, looking for some trace of another joke behind his comment. There was none. Before Father McDermott could think of a response, Mickey quietly said, "*No one*, and I mean *no one* knows that. *No one!*"

Father McDermott spoke carefully, "So you've not told Caitlin or Eamonn?"

"Not a single soul. I'm not real sure why I mentioned it now, but it is…like I said, there's a few things I been thinkin' over, and I'm startin' to feel like I need to make sense of 'em."

"God bless you, son, c'mon inside and we'll talk. I'll ring up Caitlin and tell her you'll be a while yet."

"Father, thank you so much, but I need to have a little more time to organize my thoughts on all this, and I'll be back, I promise. I am so grateful for your interest," Mickey said, and he hugged Father McDermott, not just to assure him of that gratitude but also as an apology for slamming the door that he had just opened.

McDermott let go just a little laugh, then another, then stepped back shaking his head and still laughing.

Mickey, while he didn't quite understand it, was pleased to see it, and said, "Well, it gets a little worse than that, so when I come back, I'll probably have you rollin' on the floor as I cry into your box o' tissues!"

Father McDermott heaved with laughter for a moment, then said, "I don't have the slightest idea why I'm laughin', Mick," he said not quite truthfully, "but I'll figure it out. And you damn well better not wait too long before y' do come back!"

"Thanks, Father, and I'll bring the snacks next time!"

Father McDermott watched and waved as Mickey headed his truck down the lane. *Adopted*, he thought still smiling, *how could that not have occurred to me?*

∗   ∗   ∗   ∗

As is typical in Ireland's "wild west," the fickle County Mayo skies had now darkened overhead and begun to rain, a gentle rain that might continue for an hour or end in a minute. Caitlin sat on her front porch. Ellen's Ford was not in the driveway.

"Hey, kid!" Mickey called as he got out of the truck. "What's up?"

"Glad to see Father McDermott did not burn you at the stake for your sins!"

"Well, he lit the fire, but it started rainin', as y' can see. I guess God saved me to continue on as a bad example for one and all."

Caitlin smiled sweetly, saying, "He'll never have a better one, will He? How 'bout some coffee or tea?"

"Either one, whatever you're havin'. Fergus wants me to help him take down the old storage shed and build a bigger one this afternoon, so I need to offset the pint o' Guinness that Father McDermott gave me with lunch."

"C'mon in the kitchen," Caitlin said, getting up. "Drinkin' your lunch, are you?"

"Claimed he wanted to loosen my tongue so we could talk freely, but it was probably just an excuse for a pint."

Caitlin had already heated the water. She poured it into two cups, put one in front of Mickey, then playfully threw a teabag at him, and said, "Did it work?"

"Did *what* work?"

"Did it loosen your tongue?" she said, sitting down.

"No—well, hmm," he interrupted himself to wonder.

"Well?"

"Damned if it didn't." He smiled. "Are we still on for tonight at one?"

"Are you changing the subject, Mickey?"

"No, Caitlin, I'm just makin' sure we have a time slot to talk about things," he said smiling, aware that she'd not likely handle another "shutting out" too well.

"That's one thing I wanted to ask *you*, if we can still meet. You haven't found a better offer?"

He looked up, as though in thought, then counted on his fingers for a few seconds and said, "I've had seventeen better offers, Cait, but I'm a man of my word, you know!"

"You worthless shite!" she laughed.

"Told you I been drinkin', love!" he said, playfully slurring his words.

"Mickey, I need to ask you a favor. Did you talk to Seamus Kilkelly?"

"Yes, and he very candidly told me that he had decided to let things settle down, and not to ask me back for a while. But then he found that there was so much curiosity and interest, that he thinks he'll have a packed house! As always, he was—"

"Well," she interrupted, "then I need to ask if you would mind driving over to Findlay's when you're finished, and just picking me up there. I know it's a bit out of your way, but I'd just as soon not go home with Gerry...I really need to end that."

"Fallin' in love with Mitchell, are you?" Mickey asked.

"No," she said with finality, "it's just Gerry, he's gettin' out of control with his hands and such."

"With his fiddling?" Mickey asked, not smiling.

"No...well, *yes*, depending on what you mean," she laughed.

"I'll tell you what I mean, Caitlin," he said angrily, "if that little sparrowfart ever lays an unwanted hand on you, I'll see to it that he never...plays the violin again!" he said, incorporating an old joke into his threat, in spite of his anger.

"Mickey, stop it!" she scolded. "I can take care of myself where Gerry's concerned!"

There was silence for a moment as Caitlin now pondered whether she should even let Mickey come to Findlay's, but the alternative of going home with Gerry and encountering Mickey there in the dark of night...no, that seemed even more dangerous.

Mickey then instinctively—and calmly—said, "I'll behave myself, Caitlin. You know how us big brothers can be."

She smiled. She'd have rather heard that he had said it out of uncontrolled jealousy, but at least he cared. "Okay, well, then, repeat after me: I, Mickey Monaghan, understand that Caitlin O'Connor is just as tough as I am, and she can take care of herself!"

He smiled, but he wasn't about to play her game. He looked at her with mock sincerity and said, "I never said you couldn't. I just enjoy *hurting* people, Cait."

Her face clouded up. "Oh, God! I forgot! You need to ring Eamonn right now! I'm sorry, Mickey, I forgot to tell you that."

"What's wrong?" Mickey asked, surprised at her sudden urgent tone. She didn't answer.

"Talk to me, Cait."

She looked across the table at him. "Ring Eamonn. He's at home."

"Cait?" he again asked, now demanding.

She stared back at him momentarily, and then quietly said, "Bill Sullivan died."

Mickey drew back, took in a deep breath, and got up to walk to the kitchen wall phone.

Eamonn confirmed that Sullivan had had a fluid buildup on his brain, and, as Eamonn understood, around 6:00 this morning, while the doctor sat with Sullivan's wife in a hospital office discussing the need to operate, *i.e.*, to drill a sort of drainage hole to release some of the pressure, Sullivan ran out of time.

"Why don't we get together for a pint, Mick? I gotta talk to you about somethin'," Eamonn asked.

"I can't, Eamonn. Fergus needs my help on the farm."

"Let me tell you, the farm can wait, Mick, we really need to talk!" Eamonn said, sounding mildly panicked.

"About *what*, Eamonn? I don't understand this!"

"Mickey, I *got* to talk to you! Just trust me, okay?"

Mickey looked at Caitlin with a puzzled look, indicating he couldn't quite comprehend what Eamonn's pressing concern might be, what they might need to talk about beyond the fact that Sullivan had died, but said, "Well, just come on over to Caitlin's then. That's where I am."

He again looked at Caitlin as if to ask if that would be all right with her, and she nodded her assent.

Responding to Eamonn's balk at that idea, Mickey said, "Why not? I have nothin' to hide from Caitlin," as he smiled and winked at her. She knew he was making a little joke, but it touched her nonetheless.

"All right then, I'll see you here in 10 minutes or so."

He hung up, looked at Caitlin and shrugged. "He'll just stop here to pick me up, he says. Guess I better ring Fergus and tell him the Gardai need to speak to me."

Mickey argued briefly on the phone with Fergus, with Fergus suggesting a few alternatives, laced with obscenities, as to how the Gardai might otherwise spend their time, angry that they were taking his help from him. Mickey finally told him to "just leave it all, and I'll do it myself when I get home," and he hung up.

"*Be t' tunderin' Jay-sus!*" he mused, quoting from the song "Finnegan's Wake." "Twenty-two effing years old, and I still have t' put up with that! Anyway...Cait, tell me if I'm wrong, but I just can*not* see myself singin' tonight."

"Not unless you'd like to turn into a pillar of salt," she answered quite sincerely.

"Exactly! God! I hate to do that to Seamus, after he told me the place will be full!"

"Why don't you call him and tell him about Sullivan. Tell him you'll come out and sit with the folks, you know, *work the crowd*. I'm sure he'll understand, Mickey."

"You know, that's a brilliant idea! What a useful child you can be at times!"

"I've got another good one—be at Findlay's right at a quarter past midnight. I need fifteen minutes to drop the bomb on Gerry, and I won't want t' be sittin' around there afterwards."

"Sure, I'll be there," he said. "Where's the Ford?"

"Mam and Keran are visitin' Aunt Helen in Claremorris for the day, and they won't be back til 9 tonight or so."

So they were alone.

*   *   *   *

Mickey knew that he completely trusted Caitlin, but he thought he should take this opportunity to impress upon her the vital importance of maintaining the confidentiality of their discussions.

He suggested they sit on the front porch to wait on Eamonn.

"Caitlin, while we're waitin' here, there's somethin' I'd like y' to be thinkin' about before we talk tonight. I know you said there are things you need to tell me, and...well, I suspect I'll want to share some things with you that are on my mind. Things that I wasn't quite able to share last Sunday at McCarthy's."

"Like the airplane ride?" she asked with some enthusiasm.

"Like that," he confirmed to her delight. "But, Caitlin...what if I tell you our family secret is that we once had a blue tablecloth? Do you understand, sweetie, that it would not be up to you to decide that such a secret's not worth keepin' because no one else would care? Do you understand, no matter how insignificant *you* may think it is, that does *not* matter? You still can't tell *anybody?*"

"You can trust me, Mickey, as you trust yourself."

"Do you understand that I *might* tell you some things that you might be just dying to tell someone else, but you won't be able to because you've given me your word?"

"Yes, Mickey," she answered patiently.

Mickey decided he should go another step to assure Caitlin of the bonds between them.

"And...well...Cait, do you remember how you started, uh, that conversation?" He was stumbling a bit on his words now.

Caitlin studied his face and asked, "You mean at McCarthy's?"

"Yes, that's right...uh, you know, about, like, uhm, a brother or a sister...?"

Caitlin saw that he was really struggling, and smiled. "You mean, when I told you that I love you, Mickey?" she asked, understanding that he had already qualified it as "love-comma-sibling type."

Mickey seemed relieved, "Yes. Well, I just want to say that, uh...the reverse is true as well."

Caitlin beamed with joy to hear it, but as she saw Eamonn's car approaching, she decided to chide Mickey.

"You know, I could've thought for twenty-five years and not come up with a more impersonal way to say I cared about someone than '*the reverse is true as well*'!"

Mickey just grinned at Caitlin as she continued, "If human civilization depended on such expressions of affection, you and I probably wouldn't even be here!"

"Well, it doesn't," Mickey laughed, "and, oops, what a damnable shame we can't continue *this* conversation. Here comes Eamonn!"

"*The reverse is true as well!*" she scoffed, laughing, but looking ahead now more than ever to their meeting at 1:00 a.m.

*   *   *   *

"Eamonn, Caitlin and I have no secrets, so just go ahead and tell me," he said confidently.

Eamonn looked at Caitlin. He looked extremely worried, but *her* look had just changed from one of anxious curiosity to one of confident pride, with admiration for the man who had just—it seemed to her—taken a few more bricks out of the wall between them. She wanted to hug his strong arm and lay her head against it, but she stood stoically by, thinking a display of her affection might embarrass Mickey.

"Okay, Mickey…" Eamonn began. "I guess, uh, what with Sullivan dyin' and all, well, there might be more to it. They'll likely be needin' to talk to you in some depth about it."

Mickey felt Caitlin's hand on his shoulder. "Talk to me about what? I sat and talked to Detective O'Hare for two hours when this all happened! I got nothin' more to say about it!"

"Hey, Mick, I'm just tellin' you, okay? Now that he's dead, there'll be new men workin' on it. Homicide guys, y' know? When somebody dies…well, that *changes* things, they take a little harder look at it. Caitlin, I don't doubt they'll be gettin' your side as well."

Caitlin nodded as Mickey demanded, "Eamonn, what in the hell are you talkin' about—*homicide*? Harder look at *what*? And what are you sayin'…'Caitlin's *side*'? There are no *sides* here, just the truth!"

"C'mon, Mickey, I'm not sayin' anybody's choosin' sides, for chrissake! You know yourself, two people look at the same situation, and they might not see it the same way."

The irony of Eamonn's statement was not lost on Mickey and Caitlin, as they looked at each other thinking of last Sunday's breakfast at McCarthy's, and smiling a bit helplessly.

Caitlin said, "I wasn't there when Mickey caught him out in the field, you know. I ran back inside and told them to call for help, and then I was trying to help Peggy."

"Well, that's what you tell 'em then, if they ask. Mickey, d' you want to get that pint?"

"Is there more to talk about, Eamonn?"

"Just a little bit, Mick, but it might be important to you."

"Go ahead, Mickey," Caitlin said, knowing that Eamonn would have Mickey's best interests at heart. She knew Eamonn would do anything for Mickey, and she didn't want to risk keeping him from information or advice that he might need. And something was obviously worrying Eamonn.

"All right, then," Mickey said, as he ushered Caitlin inside the front door. "I'll be right out, Eamonn."

Mickey spoke quietly. "Cait, listen, whatever it is on his mind…I'll let you know tonight. I'm sure it's nothin'. Eamonn tends to worry."

Caitlin just looked at him, and said, "Okay."

She desperately wanted to kiss him.

His eyes caught her stare, and for the first time, he felt something that he had not ever felt. He looked back at her. *She is beautiful. What an incredibly beautiful girl!*

He smiled and said, "See you tonight. Remember, I'll bring the stout."

She didn't say anything…just watched as he went to Eamonn's car and drove off, leaving his truck parked.

✳   ✳   ✳   ✳

"Go down to The Fiddler's Widow, Eamonn. It's quiet, and we'll be able to talk."

Mickey sat silently, trying to put these new thoughts about Caitlin out of his mind. Eamonn was not about to help him in that regard.

"I tell you, Mick, that Caitlin, whew! She gets prettier every day, doesn't she? If I were you, I'd marry her tomorrow morning!"

"So much for your feckin' bad advice! Take me home, Eamonn!" he joked, and they both laughed.

"Really, Mick," Eamonn said, "what I need to tell you is that these homicide guys are aggressive. You know, for cops, when you get to be a homicide detective, that means like you're the Managing Director of a big company. They're ambitious, the homicide guys."

Mickey said, "So what?" as Eamonn pulled over next to The Fiddler's Widow.

As they walked in, Eamonn tried to explain carefully, "Well, they get a case, they like to make something out of it. So you need to be careful how you talk to them."

Mickey was right about the peace and quiet: not another soul in the place except Sarah.

"One Guinness and a black coffee please, Sarah," Mickey called out as they walked to the same table by the window where Mickey had sat just one week prior.

Mickey looked at Eamonn. "Look, my friend, get to the point, will you? As far as I can see, I'm one of the good guys. Out there fightin' the bad guys. What's the problem?"

Eamonn looked more worried than ever. "Mick, there's issues of excessive force, maybe even a Manslaughter or some other homicide charge."

Mickey was incredulous at the thought. "What in the fuck are you talkin' about, Eamonn? I'm out there doin' their work for 'em, runnin' down a rapist, maybe a multiple rapist, no less!"

Eamonn suddenly started to cry. Sarah put the pint and the cup of coffee on the table, looked at Eamonn, looked at Mickey, and walked away.

"Oh, God! Oh, God! Mick, listen…I'm sorry, but after I heard about Sullivan dyin', I started braggin' on you, y' know, talkin' all about my best buddy, Mickey Monaghan, all about how you dare not cross my buddy or you're goin' t' get hurt. I didn't know, but the two homicide guys standing in the room had just come to get the file on the case." He was sobbing now.

"What of it?" Mickey asked.

"I was just tellin' 'em about what a tough one you are, and they start askin' questions that I answer, not quite gettin' the import of it all, and…then they start talkin' about maybe they'll file charges against you for excessive force or man-slaughter or even murder. I'm really sorry, Mick! I might've said some stuff I ought not have!"

Mickey forced a smile and said, "Eamonn, get a hold of yourself! Calm down!"

He leaned over the table and said, "Listen, Eamonn, I'm likely the only person *ever* goin' t' tell you this, but your friend Monaghan is not completely stupid!"

"I never said…what do you mean?" Eamonn asked, trying to catch his breath.

Mickey continued leaning over the table. He whispered, "Listen to me. After I kicked Sullivan, I looked at him. His eyes were open. He wasn't moving. I knew it was bad! Eamonn, I know exactly what I told O'Hare, exactly what I wrote down. Have you seen my written statement?"

"No."

"Well, then…stop worrying. I doubt they'd charge me with murder because my friend says I'm tough!"

Eamonn looked relieved, but still not convinced. "What'd y' tell O'Hare?"

"I told him I was runnin' after Sullivan. When I had just about caught him, he turned to fight me, so I leaned to the right as I caught him in the mouth with my left fist. He fell, and *I* fell. He was grabbin' on my leg, but I managed to stand up. It was dark. I had some dirt in my eyes, and I was rubbin' 'em and tryin' to blink it out. I heard him rustlin' around on the ground, and I just flung my leg out to keep him off me. Reckon I caught 'im, but I really couldn't see him or what he was doin'."

"Is that what happened?" Eamonn asked.

"Who's goin' t' say otherwise? It was just *me and Sullivan* out there, Eamonn. And you know what? Detective O'Hare...noticed the dirt on my clothes. Because I *fell*. Fell right down there in the field. I hadn't noticed the dirt on my clothes, but Detective O'Hare, he's a good detective. He noticed it, and made a note of it!"

"So that's what happened?"

"It's what *could've* happened, Eamonn. And it's damn sure the way I remember it."

Eamonn took a slow deep breath, then exhaled. "Okay. Maybe there's nothin' to worry about. One o' the old guys, he thought those detectives were just fuckin' with me, since you were my friend and all, and I reckon that could be the truth, but—*Jesus!*—I started thinkin' about it—"

"Well, quit thinkin' about it. Only one guy can contradict me, and he's not talkin'."

"Okay, then." Eamonn smiled a little. "I was worried you maybe said you wanted to punish the guy, or some shit like that. They still might want to talk to you, but I guess things will be okay. Want t' go? I need t' get some rest before I go out drinkin' tonight."

"You go ahead, Eamonn. I'd better sit here and think a while. And I'll enjoy the walk home."

In fact, Mickey was more upset about Sullivan's death than he let on, but he wasn't really sure how he should feel about it. And despite his show of bravado, he was now worried about the Gardai's possible pursuit of homicide charges against him.

And Caitlin. *Caitlin!* If Eamonn had not been there earlier at her house, Mickey thought he might have tried to kiss her. He thought about the look in her eyes when he left her. The word *beseeching* popped into his mind, and he smiled, wondering if she saw the same *beseeching* look on his face.

He lectured himself: *Caitlin is your friend, Mickey. Everything would change if you kissed her. Everything! You can't kiss Caitlin and risk losing...well...what we have. Don't do it!*

It further occurred to him, however, that he didn't much like the thought of anyone else kissing her, either.

Once Eamonn was gone, Sarah walked over and sat down with Mickey.

"So, Mickey, y' got boyfriend problems, love? What're y' doin' to poor Eamonn, breakin' things off, makin' 'im cry like that?"

Mickey didn't miss a beat. "'Fraid so, Sarah. Too emotional. Wants to settle down, you know, get married and raise a family. I'm just not ready right now, but I told 'im if he could wait til I graduate in June, I'd consider it…but you saw his reaction."

Sarah laughed. She reached up and touched his cheek. "When y' goin' t' marry that O'Connor girl? Word is, you two are together more than ever," she said.

"Not ready for that, either, *and* we're just friends" he said, but she'd struck a nerve.

"Good," she said. "I see you're sittin' in your lucky chair," she added softly and came around to sit in his lap. "How 'bout I put a sign on the front door says I'll be back in forty-five minutes?"

Mickey had been all set to turn down any such suggestion in light of his earlier visit with Father McDermott and Fergus's ever present need for his services, but the ill feelings plaguing him about Sullivan's death, the Gardai, and these new crazy thoughts of kissing Caitlin made it seem like the perfect solution.

"Y' been timin' me, love?"

*   *   *   *

It was a few minutes before 4:00 p.m. when Mickey arrived on foot back at Caitlin's where he had parked. He stood at the front door and quietly called her name, but heard nothing and went on to the pick-up. He figured she was napping or bathing, and, knowing that he would likely be dealing with a foul-tempered Fergus Monaghan in a few minutes, he opted to go and get that over with.

He wasn't wrong. Fergus had just about completely disassembled the old shed, and he had obviously been drinking.

"Down there fuckin' yer whore, were you, when y' should be helpin' with the work around here!" Fergus scowled as Mickey walked back towards him at the shed.

"Never mind that, Pa," Mickey said, himself on edge with his worries. "I was talkin' to the Gardai down there. Now, what d' you want me to do?"

How in the hell did he know I was with Sarah? How in the hell did he even know I was down at the pub?

"You'll take this old wood out to the field and burn it."

Mickey picked up a large board as Fergus continued, "And don't lie to me...tell me you're with the Gardai when you're fuckin' yer little redhead whore! There was no Gardai car down there!"

Mickey now understood what Fergus was talking about, and he dropped the board on the ground. He walked the twenty feet or so to Fergus with fire in his eyes. Fergus's own eyes bulged as Mickey neared him.

He grabbed Fergus's shirt with his left hand, and with his right, he smacked his head so hard that Fergus went down on the spot. Mickey was instantly kneeling over him, holding Fergus's hair with one hand and clutching his throat with the other.

He leaned to within six inches of Fergus's terrified face and whispered through clenched teeth, "If you *ever, ever...ever* speak of Caitlin O'Connor in those terms again, they'll be your final words."

Fergus stared back, weakly trying to nod, but Mickey had his head pinned to the ground, and he couldn't budge. "Because I will kill you, you vile fucking bastard," he finished. He released his grip and stood up.

He walked back to the board he had dropped, picked it up and carried it out to the field.

When he came back, Fergus was gone, as was his truck. *No doubt headed for Newport to drink his fill,* Mickey thought, as he watched Marian walking toward the torn-down shed.

"What's this with you and your pa down on the ground and him leavin' in such a huff?" she asked, almost angrily.

"He started runnin' his drunken, filthy mouth about Caitlin, who's never done a thing to him, and I let him know I wouldn't have it. He's likely off to Crowley's to finish himself off for the night."

Marian looked at him with tired, sad eyes. "Yes, you defend your little girlfriend, don't you? And you'll doubtless be leavin' me here for your pa later on, when he comes home wantin' to take it all out on me! And where will you be then?" she cried, now raising her voice, "Out pleasurin' yourself, won't you? Singin' your songs and jumpin' in some colleen's bed!"

"Ma, I didn't marry Fergus Monaghan," Mickey said, trying not too hard to contain his anger. "Seems to me you made some choices a long time ago that put you in this spot...and I'll bet if you had 'em t' make over, you and I wouldn't be standin' here together now."

"What do you think you mean by that?" she fired back nervously.

"Well, now, I'm just guessin', aren't I, Ma?" he answered quietly, "because, God knows, any actual talk about the history of this so-called family is *off limits* where I'm concerned."

"Y' don't need t' be smartmouthin' me. I asked you a simple question, what you mean about me makin' choices?"

"Nothin', Ma, I just can't understand anybody marryin' him," he said sadly. "I'll try to stick around tonight and load 'im into bed before he gets to his rage."

"You better hope you don't get him so mad he drags out that shotgun after you," she warned.

Ireland's gun laws were extremely strict, requiring an applicant to show "good reason" not just for the firearm, but for the amount of ammunition possessed as well. Each firearm required its own certificate, to be renewed annually. Fergus maintained a double-barreled shotgun in a locked gun case to protect his live-stock from predators, but he had never used it.

Mickey finished carrying the old wood to the field, and he then brought the new wood from the drive where Fergus had left it. He figured that Fergus would roll in drunk by 9 or 10 o'clock, and he didn't need to be at Seamus Kilkelly's until 10 or 10:30. He'd spend a little time with the patrons, then leave right at midnight to pick up Caitlin.

He lit the old wood and stayed with it out in the field until only embers remained, then went in to shower shortly before 8:00. He asked Marian to wake him at 9:30, or earlier if she heard Fergus coming. As it turned out, when she woke him at 9:30, Fergus had already stumbled in and quietly put himself to bed.

SUNDAY 20 MAY 1990

Seamus Kilkelly walked Mickey to his car at a few minutes past midnight.

"Well, I thank y' Mickey, for comin' out. Sorry about Sullivan. Sorry I couldn't hear you singin', but I'm glad I didn't have t' pay you!" he joked.

"This is all the payment a man could ever ask for," Mickey returned, holding up a gallon jug that Seamus had filled with Guinness Extra Stout for him.

Mickey had tried to buy some cans of Guinness from Seamus, explaining that he was meeting Caitlin to talk over a few things, but Seamus wouldn't hear of it—"Fresh out of the tap, that's the only way!"

They agreed that it had been a good night and that Mickey would start singing again the following Saturday night. Seamus wished him good luck with Caitlin and suggested that he bring her out with him next week.

*   *   *   *

Mickey got to Findlay's Pub at 12:20 a.m. He looked to the right and saw Caitlin sitting on a bench with Gerry. Gerry appeared to be upset and arguing with her.

"Caity O'Connor, yer pun'kin chariot is...right here...out the door!" Mickey called out, apparently intoxicated.

Caitlin stood immediately and walked to him. "Did you drive down here all pissed up, Mickey?" she demanded angrily.

"Had to, my swee-dee pie," he said, hiccoughing, "not able t' *walk* too good!"

Gerry walked over to him and said, "Mickey, maybe you don't know this— I'm on a date with Caitlin this evening."

"Oh, I *do* know that, Ger," Mickey said, patting Gerry on the shoulder as he swayed a little; "but guess what?" he continued as he glared at the wristwatch that he held about four inches from his face, "Three, two, one, zero, *hiccough*, date's over!"

"Mickey!" Caitlin yelled.

Gerry stepped in front of Mickey to challenge him and said, "Listen, Mick, Caitlin is with *me*, and she's stayin'—"

"Don't be crazy, Gerry!" interrupted Gerry's older brother Paddy, who grabbed his arm and yanked him back a few feet. "Get away from him!"

"No, no, no, no!" Mickey said, waving his hands in the air. "No trouble from me, Paddy! Ah muh jus' go out in the pun'kin chariot...pashen-jer door...seat...and sit!"

He stumbled out and slumped down in the passenger seat of his truck.

Caitlin came out about three minutes later, looked for the keys in the ignition, started the truck, and pulled out. She was furious, but she didn't speak. She fought tears, devastated that the intimate talk she had looked so forward to had been ruined. The word "hopeless" circled around in her head.

About a quarter-mile down the road, Mickey said, "Please pull over."

"Sure," she said with contempt, "so you can vomit your brains out, if you have any left!" She immediately swung the truck over and stopped.

He turned to her and said, "I hope I didn't embarrass you, Caitlin. I'm not really drunk at all. I just thought—"

"What?!" she called out. "What are you sayin'?"

"Cait," he answered calmly, "I saw him fussin' with you, and I just thought if I made it necessary for you to leave—to drive me home, things would go a little easier. Maybe I overdid it?"

"Mickey! For God's sake!" she scolded, "I told you I can take care of Gerry myself!"

"I know!" Mickey yelled back.

They looked at each other without speaking.

Finally, Mickey said, "You weren't doin' too damn well, when the little gob-shite wants to fight me to hang on to you!"

Caitlin stared back at him, now holding back a smile. "Well, I'll try not to tell people how he backed you down—sent you runnin' out o' the place—but I'll have to be honest if they ask!" she said with brief laughter.

"Oh, and how much alcohol did you pour into that dizzy red head of yours tonight?"

"Actually, two pints. More than I would have normally, but I needed the courage to tell poor Gerry."

"How'd he take it?"

"To be honest, he was hurt. You know, Mickey, *some* men think I'm pretty, and that I have a lot to offer," she said, as though she were explaining one-plus-one-equals-two to a toddler.

Mickey's first inclination was to ask her what the connection might be between "some *men*" and Gerry Findlay, but he thought better of it.

"What I think, Caitlin, is that *you* have had two pints, and *I* have had two pints, which puts you in worse shape than I, since I'm bigger, older, and I drink more anyway, so how 'bout we trade places?"

As they opened their respective doors, Caitlin said, "So you'll drive the pun'kin chariot, huh?"

"I will. Oh, and I think I forgot to mention—I'm a better driver, too, but I don't need sobriety for that to be true."

"Oh, shut—goodness," said Caitlin as she sat in the passenger seat, eyeing the jug on the floor. "What's this a gallon of?"

"Oh, that's a gift from Seamus—Guinness fresh from the tap! You know—Father McDermott's truth serum!" Mickey said as he drove off.

"I'll rename it after Jesus Christ Himself if it gets the truth out of you!"

Mickey felt a challenge, and he said, "Well, I'm adopted, Cait, how's that?"

"That's…what?" she said, then louder, "What?", then louder yet, "Is that what this is about? My God! Mickey, did I hear you right?"

There was silence.

After a long minute or so, Mickey nodded and said, "Chicago, Illinois, U.S.A. I was three years old and got on an *airplane*…an airplane to Ireland, probably Dublin, with Fergus and Marian. They're my aunt and uncle, not my parents."

"Oh, my God! Oh, my God!" said Caitlin. She repeated it a third time, then laughed a little.

"That's a curiosity to me, that you want to laugh. Because I told Father McDermott the same thing today, and *he* laughed."

"I can't speak for Father McDermott, Mickey, but if you knew how many people had wondered how two homely souls like Fergus and Marian popped out a kid that looked like you, well…"

As they entered Westport's largest intersection, named for its shape—"The Octagon"—Mickey was watching the rearview mirror. He suddenly swung into an available parking spot.

"Caitlin, why don't we stop at Dunning's…I am starving."

"No!" she almost yelled. "I'll fix you a sandwich when we get home. If we stop at Dunning's, your buddies won't let you leave."

"All right," he said without any resistance.

Caitlin waited for a moment, and then said, "Well, what are you waiting for?"

"Just waiting for traffic to pass."

Caitlin turned around to look. "Mickey, there *is* no traffic!"

He grinned at her, then said as he pulled out, "Well, I thought there might be…can't be too careful."

"What are you talkin' about? Am I missin' something, Mickey?"

"Maybe the same thing you missed last week. What kind o' car does Gerry drive?"

"It's a Honda hatchback...I still don't know what you're talking about!"

"Let's just say you've got quite a following. Sullivan last week, and Gerry this week. I'm sure I saw him in back of us, but he spun off the Octagon onto one of the other streets."

"Oh. Well, maybe he's just comin' in to listen to the sessions at Matt Molloy's or some such thing." Matt Molloy's pub in Westport was internationally known for its excellent musicians and their traditional Irish music sessions. *Trad sessions.*

"Actually, Ms. Caity, I'm 90 percent certain that the same car went flyin' by when we stopped to switch places. Which means—"

"Who cares what it means, Mickey? He's gone now, so let's just keep moving."

She had just cut her ties with Gerry, and she didn't want to think or talk about him. She wanted to hear more about Mickey's family secrets.

"Which means he hid down some dark lane waiting for us to pass, then resumed stalking you," he continued.

She was silent. *Is she upset?* Upset, maybe, because things just keep getting fouled up, or maybe she thought he was indirectly foisting responsibility for Sullivan on her. He hadn't meant to do that.

"Which is exactly what I'd do if you dumped me!" he joked.

She smiled a little and said, "Why don't you give me the chance and we'll see!"

She picked up the gallon jug, wiggled the cork off, and took a swallow.

"All better," she said. "How 'bout a swig for the man?"

Mickey was inclined to accept her offer, but his intuition told him to wait, that joining her in passing the jug back and forth seemed...too sexy.

Jesus, I'm obsessed! Change the subject!

"No, thank you. Caity, when we talked about meeting tonight, it was because you had things to tell me."

"Oh...oh! That's right, isn't it?" she remembered. "You're doin' fine, brilliant. You just keep talkin'."

"Well, first, I forgot to mention that Eamonn's concern today was that he—bein' my close and dear friend—had alerted the homicide detectives to my propensity for violence, and because of that, they might charge me with a crime like murder or manslaughter."

Caitlin was so alarmed at this news that Mickey had to talk practically all the way back to her house to dissuade her from her fear. She had another gulp of the Guinness as she listened.

When they finally arrived, the Ford was still not in the drive.

Caitlin grabbed the jug and ran into the house to find a message waiting on the recorder: "Caitlin, we had a flat tire in Claremorris, couldn't get it fixed til half nine tonight, so Mam and I are sleeping at Aunt Helen's and heading home soon as we wake."

"Now that's a relief," said Caitlin to no one as she went to make a sandwich for Mickey.

Mickey stayed in the dark driveway. In a short time, headlights appeared down the road. The Honda hatchback sped by the O'Connor residence, and Mickey stepped to the edge of the road to watch it pull over and park about 30 yards away. He stood back a few feet from the road to wait for Gerry, but Gerry didn't appear. He thought he heard a rustling toward the back of the house, so he cautiously moved around the other side of the house toward the back.

O'Connors' back yard extended approximately twenty-five feet to a rock wall, which went across the length of the yard. Above the wall were miscellaneous shrubs and trees, all wild and uncared for.

As Mickey peered around the corner of the house, he saw Gerry standing a few feet back from the wall, in the shadow of a tree. The light from a room in the house—Caitlin's room—barely illuminated Gerry as he unzipped his pants. Mickey walked directly toward Gerry.

"I'll hear your confession now, my son," he said, and Gerry sprung from the wall like a jackrabbit.

"You sick little fuck," Mickey called out as Gerry vanished into the neighbors' back yard.

What's the use? Mickey thought, as he walked to the front door wondering whether to tell Caitlin or not. He figured Gerry probably had been doing this for a while—jerking off as he watched Caitlin undress. Certainly, tonight wasn't a first, the way he parked and assumed his station so readily. As he came up on the porch, he decided to spare Caitlin the news, at least for tonight.

She met him at the door. "What y' doin' out there?"

With that, Gerry's Honda sped by at about 50 miles per hour, an incredibly dangerous speed on a single-lane road of such poor character.

"Jesus God," said Caitlin, "these damned kids think it's a Grand Prix out there!"

She was feeling the effects of the stout now, and she apparently had not noticed that it was Gerry who had whizzed by. She told Mickey about Keran's message as he came into the house.

Mickey sat down at the kitchen table. His sandwich awaited. A *meat loaf* sandwich. Caitlin stood at the sink holding her pint glass of Guinness, almost empty.

"How 'bout some o' that Jesus Christ truth serum for the boy, Caity Lin?" he said looking at her with a curious smile.

"Oh, amen to that, bub!" she said, filling the empty pint glass in front of him.

Mickey laughed. "Has my wee sis had her fill o' the black stuff?"

"I'm all right, Mickey," she said, "just tastes good tonight."

She leaned back against the sink, smiling at Mickey as he ate his sandwich. "How's it taste, bub?"

"Like a conspiracy, bubbette! Guess you make these two at a time, huh?"

"We-e-e-ll," she smiled, "We wouldn't want your meeting with Father McDermott ruined by one of the world's lesser sandwiches, would we?" She was definitely feeling her Guinness.

"Sit down and tell me what you wanted to say to me while I eat my delicious sandwich, Caity."

She sat and talked of a few other things while he ate, finally saying, "Oh, well, I was just concerned that you were keeping so much inside yourself. And what with you comin' up on crossroads, it just seemed—"

"Crossroads?" Mickey interrupted, somewhat annoyed. "You didn't just deliver the meat loaf—you sent him the whole script!"

"Oh, Mickey, I did not!" she said smiling. "I talked to Father McDermott about you, and *he* said 'crossroads.' And I didn't say a single thing I wouldn't tell you to your face!"

Mickey looked at her smiling back at him. *What is that beautiful girl thinking about?!*

He changed his tone and said, "I'm very grateful for your concern and caring. I'm a lucky fella."

They continued looking at each other across the table.

"Are you lucky...fella?" she asked, and whether she meant it suggestively or not, Mickey took it that way, or *felt* it that way.

"Why don't we go for a walk on this lovely night, and air that stout out of your head?"

"My head is just fine...and I think it's rainin' a bit, Mickey," she said softly.

"It's a lovely gentle rain, Cait," he said with a look on his face that asked her to understand. She did, and she grabbed a jacket from a coat tree as they headed for the door.

*   *   *   *

They walked silently for a few minutes when Caitlin asked, "Why are you adopted, Mickey? Where are your parents?"

"Killed in a car accident with my older brother."

"Oh, God, Mickey, I am so sorry! You had a brother, too!?"

"Family secret. All a family secret," he replied.

"And you weren't in the car with them?"

"No. I was sitting in my front yard, diggin' in the dirt with a stick. I lived at the end of a little street with little houses. A car pulled up in front of my house, backed up, pulled into the neighbor's driveway about six feet from where I was sitting. Fergus got out of the passenger side, picked me up, and off we went. Me, Fergus and Marian. I remember screaming, but I don't remember too much after that."

"So, it's 'Mickey the American,' then?"

He laughed a little. "Once upon a time. Suppose I'd better be an Irishman by now, don't you?"

They walked.

"Mickey, I mean no pressure by this, but I'm just interested," she said, slurring her words a little, "...do you hope to be a father and a family man some day?"

"Wow, no pressure intended, none felt. Pardon me for a moment while I gasp for oxygen."

Caitlin laughed and said, "Oh, come on—don't you want a bunch of *wee Mickeys* climbing all over you some day?"

"Bunch of wee Mickeys?" he muttered, smiling, "God help us all!" And though he wouldn't say so, Caitlin had touched him. "Honestly, Caity, would you believe that this is something that I have, in fact, thought about? I've only recently been able to start understanding it."

"What is it that you understand?" she asked apprehensively.

"Well, that I may not look at all that—family—the same as most others. You know, my father, mother and brother were killed when I was three. I was yanked out of my front yard and raised by two people who haven't seemed to enjoy the experience. So, you see, for me, 'family' doesn't necessarily connote all those warm and wonderful things that others might imagine."

"Oh, Mickey, that's so sad! That's never occurred to me, but you know it doesn't have to be that way, don't you?"

"It's so easy to say 'Yes, sure I do,' but I think that—unless I'm able to work through or understand some of this—there's something inside of me that pushes all those good thoughts out of my head.

"Fergus and Marian once told me—," he then interrupted himself, saying, "Cait, you have to understand, we have not talked about any of this since I was a little kid. Fergus and Marian would get very angry if I tried to bring it up...I mean, Fergus would yell at me and even smack me."

"Why?" Caitlin said in near disbelief.

"Oh, they had these little recitations they would make: that's too painful a subject to talk about, we are your family now, don't dwell on the past, it hurts us all. They told me that adopted children are looked down upon, so I never should tell anyone that I'm adopted."

"What? But Mickey, you know that isn't true..."

"It doesn't *seem* true, but I certainly didn't know that at the time, and I didn't want to be looked down upon...and maybe *they* believe it. They said, comin' here from America, no one would know I wasn't theirs. I never really saw a harm in that. Anyway, they once told me, long ago, that Marian is my mother's sister."

"I see," said Caitlin quietly.

"My mom's name was Meg, Caitlin. *Meg McCall.*"

"They told you that?"

"No, Cait, I *remember* my mom. And my dad, Tom McCall. He wore glasses, he was a lawyer, tall, I think, and thin. But my mom, her name was Meg, and she was a pretty lady. When I think about it, one o' *them*—Meg or Marian—must've been adopted, because they don't look much alike. I even remember a picture of her that my dad kept on his dresser. Might've been her secondary school photo or somethin', because she was young and so beautiful, with long hair, like yours, only it was brown."

"Can't you talk to Marian about all this, Mickey? This is so sad!"

"Oh, God, no! That's what I'm tellin' you. They told me just a few things, and we've not been allowed to discuss it for years."

"Oh, Mickey, I just don't think I could live like that!"

"What could I do? If you were 3, 4 or 5 years old, and you got smacked and screamed at every time you brought up a subject, you'd quit bringin' it up, wouldn't you?"

"There's got to be a way to find out about all this...maybe you could go back to Chicago."

"For what? I wouldn't know what to look for. Besides, that's another thing..."

"What is?" she asked.

"I didn't live in Chicago. I'm sure that I lived in Ohio…and we even used to sing a little song about it, living in Ohio. And Chicago's not in Ohio, it's in Illinois."

"What?"

"Yeah. I looked it up on the map."

"Mickey, I'm lost. I thought you told me that you *did* live in Chicago?"

"Not really, but that's what they tried to tell me. I remember having a horrible argument about it when I was first with them. They kept after me to say it, to say, 'I live in Chicago.' I just kept repeating that I didn't live in Chicago, I lived in Ohio, and Fergus blew up. He started hitting me til Marian made him stop. Later on, she told me she'd buy me a Milky Way chocolate bar if I said I lived in Chicago, so I did."

"Are you sure about all this, Mickey? I mean…you were only three."

"What I'm tellin' you is what I'm sure of…there's more memories that I can't be so sure of. Like, I think we did *drive* to Chicago, to the airport…but I remember names of people who lived on our street. The Fergusons, the Wilsons, the Kecks. And there was an older girl named Kay Maybe."

"Kay Maybe? *Kay Maybe?* Mickey, I think you might have had an imaginary playmate!" Caitlin said laughing. "And I do mean *Maybe!*" she added, now cackling with laughter at herself.

She was doubting him, and she began wondering how much of all this new information was true and how much of it fantasy from the mind of a three-year-old.

Mickey chuckled along with her, but said, "I'm tellin' you, Caitlin, there was a Kay Maybe, and she lived on my street."

She said, "O-*kay. Maybe*," and then repeated it several times, giggling all over again. She was tired and semi-intoxicated.

*   *   *   *

At 7:45 a.m., Ellen and Keran O'Connor turned onto Treanbeg Road.

"Oh, my God!" said Keran quietly.

"Aw, for the love o' Jesus!" Ellen cried out, "Caitlin, Caitlin! Shame, shame!" They both saw Mickey's truck parked in the driveway alongside their home.

Ellen pulled in behind the truck and bustled into the house, going immediately to Caitlin's room and banging the door open. Caitlin lay across the still-made bed, alone, fully clothed from the previous night.

"Where is he, Caitlin?!" Ellen demanded loudly.

Caitlin jerked her head, and squinting at her mother, half-asleep, said, "What? What's wrong?"

"Where's Mickey?" Ellen repeated angrily.

Caitlin now raised herself up, looking frightened, and she parroted, "Where's Mickey?" as she sat up, then jumped from the bed.

"What's wrong, Mother!? Is Mickey missing!?" she cried out.

Ellen gave a quick glance to Caitlin's room, then rushed through the other rooms, determined to find him. She finally turned to head back outside, with Caitlin following, demanding, "Mother, what is wrong?!"

Ellen pushed the front door open, then stuck her head out to look at Mickey's truck, almost to assure herself that she hadn't seen a mirage. Behind her, Caitlin pushed the door a little further to see what was out there.

"Oh!" she said, surprised.

Keran was silently pointing into the cab of the truck. She rested her cheek on folded hands indicating that Mickey was asleep across the front seat. Her mother and sister walked carefully to the edge of the porch and peered into the truck to see for themselves.

Ellen and Caitlin looked at each other. Caitlin shrugged her shoulders with a helpless smile and said, "I swear I didn't know he was here!"

Keran loudly whispered, "Shall I wake him?"

"No!" Caitlin said, motioning Keran to come in.

Ellen fixed tea as Caitlin explained to her and Keran all that had happened the previous evening: Mickey picking her up at Findlay's at her request, playing the drunk with Gerry, Seamus's gallon jug; and she admitted that she had perhaps had a "bit much" of the stout. She guessed that they had been up until four o'clock or so, and she said that they had had a wonderful talk as they "walked in the soft rainfall."

Ellen set three cups and saucers on the table, then sat down with the two girls, waiting for the water to boil.

"So he didn't find his way into your room?" she asked, already relieved.

Caitlin smiled at her older sister for a second, then coyly said, "Probably could have," and Ellen moaned as the girls laughed.

With that, Mickey knocked and called in comically, "It's blocked in I am, missus!"

"Come in here, you," called Mrs. O'Connor, "and I'll tell you how well I liked seein' your truck in my drive at a quarter til eight in the mornin'!"

"Just standin' guard on your little one, madam," said Mickey as he entered the kitchen.

"Sit down, and I'll get you a cup. Do you know what it looked like comin' down this road, Mickey? At 7:45, with Caitlin alone through the night?"

"Uh-oh…like I stopped fer tea on me way t' the early Mass?" he teased. "Actually, Mrs. O'Connor, there was a bit of carryin' on out on the road here, fast cars and all," he exaggerated, "quite late—kids I suppose—but I didn't want to leave a pretty girl all alone in here."

As much as he was speaking lightheartedly, he realized as soon as he said "pretty" that he was treading new ground.

"Think I'm pretty, do you, Mickey?" Caitlin smiled.

Mickey felt himself blush, and smiled, "Well, now, *I* hadn't ever noticed, but you told me last night that there are some who think you're pretty, remember?"

"So he listens to you, Caity!" laughed Keran. "Much more than he'd ever do if he married you like you want!"

"Keran!!!" both Ellen and Caitlin screamed in concert, as Keran hooted, clearly delighted with herself.

*   *   *   *

Caitlin and Mickey were among the last to exit the church following the 10:00 a.m. Mass. They greeted Father McDermott as usual, but he appeared somber when he saw them. He motioned them to come through, turning with them as they passed, and then putting an arm on each of their shoulders, as in a huddle. He almost whispered, "Could you two wait over at the house for me to finish here? I'd like a word."

"Of course, Father," they both agreed, and walked over to the front door of the presbytery.

Mickey smiled at Caitlin and said, "Now if this is because he drove by your place last night and saw my truck, you go ahead and make your confession first, because he'll never believe me!"

"Stop it, Mickey," she giggled. "He didn't look too happy. I'm guessin' he wants to talk about Bill Sullivan."

"Oh, right, yes," Mickey said, "that must be it. Because that involves the both of us."

As a light rain began, Mickey suggested that they step inside. As they opened the door, they saw Father McDermott trotting to join them and get out of the rain. "Go on in!" he called out.

"C'mon into the kitchen," the priest said, breezing past them. "How 'bout some coffee and toast? I'm havin' some."

"Sure," said Mickey.

"Just coffee, please," said Caitlin. "Hope it doesn't make me puke!" she whispered to Mickey. She was feeling a little queasy from the previous night's stout.

"Sit down, sit down," said the priest as he dropped bread in the toaster and put three cups on the table. "Made this right before Mass, so it ought to be decent," he said, grabbing a full coffee pot and filling the cups.

He sat down with his elbows on the table and folded his hands. "I'm goin' t' tell you both right now that I know I have only one side of the story, and I have a hard time believin' it, knowin' the two of you as I do. But already this mornin', I'm told that *you*," he said, poking an index finger in Mickey's chest, "showed up drunk last night down at the Findlay pub, bullyin' poor Gerry and stealin' his date from 'im."

They both laughed, and Caitlin explained exactly what had happened, stressing that she had made a point of asking Mickey to rescue her from what she had decided would be her last date with Gerry.

"And believe it or not, Father," she smiled, "Mickey plays an excellent drunk! I'm thinkin' he's rehearsed a few times!"

"Didn't I tell you?" the priest announced proudly. "I knew very well I hadn't heard the whole story!"

The toast popped, and Caitlin went to butter it and put two more slices in the toaster. She put the toast in front of Father McDermott. He looked at Mickey, studying him, and he raised his eyebrows as if asking a question.

"Sullivan?" Mickey said.

"Mm-hmm," answered Father McDermott. "How are you with that?"

Mickey looked at Father McDermott, but didn't speak. He lowered his head then, shaking it back and forth. "I can't say…I'm tryin' not to think about it. I wish it hadn't happened."

Caitlin stood behind Mickey with a hand on each shoulder. He shrugged.

"Are we in confidence here, Father?" he asked quietly.

"Of course we're in confidence, and don't ever ask me such a thing again, Mick. You know better."

Mickey took a deep breath. "I wanted to hurt him, Father. I…uh, was angry," he said, nervously rubbing a hand back and forth on the tabletop as he stared at the wall.

"He deserved your anger, Mickey," Caitlin assured him.

"Yes, he did," Father McDermott confirmed, "but I understand your angst. Will you be able to work through it?"

Yes, Father, and yes, Caitlin. To be sure, he's a rapist. He deserved my anger. But you two aren't listening. I said I wanted to hurt him. And I killed him! Did he deserve that? I can assure you both that I could've brought him out of that field without harming a hair on his bushy head. That's what I'm struggling with!

"Yeah, I'll work through it," he sighed. "It's just comin' on the heels of all this other crap, my *crossroads*, you know, and talkin' about the adoption stuff. *Et cetera, et cetera.*"

Father McDermott opened his eyes wide, and he looked at Caitlin. He pointed a finger back and forth between her and Mickey. "You've talked?"

"Right," said Caitlin, "that's actually the reason we got together last night." She put the second two slices of buttered toast in front of Mickey and sat down.

Father McDermott had not yet taken a bite from his toast, and Mickey said, "Now, you know, Father, Caitlin's not havin' any toast, but if you and I were to take a walk, she'd eat all four slices here, and probably look for jam before she did."

"O' course, I know," he said with feigned gravity. "I've already told you, just because I'm a priest, that doesn't mean I don't understand women."

Caitlin laughed a little and said, "Guess I needn't be a lady around the likes o' you two!" She stood and dropped one more slice of bread in the toaster.

*   *   *   *

They spoke for another hour, telling Father McDermott the details and peculiarities of Mickey's adoption, all that they had discussed through the wee hours of that morning; even how it had originally come up at Kilkelly's on the night of the Sullivan incident. Father McDermott joked that Mickey should've checked his horoscope on that day and gone back to bed. Otherwise, he asked a few questions along the way, but basically listened.

Finally, he said, "Now, Mick, you know what *I'm* concerned about in your young and reckless life; and you know that Caitlin cares about you, and that she's got some common sense that gives her concern. I can't say that it's all connected, but you've got a bit of a mystery here. There's certainly somethin' underlying all of this that none of us are seeing…even given the known, uh, *idiosyncrasies*, of Fergus and Marian."

"But why? I don't understand," he said.

The priest shook his head while he thought. "You know, when I was a kid, at one time or another, I had searched through every drawer, every closet, every shelf in our home. Have you ever done that, Mick? I mean, there's got to be some clue...your birth certificate or your adoption papers."

"Never seen 'em. But, sure, I've looked through everything over the years."

"Mmm. Well, let's all keep the wheels turnin'," Father McDermott said as he stood. "One thing I'm sure of is that this'll all come to fruition in God's good time, and I don't think that's far off. I can *feel* it! But you've got your exams this week, don't you, Mick?"

"Just two more...Monday and Wednesday morning. Wednesday at noon, I'll be finished with studying and school for the remainder of eternity."

Father McDermott shook his head with a smile as he walked them to the door, and said, "Well, put this other stuff out of your head til then so you can concentrate on your exams, and oh, I should mention—I spoke to Senator O'Malley over in Westport about your political ambitions. Had quite a little discussion actually, because he had, uh, *heard* of you—which I cleared up—but at any rate, he'd be happy to talk to you any time you'd like, so just let me know, and I'll set that up."

Mickey and Caitlin thanked Father McDermott for his time and interest. The three resolved that they would share any thoughts or ideas they came up with, then said good-bye.

As they drove away, Caitlin also told Mickey that she'd be working in Castlebar all week, because Peggy O'Grady was taking one more week to rest at home, and another employee was on a scheduled holiday week. The two agreed to meet at noon Wednesday at McCarthy's to celebrate.

MONDAY 21 MAY 1990

Later that evening, past midnight, as Mickey walked Caitlin to her front door, he knew that—this time—she would not be catching him off guard with her "beseeching" look. He knew because he was ready for it. Tonight, he would be looking for it, and, indeed, aching a little in anticipation of it.

He also knew that once he and Caitlin kissed, if that were to happen, their relationship would change forever. What he didn't realize, or what he didn't yet *acknowledge*, was that *that* change had already taken place. He now wanted and *needed* that "look" from her. It was a benchmark in their friendship, relationship, whatever it was. A point of progress. To not get it...no, he had to get it, and he was willing to stand there with her until he did...awaiting the look that he had already understood might have been irresistible if Eamonn had not been needing a chat.

They reached the door, and she turned to him. *And...there it was.* Those soft searching blue eyes that had been finding their way into his every thought.

He made a feeble attempt to be humorous, intending to sound like some curious observer speaking objectively, but instead his words were quietly sincere: "There's that look again," he said, as he looked back at her. He swallowed.

They let their eyes gaze at each other for a moment before Caitlin gently tilted her head to one side and smiled. She too spoke in a low voice: "Am I gettin' to you, Mickey?"

He didn't say anything at first. She could hear his breathing. Finally, he actually *sighed* and answered, "Yes."

Their stares continued. She waited for his kiss.

He spoke in a sort of quiet desperation, "Caitlin, you've always made me feel...strong. I've *felt* strong with you, and I've always wanted to *be* strong *for* you. I don't feel very strong right now!"

"Mickey..."

"How is it that just lookin' at you, the little girl who's always made me feel so strong...all the sudden makes me feel so weak?"

She rushed her arms around him, saying, "Oh, Mickey, you've never talked to me like this!"

He gathered her closer and said, "Cait, I can't speak for you, but I know the second our lips touch, everything between us will change—"

Ellen O'Connor opened the front door to call for Caitlin, and she saw the two hugging. In less than a second, Caitlin yelled, "Go away!"—and somewhere in that same second, an understanding Ellen O'Connor slammed the door on herself.

The couple gave each other smiles of relief, and Caitlin sweetly whispered, "It wouldn't be our first kiss, Mickey."

Mickey held her close as he released a small chuckle and said, "Don't think I don't know that. I walked away from that first one tellin' myself, 'I better never let that little girl kiss me again, or I'll be in trouble!'"

Caitlin gasped to hear that he remembered the kiss that a lovestruck little six-year old had given him almost thirteen years prior. She caught her breath, put her arms around his neck, and softly told him, "Here comes trouble."

Although Caitlin simply reached her lips to his for the sake of the kiss, this kiss would not be over quickly. With her stunning beauty and charm, she had taken control of their moment and captured her man. But as quickly as she'd found her own power, it dissolved in the arms of one far more practiced in the art of physical love.

Mickey kept their kiss soft at first as his hand touched her cheek, then slid his fingers into her lush red hair and behind her neck, caressing her tenderly in one moment, letting her feel helpless in his powerful arms in the next, skillfully moving from one embrace to another. She completely surrendered to him as though she were on some magic ride. Never before had she imagined that she could be kissed like this.

Finally, as Mickey moved his hands over her, kissing her forehead, her hair, her neck, he stopped to pull her tightly to him.

He could not have been more correct about everything changing between them. The little girl whom he had rescued and befriended when their respective ages were 9 and 6, whom he had protected and shared his thoughts and ambitions with over their young years, had invited him to abandon the days of their youth and adolescence for something better, a higher place where just the two of them could go.

And he'd accepted, knowing every other relationship, indeed, every other aspect of his life would be altered or ended to accommodate this. There was not a reason to pretend otherwise. His heart and his mind were now one, and he said, "I love you, my little Caitlin Molly, and I never want to spend another day apart from you."

"Oh, Mickey," she cried, "I've loved you since the day I met you! Is this really happening?"

A light went in the front window. Mother O'Connor had apparently decided to call time on the lovebirds. They stepped inside to find her seated at the kitchen table with a crossword puzzle.

"I've kissed your daughter, Mrs. O'Connor," Mickey declared with a smile.

She put her pencil on the table, looked at the two of them, each grinning, with an arm behind the other's back, and she said, "I'd gathered as much, and I trust you're not thinkin' o' makin' my little girl one o' your whores?"

The thought startled Mickey, but he instantly deemed it a fair question, and responded, "Any man that might say such a thing wouldn't be able to protect himself fast enough. No, Mrs. O'Connor, you have my word, and—" Mickey's alarm rang.

He woke from his dream. It was 4:30 Monday morning and time to study.

"Jesus, Mary and Joseph!" he whispered as he stared wide-eyed at his ceiling.

*   *   *   *

Paul Byrne called Caitlin into his office first thing Monday morning. He was a nice-looking, naturally cordial 39-year-old man who had become manager of the bank's main office in Castlebar because of his popularity with the bank's customers and with other employees, as opposed to any level of education or technical knowledge he had achieved. A natural leader.

"Y' all right, then, Caitlin? Sit down a minute," he said as he motioned to the chair.

"All right, thank you, Mr. Byrne."

"First of all, anybody remotely reminds you of Bill Sullivan, customer or employee, let me know right away, and I'll take care of it, okay?"

"Okay."

"I never liked that guy," Byrne continued as he casually made the Sign of the Cross with his right index finger, "never liked him. Don't know too many that did, actually."

"Mm."

"Caitlin, you'll work the middle window this week, but when Ann Moore goes to lunch, you'll have move over to her window and handle the safe-deposit boxes, because Robert is usually too busy keeping the loan accounts current. So whenever you and Ann get a free moment, she can familiarize you with what needs to be done there. I've told her that, and it ought not be a problem for you…working it just an hour a day, you might never even have a customer for the week."

"That's fine."

"Did y' know this is Ann's last week with us, Caitlin? Husband found a good job in England, Manchester I think, so as soon as Jeannette Hall is back from holiday, we'll be short again. Now—what would it take to get you to transfer down here with us permanently? I think we can give you a nice raise to cover your travel expenses and then some, *and* I know Peggy'd like it."

Caitlin thanked Byrne for the offer and promised him a response by Wednesday morning. She needed to think it through.

There was constant traffic in the bank until about 10:30 a.m. Ann Moore and Caitlin had adjoining windows, so at the first available moment, Ann showed Caitlin the signature cards, the time stamp, the keys, then took her into the safe-deposit vault and turned the keys. No problem.

"Each box requires two keys to open it, Caitlin: we have one, and the customer will have one. Nothing to it."

Nothing to it, but Caitlin's heart was beating fast. She was certain she had seen a signature card for Fergus and Marian Monaghan when Ann had flipped through them.

*   *   *   *

Father McDermott turned his Peugeot sedan up the hill toward the presbytery. He noticed Caitlin walking ahead near the top of the grade, and he rolled down his window as he neared her.

"Pardon me, lady, could I get directions to the nearest Presbyterian chapel?" he called out.

"Oh!" said Caitlin, startled, then laughing said, "Sure, mister, I'm headed there meself! Could I get a lift?"

She walked around the car, got into the front seat and said, "I've got some news, Father, and I need some advice."

She told Father McDermott that the Monaghans had a safe-deposit box at the bank's main office. A *large* safe-deposit box that had not been entered since the date it was opened in October 1971, the year that the Monaghans had come to County Mayo.

"I kept thinking about what you said, Father, about looking for adoption papers or birth certificates. What more logical place…I mean, Father, those adoption papers *have* to be in there!"

"It's an overwhelming thought, Caitlin. Let me absorb that for a few minutes."

He parked, flipped open the boot and pulled out a half-barrel of Guinness. He lumbered by Caitlin with it, saying, "These groceries get heavier and heavier! Get the door, if you don't mind, and come on in."

Caitlin waited in the kitchen while Father McDermott placed the half-barrel in an antechamber.

He walked back into the kitchen, brushing his hands against each other and said, "He loved the meat loaf, by the way!"

Caitlin laughed and told Father McDermott that Mickey had charged the two of them with conspiracy when she served him another meat loaf sandwich early Sunday morning.

She went on to tell him that she had an opportunity for a better position with the bank at the main office in Castlebar, and that she would likely be working, or sharing, the safe-deposit window.

"If Mickey can get hold of Fergus's key somehow, I think I could just sneak him in there and get a look!"

The priest grimaced a little as he thought. "I don't think you can sneak Mickey anywhere in this county right about now, much less into Bill Sullivan's old employer's. And besides, you just can't do that. You'd be fired on the spot, Caitlin."

Silence.

Caitlin was immediately disheartened and disappointed at his reaction, and he knew it. Much of her own excitement had sprung from Father McDermott's suggestion to search every corner for clues.

"What might they have in there, Father? Something in such a large box that they haven't needed for nineteen years?"

"What'd you say before…" McDermott asked, ignoring her question, "that you're going to be *sharing* the safe-deposit duties?"

"Yes."

"And you're doing that now?"

"Just at lunch, yes. Do you think there's a way to do this?" she asked hopefully.

"I tell you what, honey, let's walk down to Kelley's and get a bowl o' chowder. We need to think about this, and I'm too hungry to think." He was also not averse to showing off his friendship with the prettiest girl in the county.

On the way down the hill, they acknowledged their tacit understanding that Mickey need not be bothered with any of this until his exams were finished.

Kelley's Kitchen was nestled between Dominick Kelley's butcher shop—same ownership—and Chambers' Market at the top of Newport's shopping district, and thus, immediately across the street at the bottom of the lane coming down from St. Patrick's. Kelley's was known for its excellent meat, white pudding and chowder.

After ordering, Father McDermott asked Caitlin about the procedure for adding a signer to an existing safe-deposit account.

"Well, I know a power-of-attorney will do it, and of course, if the owner of the box brings you in. I think the employees probably know most of the customers. I *know* Mr. Byrne does. He knows everyone in Castlebar."

"I'll bet y' a quid he doesn't know Fergus and Marian Monaghan."

"Probably not. I think he told me that he came to the bank about ten years ago, and the box was opened *nineteen* years ago. And Monaghans otherwise do their banking at the Newport branch, where boxes aren't available."

He asked a few more questions, particularly focusing on whom Caitlin was to replace and what times Caitlin would be working the safe-deposit window, then said, "So what if Fergus were to bring Mickey in and ask that he be added to the box?"

Caitlin waited while the waitress placed the bowls of chowder on the table.

She then leaned to whisper, "What do you mean, Father? Fergus wouldn't do that!"

"No, no, honey, here's what I'm sayin': *nobody knows* Fergus, but Fergus has a box, Fergus brings Mickey in, so…what? You get identification from Fergus and add Mickey to the box, right?"

"Oh, right! Mickey signs as a *deputy*, it's called, the card gets date-and time-stamped next to his signature, and then he or Fergus would sign on the back with another time-stamp if they wanted to go into the box."

"Caitlin, if one of those cards were missing for a while, would anyone know?"

"No…I mean, not unless they looked for it."

"Of course, all o' this depends on Mickey findin' that key and his willingness to act," said Father McDermott, "but I've got an idea…"

They finished their chowder while discussing Father McDermott's thoughts, which were aimed at keeping Caitlin uninvolved as much as possible.

Later, as they climbed the lane towards the presbytery, Father McDermott remarked, "I don't know, Caitlin, I just don't know. We're talkin' about doin' things that aren't right, and it could bring Mick some trouble—and you'll be in big trouble, too, if you're not careful—but it'll be your choice, yours and his—"

"He'll do it, Father, I'm sure he will!"

"I think I may already be in big trouble with my Boss," he mused, shaking his head, "for offerin' such counsel."

"Your boss?" Caitlin asked, then—understanding—she said, "Ooooh...your *Boss!*"

"I'll tell y', honey, the lad hasn't had it easy down there with those two, y' know, and I'm not sure I should say all this, but I had Senator O'Malley all set to give 'im a job when he finished school, and then that damn Sullivan had to up and die. Now O'Malley thinks Mickey's too hot a potato for his office to handle!"

Father McDermott drove Caitlin home, stepped in to visit with Ellen and talk about church music and other matters. He then joined Ellen and Keran for supper, while Caitlin excused herself.

*   *   *   *

At 7:30 p.m., Mickey found himself staring blankly at his business law hornbook. Earlier in the day, he had finished his Philosophy exam by 11:00, was home before noon, then read his textbook and class notes the rest of the day. Except for three hours that he had pledged to Fergus the next morning, he would have the remainder of Tuesday to complete his review for his final exam Wednesday. Plenty of time. For the moment, he was restless and low on inspiration to study.

He knew that Kitty O'Neill was working this evening, and therefore unavailable. He didn't feel like driving as far as Castlebar to meet someone. He thought about walking down to see Sarah Callaghan, but it was early, and she might well have a few customers. He finally resolved to study until 10:30, and then drive down for a late visit. As he sat in his room making this decision, he heard the phone ring. Marian came to his door.

"One of your girls, Mickey. Shall I tell her you're studying?"

"No!" he answered emphatically, practically jumping from his chair. "I'll get it!"

"Hello, Mickey, this is Peggy."

"Peg—?"

"Peggy O'Grady. How are you?"

"Oh, *Peggy!* Brilliant, what a surprise! Everything all right?"

"Sure...well, I don't know. Are you busy, Mickey? I really need to talk to...somebody, to *you*, if you wouldn't mind."

"Well, of course, Peggy! What's the problem?"

"Maybe we could meet?"

He didn't answer.

"Mickey, I'd be happy to drive over to Newport and buy you a pint..."

He spoke quietly. "I don't think that's a good idea, Peggy, for you to be seen with me in Newport. It wouldn't look right, a married lady—"

"I'm sorry, Mickey...if you can meet me, just tell me where."

He paused, then said, "How much time do you have, Peggy?"

"All night. Brian just left for a business conference in Galway. A few of them went down tonight so that they wouldn't have to drive it in the morning."

"Can you meet me down in Louisburgh in about an hour? There's a nice little lounge there in the Durkan Hotel where we could talk."

"That sounds fine!"

He gave her directions, took a shower, and headed out.

He noticed Father McDermott's Peugeot at O'Connors' as he drove by, which tweaked his interest, but his mind was *really* focused on what Peggy might want to talk about.

True enough, he thought, *she might need to occasionally cry on someone's shoulder about the fact that she had married such an ass*, but was he the one for that discussion?

Could be, he mused, *she just wants to get laid.* That thought at least made sense to him now—now that he had met her husband and heard her bemoan the lack of romance in their relationship. But, still...maybe it was just some mundane interest in taking college courses, switching jobs, or some such thing...but why *him? Maybe she wants to commiserate about the incident with Sullivan. Sure, that's it.*

Louisburgh was almost a forty-minute drive for Mickey, and about fifteen minutes less for Peggy. When he entered the lounge, which was to the left immediately inside the hotel's front door, he saw Peggy sitting on a violet-cushioned bench which ran the length of the wall, with a table for two in front of her. She held a glass of red wine, and a pint of Guinness sat waiting for Mickey.

In the front of the room, silhouetted by the remaining daylight outside the large bay window, three men sat with their ales, arguing cordially about something or other. Otherwise, the lounge was empty.

Although a wall separated the lounge from the main bar and restaurant area in the hotel, an opening in the wall allowed the bar itself, as well as the space behind it, to extend about six feet into the lounge, giving the barkeeper access to both rooms.

"I hope I wasn't too presumptuous, Mickey," Peggy said with a sweet smile.

"Well, we'll see, won't we? Whatever did you want to talk about, sweetie?" he asked, sitting in the chair across from her.

"I meant about pre-ordering your Guinness!" she said, laughing a little.

"Oh, I think you're in safe territory there, Peggy!" he smiled.

"How about Louisburgh—are we in safe territory here?"

Mickey smiled and rolled his eyes upwards a little, leaned toward Peggy and said, "You and my curiosity are killin' me, dear! Why are we here?"

"Will you let me sip my Merlot for a minute and relax, Mickey? I'm a little nervous right now. Maybe you could tell me about life on a sheep farm," she offered lightheartedly.

Mickey displayed a troubled face, and said, "That's a very bad spot you're puttin' me in, Peggy. I promised the sheep I wouldn't tell."

Peggy laughed at his silly remark, actually spraying out a little wine as she did; and Mickey backed up, making grandiose gestures, wiping off the front of himself as though he'd been drenched. He cried out, "*Jaysus, missus!* Give me a signal next time, so's at least I can open me mouth and catch some!"

"Sorry, Mickey!" she chuckled. "I thought that was just our Welsh lads with the sheep! I *do* remember Caitlin saying something about you walking the hills, singing to your sheep!"

"That's right...she insists that I couldn't *talk* 'em into anything and had to try my singing!"

They chatted amicably about school for a while, Mickey's hopes for a career in politics...the West Irish Bank...Caitlin...and Wales; he told her that he was extremely happy to see her in such high spirits, because Caitlin had told him that she had taken some time away from work to relax after the Sullivan incident.

"Actually, my husband, who treats me like an absolute *baby*," she answered as she finished her second drink, "is insisting I take a *second* week at home. So I didn't go back in today, either, even though I wanted to."

Oh, well, then, he thought, *perhaps it's just a little companionship she needs, and that's why she rang—she's bored.*

"But you're doin' all right, then, Peggy?"

"I really am, Mickey, and I was curious about you, too, since he passed. I somewhat feel that we're partners-in-crime in all this!"

So there it is…she's being considerate, checking on me, just as Caitlin and I checked on her.

"I'm not terribly crazy about your choice of words, Peggy, but if we can be partners, I'll live with it," he smiled, immediately wondering about his own choice of words—*"partners,"* as Peggy smiled back and put her hand gently on top of his, saying, "That's a nice sentiment."

"Well, whatever the reason, Peggy, you called at the perfect time," Mickey said, standing up and taking his hand with him. "I was going stir-crazy with the books, and it's great craic talking to you! Let me get us one more."

She stared at him as he signaled the bartender. He looked back at her momentarily. It was almost 10:30.

The three men rose from their table by the window and continued carping at one another as they ambled out into the night.

As he stood at the bar, Mickey looked sideways at Peggy to see her checking her face in a small make-up mirror. Earlier, while driving to Louisburgh, he had semi-rehearsed a form of warning and disclaimer about the two of them engaging in any illicit activity—if that's what was on her mind—but after quaffing two pints while looking at Peggy's pretty face getting prettier as they carried on, morality issues and worry about others—excepting *one:* Caitlin—had fairly well faded with the daylight.

As he returned to the table with their drinks, Peggy scooted to the side a little and said, "Sit here beside me, Mickey, so we don't have to yell at each other across the table." She was obviously being facetious, since the cocktail table separating them was only large enough for a candle and a few drinks anyway.

Peggy was about to remove his only remaining concern. She said, "Mickey, I know that you're discreet, but I would just ask you one favor…I wish you wouldn't tell Caitlin that I rang you or that we met. Or anybody, really, but especially Caitlin. She…well, I *am* married, and I know you two are close, and—"

"Peggy, let me assure you that I will *not* speak a word about this to Caitlin," he said, much relieved that he didn't have to make that request for his own sake. "Yes, I've known Caitlin for a long, long time, and I can promise you she wouldn't understand our meeting like this."

"Thank you," Peggy smiled. "Whew!"

Mickey put his arm on the top of the bench behind Peggy. She heaved a short breath and said, "Mickey, Brian is only 30…only 30, but he might as well be

50...I mean, after two-and-a-half years of marriage...and it's once a week, if that! And nothing since that incident."

"Well, there might be some healing time there, for both of you," he responded quietly. "I've heard of that...when a woman gets...molested, whatever, her husband, or *some* husbands, shy away. Maybe take some counseling..."

"Yes, counseling," she smiled, "on some snowy day in hell, Brian will be there at the counselor's, asking someone else how he should live his life."

She looked at him and gave a helpless laugh. "He didn't even kiss me when he left this afternoon. I mean, a *peck*, but not a kiss, a *real* kiss, if you know what I mean."

"I think I do know," he responded, now almost whispering, "...it's something heartfelt, isn't it, Peggy?"

"Yes, *heartfelt*," she sighed. She leaned into his shoulder and looked into his eyes. "A man can tell a woman everything with his kiss, Mickey, everything he wants her to know."

Mickey had heard enough. He let his right hand come down from the bench and touch Peggy's shoulder. "Things that are better left unspoken, Peggy?" he asked, their faces just inches apart now.

Peggy melted into him, putting her arms around him as his own enveloped her. Their lips and tongues played as they pulled at each other, alternately letting their hands explore everywhere they could reach. With her hand in Mickey's lap, she begged him, "Make love to me, Mickey! I'll get us a room here...please!"

"Let's!" he immediately responded. By now, he even had no qualms about letting her pay for the room. Until Wednesday, he would still be a poor college student, and she understood that, no doubt.

She gave him two twenty-punt notes, and said, "It's thirty-five for a room. I asked when I got here."

As they walked up the hall stairway, she explained, "I don't want to leave my husband, Mickey, I just need some affection!"

TUESDAY 22 MAY 1990

At 12:30 a.m., they were still under the covers. She was up on her elbows, planting tender little kisses on his face. "Mmm," she cooed, "whatever that was I said about not leaving my husband...say the word, doll, and I'll leave 'im."

He gently turned her under him again and kissed her. "Don't you want me to get a job first?" he teased.

"This will be your job!" she whispered, "and I'll never let you out of the house!"

Forty-five minutes later, they were dressed and standing at her car. "I know I can't ring you at home, Peggy, but please feel free to ring me anytime. I think you're wonderful!"

"I won't be able to resist!" she said, kissing him one last time.

*   *   *   *

His euphoria would be short-lived. He left the Durkan Hotel relaxed and satisfied, with his ego doing cartwheels. And he was truly fond—maybe *too* fond—of Peggy O'Grady, an incredibly attractive girl who was fabulous in bed.

And who is married, it occurred to him, almost as though he'd forgotten it. In truth, though, it had always been on his mind—but he hadn't ever been with a married woman, hadn't thought about it, and it just hadn't meant much. But now, his good feelings began to dissipate as he reflected on it.

From a purely selfish and amoral aspect, he knew he would be yearning to see her again, but that might not be possible. *She's married, for chrissake! Can you imagine? "I'll be back in a few hours, Brian! You remember Mickey—well, he just thinks the world and all of me when I'm naked with my legs spread!"*

And Caitlin...as much as she knows that he runs around, she—his best friend—may well be through with him if she were to find out that he was: (a) screwing her friend and workmate, who is (b) married, while she is (c) taking two weeks away from work to recover from an attempted rape.

And then there was the guilt of knowing that his own feelings for Caitlin had escalated to the point that he had even dreamed of kissing her and professing his love. *Jesus Christ! I'm cheating on someone I've never dated or courted...whatever it's called.*

Then there's Father McDermott...and all of his *sources*. He knows about Sarah Callaghan. He knows about the rest of them. *Christ, he knew about the inci-*

dent at Findlay's within twelve hours! Mickey was certain that no one *he himself knew* had seen him with Peggy tonight, but...who knows, and what about the next time?

Yes, his parish priest, too, would be sorely disappointed in him, to learn that he had interfered with the sacrament of marriage. Caitlin and Father McDermott, both of whom had been extending themselves for his benefit, and he was effectively spitting in their faces.

And yet, too, he knew that some part of him loved it entirely, was excited by the sinfulness of it all and didn't give a damn about that self-important prig Brian O'Grady or his marriage. *Order two weeks of bedrest for your Peggy, did you, Brian? Well, Bri, she got it half-right...but, my God...your poor little wifey certainly got no rest!*

By Tuesday evening, his scruples would again have disappeared, and he called a college friend, a hard-partying fellow named Kevin Feeney, whom Mickey had recently saved from harm in a bar fight. Kevin, as a gesture of gratitude, knowing Mickey's fondness for beds not his own, had spoken to him about the availability of his parents' Bed and Breakfast on the road to Mulranny.

"Anytime," Kevin told him. "Just let me know."

WEDNESDAY 23 MAY 1990

About ten minutes before the bank's 9:00 a.m. opening time, Paul Byrne emerged from his office and into the teller area wearing a polo shirt and yellow slacks.

"Hello, everyone! Listen a minute. I'm on duty babysitting a few of the old boys from the Board out on the links today…just nine holes, but the way they play, I surely won't make it back in today. I'll be here til 9:30, so if anybody needs me, better let me know now!

"Also—you probably all know this—late yesterday, Miss Caitlin O'Connor and I," he said, gesturing toward Caitlin with a smile, "completed our extensive negotiations resulting in her permanent transfer to our office, so let's officially welcome her!"

They all applauded, and Byrne disappeared back into his office.

Caitlin had intended to ask Mickey about his willingness to participate in her and Father McDermott's scheme before she actually did anything to implement it, but Paul Byrne's departure on this date presented an opportunity that she couldn't let pass.

Shortly before 10:50 a.m.—Ann Moore's scheduled 10-minute break time—Caitlin approached her and said, "Annie, my head is pounding. If I could switch breaks with you, I'd be forever grateful. I think I just need to take aspirin and sit for a moment!"

Ann was pleased to oblige.

At 11:10 a.m., *Caitlin's* scheduled break, Ann smiled at her as she reached to a lower shelf for the metal tray of safe-deposit signature cards and placed them on the countertop. She leaned to Caitlin and whispered, "Here comes Mrs. McCreary, and guess who gets to wait on her? Hope your headache doesn't come back!"

Caitlin moved to Ann's station intending to briefly delay Mrs. McCreary while she time-stamped Monaghans' signature card, but Mrs. McCreary was gabbing as soon as she was in earshot of the safe-deposit window.

"Now, missy, I'm meeting the ladies for lunch and pinochle, and I'm a bit of a hurry. I have to look at my bonds, nephew's being married in a month and expects something nice—I can't think of a thing but money, and they never argue about that, do they! I'm ready with my key, so let's get me signed in, and if you could just stand with me in the room a second—I'll only be a second—and then I can be on my way!"

Caitlin moved with all possible haste as Mrs. McCreary jabbered on, trying to persuade her to sit in one of the customer rooms, but she wouldn't hear of it. She insisted that Caitlin stay with her while she selected a bond from her box as they stood in the vault.

When it became apparent that Mrs. McCreary would *not* finish her business before Ann returned from break, Caitlin quickly excused herself, grabbed an unused desk chair from the hall, wheeled it in behind Mrs. McCreary, and said, "Sit down for a moment, dear, I need to tell another customer that I'm helping someone very important who is in a rush, and they'll have to wait!"

"Oh, yes, please do!" agreed Mrs. McCreary as Caitlin made a quick exit.

Once back to Ann's window, Caitlin found the Monaghans' card and removed it from the metal tray. She then carefully slid it into the time-stamp, aligning the next available deputy's signature line and imprinting "11:18 AM 23 MAY '90"; then, making certain no one was watching her, she slipped it into her purse.

Father McDermott and Caitlin had figured that, if the card were to be time-stamped during Caitlin's break period—or during her dinner hour—it would logically not be attributed to her. She could then smuggle it out of the bank for Mickey to sign whenever convenient, which—now—could be today at lunch after his final exam.

And there was the added bonus: Ann Moore was to be leaving for Manchester, and if there were to be any question, Ann wouldn't be around to explain that, *No, she had indeed not attended to anyone named "Monaghan" on May 23, 1990, no matter what the records showed.*

Then, once Caitlin had returned the card to its place with the others, Mickey could make a point of viewing the contents of the lockbox whenever Jeannette Hall returned from holiday and was working the window. And Caitlin's hands would remain clean, at least *per* the bank records.

"All finished in here, missy!" called Mrs. McCreary, "I'm in quite a rush!"

"Right here with you, Mrs. McCreary!" assured Caitlin as she re-entered the vault.

Caitlin returned Mrs. McCreary's key to her after replacing her lockbox, then walked her to the exit.

"Guess your other customer couldn't wait even a minute for me, missy, whoever it was! Nobody out here! People don't have patience anymore! It's a virtue, but they surely don't have it!"

"Good-bye, Mrs. McCreary!" *What a relief!*

Caitlin turned to see Ann Moore had returned to her window, with the metal tray of signature cards still on the counter in front of her.

"Caitlin, you need to put that signature card back."

Caitlin stared at her, frozen. *Oh, God!*

Ann looked back at her. "Well, honey, you waited on her, you finish the procedure!"

"Oh! I'm sorry, Annie, I thought I had!" Caitlin smiled in relief, and she thought about having a glass of wine for lunch.

*   *   *   *

Mickey was ecstatic as he headed up the road toward the bank. His exam had gone well, he thought, despite the ever-increasing mental interference from his lustful obsession with Peggy O'Grady, and he was finished with school forever!

Since it was just half eleven, he stopped at Stauntons' Pharmacy to say hello to Brigid Riley, a pharmacy intern he had recently met in a Castlebar pub.

After they chatted a while, he decided he'd walk to the bank to pick up Caitlin, rather than wait for her at McCarthy's. He was certain that she would remember their lunch date, but he was eager to see her and celebrate.

When he entered the bank at a few minutes before noon, Caitlin appeared almost startled. Mickey noted her look as he approached her window and said, "Y' do remember that you're letting an unemployed college graduate buy you a bowl of gruel today, don't you?"

"Do I ever! Let's get out o' here!" she pleaded.

As soon as they were out the door, she explained everything, start to finish: that she had found Fergus and Marian's safe-deposit box signature card from nineteen years ago; that she and Father McDermott had talked Monday night, that they didn't want to bother him during exams; that she and Father McDermott had come up with a plan, if he was willing to do it; that she was a nervous wreck from the morning's activities.

On another day, he might have been at least initially wary of the intrusion into his personal life, but he appreciated this path he seemed to be on with Caitlin and Father McDermott. He knew he was thankful for their help and their interest, and so he simply allowed himself to be enthusiastic about her entire message. And he was not about to let anything interfere with the joy of this wonderful day.

She continued as they sat down in McCarthy's, explaining in detail how he might gain access to the box, and asking if he's interested.

"Of course, Caity, I'm fascinated! But I don't know where this key might be...I can look around—"

She reached in her purse and pulled out a key—about the same size as an average house key or car key, but flat, without grooves. It was one of a few unused loose keys she'd noticed in a cup in Ann's cash drawer.

"It would look about like this, Mickey."

Mickey nodded immediately. "Oh, yes—he's got one, all right. With a bit more age on it than this, and he keeps it on his key ring that's with him at all times. Definitely. He's got one."

"Can you get it?"

"Wow...let me think...right off the top of my head...Jesus, Cait, I'll probably have to inherit it...I don't know, I'll think about it."

"Can't do anything til Jeanette gets back next week, anyway. You'll think of something," smiled Caitlin.

"Ha! Nothing Mickey can't do once Caitlin puts his mind to it!" he said as she set the signature card before him. He studied it briefly and signed his name next to the time stamp.

"So, Caity, tell me what else you've done for two days and what's going on in your life! Talk about happy things! We'll work on this other stuff later."

"First, I should tell you that your hero Christy Moore is playing up at the hotel next Friday night."

"Oh, believe it or not, I know that! I'm going!"

"Really? I am, too! With Ray. Who are you going with?"

"Brigid Riley from Stauntons'. She was going with a workmate who cancelled on her—Stateside relatives coming in or something, so she asked if I'd like to use the ticket."

"Stauntons' *what?*" There were at least five storefronts in Castlebar with the name Stauntons'.

"The pharmacy."

"Brigid...oh! *Bridie* Riley!? Bridie Riley, I thought she was a *nice* girl, but I guess you'll take care of that!"

"She *is* a nice girl, and what in the hell is that supposed to mean?" he asked defensively, but he knew the answer.

"She'll be spendin' her leisure with you, Mickey," Caitlin joked, "and if a girl spends her leisure with you, all the decent young men will shun her!"

Mickey was silent.

He had completely forgotten about Father McDermott's request that he think about his lifestyle and the harm it might be doing "*to you and to the young ladies that you involve,*" but now it was ringing in his head.

"Do me a favor, and leave that kind of talk for the others, Caitlin."

"What's wrong, Mickey, do you *care* so much about Bridie?" she asked, not masking her jealous concern too well.

"I hardly know her," he answered thoughtfully, "but she's so pretty that if the first few hours of our date go well, I'll probably ask her to marry me and bear my twelve children."

Caitlin knew that he was teasing her, but she couldn't stop herself from asking for reassurance. "You wouldn't do that, would you?"

Mickey reached across the table and pinched her cheek as he laughed and said, "Maybe not. I only want ten!"

He then went on to tell her about Father McDermott's admonitory words, saying, "I hadn't really given them a thought until you said that about Brigid, and now they're suddenly making sense."

Caitlin stared at him with pursed lips, and finally said, "Just remember it's *me* who's makin' the sense in your life and not *Brigid,* as you call her."

He changed the subject, telling her that—as much as he didn't want to talk about it—he thought she should know that it had been Gerry driving the car whizzing by at "Grand Prix" speeds early Sunday morning.

She surprised Mickey, telling him that, having caught a glimpse of the car, it later occurred to her that it may well have been Gerry "most likely seein' to it that I got home safe, for which I certainly can't blame him, with you playin' the drunk and all!"

Mickey explained that there was a little more to the story, and that he wouldn't have brought it up except that he had caught Gerry in the back yard, perched on the wall where he had a view of Caitlin's window. He omitted the part about the pulled-down zipper, but told her that, as quick as Gerry got back there, his guess was that this wasn't the first time.

"So the point is, you need to close your curtain or pull the shade, whatever you got."

"God, that makes me ill to think he's been doing that every time he brings me home!"

"Well, maybe not, Cait. Maybe Gerry thought he was in for some kind of show with the two of us."

She smirked. "To be sure, you can trust me when I tell you I've given Gerry Findlay no cause to think such things about *me!*"

"Well, I don't know, Caitlin," said Mickey slowly. "You were spendin' your leisure with *me.*"

He promised that he would try to think of a way to get the key from Fergus, and told her of his plans for an evening of celebration in the Castlebar pubs with friends from school.

*   *   *   *

An unusually heavy rain during the night had taken out a substantial chunk of Treanbeg Road in front of the Monaghan property, just a few feet from the driveway. Knowing the futility of contacting the County for immediate help, Fergus was wheelbarrowing dirt and rocks from below the road in an effort to repair the damage.

"I'll change my clothes and be out in a few minutes, Pa," Mickey said as he slowed his truck through the affected area.

"The sooner, the better," Fergus responded solemnly. Fergus was no stranger to manual labor, but the steep incline made this work more strenuous than what he was used to; and at age 61, he wasn't getting any younger. Or in any better shape.

My exam went well, thanks for asking, Mickey silently remarked as he angled his truck into the drive.

Marian came out the front door as Mickey approached it, carrying a basket of wet laundry for the clothesline.

"Someone named Peggy wants you to ring her, Mickey," she said, stopping to stare at him.

He looked back at her. "Is that it?"

"It's the same one that rang the other night. That's not Peggy O'Grady, is it, Mickey?"

"And if it is?"

"She's married, Mickey," Marian said flatly.

"Am I not allowed to talk on the telephone with people who are married?"

"You're not quite as clever as you think you are, Mickey."

"Always thinkin' the worst o' your boy, aren't y', Ma? She just wants some advice on college courses, that's all," he said, moving around her to the door.

"Be careful, Mickey," he heard her say.

As he rushed to the telephone.

*　　*　　*　　*

"Peggy?"

"Mickey?"

"Yes, sweetheart, how are you?"

"Desperate!" she whispered into the phone.

"As I am for you! Can I see you again?"

"Oh, Mickey, of course you can! Can you come now?"

"God! How I wish I could, Peggy! I have to be workin' here til at least half four or five. Any possibility—?"

"I have until half seven, Mickey. That will give us time!"

"A friend of mine owns a B&B. We can go there if that's all right?"

"Lay me on the driveway stones or the rocks in the field, Mickey, I don't care, if I can feel you alive inside me! And I have to talk to you about some things!" she said excitedly.

"Talk? I hope you don't think I'm going to let you talk!" he teased her.

She laughed and said, "I hope not much, but this is really quite important!"

"Well, then, tell me what it's about, at least, so I don't go insane wondering!"

She wanted to wait until they met, but Mickey insisted, and she said, "Well, for one thing, two detectives came by last evening to talk about Bill Sullivan."

"Oh, shit!" he exclaimed, completely surprised that the Gardai were indeed following up on the initial investigation. "What did they ask you?"

"Just a lot of the same, but I could barely contain myself in front of Brian, telling them how brave you were, charging across the field after him!"

"Oh...really," he said quietly. "You didn't see that, did you, Peggy?"

"See what?"

"Peggy," he said carefully, "you didn't see me when I caught him, did you?"

"No, just when you ran off after him...why are you asking?" she inquired, curious about his sudden mood swing.

"Oh...well," he said, as he thought of an answer, "it's just that it all happened so quickly, I'm not even sure I remember exactly every detail, in the emotion of the moment. That's all."

"I'd rather talk about the emotion of moments to come!" she said.

"Oh, yeah, sorry, Peggy, you just caught me off guard with that," he said, regaining his composure.

They made plans to meet at exactly 5:30 p.m., then changed the time to 5:00 p.m. They might need that extra half-hour, they decided.

*   *   *   *

Mickey wanted to get his mind off the Gardai and their follow-up investigation, and he actually felt glad to have some physical labor to absorb his energy. After shoveling and wheelbarrowing with Fergus for nearly an hour, he considered that another "friendly" argument—about whether or not he should ever enter politics—might work well to divert his troubled thoughts.

"Father McDermott talked to Frank O'Malley a little bit for me, Pa. The good senator says he'll talk to me anytime about a life in politics."

"Ah, Jesus! Politics!" he snorted predictably. "Why in the hell would you want a life in politics?"

"Well, for one reason, so that you and I needn't spend our days repairing roads that should've been upgraded years ago! You'd be hard-pressed to find a Treanbeg Road in Dublin now, wouldn't you? And don't the people of this county pay their taxes same as the Dubliners? If I can help the people of Mayo, it'll help Ireland altogether, and what's wrong with that?"

"Help Ireland, my arse! Bunch o' bastards helpin' themselves *to* Ireland, that's what politicians are!"

"Well, I wouldn't do that, if I were in politics."

"And they're crooks. Every fuckin' one of 'em is a crook. Y' can't be successful in politics, Mickey, unless you're a crook. Y' vote for every damn thing y' never believed in, so that the other crooked bastards will vote for what y' *do* believe in. Now what in the hell is the sense in livin' your life like that?"

"I *wouldn't* live my life like that!" Mickey stated as nobly as he could.

"The hell! And drawin' attention to yourself, there in the public eye, y' make one mistake, and your life is over! You're in the news, you're in the bleedin' gossip rags, your family is shamed…If you want to make a decent livin', you can stay on this farm, and work in the property business, if that suits you. Then you don't have to spend twenty-four fuckin' hours a day lyin' to yourself and everybody else about *helpin' Ireland,* for chrissake!"

"Methinks thou dost protest too much," Mickey said, unaware that his statement was completely apropos. "That's Shakespeare, by the way, Pa."

"Well, Shakespeare can fuck himself up the arse, as far as I'm concerned!" Fergus scowled. "You can have that as your protest."

"Jay-sus, Mr. Monaghan!" Mickey laughed. "For just a brief, fleeting moment, I had mistaken that for a conversation we were havin' there!"

Fergus stopped to lean on his shovel and said, "Listen, you're not the only one ever knew a line from Shakespeare. I went to school long as you have—didn't waste my time studyin' that crap, to be sure! But I happen to know Shakespeare didn't write it, anyway. Roger Bacon did, then Shakespeare got the credit for it."

Sure, Mickey surmised, *true or not, you no doubt heard that from another ranting, loony drunk up at Crowley's. And that's what you have to say on the subject of Shakespeare...*

"Well, then," said Mickey, mimicking Fergus as he leaned on his own shovel, "then it's Roger Bacon, don't you think, who ought t' fuck Shakespeare up the arse—for stealin' his stuff! Huh, Pa?"

With a rare hint of a smile as he went back to his shoveling, Fergus said, "The two of 'em Englishmen...he probably did."

*   *   *   *

Mickey had told Peggy that he would park his truck at the top of town, by Chambers' Market, and wait for her; but she was already there, parked a few doors down, when he pulled into a slot at ten minutes til five. He hopped out of his truck, waved a quick acknowledgement and walked into Chambers'.

He found a bottle of Merlot and took it to the counter.

"Big seller lately, Merlot," said Betty Chambers, "but I thought you stuck with the Guinness, Mickey."

"Had my last exam of all time today, Mrs. Chambers, and nothin' is off limits tonight!" he smiled, immediately realizing his comment bordered on reckless, with Mrs. Brian O'Grady sitting outside, waiting for him to undress her.

"You be careful now, Mickey," called Mrs. Chambers as he walked out with the wine in a brown paper bag.

He moved away from Chambers' front window, and then stood on the sidewalk, looking everywhere to make certain that he was not being watched. Finally assured, he let himself into the front seat of Peggy's practically new Honda Accord.

"Sorry to be so paranoid, sweetie, just looking out for us!" he smiled.

She leaned over and kissed him on the lips, and he immediately pulled back, laughing, "Jesus, Peggy! The citizens of Newport will stone us to death for adultery, if we aren't careful!"

"I'll let you get away with that for now!" she laughed as she turned the key, then backed out.

As he wondered what she meant by that remark, she said, "Brian called, and he definitely won't be home til eight o'clock, which usually means *nine*, but we've got a little room to breathe, anyway."

"Coincidence," he said, "because I've got us a little room where we can breathe heavily."

Mickey guided her right, then left, to get out of town on the road to Mulranny. He pointed out Treanbeg Road as they passed; and, as she reminded him that she had already been to Caitlin's home, he noticed a County Gardai car headed down Treanbeg toward—he assumed—either the O'Connor or Monaghan residence, or both.

Fuck 'em. I'm busy.

As she sped along the rural countryside on N59, he held up the paper bag.

"Bottle of Merlot for my sweetheart!" he smiled.

She reached down between them and lifted a similar bag from the seat.

"Oh!" Mickey laughed, as he looked inside to see another bottle of Merlot, same brand. "So that's what Mrs. Chambers meant about this bein' a big seller lately. Now we won't have to get each other's germs," he joked.

She immediately swung the Accord off the road and stopped on the berm. Without a word, she reached for him, and they kissed passionately, locked together as cars whizzed by. Finally their lips parted, but they held each other, staring still into each other's eyes, the tips of their noses almost touching.

"That was...*incredible*, Peggy, but..."

"Sorry, Mickey," she breathed, "but the thought of your germs in my mouth...or *anything* of yours in my mouth, was so...overwhelmingly delicious! You're going to know how I feel about you before this night is over, I promise you!"

"It's just up the road a bit now, sweetheart," he said quietly, again wondering if he should be reading something *extra* below the surface of her comment.

About two miles further down the road, Mickey pointed, saying, "That's it on your right, Peggy, up where the sign is."

She waited for an oncoming truck to pass, and then turned in, parking behind a hedgerow that hid the car from the road.

Once through the front door, they walked down a short hall to another door marked "Office" and knocked. A voice called, "Come in!" and Mickey turned the knob to see an older man, probably 70, with his feet up on a desk that filled half the room.

"Kevin's friend, I'll bet," the gentleman said, peering over wire-rimmed glasses.

"Yes, sir," Mickey nodded.

The old man motioned to the corner of the desk, to a small envelope marked "Monaghan #3."

"Out the door, down the hall, Room 3. Breakfast's at half eight, but tea, coffee, juice, scones and dry cereal are out at seven, if you can't wait. Enjoy yourselves." He closed his eyes to continue his nap.

Inside Room 3, Mickey locked the door, then gently pressed Peggy against it. As she looked up sweetly at him, she unbuttoned a second button of her blouse...and then, they shared a near-criminal violence in the passion of the kiss that followed. Eventually, she dropped to her knees, but he scooped her up and carried her the few steps to the bed. He lay down next to her with his face over hers.

"We have two-and-a-half hours, sweetheart," he whispered, "and I want to use every unbelievable minute of it!"

He recognized this "stage" in a relationship—not the first time, so they knew each other's bodies, and there was no doubt where they were headed, and no doubt that they both wanted it. All-out sex for the sake of all-out sex. And—*my God!*—*this Peggy O'Grady! So sensual, so voracious!* He looked forward to the best several hours of all-out sex he'd ever known.

"Strip my clothes from me, Mickey," she pleaded, grabbing at him as she squirmed on the bed, "I want to be naked with you, I want to *live* naked with you! So you can take me whenever you want me, like the two animals that we are!"

Mickey felt supremely confident and was in no hurry to rush through this phenomenal sexual extravaganza.

"If we live naked together," he teased her as he undid button number three, "we'll have to put a bell around Brian's neck, so that I can hide behind the furniture when I hear him coming into the room."

"I want to leave him, Mickey…that's the other thing that I wanted to tell you! I haven't had a single thought of anything but you since Monday! I want us to be together!"

Hello?
What?!

*   *   *   *

"Peggy—you're kidding, right?"

"No, I'm not kidding! I want us to be able to walk down the street together holding hands, or kiss each other in the car if we want, whenever we want…we can get a little place together, Mickey!"

Just as he was about to shout "Are you crazy?!", it struck Mickey that he really didn't know Peggy *that* well, and then a myriad of thoughts flashed through his panicked mind.

Christ, what if she is crazy?!

Maybe I have truly screwed up here, fooling with this young lady, this young married *lady, who is, in fact, recovering from a violent and frightening attack. Jesus!…Is it possible that Brian O'Grady—her* husband, *for chrissake—who is certainly otherwise a successful person—also knows what he's doing here, in keeping his wife at home, protected? But wait—she was apparently interested in fooling around with me before Sullivan grabbed her…God—I can't lead her on, though…let her think I'd be interested in some form of commitment to her, but I can't just humiliate her and walk out of here…Hell, I don't* want *to walk out of here, but…but…but never mind!*

Please help me out of this, God—I've learned my lesson!

"You want to leave your millionaire for a bum who's lucky to find a quid in his pocket? Except for part-time shepherd and troubadour, I don't even have an occupation yet, sweetie!" he said, kissing her cheek.

"Mickey, you'll think I'm out of my mind, but I know that I fell in love with you Monday night and that I will love you forever! I want to hear you tell me that you love me! And all those things that you said are 'better left unspoken'! Nothing else matters! I don't care about money. My job at the bank will get us a little place until we can afford something better. We'll be fine!"

"I feel so close to you, Peggy," he whispered, "so close that I can share something that I promised to keep absolutely secret!"

"Please, Mickey," she begged, "I want us to share everything!"

He explained that he didn't feel that he would be able to leave the farm any-time soon, as his father had recently begun vomiting and spitting blood con-stantly, and "the doctors" had grave concerns that he would surely be gone within months, if not weeks or days, without immediate surgery and follow-up chemo-therapy and radiation. And large doses of Vitamin C.

He went on to say that, although he'd never regarded himself as a "mam's boy," Marian would surely be devastated if he were not there to stand by her through this ongoing crisis. Indeed, this dreadful illness had made his father so evil-tempered and ornery that he sometimes actually refuses to use the bathroom, walking around for hours with his underwear fouled, staining the furniture where he sits, and cursing everything and everyone in his path. He pinched his nose shut at the thought.

"So you see, Peggy, whether Pa's dead or alive, there's a tremendous amount of work that has now fallen to my shoulders, not the least of which—for the time being—is to protect my mother from the frequent attempts at abuse by this delir-ious, woman-hating madman!"

"He...*beats* her?"

"Tries all the time, you know, with whatever strength he can gather, but I don't think he would do that to you...you know, if you came to live there in the cottage with us," Mickey said with furrowed brow.

"Came to live...in the cottage?" Peggy asked weakly.

"Yes," he went on calmly, "the four of us."

She stared at him in silence, and then began to speak.

"Mickey, I'm afraid," she said in measured tones, as she rebuttoned button number three, "I'm afraid that I have...uh, *interfered* in your life at a time of great family need, and I...uh—" Her cheeks inflated momentarily, as she sup-pressed a retch at the thought of the stained furniture.

"Oh, yes," he assured her mournfully, "it's at least a few difficult years we'll be facing."

"...and I feel that I've done a disservice to you," she continued quietly, rebut-toning button number two.

"All the work and jobs that Pa used to do...Peggy, if you could help me and Ma with all that, why, somehow I think—"

"A tremendous disservice, Mickey," she said, sitting up, "for which I cannot apologize enough..."

"...but, of course, if life in a farm cottage seems a little drab, if I could count on the wonderful friendship that we share...you, me, Caitlin...that would be a great inspiration to keep going—"

"You can count on that, Mickey, always, and I think that right now...my stomach, I don't know, all that talk of sickness, maybe it's best—"

"We should go, don't you think, Peggy?"

"I do, Mickey. I'm sorry."

"Aw, don't be sorry, Peggy," he said, laying it on thicker than necessary. "Faith, there's too much sorrow in this world already."

Peggy drove as she listened to Mickey remind her that his father's illness was an extremely private matter; then as he talked about his final exams and the great relief he felt to be done with school, so that he could deal with "the rest of life's problems."

As they approached the rise in the road into Newport, with The Fiddler's Widow ahead on the left, Mickey said, "Oh! Would you mind, Peggy, I'll just get out now and knock down a pint before goin' home."

She pulled over and said, "While I'm so close, I think I'll turn around and go say hi to Caitlin."

They leaned to each other to exchange a kiss. Not a *real* kiss, but a peck.

*   *   *   *

"A pint o' porter, please, Sarah," he said, sitting at the bar, a few stools from an unfamiliar man, maybe 45 or 50, wearing a jacket and tie. *Probably a salesman of some class, on the road.* A few others sat at the tables.

He talked to Sarah briefly about finishing exams, when the man turned to him and said with an obviously English accent, "If you don't mind, the nice lady and I were having a bit of a chat."

"A *bit*, indeed, if you think *this* lady is nice," Mickey smiled, winking at Sarah.

"Ah, now, Mickey, behave yourself," she chimed in, but she was obviously amused.

"Behave yourself, if you know how," the man added unpleasantly. He nodded to the tables and said, "Plenty of chairs, if you'd like to sit, and leave us to our chat."

"For all the good it'll do you," Mickey sneered back, now himself unfriendly.

"I don't think that's up to you," the man shot back.

"Nor is it up to you where I sit," Mickey challenged, as he stood and walked the few steps to confront the stranger.

"Mickey, stop!" warned Sarah. He looked and saw that she was alarmed, and he realized that the last thing he wanted or needed was a bar fight, especially a bar fight over his sometime-paramour Sarah Callaghan, age 42.

"Well, cheese and crackers!" he said boyishly, smiling at her. "Can't a fella stop and tell his favorite big sister how he's doin' in school without bein' run off?"

As he moved to a table, the man, now a little befuddled, glanced at a relieved Sarah, then called out, "Sorry, mate, I didn't know..."

As he sipped the porter, his mind kept going back to the Gardai car he'd seen heading down Treanbeg Road.

Jesus, am I going to graduate from college only to go to prison for murder? And what about Peggy...she isn't down at O'Connors' confessing her—our—sins, is she? Jesus!

Jesus, Jesus, Jesus! At the very least, he decided, he needed to go talk to Caitlin about every detail of the Gardai's inquiry. If Peggy is still there, maybe she and Caitlin will give him a fairly clear picture of what the detectives were searching for. As if Eamonn hadn't already done that.

Could be the detectives are still there, or maybe they're down the road talking to Fergus and Marian. And Marian is assuring them, no doubt, that her son is up to no good these days, chatting with married women on the telephone every other day.

He finished his pint and, with the thought that he might be able to get this investigation behind him so that he might later have a proper celebration in the Castlebar pubs, he bade farewell to Sarah and the others, trotted up the road to his truck and headed for Caitlin's.

*   *   *   *

"Well, look at this, a full-grown adult male at my door! Out of school, ready to take on the world, he is! Tell me about your exams, Mickey!"

"They're over, thank you, Mrs. O'Connor!"

"That's no answer! Come in and sit down for tea—stay here in the front room, though, because I've just put all the underwear on the airing rack over the Stanley. How about somethin' to eat?" she said, disappearing into the kitchen.

"No, thank you. Just tea."

He ate two large biscuits with his tea while he answered her questions about school and the future, and he couldn't resist asking for a few more. He finally found an opening in the conversation to ask about Caitlin and Peggy.

"Missed 'em by twenty minutes, Mickey," said Mrs. O'Connor. "The detectives were just about through talkin' with Caitlin when Peggy showed up. The one said they were finished with their shift, and maybe the four of 'em could wrap up the details over a snack up at the Bridge Inn."

"*Wrap up the details*, my arse!" said Mickey, rising from his chair.

"Ah!" laughed Ellen. "You don't have to tell me, Mickey! Those are two pretty girls! Of course, Peggy's married," she added, unaware that Peggy was willing to ignore that pesky obstacle to dating and sex. "And Caitlin—did Caitlin…tell you that Ray proposed marriage to her?"

"What?!" Mickey said wide-eyed. "No, she did not! When did that happen?"

"Why, Monday night—"

"Well, she'll not do it!" Mickey proclaimed emphatically.

"Oh, and aren't you just so sure of yourself, Mickey Monaghan!"

"Well…" he sputtered, "it's…it's got nothin' to do with me! I *asked* her if she loved him, and she said no!"

"Mm-hmm," Ellen seemed to agree, "and y' think that's got nothin' to do with *you*, yeah?"

"Oh…well, I don't know," he said, clearly upset with the news, "I don't know…but she has enough sense not to go marryin' someone she doesn't love."

"Hah! Women do it every day, Mickey! Every day!"

"Well, Caitlin won't! She didn't say yes, did she, Mrs. O'Connor?"

"Well, I don't think so…oh, I'm not so sure what she said. You'll have to ask her," she said casually.

Mickey turned and went to the front door without speaking, then stood there holding it open. "I think the Gardai may have questions for me," he said quickly, and let the door shut. He stopped and yanked it open again. "Bridge Inn, right?"

"Right," she answered smiling.

*   *   *   *

As its name implies, the Bridge Inn was located at the lower end of the village, the first building up from the bridge over the Brown Oak River. The first floor was a good-sized pub, the second and third, rooms for rent.

The four of them were seated at a round wooden table for six, the first table to the left inside the entrance to the inn.

Peggy and the younger-looking of the two detectives—maybe in his late twenties—were on the far side of the table, seated sideways toward each other, their knees seemingly touching as they talked and laughed. Ale bottles and wine glasses littered the table, along with oval plates with a few fried somethings left on them. The other detective had his back to Mickey, turned toward Caitlin, who sat quietly with both hands on a small half-full wine glass.

Mickey grabbed an empty chair from the table, spun it around noisily on the stone floor, and sat with his forearms draped across the back of the chair. The two men turned to look at him, both clearly annoyed. The girls were just startled.

Mickey reached his hand to the older man, saying, "Mickey Monaghan. Thought you might want to ask a few questions." Both detectives raised their eyebrows.

"Tim Higgins, Mickey," said the older one, shaking his hand. The other man stood, reached a hand across the table and said, "Foley, Andrew Foley."

Caitlin stared at him. She was unhappy. "Why did I not hear about Fergus, Mickey?"

"Yeah, sorry about your father, uh, Mickey," said Higgins.

"Yeah, sorry," said Foley.

Mickey's eyes shot daggers at Peggy.

She looked at him, then at Caitlin. "Be-cuz he wuzzen spose tuh tell. Sss private!"

Mickey rolled his eyes, disgusted with Peggy, and he looked at Caitlin. "I'll tell you all about it later."

"We, uh, aren't exactly on duty right now, Mickey, y' understand?" said Higgins.

"Yeah, well, I'm just goin' mildly crazy with worry about it all."

"Ah, Jesus," said Higgins, "we're crossin' i's and dottin' t's, that's all, makin' sure the other guys made sure. Look, son, we'll talk to you tomorrow, and if y' tell us what y' told the other guy…uh…"

"O'Hare."

"O'Hare, right! Then it's 'case closed,' and we'll be done with it." He leaned to Mickey and whispered, "There isn't one of us that wouldn't o' liked to whack that bastard! Now you go home, and take care o' your old man, and don't worry about this!"

Mickey looked back at him, nodding toward the other side of the room. "Could I speak to you confidentially for a moment, Tim?"

He knew that Higgins was trying to get rid of him, but he didn't want the Gardai finding out elsewhere that the story of Fergus's illness was all a concoction, and therefore judging him to be dishonest before he had a chance to clarify it. He also thought he saw a way to make a sort of *man-to-man* connection with Higgins at Peggy's expense—Peggy having made herself expendable, in Mickey's opinion, by her betrayal—all of which ought not hurt the ultimate outcome of the investigation.

Higgins got up begrudgingly, and they walked across the room.

Mickey put an arm around his shoulder, and said, "Just a caution, I think Peggy might be a nymphomaniac, or at least so unhappy in her marriage that she's without scruples. She rang me to come fuck her Monday night, and again today for more, even talkin' about movin' in together. That's why I made up all the crap about my father bein' sick. You maybe ought t' talk to Foley about her."

Higgins jerked his head up and stared back at him momentarily, clearly disarmed by Mickey's candor. His interest was piqued, but he understood enough to judge that it could all wait til later. He preferred to get back to his party.

He smiled and said, "Okay, well, uh…we know a little bit about *you*, and, uh…what? She's more than you could handle?"

Mickey knew that the question was at least partially in jest. He had made his point, so he just played it straight. "No," he answered quietly, "she's a friend of Caitlin's."

"And…?" Higgins asked, puzzled.

"Caitlin and I are close. We're very close," he said.

Higgins looked back at Mickey. He nodded slowly, unsure if Mickey had such balls that he was warning him away from Caitlin, or…exactly what he meant. He reached for his billfold in his back pocket, extracted one of his cards and handed it to Mickey.

"Come in tomorrow about ten, Mickey, and we'll do A to Z," he said, as he started walking back to the table, adding paternally, "and don't worry about Miss Caitlin, I'll get her home safe."

But Caitlin stood quickly as the two men returned to the table.

"Are you goin' home, Mickey?" she asked, still quite clearly unhappy.

"No," he said, "I'm goin' t' Castlebar."

Caitlin immediately screwed up her face, rigid with the most scolding frown she could manage, and Mickey added, "I mean, I'm not *staying* home tonight, I'm just going home to clean up a bit, then heading out to the Castlebar pubs."

"Will you give me a lift home, then, Mickey?" Caitlin said deliberately.

"*I'll* take you home!" Higgins interrupted.

"Don't be silly, Detective Higgins—"

"*Tim!*"

"Tim. Mickey drives right by my house," she said walking to the door, "and thank you so much. C'mon, Mickey."

Mickey looked at Higgins, shrugged and said, "Don't worry about Miss Caitlin, I'll get her home safe."

*   *   *   *

Caitlin was on fire. Raging.

As they reached the sidewalk, she turned to confront him, yelling, "I've never been so humiliated, Mickey! You'll tell Peggy O'Grady that Fergus is dying, *dying*, for God's sake, and I have to hear it from that *whore!* She's never even *seen* Fergus and couldn't care a thing about him!

"*And* she's a bleedin' drunk! She walks into my home with 'er wine and has a glassful gone in a matter of seconds! A drunk and a whore she is, and she'd have been on her damned knees right there in the Bridge Inn if Foley had let her! God knows *what* will happen to her before she gets home tonight, and she deserves every blessed damn bit of it, she does!

"But *you! You* apparently feel free to confide in such a person, while you make *me* go through hoops, do jumping jacks and swear great oaths on Bibles before you'll tell me the slightest thing!"

He stared back a little dumbfounded, took a breath to respond, but Caitlin wasn't finished with him.

"I spent my dinner hour today explaining how I'm trying to help you, and all you can do is go on and make your little jokes about marryin' *Brigid!*" she yelled, with the name like poison on her tongue. "Nothing about your precious family secrets for my ears! No—you need to find a whore like Peggy O'Grady—somebody you can *trust*, for God's sake! And then, you're *whispering* across the room in there with...with—"

"Tim."

"—yes, with Higgins, and God only knows what *that* was all about," she continued ranting, "and I under*stand*, of course, you wouldn't *dare* to let *me* hear anything *personal* about you or your family, because *I* can't be trusted, but Jesus *God!* How could you let yourself keep anything at all from your confidante Peggy O'Grady, Mickey?!"

She was furious.

What's this, Mickey, Shakespeare yet again today, as you find yourself in the "tangled web" of your deceit? Oh, boy! Despite all of Fergus's drunken abuse through the years, and all the fights of his boyhood, he knew that he was staring into the eyes of something he'd never quite seen before. *And for no good reason…okay—at least it's not what she's thinking.*

He wanted to explain, but first tried to calm her with a little lighthearted humor. He gave her a simplistic, insincere smile, and casually said, "So—the four of you went out for a drink to…*unwind?*"

"That isn't funny! And after all that we've been through together lately…" she said as she started crying. She stepped into the passenger side of the truck and slammed the door.

All right, that didn't work. I'll try returning her anger, maybe…

"Well, aren't you just pissin' me off, Caitlin O'Connor?" he said, raising his voice as well as he could, as he hopped in behind the wheel. "You hear one side and otherwise haven't the slightest idea of what you're talkin' about—and you're railin' against me like you're—like you're my nagging wife of twenty years, or worse!"

"There couldn't *be* anything *worse* than being *your* wife!" she screamed back through angry tears.

That didn't work, either.

They sat without speaking for a moment. Mickey started the engine and pulled out.

"Even the Gardai, Caitlin," he said softly, "even they are going to let me give my story before they put me behind bars."

She said nothing, just sniffled.

"First of all, Caitlin, what I told Peggy was *not* the truth. Fergus is *not* dying—unfortunately—and he's not even sick. I want to explain this to you, but I can't if you won't let me."

One thing was now absolutely certain: he did not want Caitlin to know that he'd had sex with Peggy. And he was beginning to understand further that it was not just sex, but *any intimacy* with Peggy—like sharing a confidence—that Caitlin couldn't tolerate. Because Peggy wasn't some mere girlfriend from the "other life" that Mickey had always kept to himself. Peggy was—or had been—*Caitlin's* friend. Peggy was a part of the world, and the life, that he shared with Caitlin, and Caitlin would understandably not abide being "odd man out."

But Mickey didn't know how much Peggy had said, or exactly how she had framed it. He was reasonably confident that she would not have told Caitlin that they had socialized, *i.e.*, had drinks at the Durkan Hotel, but he didn't know.

"Caitlin," Mickey said, "Peggy told you and the Gardai that I told her that Fergus was sick and dying—"

"Puking blood," Caitlin added weakly.

"Yes, vomiting and spitting blood, I said, and I'll tell you all about it in a minute. Did she tell you that at the table in there?"

"Foley rode over in her car with her, and apparently she started to tell him on the way. Then they both talked about it at the table. If this isn't true, Mickey," she said, perking up a bit, but still angry, "why in God's name would you tell someone something like that?"

"Cait, please. Just one more question. *Where* did she say we were when I told her all that?"

Caitlin now looked at him straight on, confused. "She said she ran into you at Chambers' Market."

"Right," said Mickey. *Whew!* "And did she tell you *why* she was at Chambers'?"

"For a bottle of wine," Caitlin said, now exasperated with his ongoing "explanation." "She had been out shopping and decided to come and see me."

"Listen, Caity, what she told you is lies, a pack of lies."

"Mickey, will you get to the point? You tell her lies, she tells me lies, so what's the truth, and why in the world is everybody lying?!"

"Well, Your Royal Hind-End," he said, annoyed with her impatience, "may I have instructions on the number of words I may use to get to the *effing* point? And may I remind you that it was not *I* who lied to *you*? *I'm trying!*"

Caitlin rubbed her forehead, but she did not respond.

He stopped his truck in front of her house. He spoke abruptly. "The short version of the story is this: she rang me and wanted to talk. I said, 'Go ahead and talk,' and she said, 'No, I want to *meet* you to talk.' We met, and she said, 'Let's have sex, I'll leave Brian, and we'll move in together.'"

"Oh, sweet Jesus, she's worse than I could have *ever* believed," Caitlin said, quietly seething at the thought of Peggy trying to steal away her own hopes for a future with Mickey. "What did you say?"

"I said that my father was sick and dying, and I couldn't leave the farm." He smiled a little with that remark, convinced that Caitlin would now be satisfied. But she wasn't.

"Couldn't you have mustered the courage to just tell her 'No, thank you,' Mickey?" she demanded, unhappy that he would indulge her to the extent that he had.

Mickey, on the other hand, was frustrated with her curtness and even angrier at her suggestion that he was not man enough to handle the situation.

"It's not a question of my *courage*, Cait," he said, now with genuine bile. "It occurred to me that she might be mentally ill, and that she might start acting out, maybe screaming at me right there on the streets of Newport, behaving like a two-year-old if things weren't exactly the way she wanted them! And God knows—*one* Caitlin O'Connor is enough for this world!"

Caitlin jumped from the truck and ran into the house.

He hadn't had a chance to ask about Ray Mitchell's proposal. He started to pull away, then stopped and went to the door. He asked Mrs. O'Connor to "please tell your little girl that the bleedin' bollocks who lives down the road says he's sorry."

SUNDAY 27 MAY 1990

At 9:00 p.m., with the help of a manual, Mickey had finished designing a résumé, and he rang Father McDermott to ask if he could list him as a reference.

"You probably can, even though I didn't see you at Mass this morning," he answered with a small chuckle. "Got any good prospects?"

"Actually, there are a few things around, some down in Galway. And I went to Mass this morning in Westport, thank you."

"I won't ask how you wound up in Westport, presuming you slept there Saturday night; but before I give you a recommendation, I *should* ask if you've given any thought to our talk a few Saturdays ago."

"Father, without a bit of joking, I can tell you that I have, and that I believe my heart and mind are moving in a direction that you'd approve of."

"Well, good, and if you can get that other thing o' yours in line with your heart and mind, won't you just be a splendid young man?"

"One step at a time, Father," he answered, laughing a little.

"Good! Now listen, lad, I've got about another hour's work to do here, and then I was goin' t' sip a stout and listen to the radio for a bit. If you're not busy, why don't you come up and let the Church stand a pint for you? There's another small matter that I wanted to ask you about."

"Sure, I'll finish this and come right up!"

*   *   *   *

The priest set two pints of stout on his kitchen table, then wagged his thumb toward the radio on the counter. "That's that Tommy Murphy, from up there in Ballina. Hell of a drummer, if you've ever seen 'im."

"Oh…oh, sure," he answered, nodding understanding after a moment, "but I didn't know the radio Tommy Murphy was the same as the drummer. He was down on the Westport Quay with that bunch from P. J. Duffy's pub, just a month or so back—playin' all that American jazz…they're great!"

"Yeah. Now, Mick, there's somethin' I'd like you to look into for me, if you don't mind," Father McDermott said, as he lowered the radio volume a notch, then sat down.

"Anything, Father," Mickey assured the priest, noting his solemn face.

Father McDermott grimaced and folded his hands on the table. "Well, Mick, I've received a report about one of our strong young men here in the parish." He paused.

"Yes, Father?"

"A disturbing report." Another pause.

"Yes, Father?"

"About one of our strong—well, I *thought* he was strong—young fellows." Father McDermott cleared his throat. "Well, anyway, it seems he was gettin' bullied around by a *woman*, if you can imagine that, right there in the middle of the village—" He could no longer contain his laughter.

Mickey laughed as he caught on. "This wouldn't have taken place in front of the Bridge Inn, would it have? Because if that's the case, it was worse than a mere bullyin', I can promise you that!"

"You're sayin' it's true, then, Michael?" he continued as he shook.

"Absolutely true! Good God, the little redhead can kick up her heels when she has the notion!"

"God love her! Wouldn't that lass just spit in the eye of Granuaile herself? And may it always be so!" Father McDermott said, raising his glass to toast. "Any woman worth her salt can raise hell with the best of us!"

"Well...a toast from the bloodied victim, then!" Mickey smiled, raising his glass.

"Of course, none o' my particular business, but what'd you do this time, to merit such a tongue lashing?"

"How much stout do you have? This is a long story."

Mickey related the details of his brief fling with Peggy, admitting that he had met her at the hotel in Louisburgh, even that they had kissed after drinking awhile in the lounge, but *sans* telling of the lurid finale of that evening. He also abbreviated the specifics of their second meeting, keeping their encounter to a discussion in Peggy's Honda in front of Chambers' Market, including his story about Fergus's illness that eventually lead to Caitlin's public scolding.

As Mickey told his tale, he saw the concern reflected in his parish priest's frowns from time to time; and so, as he concluded, he volunteered a fervent promise that he had learned his lesson and would "leave the counseling of married women to the counselors."

McDermott nodded slowly. He looked at the wall and waved his head back and forth.

"Must've been a hell of a kiss over there in Louisburgh, to win Peggy over like that," he said quietly, not amused. Mickey did not respond. He repeated, "A hell of a kiss"; and Mickey knew that Father McDermott did not believe him, *i.e.*, his sanitized version of the facts.

"Have you sought absolution?"

"Yes, sir, I have," Mickey barely whispered, "in Westport." He took a deep breath and said, "I'm sorry, Father…but I *did* make a full confession, I promise you."

"You don't have to tell me anything, if you don't want to, Mickey, but damnit, you don't have to lie to *me!*"

"I said I was sorry!" Mickey said, trying to smile. "And I am ashamed of what I did. I didn't want to tell you about it, that's all…but I really did learn my lesson."

McDermott reached over and rubbed his knuckles in Mickey's hair. "Save your shame for your talkin' to God, Mickey. I'm a sinner, too, and the only way we can help each other is with the truth."

After another few moments of consternation and counseling, the priest grabbed Mickey's glass and his own, and he took them to the antechamber for a refill. He returned smiling, seemingly recovered from his disappointment, and set the full pints on the table.

"I'm glad you learned your lesson, lad. I suppose that's what you meant, then, when you said your heart and your mind were moving in a positive direction."

Mickey looked back at Father McDermott, relieved to see a smile, and he cheerfully disagreed with him. "I didn't say anything about a 'positive' direction. I said a direction 'that you'd approve of.' And, no, it didn't have much to do with learning that lesson, really."

"Well, it should have," Father McDermott said, a little curious. "All right, then, dare I ask what you were talking about?"

Mickey shrugged a little and smiled. "About Caitlin, to be honest. I guess…well, I can't stop myself from thinking about her. And it's odd…to be thinkin' of her this way. Odd, but irresistible at the same time, if you can understand that. I suppose I love her. I mean, I *know* I do, I always have, but…in a *new* way."

The priest's eyes moistened as he listened. He sniffed and said, "Well, wouldn't that be the last thing I expected to hear? Have y' told that to Caitlin?"

"Oh, no, no, no! The time isn't right—" he stopped abruptly and laughed—"because we're not speaking!"

He went on to explain that, before he would ever risk jeopardizing his long-time, close friendship with Caitlin, he needed to somehow be sure that these new feelings were right—even though he knew they were.

Father McDermott smiled, rested his elbows on his knees, then spoke quietly.

"Let me tell you something, genius...women want to get married, and Caitlin's a woman now!" He gently warned Mickey, "She's not goin' t' be single for long...there's a man in this world who'll see to that, whether it's you or Ray Mitchell or who it might be! But if it's *not* you, I'll guarantee you that this *friendship* that you *think* you're protecting will be gone—non-existent! Because no self-respecting husband would put up with it, and rightfully so!"

Mickey tried to speak, but the priest continued, "You think you'll be pickin' up Caitlin for Mass and Sunday breakfast when she's married to another man? Or that she'll join you in the pubs for a few songs on weekends? Of course not! And she won't give a damn about your airplane trips or anything else, because she'll have her own life, busy with her own responsibilities!

"What *you'll* do is, you'll politely shake the hand of her proud husband after Sunday Mass, turn to Caitlin to tell her how beautiful her children are...then walk away with an ache—that you'll learn to live with!"

He leaned toward Mickey, eyes wide, and spoke quietly but firmly. "Now pull your damn dumb head out o' your damn dumb arse, Michael Peter, and make up your mind while you have the chance!"

Mickey laughed at Father McDermott's apparent frustration with him, and responded, "So as I was sayin', it sure is dark and smelly in here."

Father McDermott wished him the best in his job search as they finished their stout, and told him as they walked to the door, "Feel free to come back whenever you're ready for another earful on women and sex."

FRIDAY 1 JUNE 1990

Mickey arrived at the Gardai station ten minutes early. His first appointment with Tim Higgins and Andrew Foley had been cancelled with a phone call from Higgins, without explanation, early on the morning following their meeting at the Bridge Inn. Higgins had then rung Mickey a few days afterward and rescheduled for this morning, again at 10:00 a.m.

At a quarter past the hour, he was ushered into a small conference room, where he sat for another twenty minutes before Higgins finally joined him. If Higgins had been trying to make him nervous by ignoring him, it had worked.

The detective sat down as he greeted Mickey. He flipped through a folder full of papers, quickly reciting some preliminary matters and then a brief outline of the facts of the attempted rape, and of Mickey's ensuing chase and capture of Sullivan.

"Now, I'm sure that your friend Eamonn gave you at least some indication of what we'll be talking about?" Higgins asked, peering over half-glasses at Mickey, who immediately mistrusted the question. He knew Eamonn well enough to know that his diffident friend would not have told on himself, but what about Caitlin? Would Caitlin have mentioned that Eamonn had come to her home with a warning for Mickey? *Nah!*

"If he did, I've sure forgotten it," Mickey replied.

Higgins continued staring at Mickey, now looking mildly displeased to hear his equivocal response. "You *are* going to answer my questions, aren't you?"

"I hope they're not all about Eamonn," he said with candor. "Isn't Detective Foley joining us?"

"No, he's not," Higgins said flatly. "Why don't we start with you telling me a little about yourself, Mickey?" he continued, seeming almost bored.

After some talk back and forth about what the point of that might be, Mickey decided to simply oblige Higgins—after all, this should ultimately be a fairly perfunctory walkthrough of the facts, if he had correctly understood the detective's remarks at the Bridge Inn.

He gave a quick self-history, and then responded to Higgins' questions, which seemed designed to elicit each and every detail of the events of May 11, starting with lunch at McCarthy's, through his departure from Kilkelly's Pub with Kitty O'Neill. Higgins even insisted on knowing whether or not he had been able to "perform" with Kitty. Mickey confirmed that he had, commenting, "Again, I'm sure there must be some purpose to your questions, so I'll answer them in the spirit of cooperation."

After almost two hours of Higgins' nudging Mickey through what seemed to be a minute-by-minute accounting of the day, Higgins extracted an 8 x 10 color photo from the folder. "Look at that, Mickey," he said, handing it across the table. "That's Bill Sullivan...still alive."

It was a close-up shot of the back of Sullivan's swollen neck and surrounding area, with every shade of red and purple coloring the skin. Somewhat sickening. Mickey correctly assumed he was being shown this to make evident the excessive force he had used, and he had prepared himself to respond.

"I feel terrible about all this," he began. "I didn't intend to hurt Mr. Sullivan, but—"

"*Didn't intend to hurt him?* Did I get that right?" Higgins fired back. "Pardon me, son, but you knocked out two of his teeth, then laid a steel toe into his neck while he was down on the ground!"

"Yes. I did kick him."

"While he was down on the ground," Higgins repeated.

"I've just admitted all this to you, and it's in my written statement as well."

"And he died!"

"Did you hear what I just said? Did you read my written statement?" Mickey asked, now getting anxious.

"Yeah, and I read 'Moby Dick,' too. Great fiction! So what's your point, Mickey? Are you goin' to stop answering questions? Should I go find something to *read?*"

"I was trying, but you continually interrupt."

"Well, let's see where we are then, shall we? You disliked Sullivan from the start, you got angry with him at McCarthy's, you later had an angry confrontation with him in the pub, then you found him trying to rape your friend—which certainly added to your anger—and now we're up to the part where you're out in the field with this man whom you dislike, angrily punching and kicking him—with no intention of hurting him. Please..." Higgins said dryly, "carry on."

Mickey tried to calm himself, then continued, "When I said I didn't mean to hurt him...I only hit him twice, and both times to defend myself. The first time—"

"The first time you punched a few teeth out—why couldn't you have simply grabbed him? Why hit him?"

"Because, damnit, he turned to hit me! I wasn't really focusing on how to gently persuade a rapist—"

"He told us he turned and begged you *not to hit him.*"

"And he's a fucking liar as well as a rapist!" Mickey shouted angrily. "He didn't speak a word!"

"All right, son, but he went down. And you couldn't have left him there for us?"

"I'd have been more than happy to leave him there, but there was a fight going on, Mr. Higgins! I was tryin' to stand up, and he was trying to pull me down! All I did was fling my leg at him to keep him away! That's it!"

"Fling? The way the doctor tells us, this was no simple fling, Mickey—this was the game-winning kick," Higgins asserted.

Mickey's nervousness was turning to anger. "I wouldn't know. I don't play sports."

"Is that a fact? Your friend Eamonn told us about a boxing match," Higgins countered with a slight smile.

"Aw, Jesus! I thought you said this would be crossing t's and dotting i's!"

"And I thought you said you didn't play sports." He looked at Mickey, who was staring back at him in frustration. "Would you like a glass of water, Mickey?"

"Shove your water up your arse," Mickey yelled, irate. "I was out there doin' your fuckin' job, riskin' my fuckin' neck...well, you can be damn sure the next Peggy O'Grady will be raped til sunrise before I'll lift a finger!"

Higgins was unfazed. "How do you know this was a rape?"

Mickey's anger was suddenly subsumed by his confusion. "What?" he asked, shaking his head.

"We've a good few bits of information—some of it damned reliable—that Peggy was not exactly discriminating in choosing her sex partners, and—"

Mickey interrupted, "I don't know where you get your information, but—"

"I'll be happy to give you one of my sources," Higgins interjected. "Let's see, who was it that told me...that Peggy was a nymphomaniac...a nymphomaniac without scruples?"

"Aw, Jesus! I was trying to *help* you—you and Foley! And I didn't know all that on that first night."

"Sure you did! Or at least you surely knew that she was in the mood. You told me today *and in that written statement*—the one that you put such great stock in—that Peggy was giving you the big come-on eyes when she left the room."

"All right," said Mickey angrily, "you just go ahead and twist it all around! You know damn well there was a rape attempt, and you personally told me at the Bridge Inn that you'd have liked to whack him yourself!"

Higgins nodded. "That was when I thought he'd done another rape down in Roscahill."

Mickey looked at him momentarily, and then asked, "Didn't he?"

"No," Higgins replied, and he went on to explain that the victim in that rape had never been too sure of her identification, and then Sullivan's wife had provided an iron-clad alibi for his whereabouts—at a seminar in Belfast—at the time of the offense.

"Well, Detective Higgins, Peggy's clothes were torn open," Mickey said, now a little frantic, "she appeared to be in shock, Sullivan was running away through a farm field, Peggy's husband heard her struggling over the phone—and Peggy and Caitlin had no idea he had followed them out to Liscarney—"

"Calm down, Mickey," Higgins said. He put Sullivan's picture back in the file and closed it.

"You're all right, son. Like I told you...I had to verify a few things. We'll close this out. I'm not sayin' I couldn't get y', Mickey...maybe I could. But considerin' everything, includin' that you were indeed on the right side, and that you saved an already-troubled young woman from some fairly significant suffering, well...you'd have to wonder what the point of it might be.

"Now! You're not goin' t' be upset that I tried to get you riled, are you? I believe that when people are on edge, they can't think as well—so they can't lie as well."

Mickey looked at him momentarily with his mouth agape, then releasing a small laugh. "You're closing it out? Well...then—"

"Now, Mick," Higgins said, leaning toward him, "you say you tried to help Foley, and the bleedin' fool should've damn well listened when I passed along what you shared. Listen to this: he was out with Peggy O'Grady until two o'clock in the damn mornin', and you should've heard her husband in the Chief's office the next day—Jesus Christ! I thought the fuckin' walls were comin' down! And now Foley's got himself a nice little suspension without pay!"

"Good God," Mickey said slowly, still absorbing the happy news that the file would be closed, "wonder what Brian did to poor Peggy?"

"Told her to pack her bags and get the hell back to Wales...but you didn't hear that from me, okay?"

"Whew!" Mickey said. "Yes, sir!"

They spoke cordially for another half-hour, Mickey talking about his future and Higgins telling stories from his twelve years with the Gardai. Mickey was happy and relieved when he left, but grieving over what he had done to Sullivan.

*   *   *   *

The Castle Arms Hotel in Castlebar featured a large nightclub, one of the most well-appointed and commodious venues in the area. Popular Irish guitar-playing singer/songwriter extraordinaire, Christy Moore, was scheduled to begin his show in approximately twenty minutes, at 10:00 p.m. The preliminary act had finished, and some of the patrons were up from their tables moving about, using bathrooms, refreshing their drinks, or just chatting with others.

Mickey had spotted Caitlin with Ray Mitchell, well on the other side of the hall, shortly after he and Brigid Riley had arrived at 8:00. He had neither seen nor spoken to Caitlin since driving her home from the Bridge Inn two Wednesdays previous.

As she stood and walked to the back of the hall into the area of the bar and bathrooms, she glanced in his direction.

He said, "Brigid, if you wouldn't mind, I just saw Caitlin O'Connor walk to the back, and I need to get a message to her. I'll get us a few drinks, too."

By the time he made his way to the back, Caitlin had disappeared, into a bathroom, he presumed. He stood near the door, and Caitlin was out within the minute.

"Hi," she said with a shy smile.

"Hi. Uhm, I wanted to tell you how sorry I am about—"

"Mickey, I am, too!" she rejoined before letting him finish.

"And I miss my buddy," he said.

"I talked to Father McDermott, Mickey. I'm so sorry I didn't listen to you," she said sweetly. Then, hanging her head playfully, she continued, "I got a little lecture on my temper!"

"That's surprising," Mickey said smiling.

"Oh, I doubt that you're surprised at all!" she smiled back.

"Oh, but I am, Caity," he said, pretending to be serious, "that you'd get a *little* lecture for a temper the size of yours."

"All right!" she said laughing. "Why don't you join us for supper tomorrow evening about six? I'll tell Mother to set an extra place."

"Caitlin," Mickey said, reaching a hand to her shoulder, "you're not marrying Ray, are you?"

Caitlin was obviously caught off guard by the question. "Ray Mitchell?"

"Yes, of course!"

She looked back at him with a puzzled smile, but didn't answer.

"Caity, your mother told me that he asked. You didn't say yes, did you?"

"No...I didn't say yes, Mickey, but he didn't ask, eith—oh! I know what she's talking about!" Caitlin remembered, laughing. "Ray was talking about settling down...you know, having a family and a home on the Atlantic Ocean. He wants to live right on the ocean someday. I guess mothers count such remarks as proposals!"

Just as Mickey was about to suggest that he would take her *out* to dinner tomorrow night, on an actual *date*, Brigid joined them, saying, "Hi, Caitlin, Bridie Riley. I thought I'd come back and meet you, since I feel like I almost know you, anyway."

They talked amicably for a few minutes, Caitlin assuring Bridie that she had heard "such nice things" about her; Bridie wondering aloud why Mickey insisted on using her given name "Brigid"; and then the house lights dimmed.

As genial as Bridie had been up to that point in the evening, when they returned to their table, she had cooled down considerably.

"Wonder what caused you to forget our drinks, Mick?"

SATURDAY 2 JUNE 1990

Mickey brought his guitar into O'Connors' home a few minutes before 6:00 p.m., and he played a Christy Moore song, "Only Our Rivers Run Free," that he'd worked on when he got home from the concert the night before. Caitlin helped him with some of the lyrics that he couldn't recall, and, on the piano, showed him a "more interesting" chord change than one that he had used.

Keran came in the room and sat with them. "What'd you think of Bridie, Mickey? Did she ring your bell?"

"I don't think it matters what I thought of her. I left her for a few minutes to go talk to your baby sister, and that pretty much ended our long and glorious relationship. About one-third of a date, and I could feel myself bein' wheeled out to her launching pad."

"Sorry!" Caitlin said with a wide grin.

"Supper's on!" called Ellen O'Connor from the kitchen.

"I love that song, Mickey, did y' get all the words?" Ellen asked, as they all sat.

"Just about. Do you have them?"

"Up here," she said, pointing to her head. "I'll write them down for you later on. What'd you think of poor Peggy, or did you even hear?"

"No—" Caitlin started to answer for him.

"Yes, I heard," Mickey interrupted. "I finally got in to talk to Tim Higgins yesterday morning, and he told me that she went back home to Wales."

"What?" Caitlin asked. "You didn't see Higgins til yesterday? I thought you were going the day after...you know, after we were all at the Bridge Inn!"

"I *was*, but *that's* pretty interesting, too. He cancelled on me, because Foley wasn't available, and then we couldn't reschedule til yesterday. Turns out Foley was with Peggy til about two in the mornin'. Brian O'Grady came into the Chief's office raising ten kinds of hell. Now Foley's under suspension, and Brian booted Peggy's hard-workin' arse back to Cardigan. Sorry for my vulgarity."

"Oh, my God!" said Caitlin. "All that we heard—what Mr. Byrne told us—was that she went back home, we didn't know why, or if she'd ever be back! He had me in his office later, and told me privately that he knew she was having marital problems...but I know that he was really pushing to find out what I might be able to tell *him* about all of it. Which was nothing, of course."

"Figurin' you're her friend, right, Cait?" Mickey asked.

"Right."

"Tryin' pretty hard to find out, was he?"

"He *was*, actually, he kept askin'—why, Mickey, what are you thinkin'?"

"Nothin'," he said, and he winked back at Caitlin.

"What—?" Caitlin started to ask and decided not to pursue it. "What about Higgins, Mickey? Did that go all right?"

"Mm-hmm," Mickey nodded with a mouthful of food. He swallowed and said, "Eventually, it did, but he worked me over pretty well with the questions before he finally let me know I'd be all right. Then it was on to the gossip. Another thing he told me was that Bill Sullivan had been cleared in that earlier rape down in Roscahill."

*   *   *   *

"The Italians would've won the war if they'd had you fixin' this mostaccioli for 'em, Mrs. O'Connor!" said Mickey, as he finished a second plate.

"Well, it's lovely that someone is eating! You girls act like you're afraid of it."

"Mother!" complained Keran. "It's my second date with Jack, and I don't want to go out looking like I'm pregnant with another man's child!" Jack Talbot operated a Westport bookstore that was owned by his father, who had all but retired; and Keran had decided: Jack's the one.

"And Caitlin?" Mickey inquired, "What's your excuse? You aren't going out with your *fiancé* tonight, are you, dear?"

"My *fiancé*," she said laughing. "You see the trouble you've caused me, Mother, telling him Ray proposed?"

As she talked, Mickey stood and walked around the table. He put his hands on Mrs. O'Connor's shoulders from behind and leaned his face to hers, saying, "Now you notice I never once mentioned a word about the Atlantic Ocean, because I don't want you tellin' people I was over here makin' marriage proposals!"

Keran and Caitlin both laughed, and Mrs. O'Connor did, too, but she turned to Mickey and said, "If you'd seen the look on Ray's face when he said that—just beggin' for a smile or a nod of approval from my Caity—you'd agree with me! People communicate with more than their words, Mickey!"

"Well, it's good y' kept your face still, Caitlin, or you'd have cost your poor mother a weddin' dress!" he continued on.

"I've got to get ready," Keran said, getting up with a sudden urgency. "Come help me pick something of yours to wear, Caitlin." The girls left the room.

"Tell you what, Mickey," Mrs. O'Connor said matter-of-factly as she stood, "she'd have had me take that weddin' dress back the minute I told her about the look on *your* face when I told *you* about all that! Talk about communication!"

Ellen stood next to Mickey and looked up at him. He said nothing. She reached up and patted his cheek and said, "Mm! If I could get my roses that shade, I'd win prizes!"

He smiled sheepishly as Caitlin came back to the kitchen doorway.

"Want to get a little air, Mickey?" she asked.

No, I don't. I want to stand right here and tell you...that your mother knows I've fallen in love with you. So it's only right that you know it, too...I love you, Caitlin.

"Mickey?"

"Yes. Air," he finally responded, and they walked out to the front porch.

"Leave the dishes, Mother! I'll get them," she called back.

*   *   *   *

"So why the wink?" she asked, leaning against his truck.

"Oh! I guess it struck me that it was so obvious to you that Byrne was diggin' for information from *you.* Tell me the reason a guy in his position would be so interested in what the chatter might be about a 21-year-old teller's marital problems?"

Caitlin looked puzzled. "Mickey...you're not implying—"

"Oh, yes, I am, Cait."

"He would never do that, Mickey. Mr. Byrne is a principled man!"

Mickey smiled and shook his head. "I'm sure he's very principled, Cait, but you don't understand. Peggy is a very, very pretty girl. Most men never get a shot at somethin' like that, not in their lifetime; but if they do, principles are out the bleedin' window!"

Caitlin smiled and chuckled a little. "Well, I'll choose *not* to believe it, thank you. If Mickey Monaghan turned her down, surely a decent human being like Paul Byrne could find the strength somehow."

"I wouldn't bet on it. Not unless his father were sick and dying," he said, and they started laughing helplessly at the silly remark.

As their laughter calmed into smiles, his heart urged him, *Tell her, Mickey. Why be afraid...don't you know she loves you, too? This isn't really difficult...just say it—tell her: Caitlin, for so long now, I've loved you as a friend...*

"Mickey, have you thought anymore about trying to get that safe-deposit key?"

"I tried to get it one day..." he answered absent-mindedly. *And quit interrupting me while I'm trying to work this out—loved you as a friend, but I now know that it's become so much more—*

"What happened?"

"What? Oh—I asked to borrow his truck, told him I was working on mine. Thought I could just get his keyring and head to Castlebar, but he took the truck key off for me and kept the others. I've got another idea, though." *Or maybe, You've turned into such a beautiful—no—the funny little girl that I grew up with— no! Shit!*

"What's that?"

"Remember the key you brought to McCarthy's to show me?" *Just tell her, Mickey, you don't have to set it up or explain it.*

"I do, indeed," she replied.

"If you can sneak that out of the bank, I could just hang on to it until Fergus passes out drunk some night, then switch keys. I'll head straight to the bank first thing, and t' hell with the consequences." *Just say the words! Four words, y' bleedin' coward—Caitlin, I love you. Tell her now!*

"Stop by Monday after work, and I'll have it for you."

"All right, then I'll tell you Monday," he said quickly.

"Tell me what?" she asked.

"Oh! Uhm...I mean...I'll get the key Monday, and tell you *thanks*...thanks for the key!"

She shook her head with a smile. "I'd better go help Mother with the dishes."

"Right, and I'll go tell her thanks for the meal!"

✳   ✳   ✳   ✳

Over the next few weeks, Mickey stayed home most nights, believing that his only chance to switch the keys would come as a result of Fergus's passing out in his bed after Marian fell asleep on the sofa, which she did with some regularity. She liked to read while listening to the radio, and she'd then generally awaken in the wee hours and put herself to bed.

Fergus kept his keys and his wallet in a nightstand drawer immediately next to his pillow, and Mickey figured that "Pa" would have to be pretty much dead drunk in order to *not* be awakened by his rooting for the keys.

Fortunately, he also figured, *that's a very definite possibility in the by-and-by.*

Fergus and Marian both asked questions of Mickey—are you sick? fighting with your friends? out of money? Gardai looking for you?

Why are you staying home?

TUESDAY 19 JUNE 1990

On this most ordinary of mornings, Marian had suggested that Fergus take his noon meal at Kelley's Kitchen, as she had not yet had the opportunity to go to the market. He was in a good mood—at least, for *Fergus*—and the thought of a full-blown dinner made him feel even better. So much so, in fact, that he actually asked Marian if she would like to join him.

She politely declined, well aware that his occasional good moods were not known for their durability. And further aware—it seemed to her—that her own presence could reverse such a mood at any given moment.

She did, however, suggest that if he could wait a few minutes for her to get herself ready, she would go to Newport with him and do the grocery shopping while he ate. He agreed.

The Super Value Food Mart was less than a block from Kelley's, but since Marian would be loading groceries, she took the truck after Fergus let himself out at the restaurant.

As she parked, she heard a horn, and turned to see Mickey waving at her as he drove by. He was returning from a long weekend away at a music festival in Sligo Town where he had performed, a little more than two hours northeast of Newport. She returned the wave and watched him as he drove up the road—heading home, no doubt.

As she was making her way through the grocery aisles about five minutes or so later, however, Mickey came bounding up to her, excited, saying, "Ma, listen, uh, a friend of mine from school is gettin' married, you know, uh, in a hurry. And he's offerin' me twenty-five quid to help him move, and he's under time constraints that aren't worth explaining right now, but—mind if I just toss my stuff in the back of Pa's truck, to make more room, and I'll get it out later? He needs me down there as soon as possible!"

"What are you talkin' about, gettin' married? Who's gettin' married, and what's the big rush?"

"Ma—I told you. A *friend!* I'll explain it all later!"

"Well, you live just five minutes from here! Is he gettin' married in five minutes?"

Mickey glared at her. Clearly, he had not impressed her—as he had hoped to—with the seriousness of his fabricated emergency.

"Listen, Ma…this isn't about gettin' married…uh, it's about *moving!* My friend is moving, because…uh, he has a girl pregnant, you see…that's that one he's goin' t' marry…and move in with! But…you see, he lives with another girl! And he's movin' out! And he's just got his lunch hour to do it, because he thinks she found out about the pregnant one! C'mon, Ma, I could use the punts!"

"Jesus, Mary, and Joseph! Why don't you just put your things in the truck bed rather than comin' in here—"

"I'll do it!" Mickey interrupted. "But I need you to give me the keys to lock my guitar behind the front seat! I can't leave that in the truck bed. I'll bring 'em right back in."

"Lord, have mercy, Christ, have mercy," Marian muttered aloud as she dug into her purse for the keys. Mickey grabbed them from her before she could hand them over, then ran out of the grocery.

A store clerk stocking shelves down the aisle from Marian stood up as she approached.

"What's that, Marian? Mickey movin' out?"

"No, no. I don't know what he's doin'," she answered, shaking her head. The two made small talk for a moment about Mickey's finishing school and what he might do next, when he came rushing back in.

"Ma, you'll think I'm crazy, but I just remembered he told me he's just got a clothes dresser and a few odds and ends, so I guess I don't need to unload my stuff after all. See you for supper!" He dropped the keys into Marian's purse.

She watched him run back out of the grocery. There was something in all of that that she didn't trust, but she couldn't imagine what it might be.

After checking out, she pulled the truck in front of Kelley's, and went in to tell Fergus that she would be next door at the butcher's while he finished. She left his keys on the table.

As he noted the familiar keys just for the sake of noting them, something looked a little…*off*, perhaps. Maybe the glint from the top half of the safe-deposit key that was visible there on the table between the front-door key and the truck key? Was it the lighting in the restaurant? Just an odd little *something*…that wasn't worth thinking about. He finished his tea and read the paper.

He then retrieved a twenty-punt note, his only cash, from his billfold, and stood to pay. The waitress was in the back, and as he waited at the till, he fidgeted with his keys, unconsciously sliding his index finger through the ring and rubbing his thumb across the sides of the keys. Again, there was something…*different?*

He could see the waitress talking to one of the cooks.

Is that a sharper edge I feel?
A different shape?
What in the name o' Christ is she doing back there?
His thumb and finger separated one of the keys, and he gave it a quick rub. And then, he froze as it hit him.

It *was* a different shape that he felt. A*nd* a sharper edge. A*nd* it was on the key that had appeared to be a different color—the safe-deposit key.

✳   ✳   ✳   ✳

Mickey entered the bank at exactly 12:50 p.m. and went to the safe-deposit window, where Jeannette Hall stood chatting with another customer. He held his empty laundry bag, which he had unloaded in case he would find anything in the box that he wanted to take with him.

He stood in queue behind the customer for a short time, when Jeannette recognized him. She had never met him, but had previously seen him in the bank. And, of course, all of the bank's staff were aware of the name "Mickey Monaghan"—he was the one who had stopped fellow employee Bill Sullivan from raping fellow employee Peggy O'Grady.

"Are you looking for Caitlin, Mr. Monaghan? Because she'll be back from her dinner break in a few minutes," she politely offered. The other customer still stood at the window.

"Uhm, no thank you, ma'am," he said quietly. "I'd, uh, like to get into our safe-deposit box."

She looked back at him uneasily, obviously puzzled. She carefully lifted the tray of signature cards onto the counter, and said, "Under 'Monaghan'?"

"Yes, that's right," he answered politely.

"Oh!" she smiled with relief, seeing the card, "I didn't realize that you had signed on."

He nodded with a forced smile, as she pushed the card forward, tapping the spot where he was to sign, then handing him a pen. She clocked in the card and asked Mickey for his key.

"I'll see you next week, Jeannette," said the other customer, as Jeannette waved back and asked Mickey to follow her.

Once inside the vault, she went directly to the box. It was one of the larger boxes, 12 inches high. Mickey was too nervous to talk as she turned both keys to open the door. She reached up to pull the handle to slide the box out, and

Mickey reached to assist her. She let him take it, and as he checked its heft, gently bouncing it in his arms, he thought, *Guess it's not Spanish doubloons.*

"Follow me," said Jeannette, hurrying to one of the small customer conference rooms, a small room with two chairs facing a wooden counter. He set the box on one chair and sat beside it.

"Let me know when you're finished, Mr. Monaghan," she said, closing the door behind her.

*   *   *   *

Fergus stepped outside the restaurant after paying and stood on the sidewalk, confused. He stared fearfully at his keys.

When did this happen?! How did he do it? Haven't I been careful enough? Am I sure this is not my key? Christ-fucking-sake, of course I am! I should have killed him a long time ago. But, wait—he's gone to Sligo…maybe he hasn't used it yet…sure, that's it! He can't use it because his name isn't on the signature card!

And then, a horrifying dread enveloped him as he remembered…that Caitlin had been transferred to the bank's main office in Castlebar.

Damned fucking little redhead whore!

Fergus pushed open the door to the butcher shop, and he stepped inside. He stared wide-eyed at Marian as she chatted with Fiona Daly, a neighbor from Treanbeg Road. He had intended to demand that Marian tell him anything she might know about the key, but that was mostly out of plain meanness, as he was fairly certain she wouldn't know anything.

Seeing Fiona, he decided to say nothing about it, opting instead to follow what his common sense was telling him: go empty the safe-deposit box before it's too late. Marian turned to look at him and saw that he was ashen.

"What's wrong, Fergus, are you ill?" she asked, approaching him.

"You don't look well," Fiona agreed.

"Something has come up…Fiona, would you be so kind as to give Marian a lift home? I have urgent business to attend to."

Fiona graciously agreed, and Fergus turned to leave. Marian called out after him, insisting that he allow her to get the groceries before he drove off; but he was oblivious to everything except his fear that he was about to lose control of his very life.

*   *   *   *

Mickey carefully lifted back the hinged top of the safe-deposit box. It was packed with manila envelopes of varying sizes. He recognized Marian's handwriting on the envelopes, centered on the front of each:

"Deed"

"Insurance—Life"

"Birth Certificates"

Hmm. Birth certificates. He folded the brass clip up to release the envelope flap and pulled out three birth certificates. Fergus's, Marian's, and his.

Wait a minute…Michael Fergus Monaghan? Date of birth January 8, 1968? What? I'm Michael Peter…born February 26, 1968! Is this a mistake? What else do we have?

There were seven bulky envelopes, all about the same size, and all taped shut. The first read "July 8, 1971." *So, what's this, 1971, would that be adoption papers? More paper than I'd have imagined.* He pulled the other six out of the box, all with successive dates marked, July 9, 1971 through July 14, 1971.

He slid his finger under the tape on the first envelope to open it. It was a newspaper, a large Sunday edition. He unfolded it to see the banner *The Cincinnati Enquirer*. His eyes bulged.

"Oh, God! No!" he cried out loud as he saw the headline: "LAWYER'S SON MISSING, FEARED KIDNAPPED." He instinctively pounded his fist on the wooden counter and cracked it. He read on, "Three-Year-Old Mickey Last Seen In Front yard." "Oh, no! Oh, no!" he repeated angrily as he looked at his picture under the headlines.

He ripped the second envelope open—July 9, 1971—another newspaper, no, *two* newspapers. He unfolded the first, *The Cincinnati Post*, and read "SEARCH IS ON FOR LAWYER'S LITTLE BOY." "Jesus, Mary and Joseph!" he cried at the sight of his family picture—*Attorney Thomas S. McCall, Sr., Margaret (Meg) McCall, Tom, Jr. and Mickey, in a photo taken just six weeks ago, in front of their Girard Avenue home.*

Next was the *Enquirer* from July 9, headline: "MICKEY STILL MISSING, NO CLUES."

He closed his eyes. He couldn't stand to see another word of it. He was filled with sorrow, loathing and wrath, and he stood up and spun around in frustration inside the small enclosure.

*   *   *   *

Caitlin had returned to work and was making copies about twenty feet from the customer room where Mickey sat. Jeannette had told her, of course, that Mickey was in the room with the box. Above the low roar of the copy machine and the traffic noise outside, she thought she heard a moan from Mickey's direction. She left the machine and hurried to the room. Indeed, she heard a cry and immediately opened the door to see him now sitting on the floor, his eyes glazed over with rage.

She stepped in and immediately shut the door.

"Mickey, what's wrong!?" she said as she spied the newspapers. She turned her head to focus on the July 9 *Enquirer* headline. Her jaw dropped, and she wanted to scream. She quickly flipped through to see the other headlines.

"Oh, sweet Jesus!" she whispered, then looking at Mickey on the floor, she continued, "God, help me be strong!"

Tears streamed down her face as she knelt beside him. She hugged him and said, almost sternly, "Get a hold of yourself, Mickey. We won't let them beat us! I'm with you through this, right with you. You'll be the big winner in the end!" She didn't really know what she meant by that last remark, but it felt good to say.

He looked at her and tried to calm himself. But his head was swirling with a frustrated anger—the enormous lie that had been his life for nineteen years! How was it that he could be so unimportant, that he could be stolen and simply *used* to play a role in the lives of others? Others so despicable as Fergus Monaghan and his wife? How could these two...*odd lumps* steal him from his family, his happiness, his home, and subject him to their wretched fucking existence? What was the reason, the point of it?

Finally, he turned and smiled weakly at Caitlin. "You're with me, are you then?"

"I am."

"Thank you."

She stood to again look at the papers. "Good God!" she whispered as she looked over the front pages. "Oh, Mickey, your mother—Meg—yes, she's very pretty! And you and your brother were so adorable!" she said studying the family's photo in the Post.

"Oh, my God!" Caitlin gasped, holding the newspaper in front of her. "Oh, my God! Mickey, you were right! Did you see this!? You were right!" she said, scanning the story.

"Listen to this: 'A neighbor, Ruth *Mebbe*, M—E—B—B—E, said that her daughter, *Kay Ellen*, had seen Mickey sitting in his front yard...' Mickey," she said, her eyes filling with tears, "there really *was* a Kay Maybe!"

Mickey stared up at her from the corner, and, although he was still shaking, he somehow felt relief from the desperation and rage that had gripped him.

"Well...thanks for keepin' it all in perspective. I get kidnapped, and you're cryin' because there really was a Kay Maybe."

"I'm so sorry to have doubted you," she cried as she knelt to hug him. "What're you goin' t' do, Mickey?"

"I'm going to kill Fergus Monaghan. And his wife."

"Mickey, stop that!" she cried, afraid of the mad look in his eyes.

"They'll burn in hell this afternoon, Cait," he growled through clenched teeth, "as God is my witness, and I hope with Bill Sullivan down there fucking them both in the arse!"

His head fell back. "Oh, God, I'm so sorry, Caitlin, I've lost my mind! I never imagined it was possible to hate someone so much!" he said with eyes closed.

"Mickey, listen to me, let's pack all this up, put it in your bag. We'll take it to the Gardai! I'll drive, sweetheart. Why don't you put all this in your bag while I return this box to the vault and tell Mr. Byrne I have to leave! Just think of it—how wonderful it will be for your real parents to find out you're alive and well!"

That had not occurred to him.

*   *   *   *

Caitlin drove the short distance to the Castlebar Gardai station and parked. She talked generally about the shocking nature of the newspaper stories, but Mickey only half-listened as he thought about his options. Of course if he killed Fergus and Marian, and got away with it, he'd inherit the farm. If he didn't get away with it, he'd be liable to spend the rest of his life in prison. Stupid and pointless.

He wondered...if they were to be arrested, could they sell the farm and use the proceeds for their barrister's fees? *Jesus! What a waste!* In any event, if they were arrested on his account, they wouldn't want *him* taking over the place. But what *would* they do with it, doomed to spend the rest of their days in prison?

"I'm not certain they'll need to hang on to the newspapers, Mickey, but we need to at least show them."

"No, Caitlin," he answered slowly, "I want to go see Father McDermott. I don't want the Gardai involved at this point."

"You're not making sense, Mickey. They have to be brought to justice! It's not a matter for a priest anymore."

"I thought you said you were with me."

"How can you doubt me, when I've been with you every step of the way?" she said almost angrily.

So now he had a little repair work to do with Caitlin, and he felt aggravation at having to appease her while his whole life was at issue. Nonetheless, she was right—he had only discovered the truth because she had urged him to do it, and even then she had found the way for him.

Mickey calmly assured Caitlin that he was in control of his emotions, and he insisted that they change seats. He pulled out of the parking lot and onto the road, going through an alley and down some back streets that would eventually put them back on the main road to Newport.

He said quietly, "Caitlin, this isn't the time or place for me to tell you how much you mean to me, and even if it were, I don't know that I could find the words...I don't even know if they exist."

"Try," she smiled, a little surprised at him. She certainly didn't want to let this opportunity go by, no matter what else might be at stake.

"Listen, sweetie," he smiled back for a second, then went on, "these two are criminals. There's something I saw in that box that makes me think that kidnapping might not be the worst of what they've done. I need some answers, answers that the Gardai might never get, and might not tell me if they do."

"So where does Father McDermott fit in?"

"He'll look after you while I go talk to Mr. and Mrs. Monaghan, Cait. This is my life, and it's my fight now." He saw her unimpressed reaction and continued emotionally, "And if they were to hurt you on my account, I wouldn't want to live another day."

"So Father McDermott is to *look after* me like I'm your child or perhaps your sheepdog!" she scoffed. "I want to be with you, Mickey!"

"Aw, Caitlin!" he yelled. "Damnit, anyway! Stop being such a fearless eejit!" Then immediately calming his voice, but still breathing rapidly he said, "Sorry...listen to me, honey! Once Fergus and Marian know that I've been in the box, they may well believe that their only way out is to get rid of me! *Kill* me! But if they get me in a bad spot, I can tell them that you're on to them as well, and that unless I'm back to you within a certain time, you'll have the Gardai swooping down on them, so you see there's no point to their harming me—"

"Shit! Oh, shit!" Caitlin interrupted, as they waited for a green light at the intersection with the main road, "Fergus just drove by, Mickey!"

"On his way to the bank, no doubt!" Mickey said, as he yanked the wheel to turn left, heading back to Newport.

He assured Caitlin that, with Fergus away from the cottage, he would be safe. He needed to talk to Marian, and when Fergus returned, he'd be ready for him. He told Caitlin that her comment about him coming out the winner had given him a good idea, and he promised to call her if he felt he was in danger. She finally relented.

Upon arrival at the presbytery, he assured Caitlin and Father McDermott that he'd rejoin them as soon as possible, and in return they promised not to interfere or to ring the authorities.

*   *   *   *

He sped past the Monaghan cottage about fifty feet and parked his truck in a grassy layby, where Fergus would not see it as he approached.

Once back to his yard, he peered in the kitchen window and saw Marian stepping up on a stool by the corner cupboard. The shotgun lay on the kitchen table. He rapped on the window to briefly distract her, then ran to the door and entered.

Marian grabbed the shotgun from the table and held it with the double barrel pointed toward Mickey. "You'll have to stop there, Mickey!" she shouted nervously. "Sorry, Mickey, but you had no right to do what you did!"

"Am I correct that Mr. Monaghan called from the bank?"

"Never mind, Mickey. He'll be here soon. You shouldn't have done what you did. Sit down in that chair!" She kept the shotgun pointed at him.

"Well, I hate to disobey such a wonderful mother, but I don't think I'll sit down, Mrs. Monaghan. I think I'll come over there and take that shotgun from you," he said calmly.

"No!" she barked. "You'll regret it!"

"Goin' t' shoot me with an unloaded gun, Mrs. Monaghan?"

She stared at him, eyes wide and her breathing now audible. "It's loaded! Stay away!"

"You've got a lot of terrible qualities, Missus, but lying well...that's not one of 'em."

He walked across the room and lifted a hand into the cabinet that she had been attempting to reach from the stool, and he pulled out a full box of shotgun shells from the back corner of the top shelf.

"Your curious little boy knew exactly what you were reachin' for up there, Mrs. Monaghan. I've looked around the place, you know."

He walked the few steps to her and took the gun out of her hands. She was too frightened to resist.

"Now *you* sit down, and while you and I wait for the Lord of the Manor to show up, I am going to load this gun, and you are going to answer my questions. And in case you're wondering—if you *don't* answer my questions, I'll start fracturing your bones with the butt of the gun until you do. Understood?"

*   *   *   *

Marian explained through her tears that Michael Fergus Monaghan was their son, hers and Fergus's.

She had met Fergus at an automotive parts manufacturing company in Dublin, when he was right out of college with an engineering degree. She was a part of the clerical staff, working in the same area.

"He was a quiet young man, and he seemed so diligent. I felt sorry for him because he rarely spoke with anyone, so shy he was. I was just 17 when we met in 1951."

They married a year later, and shortly after that, a German company bought out their employer. Fergus was transferred to West Berlin in 1954, and then in 1963, to a newly acquired transmission manufacturing company in the United States, in Cincinnati, Ohio.

"He had continually put me off on the matter of having children. He worked long hours, then came home and worked many nights after dinner. By 1967, I was getting desperate and took it upon myself to quit using the pills and to get pregnant. Our Mickey, Michael Fergus, was born January 8, 1968. Fergus wasn't pleased about it, but I was sure he'd come around and love the child.

"Instead, he only grew more cross and more short-tempered than he was already, so unreasonable and impatient he was with me and with the little baby and his cryin', and I constantly had to protect the child from him. Instead of one or two beers when he finished his work at ten o'clock or so, he started at dinner.

"I would spend every evenin' when the weather allowed, out in the various parks and playgrounds with little Mickey, tryin' my best not to irritate him. That's where I met you and your mother, in the Pleasant Ridge Park. She was there with her two little fellas, you and your brother, and it was so unusual there in the States to have two little Mickeys together, especially so close in age.

"It was on Memorial Day in 1971," she said, now starting to weep, "May 31st, a Monday, and he was home from work. Some neighbors had invited us to a picnic, but, of course, he had to spend the day working! I was going to take Mickey by myself, but by four in the afternoon, he was drunk..." She was now sobbing out of control.

"Get a hold of yourself, Mrs. Monaghan. I expect that he'll be here soon, and I need to hear this—"

"He threw him down the stairs!" she screamed through her tears, near hysteria. "He murdered him!"

So there it was. The lowlife bastard had killed their own son. Mickey felt sick inside to hear his fears about Michael Fergus confirmed, and he fought the natural compassion that he wanted to feel for the pitiful creature weeping before him, whom he now held at gunpoint. She had raised Mickey, no doubt, pining every day for the dead little boy that she had loved, the one that she had brought into this world and worked so hard to protect, all to no avail.

"All right, now, take a deep breath...and you took me as a replacement?"

She nodded. "It was his idea. He said we could leave the area, where no one knows us, and tell people that you were ours, using our son's birth certificate. He believed that someday, somehow, we'd run into people who knew we had had a son...he was sure of it. He told me he'd kill me, too, if I didn't go along. I told him about you, another Mickey, and that you were so close in age."

"And that's why we're here? On a sheep farm in County Mayo?"

"Yes," she went on, "Your fath—Mr. Monaghan, I mean, cashed in his retirement plan and his savings and bought this place. He thought we should come back to Ireland and live in seclusion—as much as possible. We weren't really in contact with the few relatives we had left in Dublin, and they've never been told we're back here in Ireland."

Mickey tried to absorb it all, but his head was spinning. "How...how did you know to just drive up the street...how did you know I'd be there?"

"We didn't. I just remembered that your mother had said you lived on Girard, and it was actually the sixth or seventh time over a period of a few weeks that we drove by before we finally saw you sitting there. We were ready to give up and look elsewhere, but that last time you were there."

"Where is your son?"

"Buried in the back yard," she sobbed.

"In Pleasant Ridge, too?" he asked as he winced at the thought.

"No, but nearby. It was called Golf Manor."

"Why in God's name would you have saved those newspapers?"

"We left the area as soon as we...took you. We put our house up for sale and went to a hotel in a city called Dayton, up the road about 50 miles. Mr. Monaghan would buy the newspapers every day when he went in to conclude his affairs at work, to see what progress they were making on the investigation..."

"But you *saved* them..."

"Well, don't you see, there was so much...not just the news, but stories about you and your family, and this was the one and only source of information we had about you. And of course we had to know enough to convince you that we were your aunt and uncle.

"They were already put away in the box, when he decided—Mickey, we kept you sedated until we got to Ireland. And it was shortly after we got here, when you started talking a lot and being contentious about this and that—"

"Like living in Chicago?"

"Yes, just exactly...that Mr. Monaghan decided it best to tell you no more, to say that it was too hurtful to talk about and such."

"Well, why *did* you tell me I had lived in Chicago?"

She explained that they were trying to make him lose track of who he was and where he was from. They had also intended to tell him that his name was "Michael Fergus" and that his birthday was January 8; but since he knew his name and his birthday, and since he had raised such a stink about Chicago, they decided to let it go, and when the time came, "just tell you that mistakes were made on your re-issued birth certificate after your adoption."

Mickey sat silently, shaking his head, when Marian continued, "And, Mickey, God strike me dead if it isn't true—I wanted you to have that information when we were gone—"

"Oh, stop it for chrissake!" he shouted, disgusted by her attempt at mitigation. He was feeling hurt and anger, not so much for his own sake, but for his mother's, his *real* mother's—that Marian could have actually met her and been friendly with her, and then—to have been willing to tear her life apart and steal her child...*my God, Marian, how could you do that to someone?*

They heard Fergus's truck skid to a halt and the door slam.

*　　*　　*　　*

"I've emptied our accounts and got the money!" he said excitedly. "We need to go now…no time to pack. He'll have the Gardai here any time now! Have you seen 'im? Don't just stand there! Did you load the shotgun? Where is it?"

From behind him, Mickey spoke quietly: "Aimed at you, *Uncle* Fergus."

Fergus stood still as his eyes bulged. Slowly, he turned to see the shotgun held casually in Mickey's right hand. He then suddenly swung around and lunged behind Marian, grabbing the butcher knife from the wood block on the counter as he did, and holding it then at her throat with his left hand, as he squeezed her neck in his right arm.

"Put the gun down, or I'll cut off her head!" he shouted.

Mickey was shocked at the thought but able to maintain his composure in spite of Fergus's desperate—albeit futile—maneuver.

"Go on, then, Fergus. Slice away! And when her head bounces at your feet, I'll send yours out that window with two loads of buckshot in it."

"You don't…care about your Ma?" an instantly deflated Fergus asked weakly, as Marian choked, moaned and gasped for air.

"About as much as you do. How do you like that, Mrs. Monaghan? After your years of fealty and selfless allegiance to this bastard, *his* first thought is that maybe lopping off your head is the answer to his problems."

Fergus stared at Mickey, powerless, too frightened and too disheartened to move. He continued to hold Marian by the neck.

Mickey saw that Fergus understood the uselessness of his tactic. He saw that Fergus—who had obviously come home willing to kill him with his shotgun—was out of answers; and, although Mickey hadn't meant to, he allowed himself to be overtaken by rage.

"Come on, Fergus!" he screamed, "Give me a reason! Let's get it over with! Off with her head! Because we're just killers, the two of us, aren't we? Let's play out our lots! Kill her, Fergus! And I'll kill you! Come on, *Pa*, call me a cocksucker just one more time! Or let me hear you say 'redhead whore'…will you do that for me, Mr. Monaghan?"

Fergus carefully released Marian and set the knife on the counter. He stood rigid and mute beside Marian as she choked and coughed.

"Oh, that's right! You two just kidnap and murder three-year-olds, don't you? What was he doin', Mr. Monaghan, little three-year-old Michael Fergus?

Demanding attention from his busy father? Makin' too much noise? What'd you do when he cried? Call him a cocksucker and threaten to cut off his head?

"Guess I've got the edge here, don't I? Because I kill full-grown adults, isn't that so?! Well...you two...you two *sweethearts*, do you want to kiss each other good-bye, or would you rather wait five minutes and shake hands in hell?"

Marian now clutched the back of a kitchen chair for support, her head bowed and her body shaking with a series of low moans, shrieks and sobs. She repeated the words "I tried" through her anguish.

Fergus stood still in the corner, his eyes wide open, but looking at nothing. He had no strength, no will, and no way out. He was waiting to die.

Mickey walked forward, around the table to Marian, and gave her a hard shove toward Fergus. "Get over there next to him...one big mess is better than two, right?"

Fergus urinated down the front of his trousers.

Mickey raised his voice again, commanding, "Kneel down, both of you!"

Mickey walked around the table. Holding the shotgun in his right hand, with his left arm and hip, he heaved the table and a chair onto their sides, out of the path between himself and the kneeling couple. He backed up and raised the gun to aim it.

"Now put your faces on the floor, I don't want to have to look at you." They obliged, both now weeping and shaking.

"Start sayin' your prayers to Lucifer, Ma and Pa Monaghan! Tell 'im you're on your way! Tell 'im—"

With that, Mickey rested the butt of the gun against his shoulder and tilted his head into the barrel to aim. He turned the gun toward the cupboards on the wall above Fergus and Marian, and pulled both triggers.

The resulting tremendous explosion sent the cabinetry crashing to the counter below it, shattered into pieces, with fragments of wood, plaster, dishes and glassware raining over the backs of Fergus and Marian. The blast caused a wave of shock so enormous that, for the moment, Fergus and Marian did not know whether or not they had been shot, or even if they were alive or dead.

Mickey threw down the shotgun in front of them. He picked up the kitchen chair that he had overturned and sat on it. Fergus and Marian stayed low, but eventually both peered up at him. No one spoke.

Mickey didn't look at them. He didn't look at anything in particular. He just sat, waiting for the impact of what had happened, what he had done, to pass through him. He was calm now, but wary of the two who knelt before him. He knew there was more to do.

Five minutes passed, then ten. Finally, Fergus quietly asked, "What would you have us do?"

Mickey took a breath and spoke calmly. "I'm going to make a phone call, Mr. Monaghan. It will be your choice, yours and your wife's, whether I'll ring the Gardai or the solicitor.

"If I ring the Gardai, they'll take you away to a prison where you'll stay until you die, if there's any justice at all in this world. And I think I noticed in your Cincinnati newspapers that Ohio might have an electric chair waiting on you.

"If I ring the solicitor, we'll go to Newport right now, and you'll deed this property over to me. I'll stay elsewhere while you'll have one week to clear out...then you can go live in Dublin, or England or Germany, wherever you want...you just can't come back here...ever."

After a brief silence, Fergus asked, "You wouldn't report us?"

"No. Not if you sign a deed to me."

"Why...why didn't you kill us?"

Mickey turned to Fergus with steely eyes. "I think I'd rather that this hatred you've put inside of me...I'd rather that be for you...than for myself."

*   *   *   *

Fergus agreed that they would deed the farm to Mickey. He asked if he could change his trousers, but Mickey would not let him. He would later privately explain to the solicitor, before leaving his office, that Fergus had serious health problems, that he was going away for treatment, and that it was agreed by all that a transfer of the property at this time would be prudent. The solicitor remarked that Fergus and Marian were "thoughtful and considerate parents" for taking these measures.

The solicitor assured his three clients that he would see to the recordation of the transfer, and he thanked them for entrusting this most significant and critical matter to his care.

It was 4:30 p.m. when they left the law office. Once outside the door, Mickey handed Fergus the keys to his truck. "You have one week. I'm sure you'll be gone, but if you're not, I'll have you arrested. I trust that these words are the last I'll ever speak to either of you."

Mickey turned and walked away, down the street toward the river. He heard Marian crying his name, but he didn't look back.

At the bridge over the river, he stood with an old man, watching a dog swim after fish, diving...then re-appearing somewhere down the stream.

*   *   *   *

It was a few minutes past 5:00 when he finished the ascent to the presbytery. Father McDermott sat on the front steps, head bowed and hands clasped together, as in prayer, wearing his black slacks and a white T-shirt under his black braces. When he heard footsteps and looked up to see Mickey, he stood and hurried toward him.

"Where's your truck? Why didn't you ring me to come pick you up?"

"Oh, I was just down the road...at the solicitor's," he answered quietly.

"Solicitor's," McDermott repeated, as if trying to understand it. "Never mind that, are you all right?"

"I am. But I've got a lot to tell you."

The priest looked him up and down, then nodded toward the door. "Well, get on in there, then! She's half out of her mind with worry!"

Mickey heard Caitlin at the piano as he opened the door. "It's all right, Caity. Everything's all right," he called out as he stepped through the vestibule. Caitlin said nothing, but leapt from the piano and ran to him.

"It's all right," he assured her as they hugged. "I've got...quite a story for you!"

Father McDermott came in behind him, saying, "I imagine you're hungry, and Caitlin's made us a wonderful casserole."

"Mickey, we found the name of your parish—*Nativity*—in the news stories, and Father McDermott called," she said. "Your parents are both living, still in Nativity parish. And your father is still a practicing lawyer."

"Thank God for that great news! And thank you both!"

Father McDermott added, "We just made inquiries—didn't say who we were. Now, Mick, I've been back and forth with Senator O'Malley and his staff. I'll give you the details later, but he can arrange for a passport, a discounted ticket, and you can be Stateside by the weekend, if you're ready. You'll need to be in his Westport office tomorrow morning at 10 sharp and then on the noon bus to Dublin."

"My God! How did you do all this?"

Father McDermott grinned at him and said, "Never mind that. Don't you have a story to tell? Let's get on to the kitchen."

Mickey recounted Marian's long and woeful tale as they all dined on Caitlin's tuna casserole and drank Father McDermott's Guinness Extra Stout. As he finished, he told them, "It was Caitlin's comment about me coming out the winner that made me think about having the farm transferred to my name. I didn't know exactly what you meant by that remark, but it kept floating around in my head."

Caitlin laughed and said, "I didn't know what I meant by it, either, but I'm glad you made good use of it."

Father McDermott looked confused. "How in the hell did y' get 'em t' transfer the property to you? Appeal to their murdering-and-kidnapping sense of decency?"

"No. I promised that I wouldn't turn them in to the Gardai, long as they moved away from here."

"What!?" Caitlin and McDermott both exclaimed. The priest continued, "You can't do that after what they've—"

"Bless me, Father, for I have sinned," he interrupted. "I lied to my Ma and Pa. I have no intention of letting them keep their freedom. I just want to make sure the property transfer is complete, so they can't dispose of it otherwise."

Father McDermott informed Mickey of the details of the arrangements made through Senator O'Malley's office, explaining that, "When the time comes, you'll have to let them manage the publicity and press releases and such…so that Senator O'Malley can take as much credit as possible for the undoing of wrong and the apprehension of the villains, *et cetera*."

Mickey had enough money in his savings to pay for the discounted airfare, as well as to provide lodging and spending money in America. He would leave Dublin International Saturday morning and, gaining the five-hour time difference, arrive at Northern Kentucky-Greater Cincinnati International via Chicago on Saturday evening. He promised to call Caitlin the day after his arrival, *i.e.*, Sunday, at 10:00 p.m., and give her a full report.

Shortly past 8:00 p.m., Mickey apologized, saying that he was exhausted, not just from the day's events, but because he had stayed up all through his previous night in Sligo, partying and playing music with trad singer Mai Hernon and a dozen or so other assorted musicians.

He had intended to rent a room at the Bridge Inn, but Father McDermott told him to go on and sleep upstairs; that he would take Caitlin home, then stop at Monaghans' cottage to bid farewell to Fergus and Marian, and to pick up clothes for Mickey.

Mickey went to the stairs and paused. He turned and went back to the kitchen doorway. He looked at Caitlin and then at Father McDermott for a moment, and said, "I love you both."

After Father McDermott dropped off Caitlin, he went to the Monaghans' cottage. There was no answer when he knocked, so he carefully entered.

Although Mickey had warned him of the damage, he was shocked to see it. He determined that Fergus and Marian had apparently taken what possessions they could, and were gone.

After filling his suitcase full of Mickey's clothes, Father McDermott stopped and got an assurance from Johnny and Fiona Daly that they would look after the Monaghans' sheep while they were away.

WEDNESDAY 20 JUNE 1990

Caitlin greeted Robert and Jeanette at 8:30 a.m., as usual, as she placed her purse in a file cabinet drawer.

"Mr. Byrne wants to see you," Jeanette said.

"Oh, sure, soon as I get set up here," Caitlin said as she unlocked her cash drawer.

"He said 'the second she gets in,'" Robert whispered, making a comic frightened face.

Oh, boy! She walked to his office and knocked.

"Come in!

"Have a seat, have a seat...Y' all right, then, Caitlin? Rough day in here yesterday, and I'm hoping you can help me out. Help me understand what's going on!"

"Certainly, Mr. Byrne, what's the problem?" she asked apprehensively, dreading his response.

Byrne said nothing. He looked at Caitlin for a moment, picked up a card from his desk and tossed it in front of her. It was the Monaghans' safe-deposit signature card.

Shit! Ready or not, here we go!

"Yes, Mr. Byrne?"

"Well, first of all, Caitlin, your boyfriend cracked the wooden counter in our customer room. *Broke* it, actually. I know that he was upset, we all know that. Did he drop the box on it, or hit it, or what? Do you know?"

Caitlin considered her answer for a moment, and then said, "Yes, sir, he was upset. Upset about a *personal* matter, and I assure you that he will pay for the damage. And he's my *friend*, not my *boyfriend*. Is that all, then, Mr. Byrne?"

"Oh, no...no, no! There's much more! A personal matter, you say?"

"Yes, sir, deeply personal."

"Mm-hmm. Would you take a look at that card, Caitlin?"

She glanced down at it. "Yes, sir."

"No, no," he tersely rejoined, "pick it up! Pick it up, and look at it!"

She picked it up, looked at one side, then the other. "Yes, sir?"

"I'm not sure if you can help me with this or not, Caitlin," he continued, now with a deliberately insincere smile, "but I see that your boyfr—pardon me, your *friend*—signed on as a deputy on May twenty-third." Byrne glared unhappily at her as he went on, "Do you know—was it his mother...or father...or both that came in with him?"

Caitlin nervously picked up the card again and looked at it. "Well, no, sir, I see that the card was signed at my break time, and I didn't—"

"Yes, I saw that, Caitlin," he quickly interrupted, "*two minutes* before your break was to be over, so that's why I say that I'm not sure if you can help me or not. And you're tellin' me that you can't, is that it, Caitlin?"

"Yes, sir, that's it. I can't," she said quietly. Caitlin heard the weakness in her voice. She felt that Byrne was toying with her.

"Mm! Missed him by two minutes! And so it must've been Ann Moore who would have waited on him, right, Caitlin?"

"Yes, sir, I guess so."

"Well, let's not guess! You were here. No one else was working safe-deposit that day, were they, Caitlin?"

"No, sir."

"Of course, Ann can't help us, because she's gone off to Manchester. And Jeanette was on holiday, right?"

"Right."

"And of all the unlucky coincidences, I was off playing golf with the directors that day, remember?"

"I remember that you went golfing one day, yes, sir."

There was a silence as Byrne rubbed his temple. He reached across his desk, picked up the card to look at it, and put it back down.

"Robert was here on the teller line, but he doesn't remember seeing Fergus, Marian, *or* Michael in the bank that day," he said, reciting the names he had just seen on the card.

"It was almost a month ago," Caitlin offered quietly, praying this torture would soon end.

Byrne took a deep breath and sighed, "Yes, well, let's just forget about that for the moment."

"Is that all, then, Mr. Byrne?"

"Uh, no, Caitlin, that's not all. Fergus Monaghan came in here yesterday shortly after you and Michael left. Came in and asked to see that card," he said, nodding to the signature card. "And he was...uh, *distressed*, to say the least."

"Yes, sir?"

"Caitlin, that card—and everything on it—is nineteen years old. Everything, that is, except your boyfriend's two signatures. Now, I have to believe that whatever it was that upset Fergus Monaghan—who is, by the way, the *owner* of this box—whatever upset him when he saw this card, it wasn't the parts that are nineteen years old!"

Caitlin did not respond, and Byrne was losing patience.

"Caitlin, let me remind you that your first loyalty is to this bank. There could be some very serious consequences for this bank, and for anyone involved, and for anyone *responsible*, and that includes *me*, if Michael Monaghan was not properly authorized to sign this card and to enter that box!"

Caitlin was crumbling under the pressure, but she was at least able to piece together that Fergus apparently had not specifically stated to Jeannette or to Byrne that Mickey's signature had not been authorized.

Of course, Fergus's chief concern at that point would be to save his own skin and get out of town! The last thing he'd want to do is to sit around filling out complaint forms or police reports about an unauthorized entry into a safe-deposit box holding the newspaper accounts of his own criminal activity!

"Mr. Byrne, I don't want to tell you your business," she began politely, "but I can't see how there could be a problem unless there's a complaint from the Monaghans, and I believe that I can assure you that there will be no such complaint."

"Oh, really!" he shot back. "And pray tell, why is that?"

Caitlin shook her head as she tried to think of an answer. "Mr. Byrne...as I told you, these matters are deeply personal."

"And let me tell you something, young lady. When it has to do with the business of this bank—*your* first loyalty and *my* first loyalty—I need to know what in the God Christ is going on! Now, I'm through playing around here, Miss O'Connor, and I want some answers!"

Now Caitlin allowed herself to show anger, as she had satisfied herself that, by virtue of the Monaghans' disappearance and circumstances, the bank would most likely never even hear from them again.

"Mr. Byrne, I only know what I know because I have a personal relationship with the Monaghans, which I have no obligation to discuss with you or anyone else in this bank. As far as the *business* of this bank is concerned, our records indicate that an authorized deputy made an authorized entry into a safe-deposit box, and that's that!"

Byrne nodded and smiled politely as he sat back in his chair and rocked slowly.

"Caitlin," he began, calmly and quietly, "I'll tell you what our bank records indicate. Our bank records indicate that for nineteen years, the Monaghans had a safe-deposit box that was never touched. Not once. Then, a few days after Miss Caitlin O'Connor starts working here, what do you know? Your boyfriend, or your deeply personal friend, whatever you want to call him, becomes a deputy under the most peculiar of circumstances. *Everybody's* gone! And he signs the card, but for some reason, he doesn't go into the box. As a matter of fact, he can't even wait *two minutes* to say hello to his deeply personal friend—who seems to have no idea that he was in the bank that day.

"Next, the bank records tell us that our new deputy shows up with a key, yesterday, and he enters the box. Now, it may not be my business to know what's in that box, but it's certainly my business to repair the counter that he broke when *he* saw what was in that box, isn't it?

"Then, Fergus Monaghan, the owner of the box, comes into our bank—I'll just bet for the first time in nineteen years—and he looks at this card, and my God, he looks like he's just read the news of his own death!"

Byrne slid to the edge of his chair and leaned over his desk, now threateningly.

"I'm not in the business of repeating myself, Miss O'Connor, so let me conclude by saying this: I'm not a fool, and I won't tolerate being treated like one. I have always enjoyed a trust between myself and my employees. Now, if you or your friends have some problems, perhaps I can help. But I'll not allow this bank to be used illegally, unethically, or in any other unsavory manner to help *your* friends or anybody else's. And if that doesn't sit well with you, Miss O'Connor, then I am afraid we'll have to part company."

"Mr. Byrne…" Caitlin said in a trembling voice, "you're not talking about dismissing me, are you?"

He hesitated a moment, then slumped back in his chair. "I'm sorry, Caitlin. But if you won't trust me, I don't see how I can help you."

Caitlin felt shame, and she wanted to cry. How could she tell her mother and Keran that she had been fired? Where would she find another job…everyone at church, everyone in Newport and Castlebar would know that the bank had terminated her. And for now, at least, she wouldn't even be able to explain that it was for Mickey—that he had been kidnapped, that another child had been murdered…

All my promises to Mickey and his faith in me…I couldn't possibly betray him and "trust" Mr. Byrne with all this…certainly not without asking Mickey first, and I know he'd never trust him—he even thinks Mr. Byrne slept with Peg—Wait!—Peggy…maybe he really did…

Byrne stared back at her patiently, knowing that he had beaten her, and he slowly formed a confident—almost benevolent—smile as he anticipated a full and complete confession from his fearful employee. But she took a breath, straightened her shoulders and looked back calmly at him. She figured that she had one card left in her hand and nothing to lose.

"How can I trust you," she said icily, "when I know what you did to Peggy O'Grady?"

Even as the words came out, she calculated that—if Byrne denied it—she could say that Peggy had *told* her that she and Byrne had had sex, whether it was true or not. A bit lame, perhaps, but it certainly wouldn't get her in any *more* trouble.

As Byrne sat mute, however, staring back at Caitlin with his face now red and an obvious fear in his eyes, she knew that further explanations wouldn't be necessary. She had hit paydirt.

She forced herself to maintain eye contact with him, as he stared back at her, clearly unable to come up with a response.

She spoke with an edge to her voice, "I had kept quiet, Mr. Byrne, out of respect for you, for your *position*, but quite frankly, when you called me in here this morning, I was scared to death that you wanted the same thing from me!"

"Oh, my God, now, Caitlin, no, please..." He had really not expected this.

"I understand that anyone can make a mistake, Mr. Byrne," she continued, her voice rising, "I know how Peggy was, and I know—"

"Hang on, there, Caitlin, hang on!" Byrne interrupted. Perspiration was already forming on his forehead. "We'll work this out," he said quietly as he yanked at his collar. "Uh...let's just forget it for right this moment, forget that we talked. I need to make a few phone calls, and I'll see you again in a little bit."

Byrne called Caitlin back to his office shortly before noon, and he told her that she would be transferred back to the Newport branch, effective immediately, keeping her pay raise, even the part added for her travel expense. She was to report to work first thing the following morning.

Without specifically admitting anything, he humbly acknowledged that "trust is a two-way street," expressed gratitude for her understanding of "everything," reminded her that he was a family man who loved his wife and children very much, and said he hoped he could count on her "continuing on the same road."

Caitlin assured him that he had nothing to fear from her. She retrieved her purse from the file cabinet, collected a few personal belongings from her teller station, and called her mother to come pick her up.

Book Two
Cincinnati, Ohio USA

SATURDAY, JUNE 23, 1990

I am Mickey, the one you called Mickey—Michael Peter McCall. When I was kidnapped at age 3, I was taken to Ireland, where I've lived ever since. My two kidnappers told me that you had all died in an accident, and that they were my uncle and aunt who were adopting me.

Before I say another word, let me assure you that I don't want a thing from you, not a single U.S. penny. It's only been recently that I've been able to find out that I was not adopted but stolen from you, and that you're still alive. I didn't want to ring you on the phone and have you worrying that some crackpot might be pulling some perverse stunt.

So here I am.

From that point, the conversation would flow, he thought. *I just need to establish the basics...who I am, let them know I don't want anything, and why it's taken me so long to find them.*

It was now 7:30 p.m. He stood and stretched, tired but excited. Home! Cincinnati, Hamilton County, Ohio. He looked ahead...everyone standing, no one moving. *Be patient...no hurry.*

He grabbed his bag from the overhead storage and waited. Finally, those at the front of the plane began to amble forward. He was exhilarated. As he waited for the chance to walk, he silently recited the greeting he had prepared: *I am Mickey, the one you called Mickey...*

The passengers all boarded a shuttle bus that took them about a quarter-mile, where they entered a building with a huge room, featuring a baggage carousel and people in numerous lines already formed, moving through customs.

A wave of gooseflesh covered Mickey's entire body as he looked at the aluminum letters on the wall ahead of him: "Welcome to the United States of America."

"Jesus God!" he whispered as he stood briefly in awe. He wished Caitlin were with him. *Look, Caitlin*, he'd say, *the United Almighty States of America!*

He got his suitcase and within twenty minutes, he was walking through the terminal. He stopped at the first shop selling books and magazines, and he purchased a street map of Cincinnati and a newspaper, *The Cincinnati Enquirer.*

He looked in the local telephone book to confirm that "McCall Thos S" did indeed still reside on Grand Valley Road. No listing for Tom, Jr., however.

He found an airport restaurant, got a cup of coffee, and studied his map. *Yes, Grand Valley Road is in Pleasant Ridge*, maybe a mile northeast from Girard Avenue, and about the same distance northwest from Nativity Church, located at the intersection of Ridge Avenue and Woodford Road.

The *Enquirer* front-page headline indicated that Iran was digging out of "the world's deadliest earthquake since 1976." Flipping through the paper to the sports section, the big news seemed to be that the Cincinnati Reds baseball team, although protesting a 7–6 loss to the Los Angeles Dodgers, was nonetheless in first place in the National League West Division by seven games.

He considered ringing up his parents, the McCalls…it was still daylight. *No, they might, they* would *insist on seeing me…I need to get a hotel room where I can shave and clean up. I need to sleep, so I can be at my best. I can't appear at their doorstep with my baggage like some itinerant beggar. I need to find a Guinness.*

SUNDAY, JUNE 24, 1990

I am Mickey, the one you called Mickey—Michael Peter McCall. He lay awake in his hotel bed reciting his greeting. It was 5:00 a.m., and he knew he had slept, but not much. He had kept the radio on through the night, loud enough so that he could hear what was on, but not loud enough to wake him if he should fall asleep.

He heard the news come on and reached over, flipping the dial until he found a station playing music—what the announcer called "old timey" country music. Hank Thompson was singing, "I didn't know God made honky-tonk angels...," then Ernest Tubb and "Waltz Across Texas." Mickey wished he had his guitar to strum along. He liked American country music and had heard plenty of it on Irish radio stations.

When he realized that more sleep would be out of the question, he decided to take a hot shower and dress for the day. The day he would be reunited with his American family! He dressed in new clothes, a pair of khaki slacks and a light blue knit shirt that Caitlin had recently picked out for him, noting that the shirt would "bring out your pretty blue eyes."

Shortly after 6:30 a.m., he decided to hike up to the church and see at what times the Masses were held. About three-quarters of a mile up Ridge Avenue, he spied a large sign in a brick encasement. Across the top, it read "Nativity of Our Lord Catholic Church." As he got closer, he saw that Sunday masses were held at 8:00 a.m., 9:30 a.m., and 12:30 p.m.

He decided to walk to 6421 Girard Avenue, to look at the home and yard from whence he'd been kidnapped, and then perhaps walk around Pleasant Ridge for a while.

He figured that he'd go to either the 8:00 or 9:30 Mass, whatever worked out, betting that Meg and Tom would be at one or the other. He wasn't completely sure that he wanted to have his initial encounter with his family at church; but then he thought an open setting such as the church parking lot, where they'd likely be surrounded by friends and acquaintances, might provide a less threatening atmosphere or...something. One way or the other, it didn't matter. It shouldn't matter.

He stood on the sidewalk and looked at Nativity Church and the adjoining school, trying to imagine how his life might now be different had he been here all his life, growing up with a big brother.

He smiled as he thought, *Maybe I'd have been a baseball player, playing for the first-place Cincinnati Reds! Maybe I'd be heading for some corporate job in New York City…maybe starting law school in my father's footsteps, just having graduated from the university! Or, God help me,* he mused, *maybe my father had quit lawyering to operate the one and only sheep farm in Hamilton County!*

As he stared at the church and school buildings, the thought hit him: *What about Caitlin?* Despite everything else, every nefarious and unhappy circumstance that had taken him away from here, his real home, his real family, a "normal" upbringing in Cincinnati, Ohio in this incredible U.S.A.—it occurred to him…*Jesus!…my life without Caitlin?* And he turned to walk away. He missed her. Oh, how he missed her.

He went left on Woodford Road, walked a short curved block to Montgomery Road and crossed, continuing on the same street that—just as the map indicated—was now named "Losantiville." He thought that *maybe* he remembered that name—*Losantiville*—and a little store, perhaps a few blocks past Girard, where his mother would take him and Tommy to get a Popsicle.

He walked past a golf course on the left. Losantiville curved and sloped gently up and down as he walked; and as he came atop a short incline, he finally spied a corner lot with a tan-brick four-family apartment building…*where the Kecks lived! Billy Keck!* He remembered it.

At this point, even the lay of the land was familiar—the road dropping as it came to Girard at the bottom, then rising immediately for the next block, disappearing around a bend to the Popsicle store, if it's still there.

He stopped at the corner and looked up Girard, at the two rows of six little Cape Cods on either side. Amazing. It was as he recalled it. He walked past the Fergusons' and Mebbes' houses on the right-hand side, and saw the Wilsons' on the left. *Is their back yard still completely a vegetable garden?* That's what he remembered.

And there it was: 6421. A nice newly painted turquoise front door, but otherwise pretty much the same house he had pictured.

He stopped on the sidewalk at 6421 and stared at the little house for a moment. Memories flowed through his head—dipping toast in a yellow soup bowl of cream-and-sugared coffee with his dad and brother; eating a too-runny fried egg that Mrs. Wilson had fixed for him (he didn't remember why) as he sat on the side of her driveway; Mrs. Wilson's gummy smile; riding on a Shetland pony that was for some reason in his side yard; being stung by two bees at once in the back yard; Jim Ferguson dripping hot candle wax on his and Tommy's hands as a rite of initiation into his "club."

He squatted to examine the ground where he sat hacking away with his stick immediately before Fergus yanked him up and took him away nineteen years ago. He looked, even wondering if he'd see marks in the dirt where he had stabbed it.

It was now about 7:20 a.m., and a young man in a bathrobe, about 25, opened the front door of the house, bounded down the three front steps and grabbed the morning newspaper from the lawn. As he turned to go inside, he gasped, startled to see the crouching figure on his sidewalk.

"Oh, sorry," said Mickey, "just out for a walk and had a bit of a kink in my back!"

The man nodded and hurried back inside without speaking.

*　　　*　　　*　　　*

Back at the intersection of Losantiville and Montgomery, Mickey went left into an area of shops, storefronts and commercial buildings. He strolled leisurely along, looking in each window like the curious tourist that he was.

Gil's Barber Shop! Wow! I know I've been here!

A few doors beyond the Ridge Avenue-Montgomery Road intersection, a Coca-Cola sign above the sidewalk said "J&J Grill." A neon sign in the window glowed "Open." He was hungry and decided to load up, unsure what the rest of the day might hold for him.

As he opened the door to enter, silently reciting *"...the one you called Mickey, Michael Peter—"* Tom and Meg McCall sped by in a Cadillac, turning left onto Ridge Avenue, headed for the 8:00 Mass at Nativity.

He ate eggs, sausage, hash browns, toast, coffee, and orange juice. *About the same as a glutton in Ireland might eat,* he thought, except for the lack of a tomato, baked beans, and the black and white puddings. He felt better, but he was getting increasingly nervous as he mentally prepared to meet his family.

What if they're quite content with their lives at this point, and they view me as some unwelcome interruption? What if they don't believe me and tell me to hit the road? What if Tom, Jr. is offended that he must share his parents with me? What if they think I'm here to extract U.S. dollars from their pockets? What if they simply don't like me? What if I don't like them? Nah!

He looked at his watch: 8:20 a.m. He saw a newspaper on a vacant nearby table and went to get it. It was yesterday's, the one he'd already seen. Maybe he'd work the crossword puzzle. No, too nervous for that.

Figuring that the church would empty at 8:45 or after, he decided to walk through the area a bit more, then get back to Nativity where he could stand guard at the door, hoping to greet his parents and/or his brother. Would he even recognize them?

What if my parents are gray-haired and wrinkled? Will I look like my brother? Should I block their path or walk along beside them? Yes, I'll walk with them, saying, "Pardon me, please, are you the McCalls?" Then, "I am Mickey, the one you called Mickey..."

What if they scream and cry, or drop dead from the shock?

What if they say, "Good to see you, Mickey. How long you in town? Perhaps we can arrange a lunch. Separate checks, of course."

And if I don't quit all this worrying, maybe I'll be found foaming at the mouth in the Montgomery Road gutter, ready for a lunatic asylum where they'll come to visit and pray by my bedside. He laughed to himself. *It'll be brilliant. It'll be wonderful!*

He walked north on Ridge Avenue, away from the church, past large frame houses set back among enormous oak, maple, poplar, and sycamore trees, wondering what size and type of house the McCalls might occupy, and hoping that these minutes would pass quickly.

*   *   *   *

Tom and Meg McCall attended the 8:00 a.m. Mass at Nativity Church on this Sunday morning, as usual. And, as usual, when Father Jerome Bartel called for a moment of silence to pray for special intentions, they bowed their heads, each in their own way asking God to protect their long-lost son from all harm, to return him to them if possible, and if not, to hold him close in Heaven.

Tom reached into the pocket of his sport jacket and found a small bracelet-sized circle of beads with a St. Jude—patron saint of hopeless cases—medal attached, that he kept with him at all times. He recited a silent prayer on each bead and returned them to his pocket.

Both now added a prayer for Tom's health, as recent tests had indicated the presence of cancer in his colon. He was three weeks from surgery. Tom was 53 years old and Meg, 48.

Thomas Steven McCall, Jr., age 23, roused shortly after his parents left for Mass, fixed coffee, lit a cigarette, and read the Sunday *Enquirer*. Tom was a liberal arts graduate of Xavier University, a Cincinnati institution operated by the Society of Jesus, a.k.a. the Jesuits.

Tom, Sr., because of his son's ample talents and gifted intelligence, would have preferred that Tom had attended one of the prestigious eastern universities, or his own alma mater, Notre Dame University; but young Tom had never found sufficient motivation to do well enough in high school to make undergraduate study at a Harvard, Yale or Princeton even a remote possibility.

Generous donations from Tom, Sr. to St. Xavier High School, the Jesuit-operated local sibling to the University, and the resulting enthusiastic recommendations from young Tom's teachers and counselors at "X High" no doubt weighed heavily in allowing his matriculation to "XU."

Because his seventeen-month-younger sibling had been kidnapped when Tom was not quite 5 years old, leaving him an "only child," he may have been both ignored *and* overprotected, a not-so-good child-rearing combination.

Certainly, Tom, Sr. had come to learn that his demanding law practice was his safest haven from the anguish and torment of thoughts about his stolen son: the possibility, no, God help us all, the *probability, the near certainty at this point,* that he had been murdered, the unbearable thoughts of how that might have happened, *why* that might have happened, why, why, why, why, endlessly *why?*

Tom's miscellaneous clients, whether they knew of the tragedy in his life or not, did not expect anything to interfere with his attention to their legal needs; and this provided an unsympathetic and sometimes frustrating therapy, but therapy nonetheless. Indeed, Tom frequently acknowledged with a smile that his law practice was a substitute torture, and oddly he believed that to be true.

Perhaps odder yet was that losing one son may have effectively caused him to lose the other in his self-imposed exile from family and home. He worked six days a week and was rarely home on weeknights before 7:00 p.m., usually closer to 8:00 or 8:30 p.m. He generally cut out "early" on Saturdays at 3:30 or 4:00 p.m., unless Notre Dame football was to be televised at 1:00 p.m. He would not miss a Notre Dame football game.

Tom, Jr. had no interest whatsoever in a legal career. And although he had been a reasonably good athlete through elementary school, he had always been naturally thin—now 5'11" and 150 pounds—and not primarily interested in sports. He had played baseball, football, and basketball for the simple reason that that's what his friends did. But he'd have outright laughed at any notion of his doing any sort of physical training that might allow him to continue competitive athletics through high school.

Young Tom was, however, a natural artist, and without any training, he was able to produce excellent oil paintings, acrylics, pencil sketches, cartoons—whatever he tried. He also was a talented writer, a voracious reader of the great works as well as the current bestsellers, and unquestionably better read than all of his friends—even those whose academic and life achievements would dwarf his own.

No, it had been obvious shortly after the birth of the huskier second son, that Mickey, not Tom, would be the athlete. "You'll be a Notre Dame fullback someday, you fat little devil!" his dad would say as he tickled the stocky toddler.

Tom, Jr.'s current employment as a third-shift bank security guard allowed him much quiet time, which he used for writing, most often working on a screenplay about modern-day vampires. Whenever he thought he could get away with it, he actually claimed to be "a writer," using that as his excuse for a college graduate's acceptance of such menial employment. His father, however, was becoming increasingly impatient with his lack of ambition and his continued residence at home.

Meg, on the other hand, reasoned or rationalized that their son's high intelligence and aptitude didn't constitute some type of contract with the rest of the world *or* with his parents that he would achieve financial independence right out of college, or ever. She would argue with her husband, sometimes bitterly, that Tom, Jr. was an artist, a writer, and that he needed their continued financial and moral support if he were ever to be a success. And she warned Tom that she would not allow him to drive away her only child.

Part of Tom, Sr.'s general dissatisfaction was the fact that he had grown tired of the burdens of home ownership, and he had been pressing Meg to consider moving to an apartment in the city. Two new apartment buildings had been constructed in the heart of the downtown area, and several other buildings were in the process of being converted to upscale apartments. He argued that living in town would allow him to walk to his office and to the Hamilton County Courthouse, most days never needing a car. He promised that they could continue as Nativity parishioners, and that Meg could maintain all of her friendships, committee work, and associations.

Tom, Sr. was well aware of the high quality of life possible in a city apartment, as he had made frequent visits over the past two years to one of the two brand new buildings, Gibson Towers, to call on and have sex with his girlfriend, Cindy Reis, a Golden West Airlines flight attendant. Tom had met her on a practically-empty flight taking him to a deposition in Phoenix, Arizona; and sparks flew immediately, for reasons that Tom had never quite fully understood. Nor had he ever questioned them.

Cindy had been transferred to Denver about six weeks earlier and had ended their two-year affair, which had been Tom's only extra-curricular indulgence during his marriage. Although somewhat saddened by this abrupt termination, Tom was glad that it could be concluded without Meg's getting hurt, or even suspecting that he was cheating. He figured, however, that the cancer in his colon was God's chosen punishment for his indiscretion instead.

Meg absolutely hated the idea of apartment life, downtown or otherwise. A trim, good-looking and bright young law school graduate had once promised Miss Margaret Rita Phillips—a beautiful 20-year-old teller at Midwest Federal Bank where his father was president—that if she would be his wife, she would one day have both the piano and the swimming pool that she had told him would be required of the man she would marry.

She had those things now, and she proclaimed, "I'm not sitting in some dismal downtown apartment playing an electronic keyboard with headphones on, Tom. And the day you spend more than a half-hour raking leaves or cleaning the pool, then I'll listen to your complaints about taking care of the yard!"

At any rate, the issue of a change in residence had certainly been shelved for the time being, at least until Tom's health was restored. The cancer crisis—and for Tom, understanding the meaninglessness of his relationship with Cindy— had realigned their priorities and renewed their love for one another. As they left Mass arm-in-arm and exchanged greetings with their friends on this warm summer morning, they felt this closeness to one another, a closeness that they had not shared for years.

*   *   *   *

He was the first to enter church for the 9:30 a.m. Mass, seating himself in the last row center. No one exiting the earlier Mass had looked even remotely familiar. In fact, Tom and Meg had gone out a smaller doorway at the front of the church as Mickey stood at the three double-doors in the back, where most of the congregation passed through.

He studied the next group as each entered. He noted a very pretty blonde girl and a blonde woman who was obviously her mother, as they went all the way to the front, to a small section of pews to the side of the altar, maybe the choir. Only one couple piqued his interest momentarily, until Mickey decided that they were certainly in their thirties, and therefore could not be his parents. Mass began. *Yes, that's the choir.*

At the Mass's conclusion, he saw the priest stop at the back of the church by a baptismal font, to greet the parishioners, just as Father McDermott does back in Newport. He would exit last, once again scrutinizing each passerby, and then he'd perhaps ask the priest about Meg and Tom. He certainly did not want to give up his identity and have someone calling ahead, but thought he might get specific directions to their house.

As the church was nearly emptied, the two blondes moved with the last of the crowd down the aisle toward the exit.

Would I rather meet a pretty American blonde or spend my time explaining my Irish accent to the good Father?

Easy enough.

He smiled and silently nodded to the priest after the ladies exchanged greetings with him, walked along behind them for a few feet, and then said, "Pardon me, please, but I wonder if I might make an inquiry?"

The mother and daughter turned, glanced at each other as if to ask if this fellow might be putting them on with the accent, and the daughter said, "Sure!"

He explained that he was from Ireland, traveling through the area, and that he hoped to locate a family to whom he was related, the McCalls.

As the younger replied, "Mom knows them," the older woman said, "Do you mean Meg McCall? Meg and Tom?"

"Yes, that's exactly right. Meg and Tom."

"And you're related?"

"Indeed, I am. My name is Michael Monaghan, by the way," he said smiling, bowing slightly. He didn't much care to call himself "Monaghan" anymore, but it served the purpose this morning.

"Oh, how nice, Michael, I'm Dorothy Mueller, and this is my daughter, Donna. I've been friends with Meg for years!"

"Hi, Michael, so the charming brogue isn't fake?" Donna asked with a smile.

"Now if I were faking, wouldn't I try to talk like John Wayne for you, rather than soundin' like some leprechaun?" he responded laughing. They laughed. "I had hoped you might point me in the direction of the McCalls' residence."

"I sure will, Michael. Depending on which drive you pull out. Where are you parked?"

"Oh, no, I'm on foot right now. I'm staying down at the Foster House by the carriageway and walking from there."

Donna looked at Dorothy and quickly said, "We'll give you a ride. We're going that way!"

Mickey noted real concern in Dorothy's face and immediately protested, saying he was happy to walk. After a little further back-and-forth, Donna argued, *"Mom! He just went to Mass!"* and Dorothy relaxed, then insisted that Mickey ride with them.

As he opened the driver's door for Dorothy, he cautiously asked, "Are they all fine—Meg, Tom and Tom, Jr.?"

"I've never seen much of Tom, Jr., but, yes, Meg and Tom, all of 'em are fine as far as I know."

"Good! Good!" Mickey said, relieved.

"Now, you know," Dorothy continued as she turned from the parking lot, "I don't know how close a relative you are, but years ago, they had a little one kidnapped, a younger boy. Did you know that?"

After a short pause, he replied quietly and sadly, "I do know that, yes." Even though it made sense that Meg's friend-for-years would know about him, it almost shocked him to hear it.

"He'd have been my classmate at Nativity," said Donna, turning to look at Mickey. "Same age."

"And if he'd been a right smart fella, probably chasin' after you all through the schoolyard, don't you think, Donna?"

Donna blushed as they laughed a little, and Dorothy said, "This is Grand Valley, their street. It'll be coming up on the left when we go down the hill."

There was silence as they approached the downgrade. Once there, Dorothy pointed ahead and said, "It's down there where the road dips."

She slowed at the bottom of the hill and said, "That's it. Right there."

Mickey looked at the wide front yard with the large and well-appointed ranch-style house sitting back perhaps seventy-five feet from the road. He saw a trim, attractive woman in a white blouse and shorts kneeling at one end of the house.

He saw her stand up.

He knew. *It's her.* His eyes burned, and his heart pounded.

Dorothy pulled in the driveway to let Mickey out. "There's Meg right there, Michael."

He took a deep breath. He spoke as calmly as he could. "You have been so kind, and I hate to impose on you even one more second, but I wonder if I might ask you to just walk up with me, since she doesn't know me...and I certainly don't want to frighten her."

*   *   *   *

Meg McCall was ready to start her Sunday gardening. Tom was doing the dishes after the usual big Sunday breakfast, and Tom, Jr. was pulling out of the driveway—headed down to the Ohio River to go boating with friends—in his 1984 Volvo 240, the Volvo that had been Meg's until some five weeks earlier when Tom, Sr. had replaced it with a new Cadillac, probably not *un*coincidentally on the heels of Cindy Reis's sudden departure from his life.

On this characteristically hot and humid Cincinnati summer Sunday, the flowerbeds across the front of the McCalls' home had become weed-infested. Meg was looking forward to cleaning them out, and, if she had time and if the day didn't get too hot, putting down the new mulch she had bought the day before.

Let's see...Mary Beth and Paul Rieger are coming over to go swimming and grill steaks at 4:00 p.m., it's now about 11:00, I can work until 3:00, so I ought to be able to do it, she thought, as she walked her bushel basket of garden tools up the driveway and around to the front of the house.

The McCalls' driveway was on the right, as one looked at the house, curving a bit as it went down one level to a large apron in the back, where the three-car garage was located as a portion of the lower level of the residence. About twenty feet from the street, there were two stone steps from the driveway to a walkway going diagonally across the generous front yard to the front door at the center of the house.

Meg was wearing a white sleeveless blouse and white Bermuda shorts with a multi-colored belt, and white tennis shoes. Not a typical gardener's outfit, but all of it getting a bit old, just not yet ready to be thrown out. Her makeup was still there, but she had begun to perspire a little.

As she knelt at the far end of the house and unearthed a few dandelions, she decided that the unusually coarse June grass and hard dry ground were a little too much for her 48-year-old knees, and she opted to return to the garage for a set of kneepads.

When she stood, she saw Dorothy Mueller's Pontiac Bonneville pull in her driveway and stop at the steps. If she'd thought about it, she might have concluded that this—Dorothy's coming by on a Sunday morning—was highly unusual. But Dorothy and Meg had been cordial friends through the years, had worked together at church functions, been members of the same church groups, and had always enjoyed each other's company; so she really thought nothing of it, except that it was nice to see Dorothy.

She waved and smiled, but she could see that Dorothy was talking to someone in the car and was turned away from her. As Meg walked toward the center of the front of the house, three of the Bonneville's doors opened, and three people got out. Meg stopped when she reached the walk at the front door, thinking that Dorothy perhaps might want to come into the house.

Once out of her car, Dorothy waited a moment until the two others joined her at the steps, and then walked up.

*   *   *   *

Meg recognized Donna instantly, of course, and, as she became curious about the purpose of Dorothy's visit, somewhere also in her mind—seeing the strapping young man with them—was the vague thought that Donna had really landed herself a good one this time. As the three people came up the steps, Meg smiled, ready to say hello to Dorothy, Donna and the young man.

They were now about five feet apart, and she glanced over at the young man again.

Her head turned a little to the side as she inventoried his features. Her eyes squinted slightly to focus. Suddenly, she drew a quick, deep breath and held it.

And nineteen years of endless night...became day.

Dorothy expressed some form of greeting, but Meg ignored it. She didn't hear it. In her mind, a gong had been struck, with its deafening hollow vibration signaling that all the world should stop. The young man was staring at her, and her own eyes were now locked to his. He appeared nervous. *Uh-oh...uh-oh.* As he stood motionless, she saw the tears well up in his eyes.

In that instant, her whole body shuddered and her breath rushed out. And the thousands of times over the last nineteen years that she had looked at boys and young men wondering *"Could it be...?"*, the thousands of times that she had said, "Tom, look at him, doesn't he look like...?"—none of them meant a thing now. Like so many matchlights against a hurricane, those moments were blown out, blown away, and forgotten.

In this mother's mind, the calculations and computations done in that very second were conclusive: A lot like Tom, Jr.—the hair, the eyes, the nose, the mouth—but bigger boned, taller, and a gentler appearance. And, yes, he looks twenty-two…a little like Tom, Sr.…but more like her!

Her mouth twitched, unable to speak. Indeed, *unwilling* to speak as though a noise might change this fragile truth swelling her spirit. Her breathing was now out of control. She felt her scalp go numb as every hair raised. She bent slightly and clasped a hand over her open mouth as she stared wide-eyed at the young man.

All of her body now shaking, it appeared to Dorothy and Donna that she was for some reason terrified by Michael Monaghan. They, too, were dumbstruck and unable to move, fearing—illogical as it all seemed—that they had brought some form of evil to their friend, and feeling entirely helpless about it.

But it wasn't any form of evil, and she wasn't terrified. It wasn't anything like anything else.

These few paralyzing seconds were beyond what any words might ever be able to describe to Meg. This…this was *it*.

This was the single, specific moment in time that, for every day—without exception—of the last nineteen years, she had thought about, dreamed of, hoped for with all her might, prayed for with all her heart and soul, the moment she knew had to come some day, the one that she knew could never come—no matter…it was here!

It was here, standing before her in the form of a strong 6'1" male physique more handsome than she would have dared imagine.

The young man, tears streaming down his face, in an unsteady voice spoke the words, "I am," and his throated locked shut as he gulped back emotion.

Meg tried to finish his sentence for him, but her quivering lips could barely come together to begin to form an "M." He understood what she—his mother—was attempting, and nodded a quick affirmation as he mouthed the single word "yes." And, *yes*…her years of *not knowing*, her years of heartache, sorrow and anguish had now, finally, ended.

They threw their arms around each other and sobbed.

Dorothy heard Meg scream a muffled "Mickey!" into the young man's shirt, and now herself crying, she turned and hugged a confused Donna, almost squealing as she said, "Oh, my *God*, Donna! *That's her boy!*"

*   *   *   *

Mickey had by now completely forgotten about his scripted message as he hugged his mother and continued to cry. At one point, he stepped back to look at her and said the only thing he could think of through his tears, "I remember you...you're my mother!"

She simultaneously burst into new tears and laughter, squeaking out the words "I know that!" as they hugged again.

After a moment, she stepped back and, as loud as she could, she yelled out Tom's name twice. She was most certainly not about to leave the spot where she stood with her baby boy.

Tom was immediately present, swinging the front screen door open and holding it as he viewed this inscrutable scene: Dorothy hugging Donna, Meg and some young man hugging, everyone apparently crying. "What!? What's going on?" he demanded.

Meg turned to the door and screamed, "It's *him*, Tom! It's our *Mickey!* He's here!"

Tom face registered shock. *Did she say Mickey? Our Mickey? Isn't this...impossible? Does she mean our son Mickey?* He felt faint and unable to think or move.

Mickey looked at him, and, with one arm around his mother, coaxing her the few steps to the door, he extended his other arm to his father. Meg wept, repeating, "It's true, Tom, it's really true! Our Mickey, our baby, he's home!"

For just another split second, Tom wondered if poor Meg had cracked—or what proof there might be that this miracle had occurred—but even through Mickey's blotchy, red face, he saw the familial resemblance and whispered through his now-labored breathing, "Great God almighty! Thank you, St. Jude!"

He released the door handle to reach for his son, but instead momentarily collapsed, fainting into Mickey's strong arms, which held him as he regained his composure and began to cry, hugging his son, causing everyone to renew their own tears.

Finally, making certain that his father was now stable, Mickey broke away and stood back a step, saying, "I certainly apologize for bein' such a crybaby. I assure you, your son is more of a man than what appears. I had no idea I'd react this way!"

In the overwhelming emotion of the moment, Meg had ignored what she thought might have been an "accent" in the few words her son had earlier spoken, but this statement left no doubt that he had not spent the last nineteen years near Cincinnati, Ohio.

Her hands folded as in prayer, she pleaded, "Mickey, what is that accent? Where have you been?"

"Is that an *Irish* accent?" Tom asked at the same time.

"To be sure, 'tis Ireland where I've been since age 3," Mickey said, collecting his emotions, "and I'll tell you all about it, if y' have a few months, but let's get one thing clear," he continued with a tear-covered grin, "*you're* the ones with the accents!"

They all laughed, not just at the good humor of Mickey's remark, but at the absolute relief of knowing that he was not just alive, not just an attractive mass of flesh and bones, but at the realization that this was an actual functioning three-dimensional human being, a presence of love—*their love*—who will even contribute something and share in their lives!

In a magnificent contrast to their occasional grim prayers that they might at least "find the body" so that they could "experience closure," this little bit of humor—well, my God, if this is going to be *fun*, too…if that's the case, then prayers that had never been prayed had been answered a thousand times over!

They spoke in loud, excited voices for the next fifteen minutes, often through tears, Dorothy explaining first how "this gorgeous young man" had approached her and Donna for directions; then, after carrying on with whatever came to mind, Mickey imploring everyone not to contact the press or police for the time being, "as there are people that I love, who are in grave danger as long as my kidnappers are on the lam."

Finally, with a promise from Meg that she'd be in touch shortly, Dorothy and Donna graciously excused themselves to allow the three McCalls to share their new and profound joy.

*   *   *   *

The front foyer took them into a large living and dining room el, where he was immediately struck by the richness of the decor. To his right, there was an ebony Baldwin grand piano that appeared to be brand new, with an ornate silver floor lamp next to it that—by Mickey's quick appraisal—probably cost more than every stick of furniture combined, back in his cottage on Treanbeg Road. *For that matter, the piano probably cost more than the whole cottage!*

"My God! Who plays?"

"Your mother—she's about ready for the concert circuit, right, Meggy?"

"Just another forty or fifty years' practice—do you play, Mickey?"

"A little, but guitar is my instrument of choice. My friend, Caitlin, she plays well, as do her mother and sister—you'll hear quite a bit from me about Caitlin."

"Girlfriend?" asked Tom.

"Oh…uh, no, but we're close. Long-time close friends. *Best* friends, really."

Meg pulled his hand across the room and to the right, into the dining area. "C'mon along, Mick—should I call you Mick or Mickey?" she asked, stopping herself from re-bursting into tears at the implication of her words.

He smiled shyly as his eyes moistened. "Well, you named me...call me what you like. By the way—where is my brother?"

"Oh! You just missed him. He's out with friends for the day," Meg answered.

"So he still lives here?"

"Yes, and 'still' is definitely the correct word," Tom smiled.

"Tom!" Meg scolded.

"Whoops! Everything okay there?" Mickey asked.

"Sure!" Tom answered quickly, then turning him through a door to the left, said, "Check out this new addition—my home theatre room!"

They entered a large room with a long leather sofa facing a huge television screen and an array of other electronic lights, components and appliances, with speakers of every size on either side of the screen and attached at ceiling corners. As Tom grabbed several remote controls, Meg said, "Tom, don't you dare think you're playing that scene from *Star Wars!* We've got far more important things to cover!"

"You're right!" he said, dropping the remotes on the table and turning to usher them out of the room. "It's pretty incredible, though, Mick, gives you the full effect of the room, and I'll show you later. What about coffee on the back porch, Meg?"

"Just what I was thinking! Do you drink coffee, or how about iced tea or lemonade, Mickey?" Meg called as she entered the kitchen.

He didn't hear the question. He had stepped to the back porch—what they called the "back porch"—and was staring out the window at the swimming pool.

"It's feckin' blinding!" he said quietly as he gazed out at the crystal-clear sunlit water in a kidney-shaped pool and the decorative-stone patio and walkway surrounding it.

As much as he was astounded by his parents' obvious wealth, he began to get a sense that everything was a bit much. *Why would anyone need to shower themselves with all this?* He shot a glance around the porch—jalousied triple-pane windows shut tight for the air conditioning, matching rattan furniture throughout the room—sofa, loveseat, chairs, ottomans, end tables, dining table and chairs, lamps...all of it appearing new, as in a showroom. Overwhelming. Nowhere in the house had he seen even a trace of what he'd consider "modest" taste.

"What's that you say?" Tom asked, following Mickey onto the porch.

"Well, I've seen pictures before...but, that water! You can barely look at it!"

"Oh...yeah. Do you want coffee or iced tea, Mick?"

"Iced tea would be lovely."

Mickey asked Tom about his law practice as they waited for Meg, curious about his father and the kind of work that would produce such abundance.

*   *   *   *

"Here we are, gentlemen," Meg announced after a few minutes, entering the room with a crystal pitcher of iced tea and three matching goblets on a tray.

"Why don't we just listen, Tom?" Meg suggested as she poured the tea.

"Sure, but first things first—where's your baggage, Mickey?"

"Oh, I'm staying at a place called the Foster House down by—"

"Like hell you are!" Tom interrupted.

"Right!" Meg agreed. "We can go get your stuff as soon as we finish the tea—oh, and what about the Riegers?"

"Impossible!" Tom said.

"Yeah, let me go call them!" Meg said, leaving the room, but the phone was ringing before she could get to it.

It was Dorothy.

"Meg, just one thing, and I'll leave you alone—Donna was just *gushing* about that boy of yours, so if he gets bored or lonely—"

"Oh, how perfect! I'll be sure to work that into the conversation, Dorothy!"

Meg returned to the porch, forgetting in all her excitement to call the Riegers to cancel their afternoon grill-out.

Mickey spoke for the next two hours, starting with his actual kidnapping, talking about the Monaghans' strategy in refusing to allow him to speak of his family, counseling him to never "draw attention" to himself, not allowing him to participate in sports, keeping him at work on the farm, and so on.

He told of the unraveling, how it began at Kilkelly's pub with Caitlin, continuing with Father McDermott and his "crossroads" luncheon as Mickey neared graduation. Meg and Tom were particularly astonished as he related the tale of his last day with the Fergus and Marian: the safe-deposit box, the confrontation, and the transfer of the property.

Meg gasped, horrified, as he told her of the Irish woman with a child named Mickey that had met her in Pleasant Ridge Park.

"Oh, my God! I *do* remember her, I do! How could she ever have been a kidnapper!?"

"And complicitor to murder," Tom added, shaking his head. "To think that, to this day, that little guy lies buried right over here in Golf Manor!"

"How incredibly chilling!" Meg agreed, then quietly offered, "Well…sounds like we owe you a graduation present, anyway, Mickey."

"Absolutely not! Not a thing, and I mean it."

Tom said, "Sounds like we owe Miss Caitlin and Father McDermott—but especially Caitlin. We wouldn't be having this glorious day without their help."

Mickey looked at his watch and smiled. "To be sure, I'd likely be trampin' through sheepshit in my Wellies or footin' the turf, rather than sipping tea out of crystal."

"What's that…'Wellies' and 'foot-in-a-turf'?" Meg asked, amused.

"Wellington boots, high-top rubber boots, and *footing the turf,*" he pronounced carefully, "well, *turf* is what we cut out of the bog for heating fuel—sods of turf, *peat. Footing* is just a way of stacking them to dry out. And I guess you know what sheepshit is?"

They laughed, and then sat silently for a moment, looking at each other.

Tom asked, "So how many sheep you got, Mick?"

"O-o-oh, I've a good few!" he said with gleaming eyes.

"And…the bog, do you have to *travel* to the bog?" Meg continued politely. "I mean, do you all go to the same bog?"

Mickey grinned widely at his mother, and said, "Yes, that's right, it's six days by mule cart," realizing his lifestyle might border on incomprehensible to one who had so much material wealth. "Actually, *no*, Mother, I'm teasing you. We have—or I should now say, *I* have my own bog, as do most of the farms in my area."

He smiled, then laughed at himself, to think that he was bragging about his "own bog" to this rich American lawyer and his spoiled wife—his Dad and Mom!

"There's so much I'd like to say," Tom began, looking away, "but I don't think I'd be able to finish a sentence. This is…beyond belief."

Mickey nodded as Meg sniffled and said, "C'mon, boys! Let's go get that luggage!"

*　　　*　　　*　　　*

They went to the basement. A recreation room filled one side, complete with oak bar and polished brass foot-rail, oak cabinets and built-in furniture, a fireplace and a billiard table. Behind the billiard table was a wall of windows looking out to the patio and pool. The other side held a shower and changing room for pool guests.

A corner door opened into a three-car garage. Tom's BMW and Meg's Cadillac sat impressively before him.

"Jay-sus! It never ends!"

"You haven't had it quite so easy, have you?" Meg asked sympathetically.

Mickey laughed. "I can tell you that the cottage I've lived in for nineteen years would fit quite handily into this garage of yours! I'm really just amazed at everything altogether."

"Sit in the front, Mickey," Meg said, opening the passenger door to her Cadillac for him. He briefly hesitated, but quickly recalled that the driver's seat was on the opposite side in American cars.

As Tom backed out, Mickey saw a pile of fresh wood laying in the back yard, and he asked about it.

"It's a replacement for the split-rail fence that's around these outer two sides of the pool," Tom said, twisting around to point. "You can see that old one has just about had it, all gray and rotten, broken in spots."

"Wish we could've had it done for you, Mickey," Meg added, "but I can't get the man out here to put it in. Claims he's been sick, but he probably just has bigger fish to fry."

"Well, it's a horror," Mickey said through his laughter as he turned to look at Meg, "to see that you've had to carry on with that dingy old thing alongside your pool! What is it about that fence that requires you to pay someone to put it in? Not to butt in, but why wouldn't Tommy just do it?"

"Hah!" Tom, Sr. responded as he pulled onto Grand Valley Road.

"Tom!"

"Oh, c'mon, Meg. You gotta admit…"

"Oh, I suppose. Your brother—well, your father *and* your brother aren't much for yard work and things physical in general."

"Not that my father doesn't work hard," Mickey offered in defense.

"Oh, believe me," Meg agreed, "you caught him during one of his rare personal appearances at home—"

"Well, never mind that," Mickey interrupted with a smile. "Let's get my luggage, and that fence will be finished by four o'clock, I promise you!"

Tom and Meg both protested vehemently, but Mickey was resolute. "Four o'clock, or I'll pay the other man meself, I will!"

"Uh-oh, Tom, four o'clock! I forgot to call the Riegers!"

"Oh! You know, Meg," he said thoughtfully, "what with introductions and such all out of the way, it might be great fun to show off our son to our best friends! What do you think, Mickey? Could you stand some company a little later?"

"Sure, whatever you like. You know, I think I remember the Riegers," he answered.

"Oh, my God, of course!" exclaimed Meg. "We were all friends before you were born, and, well...they were a great help to us through the time—"

"I *did* promise Caity—that's Caitlin—that I'd ring her at five, which is 10 p.m. back home in Ireland...but I'll pay for the call, to be sure."

Tom rocked his head back and forth and said, "Lemme see if I understand this: you're putting in a split-rail fence this afternoon, then leaving us some change on the table for your phone call. You do realize that you forgot to pay your parents for your iced tea, don't you?"

Mickey let out a laugh and turned to Meg, saying, "'Tis a saint ye are, missus, to put up with such a sarcastic individual fer yer mate day-in and day-out!"

"I ignore him," she said smiling, as Tom pulled into the Foster House parking lot. "Mickey, if we're having company, anyway, would you like it if I asked Donna to join us? She apparently thought you were—"

"No! Thank you," he said quickly, thinking only of Caitlin at first, then considering that he ought not involve himself with his parents' friends, anyway. He imagined the priest he had seen at Nativity that morning telling him to *think about the harm he was causing himself* and that lovely young Donna Mueller with his immoral ways. "Not now, thanks. I'll be back momentarily," he said, hopping out and heading to his room to collect his suitcase.

Meg cried immediately. "Oh, God, Tom! Can this be true? Isn't he *wonderful?*"

"He is," Tom said, getting out, "and I'm going to go pay for his room."

*   *   *   *

Using a sledge, a spade, and his hands, he knocked, dug, and jerked the old fence posts out—fifteen of them—in as many minutes. Gratified for the opportunity to fill an apparent void in his new family, and well aware that he was "on stage" with a chance to show off, he pounded the post-hole digger relentlessly, cleaning out each slot for its new wood and moving on.

Meg called her parents in Naples, Florida with the joyous news, then her sister in Fairfield, Iowa. They decided to hold off on talking to their miscellaneous local relatives.

Tom called his answering service, quickly returned a few phone calls, placed a few more, then found Meg in the kitchen, preparing a salad and peering out at her son every other minute or so.

"Look at him, Tom," she said, nodding to the window.

Tom stood focused on Mickey for a long moment, then shook his head. "Jesus! No kryptonite around here, for sure! He's a damn machine, a jackhammer! Meg—can you bring him down to my office about 10:30 tomorrow morning?"

"Sure. Why?"

"Press conference at 11 o'clock. I gotta work out a few more details, then I'll go tell Mick."

"He wanted to keep it quiet, Tom."

"I know," Tom smiled as he hugged Meg. "Wanna tell me what the odds are on *that?*"

*   *   *   *

By 3:30 p.m., he had tamped down the dirt around the fifteenth post and was stacking the old wood where the new wood had been. Tom had come out in his bathing suit and a T-shirt, admiring Mickey's work and even carrying a few of the rails.

"I honestly don't think I've ever seen anyone work so hard, Mick! This is fabulous!" he called out, extending his arms toward the ends of the new fence.

"Thanks, Pop. It's an honor!"

"Now, Mick. If I were a betting man, I'd put down a hundred saying you didn't pack a swimsuit for this trip. Right?"

"That's a bet you'd win," Mickey said chuckling.

"Well, not to worry. Mary Beth Rieger called a little bit ago from the mall to say that they're running a few minutes late, so I gave her power-of-attorney to pick out a swimsuit for you. Not that she knows who it's for, but just wanted you to know, okay?"

"Sure," he answered a little sheepishly, "but I don't know how to swim."

"Oh, well," Tom assured him, "we don't *swim*—we drink, we eat, and we cool off!"

"I can do all of those things," he laughed.

Tom took on a serious demeanor and said, "Listen, pal, we need a second to talk about something before you go in to clean up."

"All right," Mickey said, concerned about his dad's frown.

"I appreciate what you said about not contacting the news people and the authorities, but this—your coming home—is going to be big, no—*huge, enormous*—news, and we are not going to be able to keep it quiet for long. It was big news when you were kidnapped—as you well know from the newspapers those bastards saved—and it'll be big news when the various media find out you're back. You with me?"

Mickey nodded. "I am." And as much as he completely understood it, he wondered why he disliked hearing his father call Fergus and Marian "bastards." *They are bastards.*

"Now, there's a deal in town that one of the TV stations runs, called *Grand Scoop Hotline,* and they pay a thousand bucks to the first person who calls in a worthwhile news story—you know, a 'grand' for the 'scoop'—anyway, I don't know if that would interest you or not—"

Mickey looked back at him and said instinctively, "No, it wouldn't." He didn't care to draw attention to himself.

"Right," Tom nodded. He rubbed his chin. "Look…okay, let me put it this way: Dorothy and Donna? And this Mary Beth who's coming over this afternoon? And, what the hell, even your mother! As human beings—capital A plus. Absolutely. As friends? A plus! But they're *women,* Mick, and on their good days, they get a D plus for keeping secrets. You know what they get on all the other days?"

Mickey laughed and shook his head. "Mm, I'll try…F minus?"

"F minus is the correct answer, yes, indeed! And tomorrow when your blessed mother, the love of my life, is at the grocery, and somebody says, 'Hi, Meg, what's new?'—what'll be the first thing out of her mouth—if she even waits *that* long? What I hate to tell you is that tomorrow at this time, there's no guessing how many 'grand scoopers' are gonna be lighting up that line."

When he stopped laughing, Mickey said, "All right, I'd better warn Caitlin about it, then." *Oh—and remind her to call Senator O'Malley's office to let them know.*

"Absolutely, but Mick, why don't you consider this—let's do this right. We'll set up a little press conference in my office tomorrow, and I'll personally make arrangements with the Cincy cops and the FBI—you know, we'll keep some sort of *control* over the process, rather than just wondering who'll be jumping out of the bushes at us next."

"All right, that's brilliant, Dad," Mickey said soberly. "I really appreciate your thoughtful help, and I suppose I just need to defer to your judgment here."

He left his dad to go shower. He was eager to ring Caitlin and considered calling her early, but they had sort of *pledged* to each other to be by their phones at 5:00 p.m. Eastern time, so he waited.

*   *   *   *

Tom had met both Paul Rieger and Mary Beth Brown in the summer of 1959 when they were all college graduates, working in the credit department of Midwest Federal Bank as management trainees. Tom then continued part-time at the bank after starting law school in the fall, and Meg Phillips started as a teller after graduating from high school in 1960.

Paul and Mary Beth had been sweethearts since high school, and by the time they married in 1961, Tom had started dating Meg. They had all been close friends ever since. Paul was now executive vice president of the bank, and Mary Beth operated her own gift shop. She had bought it a year after her marriage—as a hobby—but had never once failed to out-earn her husband in a given year.

They showed up at 4:30 and got the shock of their lives to meet Mickey. Tom had simply referred to him as a "houseguest"—casually telling Mary Beth, "Oh, you'll meet him later"—when he spoke to her on the phone about buying him a bathing suit. The four of them were now out on the patio making small talk when Mickey came down the steps to join them.

"Here's our houseguest, if you've got that bathing suit, Mary Beth," Tom said without emotion.

"Oh, sure," Mary Beth answered, digging into a paper bag by her chair, then handing it to the young man, who said, "Thank you, Mrs. Rieger."

She laughed and said, "You're welcome, mystery houseguest," then continued, "Gosh, why, don't you look exactly like a bigger version of—" And she stopped cold. She stared in disbelief for another moment, then slowly turned her head to the right to look at Meg, who now held her trembling fingertips over her mouth, nodding as tears again rolled down her face.

There was more crying while Mickey told as much of the story as he could, carefully watching the time, then excusing himself a few minutes before 5:00.

*   *   *   *

He didn't know if he was relieved to get away from all the emotion or just anxious to talk to Caitlin, but he knew he was happy to be heading for the telephone. He couldn't wait to tell her about his fantastic parents and their fantastic home. And the piano.

Keran answered the phone and asked Mickey a few questions, which he answered.

"Are you all right, Keran? You sound a little off."

"I'm all right, Mickey, but Mam needs to talk to you."

"What—hello?" She had already set the phone down.

He waited nervously, and then heard Mrs. O'Connor pick up the phone.

"Is Caitlin all right, Mrs. O'Connor? What's wrong?"

"She's all right, Mickey, but she's not here. I just looked out again. She went out with Ray earlier, and then they were back here, sitting out front in Ray's car. And they were gone again."

"Well...well..."

"I know she was lookin' forward to hearing from you, but..."

"But she's gone," he said, dejected.

"Yeah," said Ellen quietly. "Now you know, Mickey," she continued, "you were right, what you said to Caitlin about Mr. Byrne over at the bank, him and Peggy. So Caitlin's workin' back here at the Newport bank. She'll have to fill you in on that."

"Oh...okay, well, listen...uhm, maybe I'll try again tomorrow morning—"

"Mickey," Mrs. O'Connor interrupted in a sad voice, "I've got to tell you something."

Mickey immediately knew that Caitlin had either become engaged to Ray, or maybe that she had been hurt...something horrible. He heard Ellen take a breath.

"They found...Marian."

"Found...has she been arrested?" he asked, but he knew even as he asked the question that she had meant something else.

"No, Mickey, I'm so sorry. She was there in the bed, in a B&B a few miles outside of Tralee. Eamonn rang this afternoon, right after Caitlin left. The Gardai think that she...well, that she did it herself. With pills. There were empty containers. I'm sorry, Mickey, is there anything I can do?"

"What about *him*?" Mickey demanded, "Where is he?"

"Gone. Is there anything I can do, Mickey?"

"Heartless cowardly bastard! Jesus...no, Mrs. O'Connor, there's nothing, thank you, and I'll ring again first thing in the morning."

*   *   *   *

He sat down in the kitchen, numb at first, trying to tell himself that Marian was a criminal, a cold and unfeeling mother who gave him no love or support, who robbed him of his own life and hurt his parents, and who devoted her life to a baby killer. But he couldn't. And he cried, because all he could think about was his last hours with her, how cruel he had been, especially at the end, when he had refused to even acknowledge her as she called out his name.

She wanted to love. She tried to love Fergus, but he couldn't have let her know any more clearly how little that meant to him. Surely, she loved her little boy, only to have Fergus murder him. And after she poured out her heart and sorrowful soul to me, where was she? Standing between the two of us, her husband with a choke hold and a knife to her neck, and me with a shotgun aimed at her, telling her I'm about blow her into eternal hell. What a pathetic and horrible life. And I did my part to get that point across, didn't I? God, forgive me, if You can.

He walked to the bottom of the steps and stood by the iron-gate entrance to the pool and patio. When Tom and Meg saw that he would come no further, they went to him.

"You don't deserve this, I know, but I have to excuse myself. Uh...I can't be much company right now. Uh, Marian...you know, *Marian.* She killed herself, and...well, I know how much heartache she's caused you...and all of us, but..."

"Killed herself?" asked Meg, stunned.

"Yeah. Pills. And I'm sorry, but—"

Tom put his hand on Mickey's shoulder. "You don't have to explain a thing, Mick. Why don't you go on and get some rest?"

"We'll visit a while later, if you're up, Mickey," Meg said, and gave him a hug.

*   *   *   *

McCalls' home had four bedrooms: the master, Tom, Jr.'s, and two others that were used as the private retreats of Meg and Tom, Sr.—both like home offices with beds. Tom did some minor straightening up, and then turned his room over to Mickey with the pledge that he'd soon spend some time clearing the room of his personal items. Mickey decided not to mention that he would only be staying ten days, intending to leave Tuesday after the next weekend.

He slept until about 8:30 in the evening, then found Meg and Tom on the patio by themselves. He grabbed a chair and walked to them.

"Riegers gone?"

"We drank, we ate, we cooled off," explained Tom.

"Mind if I join you?"

"Mind? You're lucky we didn't come up and hop in bed with you. We were getting anxious to see you again," said Meg smiling.

"How are you?" asked Tom.

"Oh, well," he shrugged, "you know—I swear I'm not a moody person, but…Jesus! What a day. Suppose I wouldn't be a very good Catholic if I didn't feel guilt for everything."

"Glad to see *that's* the same all over the world," Tom said with a smile.

Mickey explained the circumstances of Marian's death, as much as he knew, and his feeling that she was, in many ways, a victim of Fergus, just as they all were. Meg and Tom were understanding—chiefly for Mickey's sake, of course—and they all smiled as Mickey acknowledged, "There couldn't be a much more unlikely scene than the three of us holding this eulogy."

"On this otherwise wonderful day," Tom offered to conclude the thought.

Meg put her hand on her son's knee. "Mickey, your dad and I were talking, and…you said you play the guitar?"

"Yeah, I do," he said, perking up.

"Well, your dad has a good client who owns a music store—"

"We want to do *something* for you, son, and you can pick it out—the best guitar in the place—nothing gold-plated, okay?—but, whatever you want! It's yours."

"Oh," he smiled, "I play the guitar, but I was just about to switch to the tuba."

They looked blankly at him.

"Joke," he shrugged. "But I really like the guitar that I have, and…"

"Well, fine," said Tom, laughing a little, "you think of something we could do for you. You must want *something* within reason."

"Something that will mean something to you," Meg added.

"There *is* something that would mean something to me," Mickey said immediately. "I haven't had time to make a lot of plans, but with that farm, I'll have money, one way or the other. I don't know if she could get away from work, but if I could just borrow—*borrow*—the money for a plane ticket, for Caitlin...I know you'd love her."

"Done," said Tom. "I've already set your press conference for 11:00 tomorrow. You and your Mom can call for the ticket first thing, then she'll bring you downtown. And one more thing—we're having a party for you this coming Saturday night, whether you like it or not, so maybe you can get her here in time for that."

*   *   *   *

Mickey sat in one of two matching leather recliners in the living room, reading the newspaper. It was 11:00 p.m., three hours before he could call Caitlin, and he was going crazy with worry. He prayed that she hadn't accepted a marriage proposal from Ray Mitchell, and he cursed himself for not having the sense to tell her how he felt about her before leaving Ireland.

How could you have let her get away, you moron, you damnable stupid fucking moron? he asked himself over and over.

Indeed, Caitlin hadn't been there to take his call. That wasn't like her. Not at all.

What could have happened? Did she decide that my call didn't matter? It mattered, and I mattered, the other day. So what's changed? Face it, Mickey: she's marrying Ray. Your friendship is over, just like Father McDermott said it would be. And isn't it my own fault, taking her for granted the way I always have, even knowing that I loved her? But I certainly gave her no reason to hope for a future for us...just the opposite, calling myself her "big brother" or her "best friend"...Jesus! What a fool I've been!

As he sat thinking of ways to talk her out of marrying Ray, he heard the whirring of one of the garage doors powering open, and then closing. Then the footsteps up the stairs and through the kitchen. The French doors swung open, and Mickey saw his brother—as an adult—for the first time.

"Tom?" Mickey asked, and the startled figure twisted around to face him.

"You must be Tom," Mickey said quietly as he stood, holding the paper in one hand and extending the other to Tom.

"Right," Tom answered cautiously, giving Mickey's hand a light shake as he stared back and then quickly looked around, seemingly to see if anyone else were present.

"They've gone to bed," Mickey said.

Tom nodded, and they both started to speak several times, but stopped to let the other continue. Mickey was amazed to see that they did, in fact, look quite similar.

"You go ahead," said Mickey, smiling, "I didn't mean to interrupt."

Tom returned a circumspect smile, backed up a few steps and sat on the corner of the piano bench.

He raised his eyebrows and laughed, "Well, you're much too polite to be a burglar."

"No, I'm not a burglar," Mickey smiled.

Tom lost his carefree look, squinted and shook his head.

What else could it be? He's reading the paper after they've gone to bed. They wouldn't let a stranger sit in their home. I certainly don't know him...but he looks like me.

He spoke quietly, almost as though he were channeling the words in a trance. "You know, I've got about a thousand things going through my head right now, and the only one that's making sense is the most bizarre of all."

"It's probably right, then" Mickey assured him.

"But...Irish?" Tom asked, apparently referring to Mickey's accent.

Mickey nodded. "For the last nineteen years."

"Oh, Jesus!" Tom said, his voice trembling. All he needed to hear was "nineteen years." He stood to hug Mickey and asked, "What happened?"

"Kidnapped," Mickey said, sniffling, as he hugged Tom. "God, I'm so sick o' cryin', I think I'll be made an honorary woman soon."

"Let me get us some Kleenex," Tom said, leaving the room momentarily.

When he returned, Mickey asked, "Anywhere around here we might go get a pint?"

"A *pint...?* Oh! A *pint*—a pint of beer, sure!" Tom answered, laughing, then blowing his nose. "Down one flight of stairs, our father—who art in bed—has enough beer and liquor to open a night club! Follow me!"

MONDAY, JUNE 25, 1990

Tom had been scheduled to work at midnight, but he called his employer, Everguard Security, and took the night off to be with his brother. Although Mickey found the two of them to be "different as night and day," he was fascinated with his brother's conversational talents and his knowledge of all things in general. And, without being asked, Tom, Jr. confirmed that he and Tom, Sr. were not exactly "pals."

"So you tolerate each other?" Mickey asked.

"That's an apt description—for the times we're in separate locations," Tom laughed.

At any rate, after a few stories, Mickey had him convinced that he was better off than if he had been the one sitting in their Girard Avenue front yard when the Monaghans turned that corner some years back.

Mickey asked Tom about his friends, about Nativity, about the neighborhood, when they moved from Girard, the old neighbors from Girard, whatever he could think of to find out what he might have missed.

As 2:00 a.m. approached, he tried to tell Tom about his relationship with Caitlin, that he'd be ringing her in a few minutes, and that he feared that he'd "almost certainly lost her to the boring chump she's been dating." Tom reached to a lower shelf, grabbed a phone, and placed it in front of Mickey.

They spent a few more minutes talking about the possibility of Tom's going with Mickey back to Ireland; and then Tom excused himself, wished him good luck with Caitlin and went upstairs.

*   *   *   *

Mickey looked at the phone. He closed his eyes, said a prayer, and placed the call.

She picked up the phone before the first ring ended.

"Mickey?" she asked quietly.

"Caitlin, what a surprise you're there," he tried to joke, but there was no joy in his voice.

"Mickey, I'm so sorry about last night. And about Marian."

"Thanks, but…what happened, Cait? Your mother said you were home, and then left."

"Yes…I'm sorry," she whispered.

"Are you goin' t' tell me?" he asked.

She paused and said, "It was Ray. He had asked me to marry him—he'd been askin' ever since you left—will you promise me you won't be upset if I tell you?"

Shit! I knew it! Shit-fuck-damnit! You moron! Out fucking anything and everything while the girl you love—and who once loved you—finally gives up!

"Well, I'm already upset," he answered impatiently, "so why don't you just tell me?"

"Mickey—*please*—promise me," she said, sounding like she might be crying.

"I'm sorry, Caity. I have no right to act this way," he said, yet again on the verge of tears of frustration himself. "I guess I'm supposed to be happy for you, or something."

After a momentary silence, Caitlin asked, "Happy for me? What in the world are *you* thinking?"

"Well…are you marryin' Ray?" he asked, hoping…

"Jesus God! No, Mickey! He grabbed my arm and wouldn't let me out of his effing damn car! He knew you were goin' to ring me, and he was pissed off that I wouldn't talk to him about marriage! And he drove off, like the bleedin' arsehole that he is, so that I couldn't be at the phone for you."

There was silence while Mickey considered what she had said. Then he spoke slowly, his ragged nerves now reassembling.

"First of all, Caitlin, is your arm all right?"

"Yes," she pouted, "but a little sore."

"All right…now—second—for the record," he continued deliberately, his voice now steadying, "if you want a man to *be* a man, you don't ask for promises like the one you just asked for. And third, third!" he said, yelling it the second time to stop Caitlin from interrupting him, "Clean up your bleeping language a little bit, and *fourth*," he said loudly, now speaking quickly as joy and relief electrically surged through him, "my parents are rich, and they want to thank you, and they are paying your airfare to come to America—to their party next Saturday night, and let's assume that you've already asked me if I'm serious, and I've already assured you that, yes, I am dead serious, as serious as I can possibly be, what is your answer, Caitlin O'Connor—will you be here?"

"Yes!!!" she screamed into the phone.

* * * *

Mickey told her quickly about the press conference, and he asked that she call Senator O'Malley's office to let them know. He reminded her that, with the Senator's help, she could get a passport within a few days, but she reminded him that she already had one—Ellen had taken her and Keran to Paris several years back when Keran was performing in a string quartet competition.

She told him that Byrne had tried to fire her, but that she suddenly remembered Mickey's suspicions, and threw them in Byrne's face.

"I'll tell you the whole story later, but I wanted to thank you for sharing your dark and cynical view of your fellow man with me," she laughed.

"I'll tell you what occurs to me, Cait. Remember—Higgins told me that Bill Sullivan had been cleared on that other rape?"

"Sure."

"Well, it never did make much sense to me—that he would try to rape somebody that he works with, somebody who *knows* him! Either Byrne told him, or he somehow must've been aware that Peggy was puttin' out, and—klunk that he was—maybe decided it was just a matter of queuing up, and then lost control when Peggy wouldn't go for it. Or—equally likely—he may've already been with her."

Although he spoke casually about Sullivan, knowing now that other factors might be involved—such as Peggy's known promiscuity—was increasingly weighing on his conscience. Sullivan and Marian. Both dead, and, to some degree, because of him.

"And then," she said, gleefully unaware of his concerns, "there's my holiday to America we can talk about!"

After a half hour, Ellen finally forced Caitlin off the phone, to get ready for work.

Mickey sat alone at the oak bar, smiling and relieved. He *still* hadn't told Caitlin how he felt about her, but he figured, *As enthusiastic as she is, I'll wait til she gets here. I'll do it right—not over the phone.*

*   *   *   *

The videographers were already breaking down their equipment, but the camera clicks and flashes continued as Tom escorted Meg and Mickey into his office and shut the door.

Mickey dropped into a chair. "Whew! I may tend toward exaggeration when I want to make a point, but I know for a fact that those people took more pictures of me than have ever been taken in all of my life! Wow! Nice office!"

"Thanks. Well, when you spend as much time as—"

Tom's door opened suddenly, and a striking young female reporter from one of the local television stations stuck her head in.

"I know I'm being nervy and obnoxious, but Michael—if I could just ask you a few more questions on camera—you're such a sweetheart, and I think we can make this city fall in love with you!"

Tom said, "Angie Adams from the late news!"

"Right, Mr. McCall!" she answered.

"May I see your left hand, Angie?" Mickey asked with a smile.

She lifted her hand from the doorknob, and Mickey grinned and said, "No rings. Obviously dedicated to her career, and I'd like to help her. Be right back."

Tom and Meg looked at each other after he closed the door.

Tom smiled. "I gotta say—I'm relieved to see it."

Meg shook her head back and forth, smiling in spite of herself. "You're so unfair, Tom. He's barely been with us for twenty-four hours! One *day!*"

"Now, now, Margaret—he's my son, and I love him! But his best friend is a *girl*, and she's not his *girl-friend!* And you *tried* to tell him that this little hottie Donna Miller thinks he's—"

"—Mueller," Meg corrected.

"Whatever. I mean, he couldn't say 'No!' fast enough when you brought up her name. And she's an absolute dish!"

"Maybe not *everybody's* dish, Tom. Give him a chance!"

"Yeah...I will. Damn, I just hate to think that *both* of them, Tom and Mickey—"

"Oh, stop it! Tom, Jr. is just *shy*—"

"...and if Mickey *did* have a girlfriend, he damn well wouldn't be sending for this *Caitlin* broad! The *piano player!*"

"Hey!"

Tom laughed and said, "I apologize, Meggy my sweetheart, but what I'm saying is—I think she's maybe an actual musician-type...you know, actually plays?"

Meg leaned toward Tom as they both laughed, and said quietly, "Do you *ever* want to get laid again, buster?"

Meg told him how much Caitlin's ticket cost, and Tom bit down on an index finger. "Ouch!" he said, having deliberately forgotten that Mickey was *borrowing* the airfare. "Well, cheaper than college! Seriously, I have no complaints, and, hey, maybe she can bang out a little Mozart at the party."

"Right! A little Mozart, and maybe she can show me how to play the piano?" Meg asked, tongue in cheek.

"*There* you go!" said Tom, slapping his hand on his desk, "now you're talking *bargain* for that ticket!"

Mickey stepped back into his dad's office as Angie Adams handed him a business card, saying, "Call me if you change your mind about that drink, Michael."

"Sure I will," Mickey said as he closed the door and resumed his seat next to Meg.

Tom looked quickly at Meg, then at Mickey. "Did I hear that right? She asked you out for a drink?"

"Yeah, she did—hey! Did Mom tell you we got Caitlin's ticket?"

"Uh, yes! Yes, she did, and we're looking forward to that—to meeting her," Tom assured him. He wanted to ask why he didn't accept Angie's invitation, but he wasn't quite sure he wanted to know the answer.

The door flew open again, and a man—about Tom's age—stuck his head in and said, "Busy?"

"Workin' like a Jew in hell, Stanley!" Tom smiled.

"Don't start, McCall!" he laughed as he entered the office. "Hello, beautiful!" he said, kissing Meg on the cheek.

"Hi, there, handsome!" she answered, kissing him back.

"Stan Roth, Mickey," he said, extending a hand, "I taught your dad everything he knows about the practice of law, and don't let him tell you different! We'll see each other Saturday evening, but I wanted to tell you—great job fielding questions at the press conference! And I think," he continued in a loud whisper, "I overheard that little TV chick saying she wants to take you home with her! Anyway! Just a few minor H-bombs exploding on that *Smith* case, Tommy—the doc's urinating backwards on us about testifying."

"Fu—!" Tom stopped himself, cleared his throat, and said, "the *heck* with him. I know *ten* doctors that would testify, and I need to talk to you about that. *Later.*"

Stan excused himself, and Tom shook his head with a wry smile. "Guy's been so helpful that he's starting to get on my nerves...right, *beautiful?* Well! I'd like to get back to work, so I can be home for a family dinner!"

"Oh, my," said Meg as she stood, "I don't know if I can handle two miracles in two days! Let's go, Mickey."

"Whoa! Wait just one minute!" said Tom, jumping to his feet and patting his suit pockets until he heard the crinkle of paper. He reached in and pulled out an envelope. "Take this with you, Mick. One of the reporters asked me to give it to you. Don't know what it is."

Mickey accepted the envelope and gave his dad a suspicious smile.

"Go! I'm busy!" Tom insisted.

Once into the hallway, Mickey stopped to open the envelope. In it was a check payable to Michael P. McCall in the sum of One Thousand and no/100 Dollars, from the Grand Scoop Hotline.

FRIDAY, JUNE 29, 1990

Mickey spent the rest of the week with the Cincinnati Police Division and the FBI; talking to reporters; telling his story and listening to miscellaneous relatives and family acquaintances as they related their remembrances of the pre-kidnap days; visiting local nightspots with Tom, Jr. and his friends on Tom's night off, even reluctantly signing a few autographs for people who recognized him from local newscasts and newspaper photos.

On Wednesday and Thursday, he got a taste of the hectic life of a trial lawyer, following his dad from courtroom to courtroom in the mornings, attending a variety of pre-trials, pleas, and conferences. He then watched two afternoon sessions while his dad successfully tried a Receiving Stolen Property case in the Common Pleas courtroom of the Honorable Keith Humphrey, a Cincinnati blueblood and longtime family friend of the McCalls.

Although Judge Humphrey was twelve years younger than Tom and a well-known playboy, their fathers had become acquainted, then close friends, through Midwest Federal Bank; so young Keith Humphrey had always known and looked up to Tom, who in turn had helped him along the way through law school and given generously to his judicial campaigns. Tom assured Mickey (with a wink) that all of that had nothing to do with Judge Humphrey's verdict of acquittal on this occasion.

Once back at the office, Tom sifted through messages and correspondence, returning only the most critical calls and delegating the rest.

He took Mickey to a Reds' game, and they watched a movie in the home theatre room, and—to Mickey's great delight—they picked up a quarter-barrel of Guinness Extra Stout for the party.

Mickey also turned down another invitation from Angie Adams to come out and "meet some interesting people"; but more than anything, he counted the hours until 7:30 a.m. Friday, when Caitlin's flight was due to arrive at Northern Kentucky-Greater Cincinnati International Airport.

*   *   *   *

He and Meg left Grand Valley Road an hour-and-a-half early and cruised through light traffic, parking the Cadillac at the airport shortly after 6:30 a.m. Mickey nervously chattered on and on about one thing or another, but almost always with reference to Caitlin. Caitlin this, Caitlin that. Once out of the car, it was a fifteen-minute walk and rail ride to the gate, and at one point—certain that

Mickey would be happier if he could run all the way—Meg offered to let him go ahead, assuring him she'd catch up. He apologized and promised to slow down.

Meg thought to herself, *My God! It is odd, incredibly peculiar really, that he's so excited and so obsessed with this Caitlin—when she's just a friend, even if she is his best friend!* She considered Tom's laments, and she was now closer to agreeing with what he'd said: "I don't want to think it's true, but...Donna Mueller the hot blonde? Strike one! Angie Adams the stunning brunette? Strike two! Turning Angie down a second time? Strike two-point-nine!"

As they sat down in the waiting area, Mickey anxiously pointed out the door-way where the passengers would enter the terminal from the plane, the same one that he had come through the previous Saturday evening.

"She'll be walkin' right through there in less than an hour now!" he said with some anticipation.

Meg nodded and said, "Describe Caitlin for me so I know what to look for."

Mickey continued to stare at the vacant doorway and spoke softly as he shrugged a little. "Red hair...and, well, just look for the most beautiful girl you could imagine...and when y' see one more beautiful yet," he said, turning to Meg with a smile, "that'll be Caitlin." He turned back to the doorway.

Meg shut her eyes and shook her head. *My God!* Suddenly, it all made sense. She no longer had any doubt about why he ignored Donna and Angie. And Tom was wrong. Definitely wrong.

She put her hand on Mickey's shoulder and said, "Look me in the eye, young man, and tell me: you're in *love* with this Caitlin—aren't you, Mickey?"

He looked away as his face lit up with an embarrassed smile.

"Why on earth didn't you *tell* us?" she pleaded.

He continued his red-faced grin for a moment, waved his head around, and said, "Because...well...because I haven't told her yet. But I'm telling her tonight. For sure!"

Meg rocked in her chair as she laughed out loud. "Oh, Mickey, Mickey, do you have any idea how worried your father is about you?!"

"Worried?"

"He thinks you don't like girls," she wailed, "because you blew off Donna and Angie!"

*   *   *   *

While Caitlin and Mickey stood waiting at the luggage carousel, Meg stepped outside to call Tom on her cellular phone.

"She seems like a nice person, Tom, but she does look sort of like a *boy*. Oh, maybe it's just me…"

"Yeah…well, probably not," he sighed.

"And she looks very *strong*, you know, hmm, I wouldn't quite say *burly*, but I'm sure that her piano playing will be…uh, *athletic*, if nothing else."

"Mm-hmm. Are there plans?" he asked, ignoring the fact that he had suggested them.

"Dinner at The River House at 6:30. In the meantime, I'll take her out and see if I can get her some girl's clothing and a little makeup."

"Oh—yeah…well…okay, I'll be home at six," he said with an obvious disappointment. Then he heaved a breath and said, "Hey, listen to me whine, will you? We owe this girl the world and everything in it, and I don't care if she looks like Pete Rose—I'm gonna give her a great big kiss when I see her!"

Meg smiled as she turned the phone off. *Lord, I better make sure Mickey's with him, in case he faints again!*

"Would you look at this, Mom?" Mickey called out, as he and Caitlin came through the oversized revolving doors to join her. "See what she brought me?" he said, lifting a guitar case in front of him.

After getting a promise from Mickey and Caitlin that they'd sing and play at the party the next night, they all had a laugh as Meg related the details of her phone call to Tom.

"So please don't slap the poor old man if he gives you a great big kiss, Caitlin."

Caitlin was duly impressed with Meg's Cadillac, and Mickey assured her this was just the beginning. He said, "And wait'll we get out on the dual carriageway, Cait—this first sight of Cincinnati is just incredible!"

They all agreed that, once Caitlin had been given the grand tour of the residence and put her things away in Meg's "home office," she'd try to get a few hours' rest. She had been too wound up to sleep during the flight.

Meg insisted that she and Caitlin would then go out to the mall for a little "girl fun," to do some shopping and get to know each other. What she understandably *actually* wanted, though, was a little history on her son.

*   *   *   *

As the Cadillac cruised through the big bend on northbound I-75—called "the cut in the hill" by the traffic 'copter reporters—Caitlin was jubilant at the sight of Cincinnati's skyline nestled in the Ohio River valley below. She listened excitedly as Meg talked of the symphony, theater, and ballet, and was even more elated to see the manifest wealth of the McCalls' home.

Like Mickey, she had never experienced anything quite like it. And though he would speak to her privately, referring to miscellaneous furnishings and appurtenances as "such needless overindulgence," she loved it all.

When they finally reached the Baldwin grand, at Meg's invitation, Caitlin sat and played Beethoven's "Sonata No. 8, Pathetique." Meg was as thrilled to hear her piano played so well as Caitlin was to play it.

After helping Caitlin unpack, Meg pulled the shades and curtain, and then turned down the bed for her. Caitlin sat smiling on the side of the bed.

"There's no point in me lyin' down. I'm wide awake!"

And so…it was *off to the mall*, with Mickey pleased to stay behind and mow the lawn.

*   *   *   *

"Then it's not back to the dual carriageway to get to the mall?" Caitlin asked, as she saw Meg turn the other direction from the house.

"I *love* that!" Meg laughed. "*Dual carriageway*—we just say 'expressway,' but no, it's just as easy to drive out through the neighborhoods."

After a brief moment of quiet, Meg said, "That's the last question you get, by the way. From now on, I'll ask and you answer!"

"Oh, boy!" laughed Caitlin. "Well, go ahead, and I'll do my best!"

After now having met Caitlin, she was a little concerned—for Mickey's sake—that such a beauty might have so many options that even the advances of her handsome son might not interest her.

Gee—maybe Mickey has always known somehow that a "friendship" with Caitlin was all that she'd make available to him. And if Mickey tells her he loves her tonight, it could ruin her whole trip! Oh, well! Not for me to worry about!

In response to Meg's questions, Caitlin told her about her first day of school—the day Mickey had rescued her; that they had been close ever since; that Mickey—especially in recent years—had done the work around their home that "only a man should do."

She carefully avoided talk of his "bedhopping" and any mention of the Bill Sullivan incident, reasoning that Mickey would tell his parents whatever he wanted them to know about such things.

As they walked from the car to the mall interior walkway, Caitlin continued, "He was the big brother I never had and maybe even a daddy sometimes, showing us how to do things, but..." she sighed a little as her voice trailed off.

"But...what?" Meg asked cautiously.

"Well...don't let this scare you, Mrs. McCall, because *he certainly* knows it—but I wish he'd quit thinkin' of me as his little sister, and spice things up a bit!" she giggled a little.

"Oh, my gosh!" said Meg, now relieved to hear of Caitlin's interest, but confused again about Mickey. "You say he *knows that?* Are you sure?"

Caitlin laughed, "Well, he'd better! I've been telling him since I was six years old!"

"I gather that he's a little...*backward*, maybe, where girls are concerned?"

"Backward?" Caitlin asked. "Not unless that word means something else here in America."

"Well, *shy*...I mean, he seems shy around girls. He's had invitations from two lovely girls while he's been here, but he won't have a thing to do with them."

"*That's* interesting!" Caitlin concurred.

"And then, I know he likes *you*, I mean *I* think he's *crazy* about you—and I guess he's never asked you out? Oh, hell! I'll just ask—is he gay, Caitlin?"

"Gay?!" she yelled loud enough that other shoppers looked over at her, amused. When she stopped laughing, she quietly said to Meg, "Let's make a deal. If you'll tell me why you think he's crazy about me, I'll definitely put your mind at ease about whether he's gay!"

"Deal!" Meg agreed, holding out a hand to shake. "You first!"

They sat on a mall bench.

Now almost whispering, Caitlin said, "I'll leave the details up to your son, if he wants to give 'em, but I'll tell you this—if it weren't for modern birth control methods, you and Mr. McCall would probably be sendin' birthday cards to thirty or forty Irish grandchildren by now!"

Meg said nothing, just stared back at Caitlin. Finally, she asked, "He's that bad?"

Caitlin nodded solemnly.

"That's horrible, Caitlin."

"Yes," Caitlin agreed. "Our parish priest speaks to him about it."

Meg slowly nodded understanding, and as a smile appeared, she said, "His father will be *thrilled!*" They laughed.

"Your turn," Caitlin reminded.

Meg didn't want to break confidence with Mickey, but she couldn't resist giving Caitlin something to think about. Putting on her best Irish accent, she repeated what Mickey said when she asked him to describe Caitlin.

"He said that about me?!" Caitlin exclaimed with her eyes opening wide.

"Oh, for heaven's sake, Caitlin," Meg assured her, "you're all he ever talks about!"

*   *   *   *

When they returned at about 4:45, Meg had spent almost two thousand dollars on clothing and accessories for Caitlin. Caitlin was mildly shocked, but profusely grateful. As Mickey had expected, Meg absolutely loved her; and she was excited for Mickey, now knowing that Caitlin had such an ongoing love for him.

Mickey had already showered, and he was dressed for dinner, losing nine-ball games to his brother in the basement, when the ladies came in through the garage. After a quick but convivial introduction to Tom Jr., Caitlin followed Meg up the stairs to get ready.

At a few minutes before six, Meg asked Mickey to carry some things out of the trunk of her car and up to Caitlin's room—the purchases that she hadn't needed for tonight. As he unloaded the trunk, Tom, Sr. pulled into the garage. He appeared relaxed but a little weary as he exited his BMW.

After exchanging greetings with Mickey, he stood quietly for a moment, then said, "What a week. You know, Mick, I was thinking, the River House...what with the wait we'll have for a table—probably an hour—why don't we just go someplace a little quiet? There's a decent little steakhouse called The Chef's Hideout not too far from here...then your old dad could get to bed a little early, and be in shape to help out tomorrow."

"You're the boss, Dad," answered Mickey, "but c'mon, I want you to meet Caitlin. I think she's up there playin' the Baldwin."

Tom nodded, then followed dutifully behind.

Caitlin's long beautiful hair and trim waist were immediately noticeable as Mickey and Tom came into the living room, approaching the piano as she played "The Moonlight Sonata."

"Caity, I'd like you to meet my father, Tom McCall. Caitlin O'Connor, Dad."

Tom started to welcome Caitlin as she stood, but he stopped speaking as she turned around.

"So pleased to meet you, sir," Caitlin smiled.

Tom nodded as he stared back at her for the moment, straightening his glasses.

"Where's your mother?" he asked, with his gaze fixed on Caitlin's smile.

"She's in Ireland, in County Mayo," Caitlin answered, still smiling.

Tom took a step back, never taking his eyes off Caitlin. He smiled and said, "Oh…not you. *Him.* Where's your mother, Mickey?" He was still looking at Caitlin.

"She's downstairs at the bar," he answered, quietly amused.

"Will you tell her I'd like to see her in our room?" he asked, now on the verge of laughing as he looked up and down at Caitlin.

"I would, Dad, but she's already told me that if you asked to see her back in your room, I should tell you she'll be waiting in the basement—for you to come and fix a pitcher of martinis," he answered.

"Well!" Tom exclaimed, holding out his arms, "Welcome to our home, Caitlin!"

"Thank you so much, Mr. McCall!" she replied as they hugged briefly. "It's a beautiful home!"

"Yes! Beautiful!" he said, staring intently at her, then looking nervously back and forth at the two. "Give us just a minute, and we'll be right out with those martinis!"

As he hurried down the hall, Caitlin smiled at Mickey, then called out, "Mrs. McCall said I was goin' t' get a great big kiss!"

He turned as he walked, saying, "That was before…never mind. I'll be down in a minute."

*   *   *   *

Meg met Tom as he came trotting down the stairs.

"Thought you might like to know that your son told me he's in love with Caitlin, although he hasn't told her yet," she said. "Think that's worth a little toast?" Meg asked, sure that Tom would relish the news.

"I guess I'll have to fight him for her," Tom said, "because I love her, too!"

"Hey, McCall!" Meg protested.

"Sorry! Devil made me say that," he laughed.

"Well, here's the other thing...apparently, according to Caitlin, you and I have unwittingly produced the Warren Beatty of County Mayo, and there's barely a virgin around because of it!"

"No!"

"Yes! Well...maybe that's a stretch, but you get the idea."

"C'mon," Tom said as he finished stirring the pitcher, "we'd better get out there before our boy hurts that beautiful child!"

As he and Meg joined Mickey and Caitlin at the umbrella table on the patio, Tom smiled and said, "So the joke's on Dad, huh?" Everyone laughed.

"I want to make a toast," Tom stated as he raised his glass. "And Caitlin, if these words are inadequate—which they *will* be—please know that if I said all that was in my heart, Meg and I would have to go straight to bed and cry our eyes out for the rest of the evening."

Caitlin reached for Mickey's hand.

He stopped to take a breath and make himself smile, and then continued, "Mickey told us the story, but I swear I still don't understand how you did it. Anyway! To Caitlin—who has blessed us..." He stopped, choked up.

He looked at the three and said, "See? I can't do it—okay, it was a miracle, Caitlin, an honest-to-God miracle, and you did it. God bless you! You gave us our son back, and we love you!" Tom leaned to kiss Caitlin on the cheek. "There! Down the hatch!"

Mickey took a sip and exclaimed, "Jay-sus, Pop! Did y' mean to rub this on your achin' back? What's in this...*martini*?!"

"Oooh! I think it's tasty!" said Caitlin.

"Gin and vermouth! But, hey, these are shorties. You don't want to enjoy too much of this stuff and then go driving ten miles to The River House."

"Mickey said you wanted to go to The Chef's Hideout," Meg said, eyeing her husband.

"I'd *never* take Caitlin to a dump like that!" he immediately scoffed, then continued as he stood, "You'll love The River House, Caitlin," he said, offering his arm. "Incredible menu, incredible view."

As Tom escorted her arm-in-arm to the Cadillac, Caitlin grinned back at Mickey and Meg, then asked, "So, tell me, Mr. McCall, who is Pete Rose?"

*　　*　　*　　*

On the way to the restaurant, Caitlin delighted Meg and Tom as she regaled them with stories about Mickey in Ireland. Knowing Mickey's dad would want to hear it, she repeated the story of his son's bravery on her first day of school, then went on to explain how she would often go chasing after him at the end of the school day, to find him so she could teach him a new song as he walked her home.

Once at The River House, Tom found a table for four overlooking the river in the second-floor bar, and then it was only a few minutes before the animated foursome attracted their first visitors, two girls in their early teens.

"We think you're the one we've seen on TV. Are you?"

"Indeed, 'tis I," Mickey said in his best Irish brogue, then pointing to Caitlin, continued, "but the oul' missus here'll fetch me a belt in the gob, she will, if she catches me sparkin' with the likes o' you two, so pretty y' are!"

Caitlin laughed loudly and said, "Be careful, now, this one'll tell y' nothin' but lies!"

The girls stared for a moment, when one said, "Good luck!" and dragged the other one away.

Three beers and Caitlin's second martini were then delivered to the table, as Meg said, "Mickey, if those girls didn't have the slightest idea what you said, that makes three of us!"

"Well, it's not important," he laughed, "but it's lovely that someone gave poor Caity a chance to rest her jaw, don't you think?"

"They love my stories!" Caitlin proclaimed, with Meg and Tom agreeing completely, "And I've got a thousand more!" she laughed, as she tried to tickle him.

A man in his late thirties stood by their table and said to Mickey, "I hate to bother you, but my two daughters who were just over here asked if I could get you to sign this napkin for them."

"Sure I will," Mickey said, taking his pen and the napkin, "those are nice little ladies."

As the man thanked him, two older women approached the table, stepped up and proceeded to tell him that they remembered the news accounts of his kidnapping "like it was yesterday," and how "incredibly thrilled" they were to have seen and read the stories of the happy ending.

Behind them, a tearful woman, maybe 30, stood with her husband, waiting to tell Mickey that his story had "filled them with such hope," because they had a "very, very close friend" whose child had been kidnapped some years ago, but never found.

As the couple turned to leave, Tom rolled his eyes and leaned forward to whisper, "Their *very, very close friend* is probably a classmate of their second cousin in North Dakota or some such thing. People just love to be a part of it all!"

By then, a short line had formed behind the couple, and a few others stood and walked to the table to see what the fuss was about. Tom excused himself, found the second-floor headwaiter, and arranged to be moved to a private room, where Caitlin was able to resume with her tales of County Mayo.

As they walked back to the car after dinner, Mickey suggested that he and Caitlin should take a walk around the neighborhood when they got home, and she agreed. He would then—finally!—as he had longed to do, tell Caitlin that he had fallen in love with her. Meg turned to glance briefly at Mickey, smiling. She was happy for him.

But once in the back seat, Caitlin asked, "Do you mind if I borrow your big celebrity shoulder for just a moment?" A transatlantic flight with no sleep, a day of shopping, a full meal and her first two martinis—all of it kicked in as she rested her head, and she was out for the night. Once home, Mickey carried her to her room, put a blanket over her and turned out the light.

SATURDAY, JUNE 30, 1990

Meg had wisely kept all of the food inside on the enclosed back porch, fearing the "remote possibility that the weatherman might actually be right this time" about the occasional thunderstorms he had predicted on the 5:00 p.m. news. It was now almost 8:45 p.m., and the wind gusts were picking up, with black clouds and lightning coming in from the west.

A few of Tom's clients, some relatives, and most of the lawyers from his law firm, with their significant others, were on the patio with Tom, Meg and Mickey. Judge Humphrey had stopped briefly, but excused himself after a few quick Manhattans.

Meg urged Tom to escort their poolside guests into the house, and told him that she and Mickey would collect the patio chairs and put them in the garage. Caitlin had taken a nap, and she was still applying her makeup, not quite ready.

As Mickey folded the chairs, he said, "Mom, this rain'll be nice for me and Caitlin, you know. We don't get to see it much over there in Ireland."

Meg nodded as she walked by him with a chair under each arm. She suddenly stopped and turned smiling to say, "Your sense of humor takes a little getting used to, Mick."

"Glad you caught that, dear!" he smiled back.

Dorothy and Donna walked down the driveway with several trays of hors d'oeuvres in aluminum wrap. Donna was a shade tanner, and her hair a shade blonder, than on the previous Sunday.

While Meg admonished them for bothering with food, Donna walked up to Mickey, kissed him on the cheek, and said sweetly, "Good to see you're alive, stranger. I've been wondering if I should go up to the schoolyard, and see if you'd show up to chase after me," she smiled, referring to his earlier quip.

Mickey returned her smile, but he wished he hadn't said that.

"Let me help you," he said, taking the tray from Donna, then another from Dorothy. "Go on inside now, before this rain hits."

Tom, Jr. and his friends—Eddie Bonavita, Dave Anderson and his fiancée Beth Murray, and recently married Joe and Nancy Maschek—were already in the living room chatting. Eddie, Joe and Dave were Tom's closest friends, all of whom he had met at X High, all class of '84. Joe continued on to XU with Tom, and Dave attended and graduated from Holy Cross in Massachusetts.

Nancy had just mentioned to Tom that she had recently seen a book of Van Gogh's paintings, and "…for the life of me, I can't figure out what's so great about him! Your stuff is much better, Tom."

Tom, sometimes a lecturer by nature, began to set the stage: "Whether you're speaking of Van Gogh, Augustine of Hippo, or Elvis Presley, in order to appreciate a given individual's impact and contribution, you must first understand the state of the civilization in which that individual lived." And, unfortunately for Nancy, it was Tom's present intent to help her achieve that understanding.

Eddie, a now-single parent whose wife had disappeared three months after the birth of "Little Eddie," had started at XU with Joe and Tom, but had to drop out his freshman year to get a job in anticipation of the birth of his child. *And* to quickly and unceremoniously marry the young lady he had fertilized on the occasion of their first meeting, when they were both drunk, at a Hamilton County Young Republicans outing to the Cincinnati Reds Opening Day baseball game.

Everyone agreed that Little Eddie was precocious, but Dave Anderson had qualified his agreement by saying, "If 'precocious' means 'spoiled rotten little loudmouth sonofabitch from hell,' then yeah, he's precocious." At any rate, as a result of a last-minute babysitter cancellation, five-year-old Little Eddie was along with his dad this evening.

Donna Mueller followed her mother out of the kitchen and into the living room. Eyeing her, Eddie immediately scrunched himself down on the sofa between Tom, Jr. and Nancy Maschek.

"So, Tom! Got a name for that California girl over there?"

Nancy immediately took the opportunity to quietly excuse herself to refresh her drink.

Tom studied Donna for a moment, smiled and said, "My guess would be 'Misty,' but I can't say that I've ever seen her before…sorry!"

Eddie shook his head as he stood, then leaned back to Tom and whispered, "What kind of a useless, lame-ass co-host are you, anyway? I guess this is all up to me."

He walked over and introduced himself to Donna and Dorothy, then asked them to join him with Tom, Jr. and the others. Dorothy said, "You go ahead, honey, I'm going back outside to see if I can help Meg."

After placing Dorothy and Donna's trays on the back porch table with the rest of the food, Mickey came through the kitchen and into the living room. He heard Caitlin call his name, and he looked to see her walking down the hall toward him. She handed him an empty martini glass, smiled and said, "Guess I'm ready to party!"

She wore one of the two designer dresses that Meg had bought her, orange on top with a white sash and a full-length lime-green slit skirt. And he knew beyond question that this was the most beautiful girl he had ever seen.

"Will you stay with me and introduce me to people, Mickey?" she asked anxiously.

"I'll do whatever you want," he answered, but she was too nervous to notice that he was thoroughly entranced.

Mickey called out loudly, "Pardon me, everyone! Hello! Listen please! I want to introduce you all to my dear friend, Caitlin...Caitlin O'Connor from back home in Ireland. She has been my dear friend for the last thirteen years, and she's ninety-nine percent of the reason I was able to find my way back here! So please feel free to introduce yourselves!"

Doing his best Gomer Pyle imitation, Dave Anderson quietly exclaimed "Shazam!" Beth Murray promptly gave him an elbow to the ribs.

Donna Mueller stared across the room at Caitlin and Mickey for a moment, then leaned toward Beth and whispered, "How well do you have to know a red-head before you really, really hate her?"

Beth whispered back, "I'd say if you're in the same room with her, *that* qualifies!"

Mickey escorted Caitlin through the crowded room, making introductions, until they made their way to Tom, Jr. and his friends on the other side.

*   *   *   *

Eddie asked, "Caitlin, you got any sisters back there in Ireland?"

Caitlin, buoyed by Meg's assurances that Mickey is "crazy about" her, decided to flirt a bit and said, "Yes, I have a sister, but why?"

"Well, you know...I need a date!"

"Whyever would you want my sister in Ireland, then? I'm just a house guest here, and I don't have a date, do I, Mickey...my *dear friend?*"

"Well, Caitlin, yes, I think you are *my* date this evening," he said, both mildly perturbed and amused at her.

"Oh, I don't know, Mickey," she said, moving away from him with feigned concern, "I don't think my mother would allow me to have a date with you!"

As everyone laughed, she continued, "Oh, it's true, you know," speaking as though she were telling a secret, but at this point, practically everyone had turned to listen to the amusing colloquy with this dazzling Irish goddess.

"He's rather well known as a rounder and a bad, bad boy in County Mayo, makin' so many o' the young girls cry, himself with quite a trail o' broken hearts behind 'im!"

"Certainly no more extensive than your own, Miss O'Connor!" he rejoined.

She hesitated just a second, then laughed and said, "The difference bein', Mickey, that I don't screw 'em first!"

People smiled at her comment, perhaps taken aback somewhat by the remark until Mickey put his hand on his chest and said, "And therein lies the cause o' their broken hearts!"

As everyone laughed, Meg said, "Hey, I want to hear a song! You promised me you'd do the one you sang at your graduation, when Caitlin played piano."

"It's rather a long and mournful song, Mother—"

"No! You promised!" she said.

"I don't even think you'd like that one," he tried to protest, quite sincerely thinking that the words of the song, which reflect with fondness and melancholy on the place where the singer grew up, might sting a bit, with him singing to the parents who had missed virtually all of his childhood. He wasn't opposed to singing, just to singing *that* song.

"C'mon, Mickey," Caitlin said as she walked to the piano. "'The Village of My Heart,' key of F."

"Well, okay," said Mickey, thinking *it's just a song,* and then adding as he watched her sway by him, "Pumpkin."

Tom, Jr. stood by Caitlin at the piano and said, "Oh, he calls you *Pumpkin?*"

"No, he does not!" Caitlin giggled. "I suspect he said that because I'm wearing orange."

"And because you're round," Mickey smiled.

Caitlin blushed, "Oh, hush! As if you've *ever* noticed if I'm round or square or what I am!"

In truth, that comment *and* his claim that they were on a date, on top of all that Meg had told her, had Caitlin believing she was about to snare her man! *Welcome to the United States of America!* she thought to herself.

Caitlin played and Mickey sang.

In fond, unfaded memory
It's Mayo's rolling hills I see

Its emerald fields where blackbirds fly
'Neath rainbows crossing endless sky
And down the lane, around the bend
The shops, the pubs, and all my friends
Are there, and though we're long apart
Sure it's still the village of my heart

Mickey wasn't wrong. Meg was sniffling and tearing up by the third line, and said, "Oh, Tom! We were robbed of so much!"

At one point in the song, as Mickey sang, *"And there with me, close beside, The girl who might have been my bride,"* he touched Caitlin's shoulder on the word "bride," and although she thought, *Ah! More proof!*—she whispered to Mickey with a smile, "Don't use me as your stage prop, bub!" She was on top of the world.

There was robust applause following the song, along with compliments and questions about whether the two intended to pursue a career in music, to which Mickey replied that he didn't think that would be realistic.

Then came a flurry a questions, the group's curiosity piqued.

What career plans do you have, Mick?

"Well, I was intending to go into business, maybe real estate, and then I hoped to go into politics some day."

You mean politics here in the U.S.?

"No, no. I don't know what your issues are here. I meant in Ireland."

Are you going back to Ireland or staying here?

"Well, I really need to talk to someone about that before deciding. I just don't know," he answered, being cordial but a little dishonest. He needed to share his intentions with his parents first, but he had already envisioned them coming to Ireland in a month or two—for a wedding.

Meg jumped in, "Mickey! I can't believe you'd leave your mother again after I just found you. You wouldn't do that, would you?"

"Well, I haven't—"

"I'm thinking we might get his credits transferred and get him into law school here!" said Tom. "You could walk right into my practice, and let me ease into retirement! You can make as much money as you're willing to work for practicing law!"

Fred Middleberg said, "He said he wanted to go into real estate, Tom. You come to work in my real estate office, Mickey, I'll have you making a million dollars in no time!"

"Whatever you do, this is still the land of opportunity, Mickey!" said Stan Roth.

"What about citizenship, immigration and all that?" asked Donna Mueller.

"Oh, no problem," said Tom, "of course, he's a U.S. citizen, he was born right here in Cincinnati, Ohio!"

Meg moved in front of her son and wagged a finger at him, saying, "You can be a shoestring peddler or president of General Motors, I don't care, you just *can't* leave your mother and go back to Ireland again!"

Tom, Jr. observed, "I think he'd have to move to Michigan to take over General Motors, Mom."

$$* \quad * \quad * \quad *$$

Caitlin now slipped behind the gathering, to a large bay picture window, where she turned away to look out at the lightning and the thundering downpour.

"Hey, how about another Irish song?" Dave Anderson said.

"How 'bout an Irish stout? C'mon out to the Guinness barrel," Mickey said, and he left the room.

Eddie Bonavita, who had played in a high school rock band, sat at the piano and played "The Rockin' Pneumonia and the Boogie Woogie Flu." Little Eddie was trying to make it a duet until Donna Mueller mercifully pulled him away and picked him up.

Tom, Jr. asked Caitlin to play "Danny Boy," but as he looked at her, she was walking from the room. She appeared to be on the verge of tears. Tom watched as she walked down the hall to her room and closed the door behind her.

Eddie said he knew "Danny Boy" and started to play.

Mickey stood at the Guinness barrel on the back porch with Dave Anderson and Beth Murray. They were amusing each other, trading beer insults, with Dave—a Bud Light drinker—telling Mickey that, "…here in the U.S., we use Guinness mostly to patch cracks in the roads," and Mickey telling Dave that Bud Light looks like beer, all right, but beer that's already been drunk once.

Tom, Jr. stepped out on the porch and motioned for Mickey to come to him.

"Like a Guinness, Tom?"

"No, c'mere a minute."

They stepped away from the others, and Tom said, "Something's troubling Caitlin. She went to her room looking like she was ready to start bawling. Crying."

"Why?" Mickey asked.

"Dunno. She just walked down the hall and shut the door."

*   *   *   *

Mickey knocked, then opened the door to see Caitlin sitting on the side of the bed crying, her face buried in her hands. He ran to her and knelt beside the bed. He raised his hand to gently touch her hair, quietly asking, "Caitlin? Caitlin! What's wrong, sweetheart?"

He had pushed the door shut, but it remained opened a few inches, allowing enough light in the room that he could see her face.

"Mickey, what have I done?" she sobbed. "I helped you find your family just so they could take you away from me forever!"

"Oh, Caity! That's not true!"

"It is true! Of course, it's true! Your mother will never let you leave, and everyone wants to make you a millionaire!" she cried. "I've lost you forever!"

"No, Caitlin, didn't you hear me say there's someone I need to talk to before I decide?"

"So what? You're an American citizen, and you'll never come home. I know it!"

"Caitlin, it's *you*," he whispered. "*You're* the one I have to talk to."

"That's ridiculous!" she said, still weeping inconsolably. "You *know* I would tell you to come home...home to Ire—" She stopped to look at him. He stared back at her and touched her cheek with his hand. She swallowed. "Unless...is there more to it, Mickey?" she asked with a frightened smile, "What you want to talk to me about?"

Mickey looked at her for a moment, with an expression that somehow told her not to worry, that—as always—he was there for her. He stood, offering his hand.

"Stand up, Cait," he whispered. The revelers were still singing "Danny Boy" at the piano.

She felt oddly comforted, standing, as he had told her to do. She felt a wave of trust that he would take care of her, that he would not disappoint her. Her heart ached for answers, but...*this is right*, she told herself, *I'll do as he says, and he won't let me down.* She was worried, all right, but she put her faith in him. Her guardian, her hero, her best friend.

"I want us to dance, Caity Lin," he said as he pulled her to him. They had never danced before, but she said nothing.

She fought off the notion that he was simply consoling her. *He wouldn't do that, would he?* Toy with her like that while she cried for him? She closed her eyes and gently rubbed her head against his chest as they moved slowly to the music.

Mickey was ready to tell Caitlin about kissing her in his dream, but she turned to look up at him with a small, worried smile. She draped an arm over his shoulder, nestled her head back on his chest and whispered, "I would tell you…that you're holding me awfully close, Mickey," then looking back up at him, she said, "but apparently you know that." She breathed deeply.

"Close to me, Caitlin," he answered softly, "…is where you belong. I lied to you when I asked you to come here because my parents wanted to meet you and thank you. They did, but I asked you to come…I *needed* you to come, because I had found this new world and what should have been all this happiness, and…it just didn't mean much…because you weren't here to share it with me. It's a feeling I've never known before…just like everything that you make me feel…Caitlin?"

"What, Mickey?" she asked, barely audible.

"I would be kidnapped a thousand times knowing someday I could hold you this close. When you first walked into the living room this evening…you were so beautiful…it actually seemed that you were glowing. I've never known a prouder moment in all my life."

He stood still. He put his hands on her shoulders, leaned back to look in her eyes and said, "Not like a brother…not like a sister."

She was right!

Her dream was coming true, and she pulled him close as she cried again.

He said, "You know this, I'm sure, but I'll tell you tonight, and I'll tell you every day for the rest of my life, if you let me: Caitlin Molly O'Connor, I love you—now and forever—I love you!"

She tried desperately to stop crying, and finally as she sniffled and gulped, then giggled through her tears, she said, "The reverse is true as well!"

"Sweetest words I've ever heard!" he said, and he stared through his own tears into her eyes.

"Is this really Mickey Monaghan finally sayin' he loves me after thirteen years?"

"No, Caitlin, my name is *McCall*," he said, gently cupping her chin in his hand so their lips were now just an inch apart, "and I'll be the happiest man in all the world when it's yours as well."

"I love you, Mickey!"

"No more talk," he whispered; and for the first time, their lips touched, softly at first, then with a furious passion that had been building for thirteen years.

✳   ✳   ✳   ✳

Little Eddie Bonavita snuck quietly down the hall to Caitlin's bedroom, peered through the slightly opened door and watched Mickey and Caitlin. He charged back to the living room and announced to one and all, "They were *lyin'* about just bein' friends!"

The crowd looked at Little Eddie, amused, as he crossed his arms in front of himself as if holding an invisible partner, smooching at the air with his eyes closed. They then looked back up to see Mickey and Caitlin walking arm-in-arm back into the room.

Their appearances had changed dramatically for the short time they had been absent—their hair mussed, their eyes red and faces blotchy from crying, Caitlin's lipstick gone and most of her makeup wiped on the front of Mickey's shirt—but both wore broad smiles.

"I believe we've reached an understanding," beamed Caitlin.

"Let me guess," said Tom, Jr., "that you *are*, in fact, on a date tonight?"

"Tonight, tomorrow, and ever after," said Mickey, smiling and giving Caitlin a one-armed hug.

"And we're stayin' in America!" Caitlin declared, then turning to Fred Middleberg, "and we'll take that million dollars!"

"*Ah, be Jay-sus!*" Mickey cried out with an exaggerated Irish brogue, "'Tis a Yank woman ye are already, makin' decisions without proper permission to do so!"

"Listen up, everybody!" called Tom, Sr. "Let us gather at the Guinness barrel...a toast is in order!"

SUNDAY, JULY 1, 1990

"G'night, Freddie! Don't go wrappin' that new Audi around a tree now!"

"Tom!"

"Well, Meggy, he's drunk as a fuckin' loon!" Tom whispered through his laughter.

The two couples, each arm-in-arm, stood at the door as the last guest left.

Mickey said, "Mother and Dad, thank you so much. I'm sure you understand that this has been the greatest night of my life!" he said, now smiling at his bride-to-be.

"And mine as well," said Caitlin, kissing Mickey's cheek.

Tom held his hands in front of himself, framing in Caitlin like a photographer. "And here's the good news, son! You got a *better one* coming up sometime soon!"

"Thomas Steven McCall!" Meg shouted in mock horror as they all laughed.

"Hey, it's *his* fault," Tom complained with a smile as he pointed at Mickey, "him and his damn *Guinness!*"

"Well, I'll tell you, Pop, that night better not be too far off, and I think Cait and I are goin' out walkin' for a bit to talk about such matters."

"Goin' t' take your *dear friend* out walkin', are you?" Caitlin asked, radiant.

"We're so happy for you and proud of you both!" Meg said, starting to get teary. "Now don't be too late. You need to get some sleep, especially you, Caitlin, after your long trip!"

"Oh! I don't think I'll be sleeping anytime in the next month or so. Thanks to your son, I'll be wide awake, pinching myself!"

"Well, if you do get tired, Caitlin, just tell Mickey," said Tom, "and I'm sure he'll be happy to take over the pinching!"

"All *right*, Thomas!" scolded Meg, "That's quite enough!" She looked at Caitlin and Mickey with a weak smile, and then laughed. "He really *did* have too much Guinness! This is not my normal, boring old Tom McCall! He's just happy!"

"No one could be as happy as I am!" Caitlin said, catching herself as she began to cry; she squeezed her arms around Mickey and said, "I'm sorry, but he's all I've ever wanted for the past thirteen years!"

"Jesus! Let's all make a pledge that we're finished with the crying!" Mickey said, pulling Caitlin out the front door. "See you in the morning!"

*   *   *   *

They listened to the crickets and grabbed fireflies out of the night air as they walked, staring and smiling at each other, amazed to find themselves finally in love.

"Guess it's a good thing I declared my intentions, or you might be off readin' a bedtime story to Little Eddie Bonavita at this very moment!" Mickey said.

"Jesus God!" Caitlin laughed, "What a terrifying thought!"

He stopped and leaned to kiss her. As they embraced, one car passed, then another, honking at the lovers.

"I think I miss our peaceful little Treanbeg Road," he said.

"Don't talk about Ireland, Mickey, I just got here!"

"Well, I need to get back there and beat the almighty hell out of whoever taught you to kiss like this," he said, kissing her again.

"Mickey, I know you might think I'm silly, but...you won't wake up tomorrow, and regret any of this, will you?"

"Caitlin, you *are* silly...beyond words! When I wake up tomorrow, I'll be head over heels in love with Caitlin Molly O'Connor! Why would you say such a thing?"

"Well...we're here in America...it's all so new, your parents have so much, and everything is so wonderful! I'm just afraid you might be intoxicated with your new happiness, and...well, maybe when things settle down, you won't feel the same!" she said with a worried look that indicated she was making entirely too much sense to herself.

Mickey stopped walking and gently touched her cheek. "Listen to me, Caity Lin, I look at you, and, yes, it's almost *surreal* after all our years together. But I promise you...there is *nothing* about America or anybody in America that could make me love you any more or any less!"

"But how do you *know?*" she good-naturedly whined as they resumed the walk.

"I know because I was helplessly in love with you before I ever left Ireland! I know because you're all I could think of once I got here—just as you were before I left—and I know because I know!"

"Well, now I'm really going to smack you! You loved me in Ireland? And you didn't tell me? *When* did you love me?" she pleaded.

He didn't answer. He just smiled as they walked.

"Do you know, Mickey?" she asked sweetly.

"When I think about it, I know that I've always loved you, Caity. Always, somewhere inside of me I've loved that spunky little six-year-old with the pigtails. But…the day Bill Sullivan died, when Eamonn came to your house to pick me up, you and I went inside briefly, and…from that moment, I've known. Our eyes met, Cait, and I knew that it was not a matter of choice for me. My heart was gone. In your pocket."

"You are in serious trouble, Mickey! Why didn't you tell me?" she demanded as her eyes filled with happy tears.

"Caity, no more crying! I don't know why I didn't, maybe because I didn't have the money for a ring. C'mon, now, let's pick a date for our wedding!"

She sniffled and said, "It's almost two o'clock, Mickey. Mother will be up, and I'm dying to call her. I'll tell her we're getting married tomorrow morning at Nativity Church!"

"Oh, of course," he laughed, certain that she was joking.

"And you better leave the room if you don't want cryin', because—"

"Caity, ask her to ring Father McDermott about a date."

"Oh, Mickey, can't we just get married here?"

"Here? That's impossible!"

"It's not at all!"

"Caity…your mother, and Keran! Eamonn, and our friends! And Father McDermott! They can't afford to come over here!"

"But…what about *your* parents, Mickey?" she offered halfheartedly.

"Oh, for God's sake, Cait, they can easily afford a trip to Ireland! And I really want them to see it, anyway…where we grew up!"

"Well, let's talk about it later."

"No, Cait, we're gettin' married in Ireland, and that's the last we'll discuss it!"

*   *   *   *

When Mickey walked into the kitchen the next morning, Caitlin was sitting alone at the table with a cup of tea and the newspaper. He sat across from her. Neither said a word. They looked at each other, beaming smiles that grew every second. Finally, Mickey stood to walk around the table. He leaned his face to hers, and, as she closed her eyes for his kiss, he said, "Hey, Caitlin, I didn't get mad drunk last night and ask you to marry me, did I?"

She started to respond, but he was kissing her before she could speak. "I love you, Caitlin O'Connor," he said after the kiss.

"I love you more!" she whispered with a smile.

"Not possible," he whispered back.

"Yes, Mickey, I love you more, and I've loved you longer!"

"Our first disagreement!" he said, kissing her again.

"God!" Tom, Sr. said, flipping the French doors open, "Tell me you two aren't making out at 8:30 in the damn morning!"

"That's an argument we're havin', Pop!" Mickey said.

"Jesus," he laughed, yawning as he loaded the coffeemaker, "help me remember to keep a barf bag with me for the happy times!"

"O-o-oh! Just listen to you!" Caitlin chimed in. "I saw you and Mrs. McCall nuzzling last night as things were winding down!"

Tom turned to Caitlin, frowned intently and said, "I'm throwing you out of here real soon if you keep calling us 'Mr. and Mrs. McCall.'"

"Cait and I will gladly take over those names for you, won't we, sweetie? Mrs. *Pumpkin* McCall!" Mickey said as Caitlin squealed out delight.

"I love it!" laughed Tom. "And did you children pick a date for your blessed event?"

"I guess *himself* has decided he's in charge of that," Caitlin said with a mock begrudging face.

"Honestly, Pop, that's pretty much up to you…how soon can you come to Ireland?"

Tom hesitated.

"Listen, Dad, I know you've got a crazy schedule, but we'll accommodate you! So just let us know by Tuesday," Mickey offered lightly, but he immediately realized that he'd have to explain further.

"Tuesday?" Tom asked before he could continue.

"Yeah," he said, "I guess this has never come up, but, uh, that's the day I—or *we*—go back. I've got that farm and all those sheep I need to…do something with."

"Right," said Tom quietly. "Yeah, that's never come up…does your mother— well, hey, we will work all of this out, for sure! I've got some ideas I'd like to share with you guys, and maybe the four of us can powwow later this evening?"

*   *   *   *

Tom and Meg skipped Mass to clean up, but trusted Mickey with the Cadillac so that he and Caitlin could attend. Tom, Jr. was waiting for them when they returned.

Joe and Nancy Maschek had invited Mickey and Caitlin to join Tom, Jr. and come to their forty-foot cabin cruiser on the Ohio River that Sunday afternoon. The boat was docked on the Kentucky side at the Constance Yacht Club, a coved marina about forty minutes from McCalls' residence in Pleasant Ridge.

On the way over, Tom explained that the boat was actually not Joe's, but his divorced father's; but that his father, having recently found a girlfriend with a sixty-five foot houseboat, rarely used the cruiser anymore. So, lucky Joe and Nancy and their friends.

Tom parked in the large dirt and gravel lot, among other cars and the dry-docked smaller crafts. As they walked to the boat, he said, "By the way, Mick, I don't want to steal any of Dad's thunder, but while you guys were at Mass, I overheard him talking to Mom about a 'powwow' tonight, and I know he's going to ask you to come to work for him. Whatever that does for you—I hate to ruin surprises, but I thought you both might like a warning on that."

"Mickey, isn't that wonderful?!" Caitlin said, yanking on his arm with excitement.

"No, it isn't wonderful, and I was afraid he might do that. Caity, I spent two days with him down in his office. It's a pressure cooker…I didn't much care for that type of work anyway, and I think I'd lose my mind in about a week. Anyway, Tom, we're going back Tuesday, and I've already mentioned that to Dad."

"Right, but you should know this—and then I'm going to shut up—Mom and Dad are definitely taking a stab at talking you out of that, okay? There's more to it than what I'm telling you, but I'll leave that for your powwow. I just wanted you to know that you'll have a debate on your hands."

They boarded the luxury cruiser, which Joe's father had named for Joe's mother and his then-wife, Harriet, a math professor at the University of Cincinnati. He called it "Harriet *pi*", but wrote it with the symbol: "Harriet π." Either way—Mickey and Caitlin agreed—it had a peculiarly vulgar connotation.

On this hot and humid, typical July day in Cincinnati, Caitlin wore a long shirt over the bathing suit that Meg had bought her. Joe and Nancy were already aboard in their bathing suits, with all systems running.

Joe said, "Caitlin, I may choke on these words, but you'd better leave that shirt on, dear heart. With that complexion of yours, you'll be one big weeping blister tomorrow if you let this sun get you."

They cruised upriver to the city, literally able to hear the Reds' fans screaming inside Riverfront Stadium, then on to the little town of New Richmond, where they docked and ate a late lunch.

From time to time, Mickey and Caitlin would exchange private words about staying in Cincinnati *versus* returning to Ireland.

"Look at everything we've experienced, Mickey, just at your parents' home—the grand piano, the swimming pool, the billiard table, the home theatre, the Cadillac—and now a forty-foot yacht!"

"Which is exactly what I don't like," he responded. "Their *values*—this is such a materialistic world over here...I mean, *brass stands* for the toilet paper with matching brass covers for the tissue boxes? How does a person even *think* of such things, much less buy them?"

"Are you criticizing your dear mother, Mickey?" she taunted him.

"I shouldn't, but I guess I am," he said smiling.

"There's more to it than tissue boxes—there's the symphony, the ballet, the theatre!"

"Ah, Christ," he said laughing, "you've won me over now—with the mention of the *ballet!*"

"Oh, come *on!*" she responded with her own laughter. "Why would you want to plant yourself back in tiny Newport, when we have this chance—"

"We can take holidays to Dublin, or to *London*, for God's sake, if you need a bleedin' ballet or a symphony—and the crowded streets and polluted air that go with all that! Cincinnati is no London, you know, Cait."

Later, when they neared the end of their voyage, Caitlin was waiting for Mickey in the cabin below when he exited the head. She told him that Nancy suggested that they could try out the master stateroom in the bow for the five minutes it would take until they were back at the Constance harbor. She had unbuttoned the shirt she had worn over her bathing suit all day, but she held it closed.

"Try it out, you say?" Mickey smiled.

Caitlin opened her shirt and let it drop to the floor. She wore a bikini. Mickey had never seen his nineteen-year-old future bride in a bathing suit before.

"Jesus Christ!" Mickey quietly gasped, wide-eyed. "So much for criticizing how Mom spends her money! *Jesus Christ!*"

"Four and a half minutes," Caitlin smiled.

*   *   *   *

After Mickey and Caitlin absorbed the initial shock of the news—Tom's cancer surgery in two weeks, and his doctor's assurances that it's early enough to "get it all"—Tom explained his idea.

"You can start tomorrow, Mick. You'll be right there with me all day, learning as much as you can. These next two weeks will be arduous, but—"

"Sort of like the last twenty-eight years," injected Meg.

"—but I'm hoping you'll find it exciting, Mickey," he continued, after a dry smile back to his wife, "because I've been talking to people who think we can get you into law school...Mick—listen, even if I don't make it—no—bullshit—forget that. I'm gonna make it, okay? But you can stay with me part-time through law school, and you'll have a ready-made practice when you get out! And I'm not working forever—"

"You know, Dad," Mickey began carefully, "I don't know that I'd be such a benefit to you...I mean, that pace—the telephone, the stacks of paper, the running from courtroom to courtroom. I'm amazed at how you whip through it all, but..."

"Aaah, shit, you just get used to it, Mick! You're twice as smart as most of the lawyers I know, and I'll bet you can outwork any four of 'em combined! And, hell, if things don't work out, *then*, sure, you can get another job, or...go back to Ireland, if that's what you really want. Hey—we *will* work hard, yes, we will, but then we get to come home to the two prettiest girls in the world. Whattaya say?"

"First, Dad," Mickey said quietly, "what do you do if I say no?"

"Well...I mean, there *are* lawyers in the firm who'll pick up for me, but—"

"Mickey, let's give it a try," begged Caitlin.

Mickey looked at her, mildly frustrated. "Look, everybody—since I seem to be at odds with *everybody*," he said, glaring at Caitlin, "it's not anyone's fault—anyone here—that I grew up in Ireland, and...maybe it was the circumstances, but I guess the way I was living forced me to daydream about a future for myself in business and in Irish politics...and I've somewhat forged a vision of who I am and what I want for my future, and...this just doesn't fit.

"I love you both, and I never want to be out of your lives—"

"Oh, Mickey, you just can't leave us, you *can't*," Meg said, now beginning to cry in earnest.

"Mom, Caity and I will be with you forever," he tried to assure her, without success. "We will always be a part of your lives, *always*...ah, Jesus, I am so sorry, Mom." He hugged her, but she wept.

"Let me have a few minutes with this stubborn mule, if you don't mind," Caitlin said. "We'll go back to my room."

*   *   *   *

She closed the door.

"I don't want any lectures about whether I care enough about my parents," he warned.

"Not at all, Mickey, but there's a little more that you should know about...things I haven't told you. Not because I was *hiding* them, but because I didn't see the point in upsetting you.

"First is that Father McDermott told me that he had talked to Senator O'Malley about giving you a job, but O'Malley wouldn't do it because you had killed Bill Sullivan, and it would look bad for his office. Mickey, if he couldn't even have you on his staff, how could you ever stand for election? They'd crucify you!"

Mickey resented her saying that he "had *killed* Bill Sullivan." *And* her attempt to squelch his ambition. Whether true or not, she wouldn't have said those things before, and so he felt that she was being manipulative.

"I'm not afraid of that," he answered flatly.

"And, Mickey," she continued, "if we go back, there'll be no hiding the fact that we found the newspapers in that box, and we both know that what we did was illegal! We could be prosecuted for it!"

"But, Caity, we've talked about this—why would the bank or the Gardai *ever* want to come after us under these circumstances? And without Fergus's testimony—"

"But it's one more thing they could bring up if you try to enter politics—that you've broken the law!"

Mickey had already considered what she was saying. It had been reported in the media that they had found the newspapers, but of course the two had never revealed that they had gone into the safe-deposit box. So her opinion that "there'll be no hiding it" was a stretch (and, again—*manipulative*), he thought, but—*on the other hand, anyone at the bank who could add two and two, and who had been aware of the events of that day...and, of course, they'd talk...*

"Caity, I will deal with all this when the time—"

"One way or the other, I'll be dismissed immediately, Mickey. It won't be just a head game between me and Paul Byrne anymore. They can't have an employee who breaks into customers' safe-deposit boxes. I'll be fired and humiliated, and I won't be able to hold my head up in public." She smiled a little to hear herself exaggerate.

He turned from her and stared out the window. *Jesus! She doesn't let up!*

He spoke quietly, saying, "How can I take back Northern Ireland for the Irish if I'm in Cincinnati, Ohio?"

She knew he was being facetious, trying to ease the tension, and answered, "Mm, maybe become President and send the American army in?"

"Mm-hmm, then maybe cut six counties out of England," he agreed, "and station Irish soldiers there to make sure the people behave themselves."

"Sure, you can call that *Eastern* Ireland," she deadpanned.

He sighed. "Do I have a prayer of winning this argument with you, Caitlin Molly?"

She moved behind him and put her arms around his waist, and said hopefully, "Ready to give up and say we'll stay?"

"No!" he answered emphatically. "You've just got me so confused now that I have to sleep on it. But Caity—let me say this as both a promise and a warning—because if we stay, the demands on my time will be great. It won't be easy...but I'll be workin' for my *father*, and so I damn sure won't be willing to fail. Whatever it takes—"

"You won't fail, Mickey. You never fail," she said as he turned to hug her.

"No, I don't. I never fail to kill people and otherwise break the law, as you've just reminded me. Remember this, Caity Lin," he said, thickening his accent deliberately, "'twas an Irishman you fell in love with...and an Irishman who fell in love with you. And I hate the fact that we're apart on this."

"We're not apart, Mickey. I'm just expressing myself," she smiled, "as I'm sure you'd expect; but whatever decision is made, I'll be with you all the way, and that's *my* promise."

"And your warning," he laughed as he kissed her. After a moment of passion, they returned to Meg and Tom to say goodnight.

*   *   *   *

He smiled as he lay in bed thinking about his bride-to-be: *She's the one that should be the damn lawyer...she never gives up the fight!* He really believed that he had the most exciting and beautiful girl in all the world. He didn't want to disappoint her, but he trusted her promise to stand by his decision. He loved her more than he ever knew he could. And he wanted to take her home to Ireland.

He imagined the two of them picking out new kitchen cabinets and furniture as he began to realize a sense of pride—to think that he was now sole owner of the Monaghan sheep farm. *No, the* McCall *sheep farm!*

He was sure that his mother, although crying now, would be all right once they had settled into a routine of phone calls and perhaps annual visits back and forth, but he was concerned about his father's immediate needs.

He reflected on the moment that he had opened the envelope to see a check for $1,000 from the Grand Scoop Hotline...and how that had touched him. His father had looked past other considerations—even Mickey's own stated wishes—and had taken care of his son. He had done what fathers are supposed to do. Mickey wasn't accustomed to that, and it somewhat amazed him, to see a parent *being a parent* with such a natural skill.

Would his father ever understand if he were to opt to return to Mayo? Would it be fair to his dad? He prayed for God's guidance.

His mind drifted, and he thanked God for the richness of his life, and especially for Caitlin. He prayed for the repose of Marian's soul and again asked forgiveness for what he had done to Bill Sullivan, and even for his hatred of Fergus, although he struggled to imagine how God could not hate him, too. And he thanked Him again for Caitlin.

EPILOGUE

▼

By noon the following day, Mickey had been fitted for gray, navy, and brown suits; and Meg, with Caitlin, had picked out and purchased the appropriate shoes, shirts, and ties. They delivered him to Tom's office shortly after 12:30 p.m., and within fifteen minutes, he was in a courtroom with his dad for an appearance on a "Driving Under the Influence" charge against Fred Middleberg, Tom's friend in the real estate business.

When they got home at 8:15 p.m., Meg had a pitcher of martinis waiting, and it was obvious that she and Caitlin had already celebrated the couple's decision to stay in Cincinnati.

Such became the pattern for the next two weeks, with Mickey spending intense twelve-or fourteen-hour workdays with his dad, learning as much as he could prior to Tom's surgery and absence from the office.

Mickey had hoped to cut back to a semi-normal maybe nine-hour day once his dad was in the hospital, but the demanding caseload made that impossible. Stan Roth was a godsend, actively finding ways he could help.

Later that month, as the news arrived that Mickey would indeed be accepted into law school in the fall, and as he became increasingly upset with Caitlin's drinking, he took her across the river to Covington, Kentucky on a Friday afternoon, where they could be married without a waiting period. They spent a Friday-night honeymoon in a roadside motel, and returned to Cincinnati Saturday afternoon to look for an apartment.

Meg protested their moving out, but Mickey had grown impatient with his mother, gently arguing with her, to no avail, that Caitlin did not need to drink martinis on a daily basis.

Life became a blur. When Mickey started law school, Caitlin—bored stiff, with Meg as her only friend—took a clerk's position in the courtroom of the Honorable Keith Humphrey. After a few months had passed, the judge began to occasionally ask Caitlin, who would in turn ask Mickey, if he could escort her—along with other members of his staff—to some political fundraiser or another.

It did not initially occur to Mickey that this would become a problem. He was actually relieved, at first, that she could participate in these functions and go out socializing with the "courthouse crowd."

By the following summer, however, life was more difficult. Tom was back in the hospital for a second surgery. The cancer had returned. Mickey began to realize that Caitlin was no longer *asking* him prior to going out with Judge Humphrey; and furthermore, it was no longer just political events that they attended together, but a variety of judicial meetings, lectures, and society goings-on.

She refused to honor his requests to stop accompanying the judge to these functions, insisting that she had no choice—that "Keith needs me there to help keep track of who he talks to, what they talk about, and such things."

Mickey suggested that "Keith" buy a pencil and a notebook, and Caitlin wondered aloud why he cared *what* she did, since he obviously had no time for her.

When they could no longer hide their mounting unhappiness from Mickey's parents, Tom gave Mickey a down payment for a little house, just a few blocks from his and Meg's home. That helped for a while, but not much.

And though Tom compensated Mickey well, Caitlin spent every cent and filled their credit cards, most of it on clothing for herself, which she needed for her lifestyle.

She was right, though—he was not much of a husband. Working and going to school, and driven by his commitment to Caitlin, his father, and himself that he *would not* fail, all he could do was promise Caitlin that law school would someday end, and that he would then be able to establish his own practice with his own hours. And that perhaps he and Caitlin could then talk about starting a family.

But Caitlin became distant. She seemed to stop caring altogether. And her drinking at home—which she had previously tried to hide from Mickey—was open and constant.

By the time Mickey finally did graduate and pass the bar exam, their relationship was—at its best, "polite"—and at its worst, a firestorm of sarcasm, accusations, and all things hateful. Mickey's prior womanizing lifestyle and the long hours he now spent at school and the office gave Caitlin more than ample fuel to counter his objections to her time spent with the judge.

And on a cold November night in 1994, two days after Mickey was sworn in as a new lawyer, he sat alone by his father's bedside at Good Samaritan Hospital until 4:30 a.m., when the cancer finally claimed him. Thomas Steven McCall, Sr., age 57.

As he drove home to give his wife the sad news, he berated himself for wishing that his father's death would be the catalyst for a new day for him and his beautiful Caitlin.

Jesus! Is that what it takes? Does somebody have to die? And can't you just honor your father honestly, Mickey, without trying to fashion some personal benefit from it?

But it didn't matter, because Caitlin wasn't home. He drove to Mount Lookout, one of Cincinnati's finest neighborhoods, saying prayers that would not be heard. Her car was parked in the driveway of the Honorable Keith Humphrey.

Numb over the loss of his father, and now brokenhearted over his wife, he was unable to sleep. He drove to the office and prepared their divorce papers, which she signed without comment or change. He had been fair.

*   *   *   *

Within a year, Meg McCall had become Mrs. Stanley Roth, and they had retired to Sarasota, Florida; and Caitlin had become a judge's wife, with her picture in the newspaper from time to time, co-hosting this or that. Mickey's inherited law practice was thriving, so much so that he even hired a law school classmate to carry some of the load.

But as the next few years flew by, realizing that he had lost every reason to stay in Cincinnati, he heard the call of Ireland.

Fuck it all, he decided, *I'm goin' home.*

Over the next six months, he refused any new cases or clients, and he worked feverishly to conclude what he already had. He sold his car, his house and everything in it. And as the summer of 1996 arrived, so did the last day of his American odyssey.

Before going to the airport, he directed his taxi driver to the residence of the Honorable and Mrs. Keith Humphrey. He needed to say good-bye.

The bitterness now behind him, he needed—for one last time—to thank Caitlin for the extraordinary contributions she had made to his life, and to assure her of her singular, eternal importance to him. And he prayed to God that it would matter to her.

He wanted *just one more look* at the girl who, when all is said and done, will have meant more to him than anyone else in his life.

I'll never meet another six-year-old who will fall in love with me when I save her from the bullies. Or another little girl who will teach me, and learn with me, and sing with me the songs of my homeland.

I can't grow up with another best friend who will urge me and lead me to find out who I am…and where I came from. And who will love me through all of it, then marry me and be my wife, even though she's the most beautiful girl in all the world.

He needed to apologize for failing her both as a husband and as a man, and to ask her forgiveness. He wanted to tell her that he loves her today as he always had, and, *until the last breath leaves my body, I will love you.*

Finally, he wanted to tell her that she would have never had to *run* to find him after school, to walk her home. Because all along, he now knew, he had been waiting for her.

He knocked, and she came into the vestibule. She opened the glass front door and stood behind the screen door. She did not speak. Indeed, she appeared pale and sickly…listless, with her eyes open but unfocused.

A man rose up behind her—from nowhere, it seemed—grabbed her by the neck and pulled her back, dragging her down the long hall. The man was not her husband, Judge Humphrey.

He was Fergus Monaghan.

Enraged, Mickey yanked at the door, but he could not open it.

MONDAY, JULY 2, 1990

He woke in a sweat shortly before 5:00 a.m., one hand pulling frantically at the leg of the nightstand. He stared momentarily at his hand, bewildered, then released it to quickly raise his head and peer out the window…at his parents' pool, and the split-rail fence he'd put in eight days earlier.

He bowed his head to whisper, "Oh, my God! Thank You, God!"

After splashing water on his face and rinsing his mouth, he quietly let himself into Caitlin's room. He sat on the side of her bed and caressed her hair as she slept. He smiled with relief.

You love me, Caity Lin, and I promise you—I'll never give you a reason to stop.

Eventually, she woke, grabbed his hand with hers and kissed it.

"What time is it, Mickey?" she whispered, and then looked at the clock. "Jesus! What are you doing?" she quietly giggled.

He spoke with a calm confidence. "We're goin' home, Cait. And I couldn't wait to tell you!"

Her smile now changed slightly, tempered with an understanding and admiration. She wore no trace of disappointment.

"Home to Ireland, Mickey?"

He nodded.

"And we'll be married…?"

"…at St. Patrick's. By Father McDermott."

"Are we leavin' tomorrow, Mickey, or…"

"Yes, we're leaving tomorrow," he said smiling. "You know, if there's one thing I'm sure of," he said, to answer her unasked question, "it's that my dad has his law office and his responsibilities well covered. I'm goin' t' be like my dad, Cait, and take care of what's important…and that's *you*…and our future."

She sat up to hug him tightly, then asked, "Are we sellin' the farm?"

He shrugged as he stared into her eyes. "I don't know. One way or the other, we'll be busy with it, so you'll have to quit the bank straightaway."

Her face lit up as she said, "And what about that bunch o' wee Mickeys?"

He nodded. "And if we're really lucky, a wee Caitlin or two."

"I love you, and I'm so proud of you, Mickey!" she said, hugging him again.

He pulled her closer, then whispered in her ear, "The reverse is true as well, of course, and…as long as we're doin' things my way, why don't you scoot over and let me slip under those covers with you?" He leaned back—with eyes open wide—to see her reaction.

A shy smile appeared for only a few seconds before she picked up her blanket and held it to her neck.

"I will *not!*" she said quietly but firmly. "And you get yourself out of this room before I scream for help!"

He stood and walked to the door...smiled and waved at her as he quietly let himself out, went back to his bed and fell asleep.

0-595-30966-6

Printed in the United States
53105LVS00003B/99